LAND OF THE
HAUNTED DOLLS

LAND OF THE HAUNTED DOLLS

SUSAN LIEN WHIGHAM

Medical Legal Disclaimer: This story is for entertainment purposes only, and not intended to be a substitute for professional medical or legal advice. Always consult a trained professional before making any decision regarding treatment of yourself or others.

ISBN: 978-0-9858699-2-2 (Hardcover)
ISBN: 978-0-9858699-1-5 (Paperback)
ISBN: 978-0-9858699-0-8 (Ebook)

Edited by Stephanie Whigham

First Printing, 2021
www.landofthehaunteddolls.com

Dedicated to Stephanie and Sean

Contents

Dedication   v

Preface and Trigger Warning   vii

Prologue   1

Act One   3

Act Two   166

Epilogue   321

Acknowledgements   325

Gratitude   327

Appendix A: Additional
Recommended Reading   329

Appendix B: List of
Dual Roles   331

Preface and Trigger Warning

This story, part one of a trilogy, explores themes of mental health, addiction, bigotry, demon possession, gun violence, sexual assault, self harm, and suicide, among others. My intention in dramatizing these topics is not to make light of such heavy subject matter, but rather to catalyze discussion and strategies for healing.

Please note that not all human trafficking victims are trafficked for sex, nor are they all female; they should not be confused with those who voluntarily choose commercial sex work. Whether involved in the sex trade by choice or by coercion, sex workers face great danger arising not only from physical violence from pimps and their clients, but also from authorities who prosecute and criminalize them for breaking the law.

As with Christianity, specific beliefs and practices of Vodou may vary from one person or one group to the next, while still sharing certain commonalities. Out of respect for initiated practitioners of Vodou, I've refrained from going into great specificity about its rituals and practice, because my intention is not to teach how it's done, but rather to tell a story about conflicting ideologies. For the sake of a mostly Western audience, I utilize the "Voodoo" spelling that originated in New Orleans. I invite those interested in learning more about its roots in Haitian Vodou to investigate further with assistance from expert practitioners.

In spite of my decision to depict Voodoo elements in a horror story, in my view the practice of New Orleans Voodoo, or its antecedent, Haitian Vodou, is not something to fear, but has come to be so only through Western taboos which oppose it.

The effort to represent such a deeply spiritual tradition can only fall short as it scratches the surface of its meaning. And yet, the unique significance of what the practice of Vodou brings to a story about human beings and their haunted effigies is far too important to let pass without exploration. Vodou expresses something specific in a language not as readily accessible to other Western cultures. In my view, it's of benefit to all to learn to understand this language.

Although tenets of Vodou do resonate with me (as do those of many belief systems), I would not characterize myself strictly as a Vodouisant. I'm a pantheist, and I believe that Vodou is one of many valid paths to spiritual understanding. As any Vodouisant can affirm, my initiation into the world of the lwa would have been impossible without the necessary faith, humility and sacrifice to go with it.

As with any work of fiction, this story is for entertainment purposes only, and not intended to be a substitute for professional medical or legal advice. Even though different therapeutic options are talked about in the story, it doesn't mean that any one in particular is necessarily right or wrong for you. Every person has their own unique individual complexities, so it's really in your own best interest to seek professional guidance if you're experiencing any kind of disagreeable medical or legal situation.

If you're having an emergency, please seek immediate help by calling your doctor, going to an emergency department, or in the United States, by calling 9-1-1. If you're contemplating suicide, toll-free suicide hotlines are available in most areas throughout the world. In the United States, the National Suicide Prevention Helpline (800-273-8255) is available around the clock and will transfer the call to a hotline in your area. Your future self will thank you!

In the rural South of the United States, it's not uncommon to find white people speaking American White Southern English (AWSE), a dialect which shares history with and in many ways closely resembles African-American Vernacular English (AAVE). I was exposed quite a bit to these forms of language growing up, not only from Black friends but from white family as a native way of speaking. The use of AAVE in the story is born from my experiences growing up with a Southern family, and I reference it with great respect for its existence in American culture.

Please note that it's impossible to tell a diverse story without attempting to empathize with other cultures. Telling a diverse story may invite the perception that any given character is meant to assert what is typical of a particular race, religion, country, or culture. The characters in this story have been through trauma, many with absent or abusive parental figures, and this commonality of experience merely happens to be what drew them together. It's certainly not my intention to say what's typical.

Land of the Haunted Dolls, in its various manifestations, is a collaboration of kindred spirits and an examination of our intersectionality. As a storyteller, I hope to help pave the way toward a more pluralistic culture and a world where all have access to opportunities to share their stories. I'm deeply grateful to God and all those who have inspired and facilitated this work. As always, I welcome opportunities to further my understanding.

Thank you for coming along on this journey,
Susan Lien Whigham, author

https://www.landofthehaunteddolls.com

| Prologue |

I had met Ms. Titi Beaumond and her cousin Ms. Rochelle Roy more than a decade ago, when I was studying journalism at the University of New Orleans. Back when we met, she was known locally as Madame T, which was the name of her Voodoo/Hoodoo practice on Bourbon Street for readings, rootwork and spells. Many years after we had become good friends, and knowing me to be a writer, she asked me to put together a complete accounting of some paranormal events she and Rochelle had experienced which took place in the fall of 2016, two months before the United States of America would hold a historic election between the first female candidate for president in U.S. history and the first male candidate for president in U.S. history to run without any prior political experience.

She had warned me that it was a complicated story, and not just because of the sheer number of people involved—four of them were victims of a sex and drug trafficking ring, women who came from different parts of the world, and who were each manifesting multiple identities for reasons I will get into more detail about later. This was part of the reason that Titi felt with conviction that she should ask me to tell the story rather than attempt to tell it herself.

She wanted the record of it to bring to light the different perspectives of the many people involved, which besides these four women, included her above-mentioned cousin Rochelle, her ex-husband Carlos (with whom Rochelle was in a relationship at the time), her family members, some of Rochelle's colleagues at the Department of Justice, and the doctors and staff who bore witness to these events at Glen Haven Psychiatric Hospital, all of whom I've interviewed in great detail and am ready to share with you their story, with their blessing.

At Titi's request, this is not simply a story about paranormal events, but also one of relationship complexities (some already hinted at) and the strange paths we're drawn through in search of closure. Some of it may defy belief but, as the saying goes, stranger things have happened.

| Act One |

Look upon me, you who reflect upon me,
and you hearers, hear me.
You who are waiting for me, take me to yourselves.
And do not banish me from your sight.

For I am the first and the last.
I am the honored one and the scorned one.
I am the whore and the holy one.

Give heed then, you hearers
and you also, the angels and those who have been sent,
and you spirits who have arisen from the dead.

—Selected from "The Thunder, Perfect Mind"
Nag Hammadi Library
(discovered circa 4th century)

| Chapter One |

Rewind.

Replay.

Inside a darkened psychiatric hospital in the West Village, Manhattan, New York City, it was ten minutes short of 3 a.m., the witching hour. In less than seven days, four sex trafficking victims would attempt to murder their pimp.

Special Agent Rochelle Roy sat solemnly in a room dimly lit by a small lamp mounted to the headboard of a hospital bed, in a wooden chair across from a young female patient whose origins were as yet unknown. Yesterday, during her intake interview, the young woman had given her name as Abeni (which she pronounced like Albany without the "L"), unable to remember her own last name. That was when she was still conscious, before the withdrawal from the crack cocaine began to shift gears, sending her toward a near-comatose state.

Her identity was a mystery. Unaware of how long she had been in New York, or how she had gotten there, Abeni now sat catatonic in a hospital bed, propped up on pillows and staring into the empty space in front of her, oblivious to Rochelle's concerned presence and the dim sound of a small television set mounted to the corner wall casting dancing shadows on her face, the soft din of voices in the hallway punctuated by the periodic beep of the heart and blood pressure monitor. Her light brown skin was pocked with numerous scars and covered with a thin layer of sweat which clung to her face and scalp, and matted her thin, broken hair.

She and three other women, somewhere in their mid- to late-twenties, had been rescued during an organized crime bust led by Rochelle's team at the FBI Human Trafficking Unit which took down a small cocaine and sex trafficking ring in Upstate New York, operated by one Alejandro Serrano León of Juárez City, Mexico, better known to his compadres as Jandro.

Close to an hour before, Rochelle had walked four windy city blocks to the hospital, through streets strewn with autumn leaves making one last irreverent gesture in death to litter the sidewalks after the street sweepers had just passed through, straight from last call at the bar a block from her Greenwich Village loft, while anticipating another night of insomnia. The sight of Abeni's weathered face, aged far beyond her years, wrinkled like dead leaves withered and dry under a paradox of night dew, tore at Rochelle's weary heart.

"How does this happen to a human being?" said Rochelle, shaking her head, forcing herself to inhale like she was drowning in something invisible, looking down at the keys dangling from her clasped hands and then back up at Abeni. "I don't know what to say. I'm just sorry. I'm so sorry for what you've suffered. I promise you, I will do whatever it takes to bring your suffering to justice. I just need you to hold on, okay?"

Abeni failed to respond, as the vaulted ceilings hunched over them like vultures. This building filled with misfits smelled like illness and death, and seemed increasingly sinister every time Rochelle came here. The world at large was also becoming a more sinister place day by day for Rochelle, who as both a woman of color and a law enforcement officer often felt like a misfit herself, especially when thus far this year, some half a dozen high-profile cases of police brutality against unarmed young Black men had come to light. Her mother had questioned more than once her desire to work so hard for a system that attacked both her race and her gender. Her answer always came with quiet solemnity: *because this is where I can make a difference.*

A brick relic in a city bursting with metal skyscrapers, Glen Haven Psychiatric Hospital was as much a misfit as the tormented souls she housed. Built in 1847 in the West Village during the third cholera pandemic, and still dressed in her original Romanesque Revival architecture, the hospital had the look of a medieval castle, with a charcoal-gray stone facade, columned towers with Gothic stained glass windows, and masonry arches supporting her vaulted ceilings.

There on the fifth floor, where the intensive care unit was housed, Rochelle sat in silence with her black trench coat neatly folded over the back of the chair, her long, dark brown hair falling in twists over the tired shoulders of her blue blazer jacket, her chestnut brown skin darkened by the dimmed lighting of the night shift.

Her frown tensed in contemplation of the tragic state of the four victims. However old she felt, she knew that what had aged them was immeasurably more severe. If there was any silver lining to be found on this cloud of lead, it was that after receiving state-mandated rehab for their crack addiction, the victims could potentially put their traffickers away for life, if they could only recover to the point of being willing and able to testify.

Rochelle looked down at the keychain she hadn't realized she was clutching tightly in her hand. A small red yarn doll was attached to the keyring, and she ran her thumb over the texture of the doll, as she often did unconsciously to relieve anxiety. She had bought the miniature keychain doll some years ago because it reminded her of a Voodoo doll, which in turn reminded her of her cousin Titi, who practiced Voodoo in New Orleans. Having been raised in a devout Roman Catholic family, Rochelle was someone who identified as Christian, and had not intended for the keychain to honor the practice of Voodoo so much as represent a lack of reverence for it, to show that it failed to inspire fear in her. Staring at the yarn which wound round its faceless head and body, she could not escape the irony of being faced with the prospect of calling Titi to consult on this case, after a number of odd details had come up concerning Voodoo during the intake interviews. *Silly superstition*, she thought, shaking her head.

The silhouette of a hooded figure stepped into the doorway, and Rochelle looked up. The contrast of the dim lighting in the room and the brightness of the hallway light masked the details of the woman's face, but Rochelle could see that she was wearing a long, rose-pink maxi dress and a large black and gold heart-shaped pendant which had the name "Freda" inscribed in capital letters across the center of it. Alongside the pendant was a string of pink pearls, and the woman's hands appeared to be tucked into a black fur muff to protect her from the cold.

"Yes?" asked Rochelle, wondering if she was here visiting one of the patients in the hospital and had wandered into the wrong room. "Can I help you?"

The stranger stepped forward into the light and Rochelle could see the light-skinned face of a woman with Afrocentric features. Her eyebrows were tensed in anger, and she flung the black bundle of fur onto the bed. "Look what you've done," she said to Rochelle through gritted teeth, before abruptly turning to leave.

"What the…?" said Rochelle, reaching over to lift the fur object to try to figure out why she would throw it on Abeni's bed. Rochelle realized in horror that it wasn't a hand muff at all, but rather a freshly killed black cat with a long silver knife driven into its chest. Its body was limp, but still warm. Rochelle leaped to her feet with a loud shriek, her heart pulsing wildly.

A pear-shaped nurse named Maisie Laoise was shuffling down the hallway at that moment, carrying a folded cotton blanket over her arm, wearing in honor of her 47th birthday a festive scrub top with pink and yellow cupcakes on it, and coordinating scrub pants the color of Pepto Bismol. Her long, straight, sandy brown hair was pulled into a sensible ponytail at the base of her skull, and a pair of bifocals dangled on a thin cord around her neck. She jumped at the sight of Rochelle standing in the darkened room. "Special Agent Roy!" she said, catching her breath as she walked over.

"Stop that woman in the hall!" ordered Rochelle. "Please! Quickly!"

Maisie turned back into the hallway and looked around, but there was no one there. "What happened? Is everything alright?" asked Maisie.

"That woman who just left came in here and threw a dead cat on Abeni's bed. Freda! I think her name was Freda."

"A dead cat! Where is it?"

Rochelle looked down at the bed in front of her, but the cat was gone. Rochelle slid down into her chair, trying to understand what had just happened. She felt light-headed; her face was pale with fright.

Having worked more than twenty years at a psychiatric hospital, Maisie was unfazed by Rochelle's alarmed reaction. "What brings you in at this hour?" she said kindly, changing the subject, twisting her plastic pink watch around her wrist and consulting the time. She walked over to Rochelle and regarded her with concern.

Rochelle glared. *She thinks I'm crazy.* "I couldn't sleep."

"Oh!" said Maisie, catching a whiff of Rochelle's breath

and turning her face away with a reflexive cough. "Have you been drinking?" she asked, then regretted the question, quickly backpedaling out of Rochelle's personal space.

Rochelle looked down at the yarn doll without answering. She hadn't intended to go out drinking tonight. There was something that had upset her, what was it?

| Chapter Two |

Her thoughts wandered back to 7 o'clock, when she was wrapping up working late at the office. She recalled that everything was looking especially gray for some reason. Her putty-colored desk was gray, the cubicle walls were gray, the floor was gray, and even her boyfriend Carlos, staring out at her from behind the glass of a brushed silver picture frame on her desk, with his pale skin and goofy bearded smile which struggled to mask his fatigue, somehow seemed gray today. The fluorescent lights added their finishing touch to help suffocate any hint of a soul from her work environment.

Her good friend and colleague, Dr. Lin Mei Chen, the forensic psychologist assigned to the case, walked into the office just as Rochelle was getting ready to leave for the night, Lin Mei's long shiny black hair pulled back into a bun as per usual for work. Beyond the black, cat-eye frames of her designer eyeglasses, Lin Mei's eyes looked puffy, as if she'd been crying. Rochelle refrained from commenting on it.

"Hey Chelle," said Lin Mei with a lowkey cheery tone that seemed to be more than she could afford. "So glad I caught you. The network is still down for scheduled maintenance. Can

I get the case file from you before you head out? Reid said he had it couriered to you this afternoon. Did you get a chance to review the files?"

"Yeah," said Rochelle, looking away at the clock, impatient to leave for no particular reason. She briskly walked back over to her desk and unlocked the top drawer, retrieving an encrypted memory card from an envelope and handing it to Lin Mei.

"Not much to go on there. Quila González, the Latina, has a record from when she was picked up during a trafficking sting in El Paso ten years ago. She was seventeen years old back then and already a crack addict. She's the oldest of the four. It's a miracle she's lasted this long. Facial recognition identified the blonde as Olena Petrenko, aka Lena Flaxen, a former child porn star from Kiev. The sociolinguistics analysis from the intake interviews identifies Abeni's accent as Nigerian, likely from the Borno region. Then we have Eka, the red-head, whom they believe is from the country of Georgia, probably Tbilisi. She speaks Russian, but her native language is Georgian. That's all we've got on Abeni or Eka. Not even a last name to go on, but it's possible they've been brainwashed to obscure their identities. How did the pre-arraignment psych evals go? I heard the defense is considering an insanity plea? And he wants to name the vics as accomplices? Is he for real?"

"There's plenty of evidence of coercion," said Lin Mei, looking closely at the SD card and committing its appearance to memory before dropping it into her inside zippered jacket pocket. Then she noticed her button-down shirt was coming untucked, and shifted awkwardly to tuck it back in. "So naming them as accomplices won't go anywhere. His attorney is really grasping at straws. He would have been better off going with the public defender. I found Jandro competent to stand trial. There might be some substance to an insanity defense, though."

"Give me a break. He knew exactly what he was doing,

and he's been doing it for more than a decade. And what about his trafficking partners? They were insane too?"

"His cousin Danny said he's not right in the head. Says he kills people, and animals too, to drink their blood. Hallucinates, and has conversations with his hallucinations. Some other weird stuff too."

"Hm, okay," said Rochelle, glancing down to turn the information over in her mind. "Probably using too much of his own product. I mean, the vics are saying he's demon-possessed, so maybe there's some definite mental illness there. Not that we didn't know he's a real sicko. Weird that Danny would want to add murder charges to the mix. Must not be too fond of Jandro."

"I think it's fear... of something... I don't know," said Lin Mei, struggling to find the right words. "I think he's ready to shut down the family business, for reasons other than a guilty conscience."

"Not sure what you're implying."

Lin Mei wasn't convinced of the existence of paranormal activity enough to debate it, but her mind was open to the possibility. "No clues as to why they're claiming Voodoo?" she asked, instead of answering the question.

"No," said Rochelle, eyeing the clock again. "And I got a call from Dr. Varma at Glen Haven this afternoon. They're still completely catatonic, all four of them."

"Why don't you go home and get some rest," said Lin Mei, noting that Rochelle looked as exhausted as Lin Mei felt. "I'll keep working on it."

Rochelle knew Lin Mei's heart was in the right place, but the admonition rubbed her the wrong way. Obviously, Rochelle was leaving work now, what was the point of telling her to go home? "Now that you mention it, I was actually planning to ditch the dongle tonight and go deep diving for navel lint. Did I tell you? Bellybutton fluff is my new favorite hobby."

Lin Mei cracked a weathered smile. "Really. Bellybutton

fluff?"

"I got plenty of rest yesterday already," said Rochelle, glaring. "That was the whole point of Reid sending us home early. But anyway, thanks again for coming by yesterday. I know you mean well."

"Coming by? What do you mean?" Lin Mei raised a puzzled eyebrow.

Rochelle pursed her lips. She didn't have enough energy for this conversation. "You want me to repeat it? Thanks for coming by my place. I know you were just trying to help."

"But I didn't come by your place yesterday, that's why I'm confused. And a little worried."

Now Rochelle was puzzled too. "That's weird. I have a vivid memory of you coming by."

"What did we talk about?"

Rochelle sighed. "You wanted me to consult with my cousin Titi on the case. I didn't want to, for obvious reasons. Not thrilled about the idea of having to deal with the drama of working with my boyfriend's ex-wife. I did take your suggestion and call her, though."

"Well, I do think you should consult with Titi. But maybe we should schedule you a psych eval."

"Don't be ridiculous. I'm fine. Just tired. You already know, I've been having some intense nightmares since we started this case. And don't try to act like you haven't yourself. Now that Jandro is behind bars, I should be able to get a good night's sleep tonight."

"Remembering things that didn't happen is a pretty serious red flag," said Lin Mei, frowning.

Rochelle raised her eyebrows in indignation and let out a breath of scoff. "Well, you're looking pretty ragged yourself, Dr. Chen, with all due respect. Have you ever heard the expression, 'Physician, heal thyself'? Why don't you follow your own advice and go home and get some rest yourself? And partying with Molly is not what I would call getting some rest. Wait, you know what? Is it possible that you're the one who's remembering it wrong?"

Lin Mei was stumped for a moment. Could it be she was the one who had it mixed up? She did feel brutally exhausted herself. The whole team had been working long hours for months. Things weren't going well at home, either. *What did I do yesterday?* Lin Mei struggled to remember.

"Yeah, that's what I thought," said Rochelle. "If you have to stop and wonder, then this debate is over. Let's just leave it at that."

"Check your phone," insisted Lin Mei, exasperated. She wasn't about to let Rochelle get away without making sure she had made the call. The possibility crossed her mind that Rochelle was subconsciously convincing herself it had already happened to avoid actually having to do it. "See if there's a call to Titi from yesterday."

Rochelle inhaled sharply. "Fine." She opened her cell phone and checked the recent calls list. There was no call to Titi.

Looking over her shoulder, Lin Mei sighed. "Will you just call her, please?"

"There are plenty of Voodoo practitioners right here in New York City, you know that, right?" said Rochelle, glossing over the oddity of what had just happened. "There's no need to go all the way to New Orleans to find one. And I really, really don't need her drama in my life right now. I *hate* drama. Anyway, demon possession is a common delusion among addicts, like imaginary you said to me yesterday."

"Their delusions are so specific though. It just doesn't make sense. You said I had you convinced yesterday. Some part of you must see the value behind it."

"Yeah, sure, I wouldn't mind some closure from her ridiculous hostility over my being with Carlos now. It's been over a year since their divorce, and my cousin Angie says Titi's doing the online dating thing now. It's about time for her to come to terms with this. Anyway, what they need is a good psychiatrist, not a witch doctor."

"Don't you think it's weird, four crack addicts suffering from the same delusion? What does it hurt to call her and ask her what she thinks?"

"Fine. If it'll get you to shut up about it, I'll do it. And yes, I think it's very weird. I just don't know that she's the right person to ask about it."

"Were you drinking heavily yesterday? You know that having a false memory can result from drinking to the point of blackout? I'm just getting worried about you."

Rochelle sighed. "I had some drinks, yes. And I'm getting worried about you too, you know. You look pretty severely depressed, do you realize that? I'm just being straight with you. So let's admit that this case is taking a toll on all of us and leave it at that. Deal?"

Lin Mei didn't want to argue with her. Rochelle was right; she *was* severely depressed. Molly wasn't just a choice for parties anymore. She was also using it to get through quiet but difficult evenings at home. Lately it was becoming less and less effective, and she was compensating by taking it more frequently.

And Lin Mei believed sincerely that there were no better qualified agents than Rochelle to work this case. Reporting the false memory incident to Reid Shelton, their agent-in-charge at the FBI, would result in Rochelle being pulled from the case, which in Lin Mei's mind would clearly be the greater of two evils. She also risked getting pulled from the case herself for her depression. A drug test revealing illicit substance abuse would abruptly end her career.

Above all, the mystery of this case was impossible to resist; neither of them could bear to be out of the loop, and they both understood this about each other. Meanwhile, they were short-handed, as Rochelle's FBI partner Jason was taking some much-needed vacation time himself following the bust. *That's what I should have done,* thought Rochelle.

"Call Titi, okay?" urged Lin Mei. "If nothing else, maybe getting some closure from her over Carlos will free up some of your focus for the case."

"Okay, fine. That does actually sound reasonable to me."

"And let me know how the arraignment goes. I'm sure the judge will deny bail. All three traffickers are a flight risk, and Jandro in particular presents a clear and imminent danger to the community. The prosecutor's going to seek a protective order for the vics so they can be moved to Ophelia's Wing after they're released from intensive care. So your cousin will have plenty of time to meet with them and give us her thoughts. Maybe she can do some healing work with them."

"I'll give her a call later, okay? Thank you, *Mother.* Can I go now?" Rochelle knew her snarky sarcasm would get under Lin Mei's skin, which was confirmed by Lin Mei reacting with a tired sigh, for which Rochelle then ignored a twinge of guilt. The upside was finally getting her to let it go.

Rochelle's thoughts drifted back to the present, back to Maisie's concerned question about whether she had been drinking. She indulged the question, even though she didn't feel she owed this woman an answer for anything. It was more important to her to keep her interactions with the hospital staff in good standing in order for the victims to receive the best possible care. "I had a couple of drinks after work tonight." *Not that it's any of your business.* With some effort, she softened her tone. "It's been a tough case. I'm really worried about the vics… we need them to recover so we can take their pimp off the streets for good. Are they going to pull through, do you think?"

"It's kind of you to check up on them," said Maisie, reaching awkwardly into Rochelle's personal space and patting her on the shoulder. "I really couldn't say. They're in awful shape, aren't they? I've never seen catatonia this severe. But you know how it is. It's never an easy fate for addicts. What goes up, must come down and face the harsh realities they were trying to escape. Dr. Varma is the hospitalist for the early morning shift—she should be coming by within the hour. Would you like for me to have her give you a call?"

"Yes, would you, please? I'll be up for a while."

"This job really drives you to drink, don't it?"

"You have no idea."

"There's real evil in the world," Maisie nodded. "And who among us is stepping up to fight it? The world needs more people like you, Special Agent Roy."

Rochelle didn't know what to say. She wasn't feeling particularly heroic. They both stared at Abeni in silence.

"Mind if I ask you something?" said Maisie, looking to change the subject. "Do you have a daughter?"

Rochelle looked away again, as if her attention were being pulled aside by another memory. It didn't take as long this time to regain awareness of the question. She at last said with quiet resignation, "No. Why do you ask?"

"Just the way you've been looking at her. Like I've seen mothers do from time to time, when their daughters are patients here."

"They're all daughters to me," said Rochelle, growing weary of the conversation. "It's why I do this."

But she was intrigued by the observation. Abeni was the only Black woman of the four victims, and Rochelle realized that this relatability likely explained what had drawn her to visit this room in particular, of the four. But there was also something compelling and terrifying in Abeni's face, something else with which Rochelle identified, something which was gripping her with an unspeakable fear. A fear of not knowing how it's possible for a human being to fall into this emotional quicksand and not be able to find a way out. A fear that she herself, too, was teetering dangerously on the edge of a precipice.

"Why don't you go on home, Special Agent Roy?" said Maisie, patting Rochelle on the shoulder again in what was meant to be a reassuring gesture. "They're going to be okay. We'll take good care of them."

Rochelle took little comfort in the gesture. She offered a weak smile, and wanted nothing more in this moment than to pour herself a Scotch and go to bed, but her body was tired enough to fall asleep right there in the chair. It took a bit more reassuring and coaxing from Maisie to motivate her to pick up her coat and head down the darkened hall toward the elevator to go home. Rochelle battled pessimism every step of the way. *Do these vics even stand a chance? Do I?*

| Chapter Three |

Faith moves mountains, or so the saying goes. According to the words of the Christian Messiah, all you need is a bit of faith the size of a mustard seed. But how much was that, exactly? However much it was, Eka was coming up short and the mountain was clearly winning. That scripture from the Christian Bible, which Eka's father was fond of quoting when she was a little girl back in Tbilisi, Georgia, echoed faintly in the dark recesses of her memory. The idea of faith moving mountains had always inspired her, or maybe it was just the way her father used to say it, like he truly believed it. That memory of him had little substance now, having long been eclipsed by the decades of physical violence and sexual abuse she had suffered after his death. Alone and catatonic in a psychiatric hospital bed with no known family to know or care where she was, any contemplation of her situation failed to cross her mind. Her once-vibrant red hair clung to the sweat on her pallid face in tangled mats.

It was now a quarter after 3 a.m., and Maisie entered Eka's room carrying a folded cotton blanket, just as she had done for the other three victims, and unfolded it with stout fingers over the thin, gray bedspread, covering Eka's legs and feet. As she did so, she noticed the aching in her own feet from her diabetic neuropathy, and just as quickly as she noticed it, returned to tuning it out. Her shift was scheduled to end at six this morning, which couldn't get here soon enough. She was looking forward to the quiet, 30-minute bus ride home, along Central Park back to Riverside, when she would finally get to sit down and watch the world go by for a little while. Twisting her watch round her wrist to catch sight of the time, and finding that only ten minutes had passed since the last time she looked, she breathed a heavy sigh.

"Brought you ladies an extra blanket since it's been getting real cold in here at night," said Maisie kindly, but Eka didn't take notice. "You want me to turn off the TV, hun?" Again, no answer. Maisie looked up at the TV, then back at Eka, then walked over to the remote control. "I don't know whose idea it was to leave it on at this hour. You don't seem that interested in it anyway. Seems like they play nothing but commercials these days." Maisie flipped through the channels and settled on one with no picture, only white noise. "How about if I just leave on some static? Might help you get some sleep." Searching Eka's face for a reaction, and still finding none, Maisie's lips stretched into a thin smile that expressed more helplessness than warmth.

Maisie identified with Eka, perhaps in a similar way to how Rochelle had identified with Abeni, except that where Rochelle's maternal nature expressed itself by being protective, Maisie's maternal nature was more geared toward nurturing. Suddenly Maisie recalled a lullaby that her own mother used to sing to her when she felt frightened as a child. Clearing her throat, she replayed the words in her mind first, to recall with certainty how it went. Her lovely soprano voice that used to sing in her church choir came spilling out with a clear, gentle, lilting melody that caused a subtle stir within Eka's heart.

Oh baby girl, my baby world,
Baby flower with wings unfurled
Moon saw the Earth and oh how she smiled
As did this mother upon her child

Come now my darling, come walk with me
By way of the sparrow, we shall be free
I shall love you, and you shall love me
So come now my darling, come fly with me

Dr. Anjali Varma, a tall, slender woman with olive brown skin and wavy black hair cropped chicly into a bob, glided into the room carrying Eka's chart. Maisie sheepishly stepped away from the bed, embarrassed at the thought that Dr. Varma may have heard her singing. If she had, Dr. Varma betrayed no visible reaction. Her facial expression was as neatly composed as her clothing. Under her white doctor's coat, a black silk blouse was tucked neatly into a wool pencil skirt, and a thick sterling silver chain rested across her neck, matching the bracelet watch adorning her wrist. "How are you feeling tonight, Eka?" said Dr. Varma, walking over and gently pulling back on Eka's forehead with the manicured fingertips of her left hand, while using her right to shine a penlight into her eyes. After gauging the absence of a reaction, she took a step back and made a note in her chart.

Maisie stared quietly at Dr. Varma in a slack-jawed haze of envy, as she often did—envy of her style, her elegance, her figure, her youth, her intelligence, her wealth. Dr. Varma, who was accustomed to attention and usually enjoyed it, shifted uncomfortably at the thought that Maisie might be a lesbian. Not one to consider herself a homophobe, Dr. Varma was more concerned with the impropriety of sexual attention in the workplace. She might have been relieved to hear that Maisie was actually asexual, and that a sexual attraction to Dr. Varma had never even crossed her mind, although some part of her might still have secretly preferred the attraction.

Eka said nothing, seemingly unaware of their presence.

"How's she doing, Maisie?"

"Her condition's been the same over the last six hours, Doctor," said Maisie, resting one hand into the palm of the other over her stomach, like a Buddha. "She's just been sitting there, staring off into space. Doesn't even blink. Her eyes and lips are real dry, just like the other three ladies they brought in. They were so chatty when they first came in, but not anymore. All night long they've been looking like they do now. Like zombies."

"A little sensitivity, please," said Dr. Varma, her eyes narrowing, her head leaning slightly in the direction of Maisie but not quite looking at her directly. "She can probably hear what you're saying. They hadn't really started withdrawing from the crack yet, that's why they were more lively before. Obviously, they're suffering some pretty severe withdrawals now. The catatonia is quite extreme."

Maisie nodded and cringed, only enough to be visibly embarrassed at her faux pas, and catching sight of the subtle reaction, Dr. Varma sympathetically softened her tone. "Let's go to 50 milligrams on the phenytoin, Maisie, and add 10 milligrams of diazepam to her five o'clock meds."

Maisie nodded as Dr. Varma made note of the prescription changes in Eka's electronic chart and exited the room, her patent leather heels clicking on the limestone floor.

"I'm real sorry, Miss," said Maisie, patting Eka's blanketed shin in earnest. "I didn't mean to be insensitive. You hold on there, okay? You're going to get through this."

As an afterthought, Dr. Varma leaned back into the room before heading out, and said, "Make sure they're kept well-hydrated."

"Yes, of course, Doctor." Maisie walked over to a cabinet

mounted over the sink, and pulled out a small, cornflower-blue plastic pitcher, and an inspirational paper cup with the words "HAVE FAITH" factory-printed on it amidst a cheerful teal and purple floral print. "Want some water, sweetie? I bet you do. That IV hydration doesn't seem to be doing anything for your dry mouth." Maisie filled the cup and pitcher at the water cooler, and set them down on the overbed table parked across the foot of Eka's bed in the hopes that Eka might come to, at least enough to want a drink.

Caught suddenly by an uneasy concern at Eka's fixed stare, which now seemed to be pointed eerily at the paper cup sitting on the table at the end of the bed, Maisie added, "Ah yes, I see your point. You probably want a straw, don't you? That would make things a bit easier for you." After chiding herself for not having some common sense, she turned away from the table and stepped back over to open the cabinet over the sink again, pulling small white cardboard boxes out of the cupboard, one by one, to get a better look through her bifocals at what they were labeled. She found cotton swabs, tongue depressors, adhesive bandages, and a plastic spit tray, among other things, but no straws.

"I'm sorry honey, I thought we had some straws up in he—" Maisie was startled to see that the cup of water had been knocked over toward Eka, leaving a pool of water dripping off of the table onto the floor. She stared at the spill in concerned silence, then looked around the room, searching the empty space and her thoughts for an explanation. Her eyes fell upon the television set, shaking off a curious shudder at the sound of the static. "I—" she stammered. "I'm so sorry, did I bump the table when I turned around? Got so much cushion back there, I didn't feel a thing."

She chuckled nervously, reached over and righted the cup, and poured more water into it from the pitcher. "Let me go get a towel to pick up that water," she said, shuffling out of the room. When she came back with towel in hand, she found that the cup was overturned once again, facing Eka like a gaping mouth. She looked long and curiously at Eka, who only kept staring, unblinking, at the cup, and Maisie felt a sudden shudder cascading over her body. She couldn't shake the feeling of a sinister presence in the room.

Was it just the routine fatigue of working the night shift? Glen Haven had a famous reputation for being haunted, but she had never entertained the possibility with any seriousness until now. The image of centipedes crawling toward Maisie, leaving a trail of blood on the floor in front of her as if they had just crawled out of a fresh corpse in another dimension and were tracking its remains with them into ours, flashed before her eyes for a moment before disappearing.

A terrible fear washed over Maisie, fear for her sanity and fear of losing her job if she dared to report the incident. Her face was frozen into an anxious frown. Before she could find any kind of rationalization, something invisible, cold and wet slithered around her neck and tightened, and she lurched to yell but no sound came out. Was it a hand? An arm? A snake? All she knew was that it was muscled, wet and slimy. Her reflex was to reach up and pull it away, but the texture of it was so repulsive that the thought of touching it terrified her. She struggled to scream for help, but no matter how forcefully she tried to push the air out of her lungs, no sound came out. The thing slowly lifted her in the air until her feet were no longer touching the ground, and then suddenly released her. She fell forward on the ground, onto her hands and knees, gasping for air, as an ethereal voice whispered in Maisie's ear, "*No... more... sssinging. Run.*"

At that moment, Dr. Varma walked past in the hallway, saw Maisie kneeling on the ground and rushed over to her, helping her to stand up. "Are you alright, Maisie? What happened?"

24

Maisie tried to speak but her voice was gone, and she fell into silent sobs, choking on her tears.

| Chapter Four |

It was Thursday night and the air was its usual hot, heavy, humid self on Bourbon Street in the French Quarter of New Orleans, Louisiana. The smell of beer was lingering in the air like a cloud amidst the sweat and clamor of college kids making an early start of celebrating Labor Day weekend before returning to school for the semester. Police officers patrolled the thoroughfare on horseback while buskers on every corner entertained tourists. Onlookers gazed from second-story balconies, leaning over French colonial-style wrought iron railings, sipping drinks named after hurricanes.

Mingling with the light spilling through the misty air from its neon signs, the sound of a jazz band being cheered by an enthusiastic crowd could be heard from the sidewalk outside the Bomb Lounge, where Titi Beaumond did Tarot readings every week for Mystic Thursdays, where an onyx-skinned gentleman by the name of Adrian Wirth was now approaching to enter the building, sporting a short afro faded at the temples, a closely-trimmed beard and metallic gray Givenchy suit.

The muscled bouncer halted him at the door. "Strippers don't come on until eleven," he said gruffly, holding up the palm of his hand.

"I'm here to see Miss Titi Beaumond," said Adrian, taking out his wallet to pay the cover charge.

"You mean Madame T?" asked the bouncer, taking a stern read of Adrian's face before stepping aside to let him in. "She's in the back, lap dance room number three."

As Adrian made his way past the crowded bar, he glanced over at a man from whose subtext he presumed correctly to be the venue's owner, just as security was informing said owner that the strippers were ready to go on, but the audience was cheering for an encore from the band. "Let them have their encore," said the owner, who was thrilled to see a lively crowd enjoying the lineup. Swamped in applause, the band's saxophonist came up on stage for a solo and waited for the crowd to fall silent before launching into a plaintive rendition of Duke Ellington's "Satin Doll." It was so spellbinding that Adrian stopped for a minute to watch and listen, losing himself in the music before remembering what he had come there for.

He headed past the bar down the darkened hallway leading to the lap dance rooms where a group of scantily clad young women stood by loitering, waiting to go onstage. "What's poppin', playboy?" said one of them, wearing a bikini as white as her luminous teeth and embellished with rhinestones and feathers. She slid her arm around his waist and pressed her voluminous breasts up against his muscular frame. "How about some one-on-one time?"

"I'm here to see Madame T," he said, politely declining the young ingénue, who looked half his age and who was the kind of girl some part of him secretly wished his gay son would take an interest in. To her, he simply looked like money.

She pouted and then gave him a seductive wink adorned with fluffy false eyelashes as he continued making his way through. Rooms one and two already had dancers occupying them, warming up for their shift. As he approached the third room, he caught sight of Titi packing up her belongings, wearing an elegant red halter top and brightly colored floral print skirt with a slit up the leg, and was suddenly overcome by the memory of the hypnotic smell of her skin, the thought of which aroused him intensely in a way that the stripper's flirtation had not. He took a deep breath and could hear the words "Hey beautiful" come out of his mouth, but they seemed distant and unreal, drowning in the ambient noise.

"Adrian!" said Titi, clutching at her chest to catch her breath as he walked over and planted a kiss on her cheek, handing her a single orange rose. A delighted smile spread across her face as she gracefully leaned forward to inhale its fragrance. "What a pleasant surprise! What brings you out to New Orleans on a Thursday night?"

"You told me you did Tarot readings here on Thursdays, so I thought I would come hit you up for one," he said in his baritone voice that sounded deliciously like morning coffee.

"Oh, I know how it is," she teased. "You really came here to see the strippers, didn't you?"

He laughed. "I've seen plenty of strippers. I came here to see you."

Plenty? thought Titi, with a subtle raise of the eyebrow. Not quite the answer she was expecting.

Did I just say plenty? he thought, cringing.

Not missing a beat, she continued, "Well, I'm getting ready to head home for the night, but if you want, you can come up to my place for a private reading, in exchange for escorting me home?"

"Sounds great," he said, then added, jokingly, "What's in it for you?"

"You're funny," she said with a warm smile, giving him a wink that melted his heart like the Louisiana sun on a glass of iced tea.

She owed her captivating features, radiant light brown

skin and shiny, straight black hair to a vibrant ancestry that took its roots in Louisiana in the early 17th century, boasting the genetic contributions of Indigenous, Spanish, French, African, and Haitian aristocracy. Her grandfather, Charles Roy, Sr., had uncovered through the work of several professional genealogists that a revolutionary Haitian Vodou King, a Choctaw diplomat and warrior Chief, and an African American Civil War General of the Corps d'Afrique were but a few of the dignified suitors seeking and winning the affections of her famously desirable foremothers.

And when Titi said, "come up to my place," she meant literally—her apartment was directly above the nightclub. Once inside, she asked him if he had any interest in smoking a bowl with her. "I have some bomb weed from the dispensary," she said, pulling a small baggie out of a wooden box on the shelf and passing it to him to examine. The smell of it was potent and reminded him of smoking joints in college.

"Thanks, but I'll have to pass," he said. "I have to be back in Baton Rouge tonight to get ready for a deposition at 8 a.m."

"Understood," she said, smiling and gently shelving the baggie in its wooden box. "Another time."

Noticing a photo of her with another man on the end table, a white man with a beard and glasses, he wondered if it was any of his business to ask who it was. If he recalled correctly, she had mentioned previously that her ex-husband was white, and it concerned him that his photo might still be on display. He decided that now wasn't the right time to ask about it, especially considering that it was only their second date, and not even technically a date since she hadn't been expecting to see him that night. It was nevertheless disquieting.

She invited him to come sit on the couch for a Tarot reading, and deftly shuffled the deck. "Any questions in mind for the reading?"

"Sure, how about how the future of our relationship is looking?"

"Okay," she smiled, setting the deck on the coffee table. "Cut the cards."

He cut the deck into three piles, like he used to do at poker night back in law school, then reassembled the piles. She drew the top three cards from the deck and turned them face up in front of him. "Whoa," he said, frowning.

The first card said "Death" on it, and had the image of a skeleton wearing black armour and riding a white horse. The second card said "The Tower" and depicted persons falling from a burning tower that was being struck by lightning. The third card said "The Devil" on it, and showed a naked couple bound in chains, with a winged Devil figure looming behind them.

"Something tells me that's not a good sign," he laughed.

"Every coin has two sides to it," she reassured him. "Death means letting go of the past. It also means rebirth. The Tower tells us there's a radical change coming. And The Devil can mean lust, but typically it means some form of bondage or enslavement. Addiction, for example."

"Interesting," he said, rubbing his chin. "Proceeding with caution is advised?"

"Sure, you could take it that way. Or you could take it as advising us to let go of logic and proceed with wild abandon. Take your pick."

He laughed again. "Wild abandon definitely sounds tempting. Let me ask you something, out of curiosity. Or is there more to the reading?"

"There's more I could say, but we can come back to that. I'm interested to hear your question."

"Ok. What was it that interested you in my dating profile?"

"You want me to be honest?"

He smiled. "Yes, I want you to be honest."

She reflected for a moment on the memory of reading his profile for the first time. "Your dignity and class were apparent. I like that. Sharply dressed, intelligent, articulate. Emotional depth and sensitivity. A man of refined tastes. But I have to say, the icing on the cake was the fact that you don't drink."

"Really," he said, surprised. "Why did that seal the deal?"

"Long history of alcoholism in my family," she answered candidly. "I don't even want to get into it. I just don't want or need it in my life, especially now that I'm past the age of 40. Life is way too short for that mess."

"I understand," he said, nodding thoughtfully, staring at the Tarot cards. "My father was an alcoholic too. It destroyed his marriage, and took my mother's life when she committed suicide."

"Oh my Lord, that's horrible," said Titi, reaching over to squeeze his hand. "I'm so sorry."

"It's okay, I'm fine," he said, tensing his arm and resisting the urge to pull his hand away to shield himself from the unexpected wave of vulnerability. "It was a long time ago. I've dealt with the pain since then. I'm just trying to protect my son from all that with the choices I'm making right now. I've had enough crazy in my life."

If you only knew, thought Titi, reflecting on her own life, holding back the urge to say so.

"But it's hard for me," he continued, "with the work I do. The firm I work with in Baton Rouge is a real boys' club. I'm the youngest attorney there, and the only one who's Black. Excluding myself from drinking makes them see me even more as an outsider. Anyway, don't get me started. Let's talk about something else."

"Don't worry about it," she said. "You don't have to keep things light for my sake."

"It's not that," he said, tensing his eyebrows. "I just want to take things slow. I feel something powerful with us. I don't want to mess it up."

She breathed a happy sigh. "The feeling is mutual."

"On that note," he said, leaning forward to stand up. "I actually should get on the road. I need to get back and prep for that deposition."

"Leaving already?" She stood up with him and slid her arms around his neck, as he embraced the warmth of her body and breathed it in. "But you just got here. Why don't you spend the night? Head back in the morning."

"I'd like that," he said, leaning into her, and surrendering to the impulse to kiss her. His heart was alive with excitement and desire, and he started negotiating with himself how early he would have to leave in the morning if he spent the night, in order to get back to Baton Rouge in time to get a shower in before going to the office.

Falling into this woman with such power alarmed him. He could easily imagine himself relinquishing in a heartbeat all the stability and security he had worked so hard for over the last few years, in exchange for a few days of unbridled chaos with her. She was fire, and he wanted to fly into her like a moth, and damn all the consequences. It was terrifying. *Stop this foolishness,* he scolded himself. *You're not twenty years old anymore. Don't lose your head.* He pulled himself away from the kiss before lust could call any more shots. "Honestly, I should get on the road," he said again, still reluctant to get going.

"If you insist," she shrugged innocently, sensing his hesitation, maintaining eye contact and beckoning him with the infinite depths in her doe-like gaze.

He brushed a tendril of long, black hair off of her shoulder, staring at her skin like it was a pool of molten caramel he wished he could swim in. The gesture inspired another contented sigh, and she couldn't resist affectionately resting her head against his chest, with her right hand next to her face, over his heart. He was struck by the sincerity of it, and wondered what he had done in life to deserve something that felt so good. He squeezed her tight and didn't want to let go. "Um," he said at last.

She laughed and looked back up at him. "Um?"

He shook his head like he was trying to shake some sense into it and laughed too, calling himself back to the stack of legal briefs waiting for him at home. "Um, I think there's a Saints pre-season game this weekend. Any interest in coming along with me and my son?"

"Football is not really my thing," she admitted. "But I would love any opportunity to meet your son. Any interest in coming to a poetry slam on Sunday night? I wrote a new poem, inspired by Clermezine Clermeille, that I'm going to perform."

"Who's that?"

"She's a *lwa*—a Voodoo spirit."

"Ah, Voodoo. I'm not too familiar with it. I was raised Christian."

"So was I," she laughed. "Raised Roman Catholic. Let me tell you, my family wasn't thrilled about that path choosing me."

"Well, I have no reservations about it," he reassured her. "I would love to hear all about that journey sometime. But my son Jericho is in a school play, and I promised him I would come see it on Sunday. I would invite you, but my ex-wife might be there, and speaking of crazy, she's a whole mess of it that I don't want to expose you to at this point in our relationship."

The mention of his ex-wife provoked a twinge of jealousy, and Titi nodded and looked away casually to distill her reaction. He pulled himself to his feet, and took her hand in his. "And now, I really must go. Thank you for letting me know you, Miss Titi Beaumond. I wish I could spend every waking minute with you. You don't even know how much that's true."

The sting of disappointment over his leaving was eased by the warmth of his compliment.

"And," he added, "I would most definitely love to hear

your poetry sometime."

"Thank you," she said, closing her eyes for a moment and smiling modestly, taking in the warmth. Opening her eyes, she looked into his and said, "I would love to join you for a Saints game. I won't have the first clue of what's going on in the game, but the chance to spend time with you and your son sounds wonderful."

"Excellent," he said, smiling back. "I'll check the schedule and let you know. And maybe, if you're lucky," he said half-jokingly, "I'll let you hear some of my poetry sometime too."

"What! You write poetry?"

"I used to," he said. "It's been decades since I've had the inclination." For a moment, he silently conjured a particular composition of his own creation, which had spontaneously popped up in his memory.

Fear not the witching hour.
Your bleeding heart shall be your power.

It was the opening to a poem that Adrian had written his senior year in high school. He was never fond of it; he thought it sounded trite. He kept the notebook it was written in locked in an old mahogany chest in his attic, along with other vestiges of a romantic spirit he believed had left him for good when he made the decision to go to law school. Twenty years later, the words were coalescing in his consciousness like clouds drifting across the moon, their relevance slowly seeping in. He debated whether to share it and finally decided against it.

After one last toe-tingling kiss and a long, tight embrace, Adrian finally headed out into the humid New Orleans night air, and Titi went back into her bedroom. She made the bed while happily humming Satin Doll, and then picked up a book to read, although her mind was decidedly elsewhere.

Her pleasant thoughts were interrupted by the ringtone of her cell phone, and she grimaced when her cousin Rochelle's name appeared on the caller ID. *Speak of the Devil.*

| Chapter Five |

One might have expected Rochelle and her cousin Titi to have a close, sisterly relationship, being only five years apart in age and having grown up together, but anyone who knew them could tell you that things had always been strained between them. The fact that Rochelle was now in a relationship with Titi's ex-husband, Carlos, was a particular source of friction, but their relationship tension had existed long before Titi had even met Carlos.

"Titi?" said Rochelle, speaking in a humbled tone that caught Titi off-guard as she answered the phone. "I need your help."

Titi frowned, at a loss for words. She had a hard time imagining what Rochelle could possibly need help with, and whatever it was, Titi didn't feel especially inclined to help her. Her inner ice queen took over. "Are you drunk? Do you realize what time it is? Don't you have a marriage to go wreck, or something?"

Rochelle exhaled sharply. "Wow. Okay. So you're still not over this, after all this time? And Angie told me you're back to dating again, so, I don't know... I guess I just thought you would be past this by now. You still see your marriage ending as no fault of your own? And how are you going to get involved with someone new when you're not even over your ex? It's really a bad start for a relationship."

"Oh, I'm over Carlos, believe me," said Titi sharply. "I finally let go of the idea that he and I could ever get back together. It doesn't change the fact that you wronged me. You. My family. My flesh and blood. But you know what? I'd rather not get into it. I don't know why I need to waste my time explaining this to you all over again—"

"Oh, please," Rochelle interrupted. "Go ahead. Seriously, I wish you would. Let's get it all out, right now, so we can both move on with our lives."

Titi didn't want to get dragged into another fight with her cousin on this subject, especially if Rochelle had been drinking, but the idea of having a last word about it did appeal to her, so she could truly move on with Adrian without the weight of this emotional baggage. "What's so hard to understand? You and I grew up together. You're like a sister to me. So to know that you're getting intimate with someone I was once so deeply in love with, someone I thought I was going to spend the rest of my life with, just… I don't know, it just makes me physically ill. It grosses me out. I don't know how else to put it. It's like incest or something. It's wrong. It goes against my biology."

"So he's your property? He doesn't get to choose what he wants for himself? And is it me who's making you ill, or is it some kind of fairy tale conditioning that says that weddings are only ever followed by 'happily ever after'? He wasn't happy being with you, Titi. Don't you want him to be free to choose happiness for himself? Don't you want him to be independent of your need to control him?"

"You try telling Mama Ruth that honoring your vows is just a fairy tale, she'll set you straight on that attitude. I should have known you would find some way to turn this around and blame me. I knew it was a mistake to even take your call. You just happened to catch me in a good mood."

"Okay, wait!" Rochelle took a breath and reminded herself that the four trafficking victims were more important than her pride. *Suck it up,* she ordered herself as though she were one of her cadets at the Federal Law Enforcement Training Center. "Just slow down for a second, Titi, please. Just... hold up." *Does she think this is easy for me? Does she think I'm someone who likes asking for help?* "I can't help that I love him, alright? Do you think I just woke up one day and decided to pull this yeasty conspiracy out of my vagina to sabotage my cousin's marriage?" she scoffed, then quickly downshifting to a more gracious tone before Titi could take offense. "I mean, you fell in love with him, too, so you can understand that, can't you? I don't know what else to say, Titi. All I did was listen to my heart, for once. For once! Is that really so insidious to you? Maybe you find this hard to believe, but I wasn't trying to hurt you. Not at any point was it ever about you. I didn't mean for it to happen. I wish you could believe that. I'm stuck in this no-win situation, and I don't know how to fix it. And he never cheated on you, you know that, right?"

"Ha," said Titi, laughing with a raspy voice that betrayed her affinity for smoking herb. "I believe *that* like *you* believe in Voodoo."

Rochelle groaned. Maybe Titi was right, this whole phone call was a mistake that never should have happened. She was already on the warpath before she even answered the phone. *Wish her the best and let her go.*

"Believe what you want," said Titi, after the pause lingered. "I don't care anymore. So what do you want from me now?"

Rochelle cleared her throat. "I was hoping to get your input on a case that I'm working on," she said carefully. The last thing she needed was to get Titi riled up again and have her go another six months of not taking her calls. "Funny you should mention Voodoo, because it has to do with that, actually. And no, I wasn't thrilled about the idea of asking you about this. But the matter is serious enough that it was worth a try. We've taken four women into custody, human trafficking victims who were forced into the sex trade. Two of them are HIV-positive. They're also crack addicts. Right now, they're undergoing state-mandated rehab to prepare them to testify against their pimp." Rochelle paused cautiously to consider her next words. She was distracted for a moment with wondering if her work as an FBI agent made Titi feel threatened somehow. *It makes sense that it would,* thought Rochelle, *since my work makes a real impact on the world.*

"What is it that you think I can do?" said Titi impatiently. "I know I'm a healer, but you've never actually shown any confidence in my abilities."

Rochelle battled the urge to go into the kitchen to pour herself a drink. "The trafficking victims have been saying some strange things," she said, picking up the empty Vodka bottle on the floor by her feet to see if there was anything left in it. There wasn't. "I realize that crack addicts say all kinds of crazy things, and demon possession is a common delusion. But what they're saying is highly specific. They've been talking about a *bokaw nimbo*, also talking about putting a *gri-gri* on their pimp, whom we also have in custody. Does any of this make sense to you? It's Voodoo, right?"

"Surely you don't believe a word of it," said Titi, shrugging dismissively. "Unless your feelings about Voodoo have changed since we last spoke?"

"No, they haven't. These vics have this crazy idea that they're the reincarnated souls of four women who died three hundred years ago, during the Salem witch trials. Sorry to be blunt, but needless to say, I'm not buying it. But I do agree with Lin Mei, in the sense that the stories we tell ourselves can have a powerful impact on our bodies. So I—"

"Stories, huh?" Titi interrupted her with another reproachful laugh. "If they're only stories to you, then what are you calling me for? I really don't have time for this. Have yourself a good night."

"Listen," said Rochelle, losing patience. "You call yourself a healer, but you need me to stroke your ego first to get you to care about them?" She cleared her throat again and made a conscious effort to soften her tone. "Sorry. All I'm saying is, just meet them, please? I'm not thrilled about the idea, okay? I can't lie. I know you don't like hearing how I feel about your... Voodoo." Stopped short of using the word *hobby*. "But it doesn't matter if I believe their story, does it? What matters is that they believe it. And if you can help *us* find a way to help *them*, then that's what's important, isn't it? What's also important is that we need them to testify, so we can put these trafficking creeps away for life."

"Okay. Fine. You're right."

Did she actually have a change of heart, or is she just patronizing me now?

"No, you're right," Titi said again, answering Rochelle's unspoken thoughts, more convincingly this time. "Maybe there's something I can do to help. That *is* what's most important. I'll give you that. I'll hear what they have to say. And as for your doubts about Voodoo, maybe this case will be what it takes to convince you of its power."

"Yeah," said Rochelle, still obviously skeptical. "We'll see. I'll have my assistant get a hold of you about arranging your flight to New York City, and we'll meet up at Glen Haven psychiatric hospital, where the victims are in rehab. The arraignment is tomorrow afternoon, so I'd like to try to see you before that."

"Oh no," said Titi abruptly. "That won't be possible. I need time to meditate, and gather some healing and ceremonial supplies, and I also need to do an herbal bath in preparation."

Rochelle shook her head and rolled her eyes. *What lunacy did I just get myself into?* "Look, we don't have time for all that frou-frou stuff. My boss Reid isn't going to go for that. We just want your opinion, okay? Not your scented oils. I just need you to get up here as soon as possible. Please. I'm asking nicely."

"You call that nicely? You better let me get going then."

Titi hung up the phone, shaking her head in disbelief. *Some things never change.* As she swung her feet around the side of her bed in order to stand up, she suddenly caught sight of some shadowy movement in her peripheral vision, coming from the hallway just beyond her open bedroom door. She turned her head to look, and was startled by the tall, tenebrous figure of a woman who had long black curls flowing around her head, defying gravity. Draped in a ruched red satin dressing gown with a long flowing skirt and flared sleeves that rippled around her like water, the woman cradled in her left arm the dark specter of an infant, while extending with her right hand a long silver dagger. In front of her hovered a large white oval porcelain basin. Titi immediately recognized the figure as a Voodoo lwa, Mambo Erzulie Dantó, whom she had seen in visions on previous occasions, but whose powerful presence overwhelmed her every time.

Dantó said nothing, but her ire was made clear in the form of intense sonic waves that rippled outward from her, bending the air around her and shaking the room like an earthquake. Titi struggled to speak to acknowledge her, but could only gasp for air, falling backward in reverence and terror.

As Dantó tilted the dagger forward, the basin was lifted by magic and tipped toward Titi, pouring from it a flood of thick, dark red blood which defied the bounds of gravity as it crawled into the room like the tentacles of an octopus, stretching toward Titi like venomous snakes. She lost consciousness as they swallowed her whole.

| Chapter Six |

Lin Mei stared absently past her apple martini at the bottle of Midori liqueur sitting on the shelf behind the bartender, glowing a bright neon green from the mood lighting illuminating the bar. She noticed in her peripheral vision a slim, Caucasian businessman with athletic build sitting down the bar to her left, and hoped he wouldn't come over to talk to her. From his posture, tailored suit and genuine leather briefcase, he obviously came from money, but from his subtext, Lin Mei was guessing more specifically that he worked in investment banking, and from his swagger, she guessed he came from a family of old money. His skin seemed unnaturally tan and leathery, tanning bed maybe? Casting another subtle glance with her side eye, she decided he wasn't the tanning bed type. Surfer? *He lacks the aura of a surfer. Maybe he just got back from a vacation in Cancun,* she pondered. *Oh God, here he comes.*

He stood up and picked up his briefcase, and sauntered over to the empty stool next to Lin Mei. "*Konban wa,*" he said in a thick American accent while flashing a glossy smile.

Tanning bed. "I'm not Japanese," said Lin Mei politely, even though she spoke it fluently. "My wife is, though."

"Your *wife!*" he said, laughing. "I wouldn't have pegged you for a lesbian."

"Why's that?" said Lin Mei, although she anticipated the answer. She was trolling a little, but wisely had intentionally left out the part where her wife was presenting as a man when she married her. This guy didn't seem like the trans-friendly type. And in reality, she never would have pegged herself for a lesbian, either. She just loved her wife too much to let her go, even though the surprise of her coming out as a woman was still new and overwhelming to her. It was only a month ago that she was still calling her Mik instead of Midori. She was still struggling with pronouns on occasion, which she found embarrassing, just as she felt embarrassed every time she caught herself still searching for Mik's old familiar face when she looked at Midori, searching for the Mik who, it seemed, didn't want to be around anymore. To Lin Mei, Midori appeared to have a totally new identity, even though to Midori, her true self had been there all along, just waiting to express herself in full.

Lin Mei knew it to be irrational, but a grievous sadness about it consumed her, like it was a death somehow. She dismissed her grief as silly sentimentality, because obviously Mik didn't really *go* anywhere, and all the same memories and personality were still there, just breathing with a different face, a more lilting tone of voice as a result of the estrogen therapy. And Midori of course loved Lin Mei just the same as Mik ever did, even more so now that Lin Mei saw and accepted her for who she really was. As a psychologist, Lin Mei would have imagined herself to be better equipped than most to adjust to the transition. But what adjustment it did require of her, she still found hard to accept.

"You're too pretty," said the businessman, shrugging. Then, with a lecherous grin that made Lin Mei's skin crawl, he said, "I bet the sex is really hot though, right? I know how you Asian chicks are. Freaks in bed."

Lin Mei smiled awkwardly and took a sip of her martini, wondering if wishing hard enough would make him go away. *I can't even remember the last time we had sex. But it's not because of the transition,* she made clear in her mind, as though Midori could hear her thoughts. *It's because of me being exhausted all the time from work.*

"So if you're not Japanese, what are you then?"

She didn't feel like getting into it, and suspected that he had no real interest in the answer anyway. "American," she said.

"Let me buy you a drink," he said, beckoning the bartender.

"No thank you, I have one," she said, lifting her glass in a curt gesture to remind him.

"Let me get you another one. Bartender, another martini for the lady."

"No, really, it's okay," she insisted. She shot a pleading look at the bartender for him not to bring another. "It's been a rough day, I'd really like to just enjoy my drink alone."

The businessman glared at her in disbelief.

Here it comes.

"Well you don't have to be a bitch about it," he snarled.

"Come on, man," said the bartender, interceding. "Let the lady have her space."

"Fucking dyke," the businessman seethed, nostrils flaring in disgust as he picked up his drink and briefcase, and walked to the other end of the bar.

"Thank you," said Lin Mei to the bartender. "I really appreciate it."

The bartender said nothing but only nodded his head and tipped an imaginary hat as if to say, "You're welcome," and turned away to help another patron.

Lin Mei's phone rang, and she dug it out of her red patent leather purse, thankful for an escape. *This purse is such a creep magnet,* she thought, glancing at the caller ID. It was Rochelle.

"I took your advice," said Rochelle, sounding like she still wasn't sure it was the right thing to do. "I called my cousin Titi. She's flying up here tomorrow to come consult on the case."

"Good," said Lin Mei, taking a sip of her martini. "You know it was the right thing to do. There's something unnatural going on with those women. I'm curious to hear what your cousin has to say about it."

"I'd say being sold into sex slavery is pretty damn unnatural."

A garbled woman's voice on the airport intercom announced boarding for a departing flight.

"Where are you?" said Rochelle, perplexed by the ambient sound.

"I'm at Martini Moon."

"At JFK? What are you doing there?"

"Having a drink."

"I get that, that's what people usually do at a bar. What are you doing *at the airport?*"

"I'm getting ready to fly to Tokyo."

"What? Why?"

"It's a family emergency. Midori went to Tokyo a few days ago to come out to her father in person about the transition. Her father didn't take it well, which of course I didn't think he would. She didn't take it well, his not taking it well. Ended up relapsing into a meth binge at a party, now she's falling apart. Her sister called to tell me it's going to be difficult for Midori to stay at their house much longer. That's her polite way of saying they're going to put her out on the street if I don't come get her."

"You can't be serious. You know Keiko would never do that. And why is it *your* job to pick up the pieces? You're getting on a thirteen-hour flight to go literally drag her ass back here? Come on, Lin Mei. I thought you had better self-esteem than this."

"It's not about my self-esteem," said Lin Mei defensively.

"I love her, and she needs me right now. If you met her father, you would understand. Textbook narcissist. Empathy is not in his vocabulary."

"Believe me, I understand. If you met *my* father, you would understand just how well I understand. Sometimes you need to just put on your big girl panties, though, and deal with things. She's never going to figure out how to solve problems for herself with you coddling her all the time. You're enabling her."

"This isn't about enabling. There's not going to be a 'rock bottom,' okay? She needs some support, or she's going to self-destruct, and I'll never forgive myself if that happens. And yes, we all have narcissistic fathers in common. Okay, except Carlos. He has a narcissistic mother. That's why we all get along so well. But the abuse Midori suffered is different from ours. It's bound to her transness. It's just... different. It's *deeply* stigmatized. And she's capable of learning better coping mechanisms if someone will take the time to teach them to her. I happen to be in a position to help her, and I want to. Don't worry, I have a clear sense of where my boundaries are and I'm not afraid to defend them."

"Hm, okay. If you say so," said Rochelle, inclining toward changing the subject. "Speaking of Carlos, I haven't heard from him since he left for his trip to San Francisco. Not sure what's going on with us right now, but—"

"I've got to go," said Lin Mei, cutting her short. "They're about to start boarding my flight.

"When are you going to be back? I really wanted you to meet Titi. Consulting her was *your* idea."

"You don't need me there as a buffer. Don't worry, you'll be fine."

"I don't need you there as a buffer, Cray." Rochelle shook her head and laughed. "I just want you to meet her. Just so you can get to know some of my family, you know? Stop overanalyzing everything. And be safe over there, okay?"

"I will. Stay sober. I'll see you when I get back."

Stay sober? Now why did she have to go and say that? Rochelle's thoughts were racing in indignation. *Who's the one at a bar right now? You want to see an alcoholic? Let me take you to meet my father. What I drink to help me cope with the brutality of my work is nothing by comparison. It's nothing.*

"Are you still there?"

"Yeah, I'm here. See you when you get back."

| Chapter Seven |

Titi found herself floating high above the Louisiana Bayou, a crescent moon behind her, clouds and lush vegetation at a dizzying distance below her. Her heart leaped with excitement and she inhaled deeply to relish the moment, as flying dreams were her favorite. Now seemed like a good opportunity to practice her descent, which had been awkward and clumsy in previous flying dreams. Using her mind to navigate, she lucidly drifted down, down, down, clouds wafting softly past her face, not cold and wet the way real clouds would be, but soft and comfy like her cotton bedsheets.

She still didn't quite have the hang of landings, but she did manage to steer herself away from the dark, fertile water of the Bayou, and tensed her legs to brace for touchdown on dry land. Pulling in a lungful of air for buoyancy, her feet lightly touched the ground like a feather coming to rest after a magnificent journey.

Looking around in the moonlit dark, her eyes had to adjust to find her bearings. Gasping with surprise, she realized that she had landed at the estate of her deceased grandfather,

Charles Roy, Sr. During her childhood, she remembered his house mostly for the hot summer days, playing outside and running through the thick green foliage with her cousins. How different it looked at night! How different it looked in her dreams. There was a vibrant old oak tree she had never seen before, radiating some type of wave that was a mixture of sound and light. "It's you," she said, putting her hand on the tree and sensing the warm spilling out from its grooved, textured bark. "You're the one who dreamed all of this into existence."

The sound of a voice startled her. It came from somewhere close, as if right over her left shoulder, but she couldn't see anyone there. Her heart skipped a beat as she realized with astonishment that it was the voice of Papa Charles—her deceased grandfather.

"Titi Anne! Where my grandbaby at!" said the voice. "Where is she!"

"I'm right here, Paw Paw!" she announced, and on hearing her own voice, realized that she was in the form of a child—her own nine-year-old self.

"Where you at, baby girl! Come closer!"

"Right here, Paw Paw!" she called out again. She looked all around but again, didn't see him. *He's here in spirit, not in the flesh,* she realized. It was already a year since he had passed on when she was at the age of nine.

"Come over to me here, darlin'," he said. "And bring that drawing with you."

She looked down at her right hand which was holding a drawing that in real life she had made as a child. It was a drawing of four young ladies, one that had upset her mother Sheila when she questioned Titi about it. Titi had completely forgotten about the drawing until now.

"Who are these girls?" her mother had asked her when she showed her the drawing. The year was 1984.

"They're ghosts," said Titi, wearing a smocked pink dress that she normally wore to church, white tights, and black patent leather shoes with a T-strap, with her hair folding neatly into braided ponytails. She had insisted, as she usually did with great pride, on doing her own hair, since her mother always pulled too tightly against her sensitive scalp.

"Ghosts!" exclaimed her mother in dismay. "What do you mean, ghosts? Who are these two white girls? Are they girls from your school?"

"I don't know," said Titi. "I think they're sisters. And this girl here is Native American. And this Black woman is their slave. Somebody killed all four of them. And now they're ghosts."

Her mother clicked her tongue disapprovingly, snatched the drawing out of her hand and tore it up. "I don't like this at all, Miss Titi Anne Jameson. The only spirit you need to be seeking out is the Holy Spirit, you hear? Don't let me catch you drawing pictures of ghosts again, child. I've done told your Auntie Yolande I don't like you watching MTV at their house. 'Thriller' is not appropriate viewing for children." Titi wanted to tell her that the drawing didn't come from watching Michael Jackson, but she knew better than to talk back.

In the dream, Titi held the drawing up to her face and peered closely at it. Four young ladies, all holding hands. A blonde, a red-head, an Indigenous girl and a Black woman. The colors of the drawing were vivid and animated, like they were alive. On closer look, they were indeed alive. They were all looking Titi directly in the eye. As the four of them opened their mouths, an unearthly sound emerged which seemed a cross between a rumble and a scream.

"Come on in here, baby girl!" said her grandfather's voice again, startling her, and Titi realized the voice was coming from inside the house.

The front door was slightly ajar, and it pulled her toward it, as if she were floating. *I'm frightened, Paw Paw. What's happening?* She pulled open the screen door and pressed her

50

hand against the wooden door to push it open. As it swung inward, she stepped inside where a skeleton figure solemnly rested with an upright posture in the sitting room, wearing a long black Victorian dress, in her grandmother's burgundy velvet armchair. On the floor next to the skeleton was a shiny black rooster that slowly turned to look at Titi as she entered the room. *Time to wake up,* whispered the rooster without making a sound. She recognized the seated skeleton figure as Maman Brigitte, a Voodoo spirit whose role as a death lwa is to help the recently deceased transcend into spirit form.

On the long settee behind her, four women were seated, whom Titi recognized as the ones in the drawing, only now they were adults. They looked lifeless and expressionless, like dolls. Maman Brigitte raised a bony finger and pointed to the window behind Titi, over her right shoulder. She shuddered to realize that there was a malicious presence standing behind her, outside the window. She didn't want to turn to look at it, but couldn't help herself. Fear preventing her from moving any faster than molasses, she slowly pivoted her head to the right, her breath trembling as she gradually looked back over her shoulder until the demon came into view.

A tall, lanky, humanoid figure which seemed to have the head of a giant, dead fish, the irises of its eyes a blood red color with a giant black pupil in the center of each eye which widened at the sight of her, and a slimy gray tongue which protruded from its partly opened mouth, stared at her through the window glass. Its nose was long and pointed like that of a barracuda, with thin lips stretched in a snarl along the sides of its face, and a narrow row of small pointed yellow teeth lining its gray gums. The rest of its body was smooth and slick like a salamander, dark pink with purple and blue-green blotches that looked like bruises.

She wanted to scream at the sight of it, not just because it looked grotesque, but because it gave her a horrible feeling, the feeling that something menacing was invading her space just by staring from outside the window, something that didn't belong here breathing our air, something which she somehow knew intended to do her harm, and hadn't yet only for the sadistic thrill of it, wanting her to feel the full fear and dread of its intention.

The demon was motionless for who could say how long, silently gazing at her before finally raising its left hand from which branched six fingers, bulbous and round like those of a gecko, which the creature pressed to the glass near its face. Panic arose in Titi's chest. She wondered why beautiful dreams had to turn into such terrible nightmares.

The center of each of the demon's six fingers opened like a pore, and whitish-green, slithering creatures like worms or giant maggots oozed out, trespassing through the glass as effortlessly as through water, sliding across the ceiling, walls and floor toward Titi. Nauseated by their horrific odor which stung like the smell of vomit, she struggled to maintain her breathing as they took the shape of white smoky shadow figures, pacing the outer perimeter of the room, silently looking around, and occasionally looking over at her with vacant faces. At last, they lifted their arms and somehow transported the demon into the room, pulling him through the glass once again as if it were water.

The demon walked toward Titi and sniffed her face, and Titi tried to lean back away from it, but she realized that she was paralyzed and had no choice but to be subjected to its invasion of her space. "How many strippers is plenty, Mrs. Beaumond?" it asked with a croaking voice, but Titi couldn't answer.

With a wave of its hand, the rest of the sitting room disappeared, and Titi found herself standing in almost total darkness with the creature, except for a narrow, dim spotlight which lit the two of them from above. The demon pivoted to its left and gestured into the darkness, where an apparition of Adrian materialized under another dim spotlight. His eyes were open but he stood perfectly still, seemingly unaware of his surroundings. "Look what I found," said the creature. "Keys in the car and no one around. Who could blame me for taking a spin?"

Pointing one bulbous finger at Adrian, the fish-headed beast summoned a red gasoline can which materialized, hovering, in the air in front of Adrian. Curling its fingers as if manipulating a marionette, it compelled Adrian to use the gas can to pour gasoline all over his head and face, as the suffocating odor of petrol stabbed Titi in the heart. Then the gas can disappeared, and a cigarette lighter materialized in its place. Titi wanted to scream, but was helpless to do anything except feel tears escaping from the sides of her eyes.

The demon pivoted back toward Titi, as Adrian silently erupted in flames behind him. It placed its six fingers on Titi's chest and gave her an abrupt push—not hard enough to make her fall down, but hard enough to convey a threat. "Don't think for a moment that I'm going to let a little slit get in my way," it hissed in her face, the word "slit" coming out like "ssslit." It gestured back toward Adrian, and Titi could see now that the flames were gone, leaving Adrian with a blank expression, like a mannequin head without a face. "You can have him back now. He won't be much use to you, or anyone ever again, unless you manage to undo the enchantment before it kills you both."

Knock, knock, knock.

| Chapter Eight |

Titi awoke in a panic to the sound of a slow, persistent knocking at the front door. Clutching her chest to catch her breath, she picked up her phone to see what time it was. 11:17 a.m.—so much for getting to New York City by this afternoon. Rochelle wasn't going to be happy about that. There was a missed call and a voicemail from her cousin Angelique in Charleston, and two missed calls from Rochelle.

Titi dialed Adrian's number. No answer. She hung up and listened to the voicemail from Angie as she got up to answer the door. "Hey T," said the message. "Had a worrisome dream about you last night. I dreamed that Mama Erzulie Dantó was angry with you. Just calling to see if you're alright. Call me!"

Taking a quick peek through the peephole, Titi immediately recognized the shock of disheveled, peroxide-bleached hair with a crown of long black roots growing out, olive tan skin, dramatic eyebrows and the kind of naturally sharp cheekbones that many women emulate using contour, as belonging to her neighbor and friend, Lola Wheatley.

Lola had the kind of look which interested men called "exotic" and which often drew conjecture as to her ethnicity, especially after she took her ex-husband's last name which, like Titi, she had never bothered to change back to her maiden name following their divorce. She always gave, by way of a reply, an enigmatic smile, confessing no more than that she was of mixed descent. That enigmatic smile was, at the moment, nowhere to be found, as Lola faced the door with a soulless stare, raising her hand to knock again just before Titi opened it.

"Miss Lola!" exclaimed Titi warmly. "What a pleasure to see you, as always. Come on in. May I offer you some iced tea?"

Lola turned slowly to look Titi in the eyes with a desperate, pleading gaze, but said nothing. She was obviously in a bad way, and obviously no longer in the pregnant state she was in when Titi last saw her a couple of weeks ago.

"Okay, so that's a no on the iced tea. That's okay honey, come sit down on the couch here with me. You don't look too well. You had the baby, I take it? Everything went okay?"

Lola knitted her eyebrows in anguish, but still said nothing.

"Did you give up the baby for adoption, like you talked about?"

A subtle nod of yes.

"Okay," said Titi, slowly digesting the situation. "Okay. I understand now. I know that wasn't easy, but you know you did the right thing, right? You know that fool Randy wasn't going to help take care of you or the baby. At least this way, you know she'll get into a good home with parents who will be happy to have her. Maybe one day when she's grown, you can go talk to her about why you had to do what you had to do. But right now, you just need to take care of you. The lady at the adoption agency whose number I gave you—she's the one that helped me and Carlos when we were thinking about adopting. I told you that, right? They'll find her a good home, don't you worry."

Lola heaved a heavy sigh and stared down at the floor.

"Let's get you on into the tub so I can do a healing bath on you," said Titi, leading Lola into the bathroom. Lola was familiar with the routine of healing baths, and put up no objection to the suggestion. For many root doctors versed in herbal medicine like Titi, the word "bath" didn't mean being submerged in water, but rather the rubbing of the herbal "bath" treatment into their clients' bare hands and feet, and over the top of their clothes.

"Go on there, let's get your shoes and socks off, and get you onto the stool in the tub. I'll fix up a treatment for you with some rootwork for your postpartum depression." Lola knew well the routine; she had been coming to Titi for healing baths for almost a year, ever since Titi had set up a private Voodoo practice out of her home following her divorce. Supported by her family's wealth, Titi worked for tips and for karma, and as such, was well known as a healer among the poor and disadvantaged. She knew she needed to make some phone calls to let Angie and Rochelle know that everything was okay, and that she would be delayed getting up to New York, but they had waited this long and could wait another half hour. She was more concerned about whether Adrian was alright.

After the healing bath was completed, Titi rubbed Lola's feet with a towel and brought her back into the living room to sit down on the couch. She put her arms around Lola and held her tight while Lola silently rested her head on Titi's chest, heaving another heavy sigh before sobbing tears began to flow. "That's it," said Titi, comforting her softly. "Just let it on out. You're okay now, baby. You're okay."

| Chapter Nine |

"Oh God," said Dr. Silvia Gomez, a radiation oncologist at Bay Area Oncology Associates in San Francisco, California, eyeing the schedule on her laptop screen. "Dr. Beaumond is coming in today."

"Your ex?" said her colleague, Dr. Zahra Marwan Amir, leaning over Silvia's shoulder to look at the schedule.

"No, his mother," said Silvia, standing up to pick up a stack of forms she had just finished signing to carry them over to the outgoing mail bin. "Are you kidding? I would love to see Carlos."

"Still friends?" asked Zahra, taking Silvia's seat and her computer mouse to open the electronic chart of Dr. Veronica Beaumond, shifting to adjust her hijab as she leaned back into the chair.

"Not exactly. Haven't seen or heard from him in fifteen years. But I'm pretty sure I'd still hit it."

Zahra laughed. "That good, huh?"

"Yeah," said Silvia, with a wistful half-smile. "I was going to marry him."

"Didn't you tell me he was doing coke all the time?"

"That was later in the relationship, when we were already on the verge of breaking up. His mother had more to do with us breaking up than the coke."

"She's coming in for an initial oncology consult," said Zahra, scrolling through the chart. "Her x-rays look pretty gnarly."

"Yeah... would you mind taking that consult for me? I really could do without seeing her."

"Aw, I'm sorry, you know normally I'd do anything for you, but I can't today. I have a keynote presentation at the Western Psychiatry Conference this morning on how cancer impacts the treatment of mental illness. I have to get downtown by 10:00."

"Oh yeah, I forgot about that." Silvia put her right hand on her stomach, feeling a tight knot forming in the center of her gut. *I should have looked at the schedule last night like I was going to.* "I wonder if it's too late to call Anokh in."

"Maybe you'll feel better if you just take the consult," said Zahra, sympathetically. "How bad can it be? Maybe you'll feel like it's justice being served."

Silvia stared out the window at a rat lying dead on the sidewalk outside. "I don't like that idea. No one deserves cancer."

"I don't know. I'm guessing probably some people do. What about Hitler? He probably did, right?"

"She loved to talk about how she wished he would marry a white woman," said Silvia, ignoring Zahra's comment in an absent-minded state of remembering her med school days at Stanford.

"Wait. I don't know why, but I thought he was Latino?"

"His dad was French, his mom from Spain. So she identifies as white, and she especially did not like him dating me, a Chicana."

"Ugh."

"She would swing between telling me how I was never

going to be good enough for her son, and telling me what a pathetic disappointment he was all the time. And no matter how badly she behaved, he staunchly took her side, every time. She had no idea how lucky she was to have him."

"Oh, I'm sure she did. And I'm sure she conditioned him from childhood to do that."

"I don't know. I finally gave up and moved on."

"She sounds like a narcissist."

"It took years of therapy to detox from it."

"I'm sorry." Zahra came over and gave Silvia a side hug.

"What's really crazy too is when Carlos started dating someone new, Veronica suddenly started acting like I was her BFF. Wanted to invite me to every family gathering just to stir up drama with his new girlfriend."

"She sounds like a real piece of work." Zahra tightened her lips to restrain herself from making a harsher comment.

"Sorry, I could go on and on forever on this topic. I thought I had closure on this. I guess not."

"I gotta go. Be strong, okay?"

At least she's the first appointment of the day, thought Silvia, as she tried to distract herself from her emotional distress with reviewing Veronica's x-ray images online. *Let's just get it over with. Wow, she wasn't kidding. These look bad.*

"You can't go back there, ma'am!" Silvia's thoughts were interrupted by the voice of their front office receptionist, attempting to stop a patient from entering the back office where Silvia was seated at her desk. "That area is for doctors only!"

"I *am* a doctor!" shouted the woman, whose piercing voice and Castilian accent Silvia immediately recognized as belonging to Veronica. At the age of sixty-eight, Veronica Beaumond was an arresting and shrewd businesswoman with a double degree in law and psychiatry. She commanded the receptionist to step aside, and he reluctantly obliged.

Silvia cringed and took off her glasses, swiveling around

in her chair to brace herself for Veronica's entrance.

"Silvia!" said Veronica, on entering the room. "You actually work here?"

"Hard to believe, huh?" said Silvia, rising to her feet.

"Spare me your sarcasm and show me my films."

"Dr. Beaumond, we really should wait until—"

"They're MY x-rays, damn it, let me see them!"

"Please, Dr. Beaumond, let's do it in the exam room with the surgical oncologist present. Please?" Silvia gently placed her hand on Veronica's back to try to usher her from the room.

"Take your hands off of me! I'm a doctor, God damn it. I want to see the films. Now!"

"Right now you're our patient, and you're not supposed to be back here. Let's get you into the exam room, and I'll come in there right now and show you the images, okay? Please work with me here." With a sigh, Silvia picked up her laptop and escorted Veronica into an exam room.

"You haven't heard from my son lately, have you?" said Veronica, once inside the exam room.

"No, I haven't."

"I never do anymore, not since he's taken a liking to Negro women and moved away to the East Coast. Finally convinced him to divorce one of them only to have him shack up with her cousin! Such a completely worthless waste of my uterus."

"Don't say that," said Silvia, frowning. "That's not very nice. And your son's a good man."

"Who the fuck are you to tell me what I can or can't say? I'll say whatever I goddamn want. And who the fuck are you to tell me about my son? You think you're the authority on the subject? The nerve. I know what a good man looks like. A good man doesn't look like Carlos, I can tell you that much." At this, Veronica launched into an interminable coughing fit, hacking mucus into a silk handkerchief she pulled from her suede purse.

60

After a long pause, a resigned calm washing over her, she added, "You think you know him. *Nobody* knows him like I do."

"I have your x-ray images pulled up here, Dr. Beaumond. Would you like to take a look?" Silvia rotated her laptop screen toward Veronica, with a lung x-ray image at the forefront.

Veronica turned away from the screen. "I've seen enough," she said quietly. "Take it away."

"I'll step out and give you a few minutes," said Silvia, gently closing the laptop. "Your appointment is at nine. I'll come back in when the surgical oncologist gets here, okay?"

"I don't want you in here for my consult. I'll meet with the surgical oncologist by myself."

"Okay. I understand," said Silvia, making a strained effort at an uneven smile. "I know it's hard, I'm sorry."

"I don't want your pity. Just get out."

Silvia picked up her laptop and left the room like a bat out of hell.

| Chapter Ten |

"It's gracious of you to fly all the way here from New York to get my brother," said Midori's sister, Keiko, in Japanese. Keiko held her teal Burberry cardigan tightly shut around her body, with her arms crossed defensively. "You're a patient and generous wife. We offered to take him back to the airport, but he refuses. He says he doesn't want to go back to the United States. He has no money, and no place to stay in this rain. He won't let us take him to a hospital or rehab center, either. As I mentioned on the phone, he's in a terrible state. Sometimes crying out loudly in the middle of the night. *Very* loudly, waking the children. He forbade me to tell you that he's here, but I don't know what else to do. I would invite you to stay for lunch, but I think it's best if you can take him back home as soon as you can, before the typhoon gets any worse."

"It's quite alright," answered Lin Mei in Japanese. "I've chartered a shuttle to take us to the airport. The driver is waiting for us outside. We will leave immediately."

"A wise decision," said Keiko's husband, tightening his lips. "That way, you can be spared the humiliation of Mikito's embarrassing behavior on the train."

"My brother is a disgrace," said Keiko, nodding in agreement and cringing in shame. "My father wants never to see him again. I don't blame him. My father says it was bad luck to have had a fourth child. I'm beginning to agree with him."

"I respect your father," said Lin Mei kindly, "but Midori's gender dysphoria is not something to be ashamed of. I can assure you that she never had any intention of shaming anyone."

"You are kind," said Keiko, nodding cordially. "But it's not Mikito's desire to be a woman which brings us shame, so much as his drug abuse. It will be much easier to treat one disability than the other. He's been secretly dressing as a woman since childhood. He thinks no one knows, but we all know. It's just not a good time for Mikito to confront my father about it, not with Mother's passing so recent. He could have waited. Why does he have to force the issue on everyone?"

"My perspective on it is somewhat different," said Lin Mei, nodding back. "It's society's intolerance of it that is disabling. And your mother's death has been very difficult for Midori, too. But please, let us not quarrel. I don't wish to cause any ill feelings between us. I promise you, I will get Midori the help that she needs to treat her addiction and facilitate her transition. Where is she?"

"In the children's bedroom, upstairs. He's barely eaten anything for two days." Keiko's insistence on referring to Midori by her birth gender and deadname was getting on Lin Mei's nerves, but she tried not to focus on it, even though lack of sleep and terrible jet lag were making it difficult not to.

Knocking lightly on the upstairs bedroom door before entering, Lin Mei called out gently in English, "Midori? Are you in there? It's me, Lin Mei. I've come to take you home." As she slowly pushed the door open, she caught sight of Midori curled up on the floor in a fetal position, twitching and digging her fingernails into the skin on her arms. Lin Mei turned to Keiko, who was standing just behind her, and asked if she could please bring a glass of water. Lin Mei went over to Midori and sat down on the floor beside her, slipping one arm under her shoulders and lifting her up.

"Wha..?" said Midori, groggily. Her black eyeliner was smeared into dark circles around her eyes. "Lin Mei? Oh no... no... I asked Keiko not to bring you here. Leave me alone! I want to die. I just want to die."

"No, don't say that," said Lin Mei, stroking her hair. "I don't want you to die. Here, let me give you some water." Lin Mei reached over to take the glass from Keiko's outstretched hand. She tilted Midori's head back and poured a small amount into her mouth, pushing up on her chin with the other hand to close her mouth and induce her to swallow. Water spilled from Midori's mouth down her neck, onto her green sequined party dress. "Help me out, please, Midori?" Lin Mei pulled on Midori to help her sit up. "A typhoon is coming in, so we need to get to the airport as soon as possible. Do you think you can stand up?"

"Just leave me here, Lin Mei," said Midori dejectedly. "You deserve someone better than me, someone who's not all fucked up."

"I want to be with the woman I love," said Lin Mei. "That means you. So will you please help me out? I understand that transitioning is hard. Things can get better, I promise. We'll get you the help you need."

"You don't want me," said Midori spitefully. "Just zip up your vag and move on, okay? You want a *man*. With a *dick*. Just be honest. That's why you married me."

"I want you to be your true self, that's what I want. I didn't marry you for your body parts. I married you for your companionship, for your intelligence and wit, for your sensitivity and depth. Please believe me, Midori. The plumbing is not an issue."

"You're lying. You're all freaked out. Don't act like I can't see it. You've got some kind of closet transphobia going on."

"No, I don't—it's... it's just... an adjustment, yes. I never thought of myself as a lesbian. But that's not the issue here. It's just hard for me to see you in distress, okay? That's what upsets me, not your transition."

"You're lying!"

"Is it necessary to yell?" said Keiko, exasperated.

"No, I'm not," said Lin Mei calmly to Midori, ignoring Keiko's remark. "Please, just come home with me? Please? The meth is distorting your perception. You'll feel better after you get through the post-acute withdrawal. I brought you some Valium, will you please take some?" Lin Mei gestured to Keiko to retrieve two Valium from her purse, then placed them carefully into Midori's mouth. Midori tried to spit them out, but her mouth was dry, and they kept sticking to her tongue. Lin Mei poured another swig of water into Midori's mouth and compelled her to swallow.

"I'm terribly sorry for the inconvenience," said Lin Mei to Keiko. "Could you please be so kind as to let the shuttle driver know that we will be out in just a few more minutes?"

Ten minutes later, after much coaxing, cajoling, and obstinate objections, interspersed with more tears and accusations, Lin Mei and Midori emerged through the wrought-iron gate of the Kawata family's boxy, post-modern, two-story house, with Midori struggling to walk, and bearing most of her weight onto Lin Mei's shoulder.

A thick, unforgiving rain was pouring down, and within seconds they were both completely drenched. In a sudden flash of determination to escape, Midori wrested herself from Lin Mei's grasp and bolted off running down the street, toward the train tracks of Shinagawa Station. Exasperated, Lin Mei sprinted after her, thankful that she had worn comfortable shoes for the flight. *Please, God, help me out,* she begged silently as she ran. *How long must this battle continue?*

Midori was taller, lankier and notably stronger than Lin Mei, but also worn from days of tweaking, sleep deprivation, hunger and dehydration. Lin Mei threw her arms around Midori's waist and tried to drag her back toward the Kawata house where she could see from a distance that thankfully, the shuttle driver was still waiting. Midori resisted and twisted her body, planting her bottom on the ground like a toddler, and screamed for Lin Mei to leave her there, to let her die alone on the street.

Lin Mei locked the fingers of her hands together and held onto Midori's torso with a vice-like grip, her arms trembling and aching against Midori's violent thrashing, until Midori finally stopped struggling and began to cry helplessly as neighbors watched with pity from behind curtained windows, her tears indistinguishable from the rivers of rain streaming down her face, while a fierce wind beat mercilessly against their backs, whipping strands of wet hair against their faces. "Just let me die," she sobbed. "Just let me die."

"I can't," said Lin Mei, unable to help crying herself. "I can't let you self-destruct like this. Come back with me, *please*, Midori! I'm begging you. I *hear* you. I *see* you. I want to be *with you*."

These last few words finally got through to Midori, or maybe she was just too exhausted to resist anymore, or maybe it was the Valium beginning to kick in. She let out a small sigh and let all of her muscles go limp as she stared absently over Lin Mei's shoulder.

"You came all the way out here, and said what you needed to say to your father," said Lin Mei, forcing the words out breathlessly as a sharp pain formed in her chest from the exertion. "It was courageous of you. I'm so very proud of you Midori, I really am. Let's go now, okay? Let's go catch our flight before the storm gets much worse."

| Chapter Eleven |

Rochelle was sitting alone in the lobby at Glen Haven, anxious for Titi to arrive in a chauffeured car that was bringing her in from John F. Kennedy airport. She suddenly recalled having a terrible nightmare the night before about a school shooting that had jacked up her adrenaline at the sight of a man emerging from a basement window carrying an AK-47 onto a playground full of children. One of the male teachers recognized him and shouted, "Silverfish, no! Don't do it!" just as he opened fire. Blood pounding through her veins, Rochelle drew her handgun and took aim, waking up just before she could pull the trigger.

Unlocking her smart phone to read the news, she noticed a missed call from Jason, her partner at the FBI Human Trafficking Unit over the last nine years. "How was your Buddhist retreat?" said Rochelle, returning the call.

"I was the only brother of color in a group full of white women," he laughed. "It was cool, though." When Rochelle didn't respond, he realized he could sense distress in Rochelle's voice.

"Natasha didn't go with you?" Rochelle asked at last.

"Nah, not this time. She's working deep cover on a sting.

I take it your cousin didn't make it there yet?"

"No," sighed Rochelle. "Not thrilled about her being delayed an entire day. I'm sure I've told you before, she just *loves* making people wait. Said she had an unexpected consult, and then had to do some kind of ceremony to appease angry spirits. Bunch of passive aggressive B.S. On the up side, Lin Mei is stateside, on her way here. Should be interesting."

"Been catching up on sleep?"

"Never, you know me. Oh hey, let me call you back. Titi's out front, gotta go."

"Call me later, let me know how it went."

Rochelle stood up to greet Titi as she entered through the revolving door.

"Modern innovations on a building that's very old," said Titi as she looked around, sensing the presence of several ex-human spirits in the room. "There's a ghost of a woman hanging from a rope in the corner over there," she said, a ghastly knot forming in her stomach as she averted her gaze—a gesture that was equal parts discomfort and courtesy for the dead. "Committed suicide in 1952, has literally been hanging around here ever since. Over there, standing by the window is the spirit of a Norwegian man named Ben. He lost his sanity after his wife killed their only child. Died of heart failure in 1983. He watches out the window every day, hoping he'll find the ghost of his son—"

"Are these hallucinations you're talking about?" interrupted Rochelle. "Or are you just making this up as you go?" She couldn't decide which answer she would have preferred.

Titi scowled at her. "You can't see them yourself, so it makes you feel better to convince yourself that I'm delusional. Sorry to disappoint you. I can't help that I can see them and you can't."

"So, in other words, hallucinations," said Rochelle. "Which are symptoms of mental illness."

"Here we go again. Did you bring me here to ask my advice, or to insult me?"

"I brought you here to help bring some sense to this mystery. Which so far, you haven't."

"Well, let's get on with it, then."

Neither of them spoke during the tense elevator ride up to the fifth floor. Rochelle distracted herself by opening the news app on her phone. She was stunned to read that a school shooting had in fact happened that morning, killing twelve. The shooter's name was Avram Sylvrvysc. It struck her as an odd coincidence, considering the shooter in her nightmare had a similar name, but she said nothing to Titi about it. After exiting the elevator, Rochelle approached the nursing station and addressed the male nurse seated in front of a computer monitor.

"Hi Rahim, can I talk to Maisie?"

"Maisie's not here, Special Agent Roy. She's been off of work since she lost her voice on Thursday morning."

"What do you mean? I just saw her on Thursday morning and she sounded fine. Did she come down with a cold?"

"No ma'am, it's not laryngitis. Something traumatic happened to her after you left. She's gone completely mute."

"What happened?"

Rahim shrugged. "I don't know, sorry. It's just what I heard."

A frown washed over Rochelle's face. "Okay, thank you. I'll ask Dr. Varma about it. By the way, this is Ms. Titi Beaumond, who is consulting on the case. She's here to have a visit with the four trafficking victims."

"Of course, we've been expecting you both. I'll sign you in."

Rahim ushered them into a nearby patient room, where a young woman with pale skin and long, thin, stringy blonde hair was sitting upright in the hospital bed, her back resting against the pillows, her face worn and scarred like the others. On entering the room and realizing intuitively, without having met the other three victims yet, that these were the women from her childhood drawing, Titi felt a strange tingling fall over her skin like a waterfall, like a gentle gust of air that gives you goosebumps. With a clear sense of purpose, she introduced herself to Olena and asked her permission to approach and examine her. Olena didn't say anything, but her left eye twitched into a half-wink, seemingly in response.

"Did she just wink her eye?" asked Rochelle. "I think she might have heard you. I hope that's a good sign."

Titi walked over to the bed and put both her hands on Olena's blanketed feet. "I've come to help you," she said gently. "I'd like to come closer to take a look in your eyes, if I may." Olena said nothing. Titi walked over, then took a gentle but firm grip of Olena's head, cradling her skull with both hands and peering into her eyes, gently tilting her head in different directions to search for a response, and finding none.

"This is Olena Petrenko," said Rochelle, observing Titi's behavior with keen interest. "She was a famous child porn star from decades ago, known on the circuit as Lena Flaxen. Resurfaced in London a few years ago, where she was picked up for street walking. Mind you, every trafficking victim has a tragic story, and not all of them involve sex work. But child pornography is a special kind of nightmare that haunts its victims for the rest of their lives. Those pictures will still be circulating pedophilia rings long after all of us are dead and gone."

Titi turned toward Rochelle with a somber look, and declared that Olena had been zombified.

"Come again? *Zombified?* Don't be ridiculous," said Rochelle dismissively. "It's the drugs, and post-traumatic stress. All of the trafficking victims we bring in are dead in the eyes like that. It doesn't mean they're zombies."

"No, it doesn't," Titi acknowledged tersely. She didn't want to spend the whole trip bickering, and it was taking some effort to speak with conviction without being rude. "But in this case, they *are*. Their souls were dead long before they became *zonbis*. It's why the bokor chose them. They had nothing left to live for, no reason to fight back. Don't you shake your head at me. Did you ask me here for my expertise, or not?"

"She doesn't believe me," mumbled Olena, startling them both. Without blinking, she continued speaking softly. "She never believes me."

"She hasn't spoken to anyone since Wednesday," said Rochelle, astounded. "What did she say? I couldn't hear her."

Titi gestured sharply for Rochelle to keep quiet, and the two women leaned in closely, waiting for her to speak again.

"She's reading my mind," said Olena blankly, as if talking in her sleep.

"Who's reading your mind, Olena?" said Rochelle.

"*She's* reading *my* mind," said Titi, her eyes widening incredulously.

"What do you mean?" said Rochelle.

"Those were my exact thoughts. Just now. I was just thinking that you never believe me. Then she spoke the exact same words out loud. And when I thought to myself that she was reading my mind, she spoke *that* out loud."

"Oh wow," said Rochelle. "You don't actually believe she was reading your mind, do you?"

"Chelle, I'm telling you, she just read my mind, and spoke my thoughts aloud. Do you really think I'm making this up? I'm telling you the truth."

"Fine. Think something specific, write it down, and let's see if she does it again."

Titi rolled her eyes, exasperated. "It doesn't work that way. She's not a trained dog. And if you can't take my word for truth, then we have a serious problem here."

"Oh, but isn't that convenient? I'm sorry, but this is all sounding highly schizophrenic. Have you ever heard of thought broadcasting? It's a delusion suffered by schizophrenics. And why exactly is she reading *your* mind, and not mine?"

"Probably because I'm accustomed to extending and receiving psychic communication," said Titi, glaring as if the answer should have been obvious.

At that moment, Lin Mei walked into the room, looking more disheveled and puffy-eyed than Rochelle had ever seen her. "Sorry I'm late," said Lin Mei. "Midori didn't let me get much sleep on the plane. Where are we at?"

"Oh, you didn't miss much," said Rochelle sarcastically. "Just some mind-reading zombies, that's all."

"Titi Beaumond," said Titi, introducing herself. "It's a pleasure to meet you. A Voodoo zonbi is not like these brain-eating zombies you see in the movies," she explained. "Ok, well they're kind of like them, in a metaphorical sense. But they don't actually eat brains. Not literally, anyway. A Voodoo sorcerer—what we call a *bokor*—has clearly taken control of these women. They have spirits possessing them which are not their own."

"Spirits?" said Lin Mei. "You mean a demon, like the one they say is possessing Jandro?"

"No, I don't think so. It doesn't sound to me like Jandro is a zonbi," said Titi. "I would have to meet him to be sure."

"Out of the question," Rochelle interjected. "I'm not having you meet that psycho. If anyone from the cartel gets wind of your identity, it will expose you to some serious danger."

"If I'm understanding correctly," Titi continued, ignoring Rochelle, "these women said in their intake interviews that they're possessed by human spirits who lived three hundred years ago. A displaced ex-human spirit is a different matter from a demon. Demons have been in spirit form much, much longer, and the potency of their malice is much stronger."

"Is there anything you can do to help them?" said Lin Mei, feeling her grasp on reality slipping from lack of sleep, and the words coming out as if on auto-pilot.

"I would like to see their case files," said Titi politely. "And, after I have reviewed those, I would like to try interviewing each one of them. Privately. It may be possible to perform some healing spells in order to liberate their bodies from the possessing spirits. Their ability to heal—and *less* importantly, to *testify*—will depend on it. But I can't promise anything. I need to know first exactly what we're dealing with."

Rochelle grimaced. "This is crazy. Demons aren't real. They're nothing more than excuses people use to relieve themselves of accountability. I'm not buying any of this. And I certainly don't see any hope of convincing Reid, our special agent-in-charge, to release protected health information on four different witnesses to a civilian who isn't even a licensed medical professional.

"I know I can help them," said Titi adamantly.

"I'll get you the case files," said Lin Mei. "I'll have a copy made for you and have a secure courier bring them to your hotel."

"Wait, what are you doing, Lin Mei?" said Rochelle, pressing her hand to her forehead in disbelief. She felt a migraine coming on. "You're going to do that without clearing it with Reid first?"

"You know Reid's not going to give her clearance," said Lin Mei, widening her eyes to make the point. "You just said so yourself. I'll take full responsibility for the decision, okay? I'll bear the consequences."

"Okay, you're not thinking straight," said Rochelle, shaking her head. "You need to go home and take a nap. You could lose your job over this."

"I'm not going to lose my job, don't worry."

"You could stand to lose your arrogance," Rochelle retorted.

Lin Mei sighed. "These women are in a state of spiritual crisis. They need all the help they can get. This constitutes religious belief, and we owe it to them to accommodate their belief as best we can. Let your cousin help them. I believe she can."

"Thank you," said Titi, nodding graciously.

"Okay, wow. This is *your* decision, Lin Mei, let's get it straight for the record," said Rochelle, throwing her palms up as if dropping a hot potato. "I want no part of it. This is a disaster waiting to happen."

| Chapter Twelve |

"How's your wife?" said Dr. Howard Hambert, taking a hearty bite of his steak. He was a gaunt man, with short, curly blonde hair and wire-rimmed glasses. "What's her name again? Chrissy? No, wait. Is it Cici?"

"It's Titi," said Dr. Carlos Beaumond, shifting uncomfortably. "But we're divorced now."

"Oh, is that right? What a shame. Such a beautiful woman. I'm sorry to hear it, my good man. I'm sure you are even more so."

Carlos cleared his throat. "Yes... divorce is, well, divorce. Never fun. But I'm okay. I've moved on. I'm with someone new now." Carlos pushed the asparagus around on his plate, pretending he was raking his miniature Zen rock garden at home, hoping it would somehow relieve the awkwardness. It didn't.

"Wow," said Howard. "Moving fast, eh? Can't say I'm surprised. You've always been quite the ladies man."

Carlos breathed a quiet sigh. These conference luncheons with colleagues could be so tiresome. The mention of Rochelle reminded him that it had been a week since he arrived in San

Francisco, and he hadn't heard from her the entire time, nor did he really have any desire to contact her.

He knew she was working an important case when he left, one which was, at the time, about to culminate in an arrest. But knowing this didn't ease the discomfort of feeling like he was stuck in some weird limbo. He was starting to wonder if the relationship was winding down to an end. The signs were there, just like they had been toward the end of his marriage to Titi. He half-expected Rochelle to call at any moment to break up with him.

"Sorry to interrupt, Howard, but I need to make a quick phone call."

"Now? In the middle of lunch?" said Howard with his mouth full of steak.

Carlos cleared his throat. "It's an important matter I need to take care of that slipped my mind earlier. It'll only take a minute. Sorry." He stood up abruptly and fumbled with the chair before exiting the hotel restaurant. *Why am I trying to justify myself to him? What is he, my mother?* The important phone call bit was a desperate invention; Carlos was jonesing for a cigarette, and Howard was unwittingly aggravating the craving.

Once outside, his cell phone rang, as if to make an honest man out of him. It was Rochelle, and he contemplated whether to answer or silence it. He didn't want his nicotine withdrawal to start another argument like the one they had just before he left New York. *This was a bad time to try to quit smoking.* He opted to silence the call.

Startled by a shrill voice that came from behind him, he turned around to find his mother standing there. Her short, frosted blonde hair danced wildly about in the San Francisco wind, peeking out above the farmed-mink fur collar of her Gucci cashmere trench draped over her slim, Pilates-conditioned body. Through light-pink tinted aviator sunglasses, she glared at him with piercing disapproval.

"Carlos! What on Earth are you doing here in the city? You didn't even let me know. Oh, for fuck's sake."

Instant karma, thought Carlos, rubbing the back of his head. "What are *you* doing here, Mother? What's that smell? Have you been drinking?"

"Well, I assumed you would be here, even if you don't see fit to return my calls. I know you attend the Western Psychiatry Conference every year, did you think I had forgotten? I'm simply furious with you. You have no idea."

"The conference schedule doesn't leave much room for socializing, Mother. You know that. I've been busy with colleagues all week."

"What's that tone? Are you using a tone with me?"

"No, I'm just standing here in the cold, that's all. I should have brought my jacket. No tone was intended."

"I think you should at least apologize for using that tone."

Carlos sighed, staring at the sidewalk. "I'm sorry, Mother, I didn't mean to use a tone with you."

"Such an ingratiating over-achiever, like your father," she said. "In constant need of everyone's approval. Well, how about my approval? Does that mean anything to you? You certainly don't act like it does."

"I really need to get back inside. Howard is waiting. I'm sorry I didn't have time to call or see you during the week."

"Well, you should be sorry. You've been nothing but rude to me since your divorce. I blame that nasty woman you're living with now. Titi was such a sweetheart compared to her."

"What are you saying, Mother? You never liked Titi. Let's talk about this another time, please?"

"You'll be sorry when I'm gone. Mark my words. You'll wish you had taken the time. Especially now that I have stage four lung cancer."

"Wait, what? Since when?"

"Well, I tried to call you yesterday as soon as I found out, but you were too busy to care."

Carlos turned to grab the attention of a teenager walking by, wearing a red flannel shirt and toking a cigarette. "Hey man, can I bum a smoke off of you?" The kid passed him a cigarette, lit it and winked at him as he left.

"'Hey man'," Veronica said with a mocking sneer, "'can I bum a smoke?' You try so damn hard to be cool."

Carlos observed quietly to himself that anything at all can be made to sound ridiculous if said with enough scorn.

"God. This is how you treat me?" she said with reproach. "You're going to smoke a cigarette in front of me, when I just told you I have lung cancer?"

Exasperated, he went to extinguish the cigarette, but she quickly added, "Don't bother. It's not like I have any intention of quitting."

"Well, you should," said Carlos, taking a long drag on the cigarette and then mashing it out on the sidewalk before stashing the butt in the pocket of his khaki pants. "And so should I."

"I want you to come stay with me for a while, Carlos. I need your support right now, more than ever. No else gets me like you do, darling. I need you."

"And leave my practice in New York?"

"Oh, don't be such a whiny baby. You know you can afford to take a sabbatical. You can do some work for us at the firm, in a med-legal capacity. We could certainly use an expert witness in psychiatry on retainer."

"Sure, because no judge will have a problem with an attorney calling her son as an expert witness."

"You can help out with research. I wouldn't be calling on you to testify, smart-ass. And please do me a huge favor, darling, don't mention the cancer to anyone? Not even *her*."

"Her? You mean Rochelle?"

"You know I do."

"So, you want me to close up shop, move back to the

West Coast, and not give my girlfriend any kind of explanation."

"Oh, you can just tell her that you're helping the firm."

"I don't know if I feel comfortable with keeping this a secret from her."

"Of course you don't. But I'm in a terribly vulnerable state right now, darling, even if I don't know how to act like it. The last thing I need is her passive aggressive remarks."

"They're not passive aggressive—never mind. I need some time to process all this. I'll have to get back to you."

"Don't go growing a backbone on me, young man. I won't know what to do with myself."

"I'll try to keep it in check."

"Keep that sarcasm in check, while you're at it."

"I really need to get back inside."

"Call me later. I want you here for my surgery, and then I'll be starting chemo."

"I'll call you later, Mother."

Back inside the restaurant, Carlos found that Howard had picked up the check and left. "This one's on me!" said the napkin he had left on the table. Carlos sat back down at the table and ordered a bourbon. His father had died of brain cancer when he was seven years old, and even now he didn't feel he had completely recovered from that loss. Now he was faced with the prospect of becoming an orphan. As much as his mother drove him crazy, he knew she was right when she said he would miss her when she was gone. His cell phone rang. It was Rochelle.

"Hey babe," he said, wearily picking up the call.

"Hey," said Rochelle. "How's the conference going?"

"It's going alright. A couple of interesting speakers this year. It's almost over; I'll be flying back to JFK tomorrow. How's your week going?"

"Not great," she said with agitation in her voice. "Your ex-wife is here in New York City right now, creating drama. You know how she does."

"What is she doing there?"

"We flew her up here to consult on a case," said Rochelle gingerly. "I know, it's not the brightest decision I ever made. But our vics think they're under some kind of Voodoo spell. Lin Mei thought it would be a good idea to get Titi's input on it. Can't believe I let her talk me into this."

"Um, well, that's good, I guess? Seems like a good context for you and her to work out your differences?"

"No, we are not working out our differences. Our differences are getting worse. She has no sense of logic whatsoever, Carlos. I don't know how she comes up with these crazy, random ideas. She's completely lost touch with reality. She thinks one of the vics was doing actual mind-reading today. It's so completely delusional, I just can't. I think it's a really bad idea that you keep prescribing marijuana for her. She's clearly schizophrenic, and I think the weed is making it worse."

"Well, you know my feelings on it. I don't think it's schizophrenia. I think it's post-traumatic stress. Schizophrenia is a neurodivergent condition which looks very similar, but needs no wound to precipitate it. PTSD, on the other hand, is a healing response to an emotional wound, just like a scab is a healing response to a physical wound. A scab is not a disease, it's just the body's natural defense system at work. Once the wound heals, the scab goes away, just like PTSD can go away after treatment to heal the wound. Anyway. She does better on the weed than off it."

"I don't know, Carlos. I just don't know. You know I respect your autonomy, but really, she should get her meds from someone who can be more objective about it, not her ex-husband. It's questionable, ethically. And she's kind of crazy about these Voodoo spirits. It's pretty disturbing."

"Well, what exactly did you expect, inviting her up there, Ro? You wanted her perspective, you got it."

"I didn't know she was having actual *hallucinations.*

She's seeing and hearing things that other people don't."

"Not uncommon for psychics."

"Yeah... I should have known you would take her side. I don't even know why I'm calling you. I'll see you when you get back."

"Okay, I think I understand. What you're saying is, I'm a big penis head."

"Come again?"

"A penis head. You think I'm a big penis head."

"No, I don't."

"A giant penis. With a beard."

He could hear a smile in her voice. "Stop it," she said, trying not to laugh. "That's not a visual I needed."

"A penis with glasses. And ears."

A small laugh managed to escape, despite her best effort to resist. "This is serious, Carlos. Not a good time for jokes."

"Want to hear my Ode to Fuzzy Green Mold that I wrote this morning?"

"Am I going to be able to stop you?"

"Oh, Fuzzy Green Mold on my beef jerky! How you disappoint! How unwelcomely you grow! How you remind me so of those who denounce protesters for disturbing the peace, while failing to call out the crimes against humanity committed by the police! These rightly incite protest! Despicable parasites on my soul! How you molest! How I detest—"

"Carlos. Just stop, please."

"Come on, babe. Don't be angry. I miss you. I can't wait to see you. I'm sorry if T is giving you grief. This psychic stuff is how she's always been, I thought this was nothing new."

"Then Lin Mei had to go give her the case file like a damn fool," said Rochelle, not seeming to have heard what he said. "And what's worse is she did it without getting clearance from Reid. Well, I don't feel comfortable with this at all. I thought I could keep quiet about it, but I just can't. I'm going to talk to

Reid about it first thing in the morning."

"You have to do what you feel is right," said Carlos.

"Yes, I know that."

"Listen babe, I have to go. Some colleagues from the conference are waiting for me inside. Love you."

"Yeah. Love you."

He downed the rest of his bourbon, retreated into the hotel lobby restroom, shut himself into a stall and slammed his fist into the toilet paper dispenser.

| Chapter Thirteen |

"Dude, your man card is revoked." Adrian's childhood friend, Pete Hill, shot a peripheral glance of disapproval over his left elbow toward Adrian, before ordering another IPA from the bartender. Aside from a more pronounced beer gut, and a little more fat around his once chiseled jaw, Pete hadn't changed much since Adrian had last seen him. *Still playing the man card.*

"Because I won't cheat on Titi?" said Adrian, laughing. "What are you, still twenty years old? This is why I never hang out with you anymore."

"Oh, really? I thought it's because you're making the big bucks now. I saw you roll up in that Benz convertible. Too bougie to associate with us rednecks now, huh?"

"I think you have it backwards," said Adrian, laughing. "Most of the rednecks we know are the ones who think they're better than me, and it doesn't matter how much money I make."

"Okay, well you got me there. But look at you, man. You're drinking iced tea, for chrissake. You're a total vagina right now. You're getting old, man, stop acting your age. Remember how ripped we used to get back in high school? No one could hold their liquor like you. Hey, remember that time we ended up naked in Cheryl Johnson's tree, and her dad came out of the house with a rifle?"

"I really don't," said Adrian. *Entire decades of my life are a blur. Not exactly something I feel good about.*

"Aw yeah, those days were golden. Anyway, it's not cheating if you don't have a commitment. You've gone on what, two dates now? You should have nailed that shit down before she left for New York if you wanted to get all monogamous up in there."

"She's a classy lady, man. She actually sees me for me, and not for how much money I make. Crazy, right?"

"Sure she does. Keep telling yourself that."

"You've got it all wrong. She just… makes me feel happy, Pete. I don't know what else to say. Sorry if that disappoints you. I don't want to mess this up."

"Wait a minute, are you *gay*?"

"Hey, now. Better watch yourself," said Adrian, smiling with a mock tone of warning, before feeling guilty at the thought of what his son might think if he had heard him say that.

"Isn't that the whole point of getting on that dating website, so you could see what's out there? Let me hook you up with my friend Lisa. She's hot, and single. She saw your pic on my Facebook and thinks you're cute. She has a thing for nerdy Black guys. And she's an easy lay."

"You're grossing me out right now."

Pete swiveled toward Adrian on his barstool and took a more serious tone. "Listen man, I know I like to josh you a lot, and I know you think you're doing the right thing. But let me just be serious for a minute. It's way too early in the game to be whipped like this. If she's as hot as you say she is, you think if she runs into some hardbody action up there in New York, she's going to turn it down? Don't sell yourself short here."

Adrian stared pensively at his iced tea. It was true that Titi seemed to lack closure, and he still wondered if she was pining over an ex. But there was something special about her, something he couldn't very well articulate, let alone expect Pete to understand. "I know you mean well, Pete. And no disrespect toward your friend Lisa, I'm sure she's very nice."

Pete chuckled. "I didn't say nice, I said hot."

Adrian sighed. "I just don't feel like I have to sleep with every woman who comes along, like she's some kind of scorecard," he said, bracing himself for Pete's reaction. "That was the me before college. I've grown up since then, and I need to set a good example for my son. He needs to understand that promiscuity is not what makes you a man. Besides that, I just want to take things slow, and see where things go with Titi, who, by the way, manages to be both hot and nice at the same time."

"Ain't no such thing, bro," said Pete, shaking his head with a laugh. "Hot only comes with crazy."

"If you keep telling yourself that, Pete, then you're the one who's selling himself short." Adrian stood up and settled the bar tab.

"Alright, alright. Maybe so. You're the smart one here, there's no question about that. Did I offend you or something? You're taking off already?"

"Yeah, I've got a big client meeting early in the morning and another pile of legal briefs to review tonight, it's nothing personal. Good to see you, man." Adrian gave Pete a hearty man-hug with a good-natured slap on the back.

"You too, thanks for coming out. Don't be a stranger, now that you're getting some."

Adrian chuckled and shook his head. "You kill me, Pete."

The drive home from the Tin Holster Cocktail and Oyster Bar on Main Street in Downtown Baton Rouge, back to his two-story house in Roseland Terrace where he shared custody of his son, was a brief four minutes, but once he arrived home, he sat in the driveway for another ten minutes staring into the steering wheel like he was consulting a crystal ball. The steering wheel was telling him to stop running away.

"How was your AA meeting, Dad?"

Adrian was surprised to find his seventeen-year-old son Jericho home so early. With a faded Scott Joplin t-shirt hanging off his skinny frame, Jericho was standing at the kitchen island counter making himself a peanut butter and jelly sandwich when Adrian walked in and pulled up a chair. "I didn't go to AA tonight, son. Met up with an old friend for drinks."

With a short flick of the neck, Jericho flung back his locs which normally hung low over his eyes, and raised an eyebrow suspiciously.

"Don't worry," Adrian laughed. "I only had iced tea. And I got no end of grief for it, so spare me the suspicious looks. What are you doing home so early? No *Hamlet* tonight?"

"The director had to cancel rehearsal because of a family emergency," said Jericho with a mouthful of sandwich.

Adrian nodded, then casually changed the subject. "Listen, son. There's a lady I've been seeing down in New Orleans, her name is Titi. She's really special to me, and I'd like for you to meet her."

"*Me*? Really?"

A warm feeling washed over Adrian as he watched his son's face light up.

"Yes, of course you. Really."

"You could bring her to my opening night!" said Jericho gleefully.

"I would love to, son, but she's out of town this week. Plus your mother is going to be there opening night, and I don't want her getting into it with Titi. I was thinking of taking you and Titi to a Saints game. We could tailgate, get the barbecue going. Pete and I used to tailgate all the time back in the day. I'm thinking it's about time I take you so you can see how much fun it is. What do you think?"

"Wow, I'm really honored, Dad. You're not too

embarrassed to introduce your lady friend to your gay son?"

Adrian was stunned. "Why on Earth would you say that? Of course I'm not embarrassed of you, son! I don't ever want you to think that."

"I dunno. Sometimes I feel like you're disappointed with me because I didn't turn out to be, you know, like, this dudebro, football player-type. And sometimes when we're in public together, it's like you want me to, I don't know... act more macho, or something."

"Not because I'm embarrassed," said Adrian. "I just fear for your safety sometimes, Jay. Not everyone in Baton Rouge is as understanding as I am about having a gay son. It's a terrible thing as a parent to fear your child will be the victim of a hate crime."

"I'm sorry to put you through that, Dad."

"You don't have to be sorry. It's the world that's wrong, not you. But yes, you did have pegged me right on one thing. I'll admit I had a different picture in my mind of the son you would turn out to be. Maybe every parent does, I don't know. We're just human beings, after all. I guess I expected you to turn out more like, well, like me. Not because I think I'm any better than you for being straight, but just because straight is just the only way I know how to be. It just didn't occur to me to picture something else. I hope you can forgive me for that. I didn't mean to give you the wrong idea."

"It's okay, Dad. I get it. Did you tell your lady friend that you're an alcoholic?"

"Whoa there. Check the narrative, son. All things in due time. Not trying to scare her off, alright? Let her get to know me as a responsible, stable adult first. Is that alright with you?" Adrian joked.

"You should just be straight up with her," advised Jericho matter-of-factly, taking another bite of his sandwich. "It's the best way."

"Oh, is that right? You're the expert, huh? Now what does a young gay man know about romancing a woman?"

Jericho giggled good-naturedly. "A lot more than you do, Dad, trust me."

Adrian couldn't help but laugh with him, but also felt a twinge of fear in his gut at the thought of discussing his alcoholism with Titi, especially after she had explicitly condemned it.

Adrian picked up his cell phone to dial Candace, his ex-wife and Jericho's mother. "Now for the hard part," he said before sending the call. "Got to clear it with your mother."

"No comment," said Jericho.

"Oh, no advice for me now, huh, smart guy?" Adrian bumped Jericho's arm affectionately before noticing that Candace had picked up the call.

"What do you want, Adrian?" said Candace impatiently.

"I'm doing fine, thanks for asking," said Adrian sardonically. "And how are you?"

"I don't have time for your attitude," said Candace. "I'm showing an open house in five minutes. Make it snappy."

"Fine," he said. "I want to take Jericho out to a Saints game, not this weekend, maybe the weekend after."

"I have plans with Jericho that weekend, Adrian, do you remember me telling you that? Or have you been drinking again?"

"I've been sober a year now, not that that fact ever wins any points in my favor."

"You have a long way to go before you're winning any points with me, you know that. You got your joint custody, what more do you want from me?"

"How about the weekend after that, then?"

"You going to a football game sounds like an excuse for drinking. You think I don't know you well enough by now? Who's all going? Let me guess, Pete Hill?"

"Look, I know you find this hard to believe, Candace,

but I'm not trying to fuck up my life anymore. I have a good job, a nice house and I'm grateful to have Jericho back in my life again. I'm fully capable of having a good time sober."

"Yeah, I've heard that before. And watch your damn language around my son. And you didn't answer my question."

"It'll just be me, Jericho, and my lady friend, Titi."

"Oh no. No. Just, no. I don't want you bringing your ratchet hoes around my son."

Adrian had grown so used to Candace taking shots at him about his drinking that they rarely fazed him anymore. The moment she took aim at Titi, though, his anger flared up. He drew in a measured breath to restrain his frustration. "You don't even know her, so I recommend you keep your insults in check. She has more class than all of your wealthy clients put together."

Candace felt a pang of jealousy at his indignation. "The following weekend doesn't work for me either, Adrian. So you need to figure something else out. My first buyer just pulled up. Gotta go."

For the first time in months, Adrian felt himself craving a drink.

| Chapter Fourteen |

Alone in her room at the Hotel Piscean, Titi pored diligently over the case files, occasionally toking on a small glass pipe packed with bud from the nearby dispensary. For a moment, she contemplated giving Adrian a call, but she had already left him a message before leaving for New York, and reminded herself that it was better now to let him call her.

At this point, she thought it silly to continue to be troubled by a nightmare that was more simply attributable to relationship fears. For the time being, she was enjoying the company of the enchanting Voodoo lwa known as LaSirenn, "The Mermaid," who was making a meaningful appearance in the form of a painting hanging on the wall in Titi's hotel room. Titi was thoroughly captivated by it; the mermaid tail was cast in shades of dark purple and red orange, with the glint of a metallic gold. It reminded her of Hans Christian Andersen's fairy tale of "The Little Mermaid," which was a favorite story of hers when she was a child. She blissfully cast herself afloat in LaSirenn's ocean, swimming in a sea of mercurial memories and obscure, otherworldly visions. Floating beneath her was the immense sinewy shadow of LaBalenn, the whale spirit, which infused Titi with energy and insight.

Her rapturous reverie was disrupted by the sound of her phone ringing, and she quickly picked it up in hopes that it was Adrian. But it wasn't Adrian's name on the caller ID, it was her cousin Angie.

"How are things going up there in New York?" said Angie, her voice lightly muffled by the sound of a large window fan she used in her living room to stave off the fall Charleston heat.

"Oh, you know how it is with me and Rochelle. Oil and water. Nothing has changed. The woman has no sense of spiritual vision whatsoever."

"What happened with Mama Erzulie Dantó? Is she still angry with you? I tell you, that dream I had really upset me. It put the fear in me."

"I left some fine perfume and a box of cigars for Mambo Erzulie Dantó on her altar, to appease her. Maybe she's jealous because Mambo Erzulie Freda walks with me now."

"Maybe so," said Angie with a laugh. "Sisters ever at odds with each other. They remind me of you and Rochelle. So does that mean things are going good with Adrian? My girl Cynthia spilled some tea on him, I don't know if you want to know."

"I'm not sure if I do," said Titi. "But go on."

"She lives down in Lafayette, and she said she used to date an Adrian from Baton Rouge. Sounds a lot like your Adrian. He's an attorney, real dark-skinned, has a teenage son."

"What did she say about him?"

"T, I don't know if you want to hear this. She said she had to break up with him because of his drinking problem."

"What? No. That can't be him. My Adrian doesn't drink."

"Think about it. Maybe that's *why* he doesn't drink."

"Baton Rouge is a big city. Could be a different Adrian."

"She said his mother committed suicide when he was a

kid. Got him all messed up in the head. He lost custody of his son for a while on account of his drinking. Only recently got cleaned up."

Titi stared at the mermaid painting, thunderstruck. *No. Not an alcoholic. Please God, not an alcoholic.*

"Are you there, T?"

"Yeah, I'm here. I've got to get going, Angie. I got business to take care of here. I need to focus on this case file."

"You sound shook. I'm sorry to break it to you like this, but I figured you'd rather know sooner than later."

"You did right. I just can't try to think on that right now. What I'm working on here is too powerful. This bokor is working some level of magic like I've never seen before. He compelled these souls to *time travel*, Angie. These four women are going to need an exorcism, their pimp too."

"Bring them on down to Charleston. We can perform the exorcism here at our temple."

"No way Rochelle's going to go for that, but I'll put the idea to her and see what she says."

"*Ashè,*" said Angie. "Let me know how it goes."

After she hung up, Titi crawled into bed, dug down into the blankets, curled into a fetal position and surrendered to a flood of tears. Half an hour later, she got up, went into the bathroom and washed her face, staring long into her eyes in the mirror. *All you have to do is walk away, Titi Anne. God is testing you to see if you're strong enough to walk away from this.*

But it wasn't so simple. She had never experienced anything more holy in life than kissing this man. Even in his absence she could feel the strength of his spirit as if she had known him her entire life, as if he had been there all along, long before they ever actually met. The intensity she felt when she was with him was unrivaled, and to let go of that, to toss it aside as if it meant nothing, was unimaginable, unbearable.

In the mirror, she caught sight of an elderly Black man

approaching behind her, wearing a wide-brimmed straw hat, carrying a carved walking stick and smoking a dark-stained corn cob pipe. He put his left hand on her right shoulder in a gesture of affection, and she immediately recognized him as the Voodoo lwa known as Papa Legba. She reached across with her left hand and placed it warmly over his, comforted by his visit.

"I can always tell when I'm in the presence of a healer," he said with a gentle smile.

More tears fell silently from her eyes. "I don't think I'm much of a healer," she said, a small laugh breaking through her tears.

"You're a healer, whether you believe it or not. Truth is plain as day. You draw the wounded to you like a magnet."

"But can't I find a man who doesn't need healing?"

"There ain't no such thing. We all come out of the womb with a wound. The question is: will you use the gift you've been given?"

"I want to, but I also know of four queens with a deep wound. They're calling to me for help."

"Yes, I know they are, and you'll answer them. You don't have to do it alone. But who else do you know in need of healing?"

"Adrian?"

"This ain't no multiple choice quiz, child. Use your heart. Feel it."

"Please, Papa Legba, I don't know how I can heal Adrian. He said he's had enough crazy in his life. His momma committed suicide. If he only knew that I... I mean, if he only knew the half of what I've been through, he'd walk away. And there were so many others before him I tried to heal. Every time, I ended up abandoned, or abused. Some people just don't want to be healed, or they can't stand to let you see their wound. They can't handle letting someone get that close to them, letting themselves be that vulnerable. They punish you because you saw them when they felt weak."

"Adrian isn't the same as those others. You've got to keep that in mind, you hear? Otherwise your heart will never love again. Open your eyes, and see him for his true self. Who else do you know in need of healing?"

She thought for a moment. "Carlos." She heaved a deep sigh.

"Who else?"

Another pregnant pause followed by another heavy sigh. "Rochelle."

"Who else?"

Another deep breath, and more tears spilled out of her eyes. "Myself."

"Let the spirits guide you," he said, then turned and slowly walked away into the darkness behind her.

| Chapter Fifteen |

"When was the last time you went to church?" Jason asked when Rochelle called him back that evening.

"Can't remember," said Rochelle. "It's been a while."

"Might help you to reconnect with your faith," he said good-naturedly. "Natasha goes to St. Abigail's. You should go check it out. The evening mass is at seven on Saturdays. Father Pacifico Galang's the pastor there. Natasha grew up with him, he's really good."

Jason was a sensible man of quiet intensity and singular purpose. He rarely questioned Rochelle's decisions and even more rarely offered unsolicited advice. As such, she was inclined to pay special attention when he had counsel to share, but didn't think that being at church was going to make her feel any better. Something profound was ailing her on a level beyond reach. Still, on his advice she caught the evening mass that night. Father Galang gave an impassioned sermon on the topic of dreams.

"Brethren," said the pastor, "we can find in the Scripture no shortage of accounts of spirit beings, whether angels, demons, or God Himself, appearing to the faithful in the form of dreams. This leads us to the question of how much importance we should give to our dreams. And how can we recognize Divine inspiration when it comes to us in dream form? How are we to know what parts of our dreams we should pay special attention to? How are we to know if we are led by angels or demons? There's no simple answer to this question."

"Brethren, modern science proposes that dreams are our mind's way of working out problems while we sleep. In many respects, dreams can be thought of as a healing process. Anguish which has taken place in our waking lives very often translates into anguished dreams. So from a spiritual standpoint, and even from a scientific standpoint, it's in our best interest to give dreams proper consideration from time to time. If any of you have a particular dream that's been weighing heavily on you, I urge you to take into consideration how elements of the dream made you *feel*. And I encourage you to take the matter up in prayer. Let the Holy Spirit inspire you to make positive changes in your life, and let it inspire your faith."

He talked about King Solomon being visited by God in a dream, who granted him his desire for wisdom and justice. Even though she was familiar with the account, Rochelle was particularly moved by Father Galang's warm and compassionate recounting of the two prostitutes who famously had come to King Solomon with a dispute over which was the true mother of an infant child. The woman who was the impostor had no problem with King Solomon's suggestion that the child be split in half with a sword, and half given to each woman. The true mother pleaded with the king to give her baby to the other woman so long as he would just let him live. By her protective instinct, Solomon knew which was the true mother.

Feeling refreshed and spiritually fortified by the timely topic of the sermon, Rochelle went back home to the spacious West Village loft that she shared with Carlos. *I've been giving this thing way too much power over me,* she reassured herself. *I need to ease up on the drinking and just get some rest.* She put the television on, and went into the bathroom to take her makeup off.

As she opened the bathroom drawer to pull out a makeup wipe, she caught sight in the bathroom mirror the reflection of a man standing behind her in her living room. She swiftly drew her 9mm and, quickly pivoting her back toward the inside wall of the bathroom, swung around and aimed the pistol at the man's head. Perplexed as he began to chuckle and applaud her with a slow clap, she suddenly recognized the man as Jandro, the trafficking boss she had arrested.

"Magnificent," said Jandro, whose bloodied wife-beater tank top revealed sculpted muscle on his arms and chest. "It's such a pleasure to watch you work, Special Agent Roy. I don't think you'll be able to arrest me with that, though," he said, gesturing toward the Glock, then turning away casually to look around the apartment. "Nice place you have here."

"Thanks," said Rochelle, trailing Jandro's movement around the living room with her gun. "We do alright. Excuse me, but what the hell are you doing here?"

"You're really into this abstract art, huh? What's this piece, Paul Klee? Pre-1920's I'm guessing. Has your father ever seen this place?"

"No."

"Estranged, huh? That's got to be hard on you," said Jandro, glancing back at her and pursing his lips sympathetically. "You're lucky, though. I never knew my father."

"It's not something I think about."

Jandro shrugged. "I can't say I blame you. I don't think much about my mother anymore, either. She was a very, how shall I say—*angry* woman. Had a wicked way with a broom handle. I used to pray my uncle Hector would come adopt me and take me away from all that. He was a good man. Died of a heart attack when I was eleven. But enough about me—let me ask you something." Jandro stopped his eyes from wandering around the room and fixed his gaze onto Rochelle.

He seemed different to her somehow than he did at the arraignment, but she wasn't sure how at first. His tone of voice was intimate. It was quiet; familiar, like he was talking to a good friend, or a sister.

"You have all this space, but you got your cousin shacked up in a hotel? What's up with that? Why doesn't she stay here?"

"I don't want her smoking weed in here, stinking up my place, and she smokes *a lot* of weed. It's an unhealthy crutch for her. I don't like it."

"What about your drinking?"

"It's not the same at all. I drink so I can deal with creeps like you. What does she have that compares?"

"Wow!" said Jandro, clutching at his chest as if a bullet had just entered it. "You wound me, Special Agent Roy!"

"You buy and sell women like property. The violence you're guilty of should be done to you. You make me sick."

The oddness of the situation suddenly dawned on Rochelle. Her eyes widened and panic lurched in her chest as if she were watching a horror film and had just pieced enough clues together to realize the victim was about to die. *I must be dreaming. I've got to wake myself up. Wake up. Wake up!*

He turned and started to move toward her, as if in slow-motion. "I see that you're expecting," said Jandro, pointing at Rochelle's stomach. She looked down and was alarmed to see a pregnant bulge protruding from her waist. Steeling her emotions, refusing to give in to her fear, she then looked back up at Jandro. His hair was beginning to grow unnaturally out of his face, out of his forehead, out of his cheeks and his eyeballs, until his entire face looked like the back of someone's head. *This isn't real,* she thought, fighting the impulse to scream. *Just wake up. Just wake up.*

He plunged his hand into her womb and pulled out a crying baby covered in blood. "Tsk, tsk. Whose baby is this?

She doesn't belong to you, Special Agent Roy. It's time for me to give her to her rightful mother."

The sound of her cell phone ringing woke her, and she sat up from the living room couch in a lurch. It was Titi calling.

"Yeah?"

"You didn't tell me that Abeni mentioned me by name," said Titi, with a tone of accusation.

"What do you mean?"

"Are you alright? You don't sound too well."

"I'm fine, I was just having some kind of crazy nightmare about the pimp we arrested."

"What was the dream?"

"What? I don't know, never mind. Why are you asking me that? And what do you mean, Abeni mentioned you by name?"

Titi sighed impatiently. "Don't pretend you don't know what I'm talking about. Here in the file from the British Home Office," she said. "After they picked her up in London for street walking. The case worker made note of something Abeni had said to her. She said Titi would come for her. She didn't know what it meant."

Rochelle sighed too, bracing herself for more insanity. "Oh, that. I looked into it. The girl is Yoruba. Titi means 'the end' or 'the eternal' in Yoruba, something like that. You seriously think she's talking about you? You've lost touch with reality, Titi. I'm getting more and more worried about you every day."

"You're the one who's lost touch," said Titi indignantly. "Signs all around you, and you refuse to see a single one."

"How's this for a sign? I talked to my boss a little while ago, and of course he wasn't happy about Lin Mei giving you those case files. Your involvement with the case is done. I'll send a driver by to pick up those files from you and take you back to the airport."

"Oh no. That is not acceptable. Don't you understand?

Their souls are in danger."

"It's not up to you to save their souls, Sister Titi Anne. They didn't teach you this at the convent?"

Titi inhaled deeply, then exhaled. "Of course. Yes. Thank you for bringing that up. Yes, I was a nun—"

"A lot good it did you."

"Will you let me finish? Did you know there are Catholic priests who are specially trained to perform exorcisms? Well, an exorcism is what these women need. Except the magic being worked on them is Voodoo in origin. They'll be better served by a Voodoo priest, not a Catholic one."

"I didn't ask you here to heal them, Titi. We brought you in as a consultant. You know, to *consult*?"

"That's what I'm doing, consulting! During my meditation, I received some psychic insights about these women, ways that we can get through to them. Connecting to their authentic selves might be the only way we'll be able to liberate them from their possessing spirits. For starters, I had a clairvoyant insight that Eka likes to sing. If we could find a way to get her to sing, I think we could maybe get through to her. And Quila has a sister—"

"Listen, sorry if I wasn't clear. Your time for consulting is over now. And now that you're off the case, let me just say that it seems like every time you open your mouth to speak, something batshit crazy comes out of it. You're not a well person, Titi. You're paranoid schizophrenic. You need professional help. And I don't mean from a Voodoo priest, or from your ex-husband."

Too furious to speak, Titi ended the call and threw the phone down on the bed. *She's drunk and she doesn't know how she's being,* she thought, fuming. Then she picked up her cell phone again and rapidly typed a text message to Rochelle: "I REFUSE TO BOARD ANY PLANE."

| Chapter Sixteen |

FLASHBACK : December 7, 2003
Chaveña, Juárez City, Chihuahua, Mexico

"I don't know what's worse," said Quila, staring out the passenger window of a dusty gray pickup truck at the *tortería* selling sandwiches across the street, trying to ignore her stomach's growling hunger pains. "Not having a *quinceañera*, or my father having to *tell* me he can't afford one. He was crying, Jandro. I never seen my father cry before."

"He must have felt so horrible." Jandro squeezed Quila's hand sympathetically as she used her other hand to brush a tear from her eye.

"I wish you could have seen Marisela's quinceañera. We rode there in a limousine. Her dress was breathtaking. It was straight out of a fairy tale. The food, the ballroom, the dance. They had a live band *and* a DJ."

"Marisela's father is a *sicario*. He can afford all that. Your father's not like that; he won't take money from the cartels to do their dirty work. I respect that about him, you know? He's a hard-working man. But it's hard to make an honest living in this city. Especially having two daughters to take care of."

"Yeah it is."

"I worry about you too, *reina*, with all these kidnappings and murders lately. Young women disappearing every day, getting raped and tortured. It's not safe for you here. That's why you should come to El Paso with me. My cousin Danny has a real cushy job up there, working on a big ranch for an American couple. He said the wife is looking to hire a housekeeper and wants to pay $40 a week. They'll feed you, they'll give you a place to stay and everything. You should come with me, and stop being a hardship on your parents. You're old enough to get a good job for yourself, and I don't mean a factory job. We can all make a good living in El Paso and get away from these slums. We'll send for your sister Vanessa too, after we get some money saved up. Doesn't that sound nice, baby?"

"My parents won't like it at all. If they even knew I was seeing you, they would completely freak out."

"That's why you can't tell them about it, mama. Sneak out with me tonight, and we'll head up there. I know a guy who can get us across the border."

"I don't know. I need time to think about it, okay?"

"Listen, Quila. I'm not trying to pressure you, but I don't know how long this opportunity is going to last. I'm going to take my chances to get out of here now, while I can. Meet me here tonight at midnight if you decide to go, okay? If you're not here, then it's time for us to say goodbye, right now. I won't be coming back to Juárez City ever again. Whatever you decide, just know that I love you, okay? I'll always love you."

Quila turned to look him in the eye. He was dead serious. Once upon a time, she would never dare let herself dream of a better life; she was far too practical for that. But opportunity was knocking, here and now. She might never get the chance again. "Okay. Let me say goodbye to Vanessa at least," she said.

He slid his arm around her and pulled her toward him

to kiss her tenderly. "I'm so thankful you're coming with me," he said. "We'll save up and buy a ranch of our own. We'll get married and have a bunch of kids. It's gonna be beautiful. You're beautiful. You're so beautiful." He kissed her again and again, all over the golden brown skin of her face and neck, gently stroking her long brown hair and squeezing her tightly. "Midnight, okay? Don't be late."

"I won't," she promised as she stepped out of the truck and closed the door. It was a three-block walk from there to her father's shanty house around the corner, where she lived with her parents, her grandmother and her eleven-year-old sister, Vanessa.

"How was school today, *mija*?" said her grandmother affectionately as Quila sat down next to her on the small mustard yellow couch in their living room.

"It was fine," said Quila, a lump forming in her throat at the thought that this may be their last conversation ever. Her grandmother was 92 years old, and her health was failing.

"It's important to have a good education," her grandmother reminded her, as she was inclined to do quite frequently. "You're a big girl now, going to preparatory school next year. Have you decided which career program you're going to enroll in?"

"Not yet," said Quila.

"It's okay, you have plenty of time to think about these things. You speak English so well, you would make a good bilingual secretary. Better that than the factory."

"Where's Vanessa, *abuelita*?"

"I think she's out back, with her friends. You and Vanessa be sure to get that washing done and hang the clothes up to dry before your mother and father get home from work."

"We will." Quila put her arms around her grandmother and hugged her tightly.

"What's this for?" said her grandmother with a warm smile, reaching up and hugging her back.

"Just because I love you," said Quila, holding back tears. She jumped up from the couch and ran through the house, out the back door. From there she spotted Vanessa sitting outside in the back alley, gathered with a group of children around a tiny television set belonging to their neighbor. "Vanessa!" she called. "Come over here! Yes, right now! I need to talk to you."

"Save my place!" Vanessa barked to her friends as she reluctantly gave up her premium seat closest to the TV, and skipped over to where Quila was standing on the back porch of their house. "Hurry up! What is it?"

"I'm running away to El Paso tonight," said Quila nervously. "I'm leaving at midnight. So I need you to be really quiet, and not wake everyone up, when I get up to leave."

"With Jandro?"

"Yes."

"Ooh la la, he's such a *bombón*. Someday I'm going to have a hot boyfriend just like him."

"Yes you will, without a doubt. But listen to me. Jandro and I will send for you after we get settled in El Paso and have some money saved up."

"I don't want you to send for me."

"Why not?"

"I want to stay here in Mexico. I'm going to Mexico City when I grow up. I'm going to be a model, and report the news on TV."

"That's good, Vanessa. That's good. You're super pretty, I know you can make it. You have light hair, light skin and green eyes. They want *rubias* like you. You're perfect for modeling. Maybe you're the one who should send for *me*," she joked, "once you're all rich and famous."

"Maybe I will," Vanessa shrugged. "Only if you're nice to me."

"Listen, I can't risk anyone trying to stop me, Vanessa. I have to get out of here, you understand? Not a word about this to anyone, you promise?"

"Okay. I promise."

Quila squeezed her tight and never wanted to let go. "I'm going to miss you so much."

| Chapter Seventeen |

FLASHBACK : October 11, 1998
Solomianka Raion, Kiev, Ukraine

Her father had warned her many times that her mother wouldn't believe her. But Olena was a precocious six-year-old, and waited with patient silence—over days, weeks, months— for her father to let down his guard. On most days, he kept his tiny digital camera in the locked letter drawer of his vintage oak writing desk. On most days, he remembered to lock the drawer. But on this particular day in October, his routine had been disrupted by distress over the Ukraine financial crisis, and its impact on his employer, Stone Capital Bank. After hearing the alarm in his voice during several phone calls which took place before he left for work that morning, and listening from the next room as he dug frantically through his desk for reasons she could not even begin to guess, Olena prayed fervently that today would be the day he'd leave the drawer unlocked. And it was.

After ascertaining that the camera still contained the damning evidence she needed to present to Oksana, her mother, she placed the camera back into the drawer and walked into the kitchen where her mother stood washing the dishes from breakfast. She didn't want to have to show her the camera. But if it was true what her father had said, that her mother wouldn't believe her, then she might have to. Timidly, she tapped lightly on her mother's arm, startling her.

Olena spoke so infrequently that her mother had begun to wonder if she had a learning disability, and worried about how Olena was adjusting to her new semester in primary school. While Olena's father was in the house, they all spoke Russian, but while he was away, her mother was teaching her to speak Ukrainian, and she had speculated based on Olena's overwhelmingly quiet nature that she was perhaps becoming confused by the bilingual exposure. The truth was that most of the time, Olena found no compelling reason to speak. Until now.

"Mama," said Olena quietly.

"What is it, my little sun?" said Oksana, drying her hands on a towel.

"Papa..."

"Yes? You want your Papa? He was called away to work, my love. He'll be back tonight before dinner."

"Papa... takes pictures... of me."

"Speak up, Olena, I can't hear you. Papa takes pictures?"

"Papa... takes pictures... of me."

"Well, of course he does. He takes pictures of all of us with that ridiculous little camera."

"He takes pictures of me... naked."

"What? What do you mean, Olena? What are you saying? Pictures in the bath?"

"In the bedroom. When you're not home. He makes me take off my clothes, and he takes pictures."

The gravity of the accusation was beginning to sink in. "No," said Oksana, as an invisible cloud began to form around her head, and her thoughts grew distant and murky. "No," she said again. "You're lying."

"He said you wouldn't believe me."

"No! Be quiet! YOU'RE LYING!" screamed Oksana, slapping Olena hard across the face, knocking her down to the floor.

A flood of emotion welled up in Olena's chest, and her face was reeling from the sting, but her ability to dissociate had been developing rapidly ever since the naked photos had progressed into specific sex acts on camera, things too painful to describe to her mother, let alone experience. She had no recourse but to show her the camera. After rubbing her face with a show of consternation, and after shocking her mother with an absence of tears, she stood up and marched into her parents' bedroom, and pulled the camera from her father's desk drawer. She powered it on and brought it to her mother, who remained aghast in the kitchen, still covering her mouth with her hand in horror and disbelief.

As Oksana took the camera from Olena, she stared at it for a moment, as if it were an alien object from some other planet. She didn't want to look at the pictures, but driven by the compulsion to find out exactly what was going on behind her back, she reluctantly and grimly scrolled through dozens of photos before handing the camera back to Olena. With a deep breath, she then straightened out the wrinkles of her sweater, as if making herself look presentable. "Put this back where you found it," she said with a cold, impersonal tone, as she lit herself a cigarette. "What do you expect me to do with this, huh? You think I can pay for this apartment and feed two children by myself, working part-time at the department store? Stop thinking about yourself for a minute, and think about your baby sister. Where do you expect us to go? The answer is nowhere. There is nowhere for us. So go. Go now. Put it back."

Olena went back to the desk and placed the camera back into the drawer, exactly as she had found it. She closed the drawer somberly like she was closing a coffin, a sealed and silent casket with her soul inside to be buried and never again see the light of day. She kept staring at the closed drawer, paralyzed and dumbfounded, until her mother came into the room and told her to put on her shoes and coat so she could take her shopping. The toy store at the mall where her mother worked had a set of wooden nesting *matryoshka* dolls, and she bought these as a gift for Olena to take home, and asked Olena never to speak of the photos again.

| Chapter Eighteen |

FLASHBACK : June 27, 2008
Soho, City of Westminster, West End, London, UK

"Get in here," said Miles, ushering a gangly fourteen-year-old girl with pale white skin and a bushy mop of red hair into the small, barely furnished one-bedroom flat. Her birth name was Ekaterina Oniani, but most knew her as Eka. "Time for you to meet your co-workers. Lena's the only one here at night now. She's handling the walk-ups today, so we start with her. Lena, this is Eka, our new girl from Tbilisi," he said, gesturing toward the bed for Eka to go sit down. "From now on Lena, you'll be walking Sussex Gardens, you got that? Eka will take over the walk-ups."

Sixteen-year-old Olena looked at Eka with a dispassionate glance, sizing her up, and decided she had nothing to feel threatened about. Right now she only cared about one thing, and that was getting her hands on some more yay.

"It's pathetic I have to ration your crack for you," said Miles to Olena, handing her a baggie containing two rocks of crack cocaine. "You smoke way too much. You're acting too crazy with the customers. One gram at a time from now on. *I'll decide when you can have more.*"

"I don't need you to ration it," Olena insisted indignantly. "I want you to give me what you promised me. And this isn't even half a gram, Miloš. How stupid do you think I am?"

"I told you, stop calling me that. It's *Miles.* I better not catch you calling me that to the punters," he said, referring to the prostitution clients, shaking his head in frustration. "I should have left your sorry ass in Ukraine. You're not the only girl who speaks Russian here now, so you better start thinking about job security. Stop being so greedy."

"You think they mistake you for one of them? Because you change your name?" she said, mockingly. "You're an idiot! You sell twice as much rock now because of me. You should pay me twice as much!"

"Shut up!" he said, backhanding her.

The sudden violence startled Eka, and she leaped instinctively to Olena's defense. Unleashing an unearthly war cry that was half lion's roar, half screeching wraith, Eka rushed forward and jumped onto Miles, wrapping her bony arms and legs around his slender body in a futile effort to take him down. With one forceful hand to her face, he shoved her to the ground, wondering if he had made a mistake bringing her in, and contemplating how to get rid of her. He pushed back his long, blonde hair, and checked the pistol that was tucked into his waistband, pulling it out to remind Eka that he had one.

"You better kill me now," warned Eka with a seething ire, "or spend the rest of your life watching over your shoulder! Because if you EVER lay another hand on her in anger, or on me, or on ANY woman, I will FUCKING KILL YOU. You don't believe me, huh? Look me in the eye," she said, pointing at her eyes. "Am I lying?"

Miles stared at Eka for a moment in stupefied disbelief. *Who does she think she is? I could snap this skinny little twig in half with two fingers.* His body was seized by an indignant posture, while the ability to speak actual words momentarily escaped him in the face of her absurd audacity, which exhibited a kind of strength beyond the physical, more than he knew what to do with. He simply erupted in maniacal laughter. "You're a crazy bitch," he said, shaking his head. "What am I going to do with all these crazy bitches?" Turning to Olena, he said, "Supervise her while she does the walk-ups. Tomorrow you go to Sussex Gardens, and I'll give you a couple more rocks, but only if you stop acting like a crazy bitch." With an abrupt slam of the door, he exited, leaving them alone.

"What the hell do you think you're doing?" said Olena tersely, packing her crack pipe. "You think you're action movie superhero, huh? I don't want your help, so mind your own damn business."

"If I wanted to get beat up," said Eka, walking over to the window and pulling the curtain aside to look outside, "I would still be living with my mother and her shit boyfriends."

"The punters don't care about your standards, Princess," said Olena, with one especially abusive client in mind. "And get the bloody hell away from the window!" she snapped. "Last thing we need is police showing up here."

"Ha!" laughed Eka. "You think police are going to jump out of their pants over some pathetic little runaway? I wish the world was so kind."

Olena shot her a menacing glare, and Eka obediently let the curtain fall shut.

"Hey, where is karaoke around here?" said Eka. "We can go singing sometime, yeah?" She swirled around and crooned to Olena, "I've got the blues, I feel so lonely. I'll give the world if I could only… make you understand. It surely would be grand! Oh baby, won't you please come home!"

Where did Miloš find this crazy little skeleton girl? "What makes you think I want to go to karaoke? Do I look Japanese to

112

you?" said Olena coldly, rolling her eyes before hitting the pipe and letting heaven wash over her. The euphoria lasted a few too-short minutes. She fumbled to put another rock in the pipe.

"It's not Japanese song, it's jazz. 'Baby Please Come Home,' you never heard this song? You don't like jazz? You don't like anything?"

"I like crack."

Eka sat down on the bed and wrapped her arms around her knees, like she used to do as a child when her mother would lock her in the closet.

A ring came at the doorbell and Olena gestured for Eka to wait. Patrons were to only be granted entry if they knew the code. There was a pause, then two rings, then three.

"It's Friday," said Olena, tucking the pipe away under the kitchen sink. "Here come the regulars."

| Chapter Nineteen |

FLASHBACK : June 27, 2013
Borno State, Nigeria

"I have a special favor to ask of you, my angel," said Tobi Abiola, a young, charismatic, dark-skinned man, to his wife, Abeni. "It would please my mother very much if we could keep the *ere ibeji* statuette in our bedroom, instead of on display by the entrance to our home. As you know, she is not one for superstition, and she wishes for us to raise her grandchild as a Christian, not as an animist.

The wooden statuette in question was a traditional effigy which had been specially carved as a physical embodiment of the soul of their son's twin brother, who died in childbirth. It was culturally understood that the mere suggestion, not to mention her husband's failure to address the spirit by name, could be enough to offend the spirit of their stillborn child.

"How can you even suggest that?" she answered, distraught at the very idea of it. "Adisa Taiwo protects the soul of his brother." The twenty-three-year-old mother picked up the broom and began to sweep the room nervously. "I knew when

114

we married that an inter-faith marriage would be challenging. But you promised me that you would respect my beliefs. You gave me your word."

"Baby, I do respect your beliefs," said Tobi. "After five years of marriage, I think you know that's true. It would be unfair to accuse me of being intolerant, would it not? But I also respect my mother, as a man should. She said she will come by today to bring me some teaching materials for the school. It is an act of great generosity on her part. Is it not possible for the *ibeji* to keep watch over our home from the bedroom? Just for the afternoon?"

"Adisa Taiwo is here for the protection of Abeo Kehinde," Abeni reiterated adamantly. "He has watched over our home for five years, and only now your mother is expressing an objection?"

"She wants to impress the new pastor with her piety," he explained, scratching the back of his head. "And, if I can be honest with you, she is growing impatient for more grandchildren. She has suggested that I consider taking a second wife."

"If I could summon another pregnancy, I would. So she's done with me, is that what you mean to say?" said Abeni, containing her frustration. "What do you think of the idea of moving back to Lagos? As a Hausa reading specialist, you can easily find work there."

"Just to get away from my mother? It is not a good enough reason. Abeo has many friends here, and he's doing well in school."

"It's not the only reason. I'm also worried about violence from the militant groups. It's getting worse every year."

"A civilian militia is forming for our protection. My brother is a member, and they are stockpiling plenty of weapons to defend us. He will protect us, much more than your little statue will, I promise you that, my angel. And we have a good escape plan," Tobi assured her. "When we hear gunfire coming, we will have plenty of time to flee."

Her husband could be stubborn, and on many occasions, she found it to be an admirable trait. He was neither a bully nor a tyrant, but neither was he an easy man to push around. He resolved conflicts with diplomacy, most of the time. But Abeni felt ill at ease.

"Will you *please* be nice to my mother when she comes by?" pleaded Tobi, pressing his palms together into a praying gesture.

"You know that it is not necessary to ask that of me," said Abeni, picking up the ibeji statuette and cradling it like a child. She rocked it gently in her arms, as if comforting a baby, before carrying it into the bedroom. "I am much nicer to your mother than she is to me."

"I did not wish to anger you with her request," said Tobi. "But if one of you is to be angry with me, better you than she."

"It is not *my* anger that you should worry about," said Abeni defensively, picking up yams to peel for breakfast.

Just then, a man broke through their front door wearing a rifle over his back and carrying a pistol in his right hand. Before Abeni could register what was happening, he had shot Tobi in the forehead, who fell to the ground. Screaming his name, she rushed over and kneeled next to her husband's lifeless body, but he had already passed on to his next existence.

Since Abeni didn't hear any approaching gunfire—as Tobi had just assured her would happen to warn them—her immediate and only thought was that the intruder must be here alone and that his primary intention was to rape her. *If God is willing, may this man never father another child!* she thought, picking up a heavy gourd filled with rice, and swinging it with full force into his groin. "Run, Abeo!" she screamed to her son, who was playing outside. The intruder howled as he keeled over in pain, then angrily lifted his pistol to dispatch Abeni.

Before he could fire, a second man walked through the

front door and swiftly shot the first intruder, first in the hand to disarm him, and then in the head to end his life. His aim was precise. Once ascertaining that the first intruder was dead, he then gestured to some men outside to bring Abeo into the house, who was violently kicking and screaming. "*Oya!*" he said to the others. "Hurry up!" He appeared to be their leader. "Quiet!" he barked at Abeo. His voice was so powerful that the boy immediately stopped struggling and obeyed.

Abeni was bewildered that this man would shoot his own man. Whoever he was, he apparently wanted her alive. Her next immediate thought was to try to negotiate for the safety of her son, but the leader was already addressing the topic.

"Listen closely," he said, sternly but politely. "No more impulsive violence, if you please. You must think now of your son and his safety."

"What do you want from me?" said Abeni, her face tensed in anger and grief.

"Please allow me to make your acquaintance. I work for a cocaine trafficker here in Borno. Our local supplier has a contact in London, Mr. Miles Mason, who wishes to employ a beautiful, light-skinned 'African' woman such as yourself," said the man candidly. "By special request for his clientele."

"What kind of employment?" said Abeni.

"Why, the kind that ladies do best, of course," said the man with a wink. "Mr. Mason is willing to pay top dollar for your services. He has arranged your flight, complete with passport and visa. All that remains now is for you to simply take the journey, without causing any problems for us. If you try to alert the authorities, or obstruct the process in any way, I can assure you that your little boy here will die a long and painful death."

Abeni was stunned. A passport and visa meant this plan had to have been set in motion months before. *Who knew about this?* "What assurance do I have that you will take good care of him if I comply?"

"Well, now, if you do exactly as we say, you can trust reliably that your boy will be well looked after. He will make a fine young soldier. He will be a great asset to us. Do not give us a reason to harm him. It is all we ask."

| Chapter Twenty |

With clarity of purpose, Titi walked over to her hotel dresser and removed a wooden box containing her ritual kit. She hand stitched four poppets, lit four candles and began mixing ingredients in her wooden mixing bowl. Once she was satisfied with the contents, she began to chant a healing spell.

An hour later, her cell phone was ringing. It was Rochelle. "What the hell is going on?" she demanded.

"Could you be more specific?" asked Titi innocently.

"The four women we have in custody at Glen Haven are flipping out."

"And you think *I* had something to do with that? I mean, yes, I did perform a healing spell, and it should have helped them. But I wouldn't have expected to make a believer out of you, Miss Die-Hard Skeptic. Did you call to tell me that it's working?"

"*Working*?" said Rochelle incredulously. "No. If your spell actually did have some kind of... unexplainable effect, working is not what I would call it. More like waking wack. They've become angry and violent. It's like they've got... superhuman strength. It took a dozen nurses to get them into restraints. Sedatives are not helping. I don't know if you can go so far as to call me a believer, but something highly unnatural is definitely happening here." Her thoughts were racing. "I just don't know. I'm trying to make sense of it. I'm trying, I just... What the hell is going on, Titi?"

"The possessing spirits are resisting the spell," said Titi, her initial sense of smugness quickly vanishing into worry as she digested the news. "The bokor is manifesting considerable power like I've never seen. Let me talk to them, before they start doing some real damage to themselves. You want them to testify, don't you? I can help them. A conversation. That's all I'm asking."

"Okay, fine," said Rochelle, feeling her sanity slipping from grasp. She drew in a deep breath and gave herself a moment to reconsider. "Fine," she said again. "They're being transferred to a safe house. I'll send a driver for you."

Titi was puzzled when the driver dropped her off in front of Glen Haven.

"I thought you said they were being taken to a safe house?" she said, on meeting Rochelle in the lobby.

Rochelle gestured with a finger to her lips for Titi to keep quiet, and then discreetly motioned for her to follow as she turned to exit the hospital lobby through a side door which led into a long hallway. "We're meeting them there."

At the end of the hallway, Rochelle opened another door and led Titi down some stairs to yet another door which had a small panel next to it that was locked, and looked like it would have a standard fuse box inside. Rochelle opened the panel door with a key to reveal a biometric scanner which scanned her right eye and unlocked the door. On the other side was an elevator which scanned the veins in Rochelle's left hand using infrared before it opened.

Once inside, Rochelle pressed a button labeled "O" and then startled Titi with the sound of her voice as the elevator quietly lurched into a downward motion. "It was inadvisable to speak freely about this in the lobby," she explained. "This is a secure area, so we're fine now. I'm taking you to Ophelia's Wing, a maximum security annex to Glen Haven that used to house the criminally insane. It's where the vics are now."

"We're taking your car?" asked Titi, thinking it was odd to have so many security measures just to get to the garage.

"No," said Rochelle. "We're taking an underground transit system that was specially built for Ophelia's Wing. The wing was built in 1961, six city blocks away from Glen Haven, and they connected the two buildings using a decommissioned underground aqueduct from the 1800's. The FBI acquired both Glen Haven and Ophelia's Wing in 1986, then installed additional security fortifications so Ophelia's Wing could be used as a safe house. Are you okay?"

Titi's face was contorted in distress. "I'm okay. These small spaces are just triggering my claustrophobia."

"Oh, you'll feel better when we get to the bottom. It's pretty spacious down there. You wouldn't believe how huge the aqueduct is. It's amazing there's so much infrastructure underneath the city."

The elevator doors opened, and Rochelle led Titi down another long hallway to another door that opened with a vein recognition scanner. Titi's heart was thumping in her throat, and she was trying to keep a panic attack at bay. It suddenly abated as Rochelle pushed the door open, leading them out onto a small platform next to a set of train tracks which threaded the aqueduct, a massive concrete structure textured with almost two centuries worth of water erosion.

The tension in Titi's shoulders began to relax as the space opened out in front of her. *I should have smoked a bowl before I came here.*

"The sewer smell is pretty much constant," said Rochelle. "Take a look at the sides of the train track," she said, pointing along the wall of the aqueduct as it narrowed in front of them into a deep, dark hole. "There's water running through here. It connects to the Atlantic Ocean, somewhere." She unlocked a panel to call the train.

Titi squinted her eyes for a moment, peering into the darkness, then relaxed them. "I'm picking up some psychometry from this location," she said slowly. "There are people buried under here. Unmarked graves, hundreds of them. They died of yellow fever." For a moment, the image of hundreds of people pale, jaundiced, and naked, bleeding from their vacant eyes as they aimlessly wandered a darkened forest at night, haunting their graves, flashed through Titi's vision. It always unsettled her to catch glimpses of the dead, though it happened often enough that she held out hope that someday she would grow to not feel so alarmed.

"What do you mean by psychometry?" said Rochelle, interrupting Titi's thoughts.

"It's a form of clairvoyance where the reader can sense the history of a place or an object by touching it."

Rochelle looked away at the wall, stifling a reaction. She wondered how much more surreal this experience could possibly get.

Titi was wondering the same thing. "Before that," she said, "there was a dense forest right here, with a river running through it. Pine trees everywhere. Late sixteenth century."

"So if you're psychic, what am I thinking right now?" said Rochelle.

"Psychic doesn't mean omniscient," said Titi with a glare.

A single train car pulled up alongside the platform and a device mounted to its outside wall scanned Rochelle's face before opening the door. "Let's go," said Rochelle. "Lin Mei is already there, waiting for us."

| Chapter Twenty-One |

"I learned a few phrases in Yoruba from YouTube," said Titi. "Let me talk to Abeni first."

She was quickly ushered into the convalescent room where Abeni was bound to a hospital bed with leather straps at her arms and legs. The room was under supervision by four security guards. When Titi asked in Yoruba what her name was, Abeni immediately responded in English, as if to relieve Titi of the awkwardness of trying to communicate in a language with which she clearly had almost no proficiency. "My name is Kemi."

"Where do you come from?" asked Titi, validated to see that her zombification theory appeared to be correct.

"From another place, and another time," said Kemi. Titi searched the girl's unblinking eyes for any sign of Abeni, and found none.

"Please, Miss Kemi, I would love to hear more about this. What brings you to our place and time?"

"I was hanged with my sisters at Gallows Hill of Salem, Massachusetts Bay, in July of the year 1692," answered Kemi. "My sisters and I have arisen in death to seek vengeance for our wrongful deaths caused by the demon Bram Sylvrvysc."

"Did you say Silverfish?" said Titi, her eyes widening.

Rochelle, watching from the next room, was equally stunned. She turned to Lin Mei and asked, "Did she say Sylvrvysc?"

Lin Mei shrugged.

"Bram Sylvrvysc, yes," affirmed Kemi. "Bram was able to escape us, and now has taken possession of a man in your time, by the name of Jandro. We have followed him to your world with the help of Nimbeau, the bokor."

"Are your sisters also Yoruba?" asked Titi.

"My sisters are not of my blood. Abitha and Temperance are the daughters of my employer, Reverend Rufus Thorpe. Talisa is the adopted daughter of the reverend and his goodwife, Charity. Talisa is the Indian daughter of the squaw sachem of the Massachusett tribe. But she is our sister too, in spirit."

"If I may ask, how did you and your sisters come to be hanged?"

"Bram had made a compact with Reverend Thorpe. Bram promised to make him governor of Salem Village in exchange for intercourse with his daughters. Reverend Thorpe, while possessed by the demon, also forced himself upon our dear sister Talisa. When Goody Thorpe confronted him with these accusations, he denied them, saying they were falsehoods. He accused us of witchcraft, and we were all four sentenced to be hanged."

"And how did the bokor come to be involved?" Titi asked.

"The jailhouse was full of those accused of witchcraft," said Kemi. "So full that we four had to be taken to a separate, private jail. The night before our execution, we were visited at the jailhouse by the bokor Nimbeau. He promised vengeance for the four of us. He said that the demon Bram was a traveler from another dimension who would persecute more women if we did not stop him."

Rochelle stared at the conversation on the other side of the one-way mirror. She was trying to follow what was happening, but her mind was reeling. The fingers of her right hand were pressed to her forehead, as she struggled to hold onto a rational explanation.

"Bram is not a Yoruba word, is it?" asked Titi. "I've never heard of this demon, Bram Silverfish. But I think I may have seen him, in a dream."

"Bram is his Christian name," said Kemi. "Nimbeau explained to us that Bram was a *petro lwa* who decided he could have more fun persecuting the Protestants than those protected by Voodoo."

"Where is he now?"

"He has taken possession of a man in your time named Jandro, a man who trades in the services of women. Bram has a never ending lust for sexual acts, and he uses Jandro to indulge his cravings. But Abitha tells me your people have jailed him."

"How do you intend to exact vengeance?" pressed Titi, reading her intently.

"Bokor Nimbeau has provided us with instructions to create a gris-gris. We will use it to keep him trapped in human form, and then we'll make him suffer," said Kemi, clearly relishing the idea.

"If he's a demon, then his ways will not be reformed," cautioned Titi. "Torturing him will achieve nothing. It will only reinforce his malice."

"No matter," said Kemi. "We are content to see him suffer." Her face tensed into an angry scowl. "He cannot suffer enough."

"And then?"

"And then he will know what it means to be the slave, and we shall be free."

"No, my dear child, I'm afraid it doesn't work that way,"

said Titi kindly. "To act with malice is to become a slave to it. There is only one true slave here, and his name is Bram."

"You know nothing," said Kemi, her animosity rising. "With the help of Nimbeau, we too can travel in the spirit realm. You will not stop us."

"You've wrongfully displaced the souls of four other women. Who will avenge *them*?"

"They were already dead. Keep your distance, Mambo. I warn you now, for your own protection. The events which must transpire are beyond your influence."

"What if they're not dead?"

"They are."

"And if I can prove otherwise?"

Kemi ignored the question. "Keep your distance," she said again, sternly. "You have been warned."

| Chapter Twenty-Two |

Lin Mei poured the last of the coffee from the carafe into her mug, and stared at it blankly, unable to focus on the women in the room next door she was supposed to be observing. She was feeling more agitated by the caffeine than energized. *Come on, coffee. Do your damn job.* Reid wasn't happy about her giving Titi the case file, but he said the consequences would be dealt with after the case was closed. He told her to get the file back and send Titi home. Lin Mei knew Rochelle valued her on the team, but couldn't shake the feeling that Rochelle was somehow disappointed that she hadn't faced stronger, immediate discipline.

Lin Mei's neck and shoulders were aching, and her thoughts kept wandering. She felt herself drowning in a proverbial sea with a methamphetamine millstone around her neck. At the very least, she had managed to convince Midori to check into a rehab that would respect her transitional state. *Things can only get better from here. If only I could just lie down and sleep for a year.*

Staring at Abeni from the other side of the one-way mirror, Rochelle was meanwhile occupied with trying to retain some healthy skepticism, but the four women exhibiting superhuman strength had her shaken and stirred like the two martinis she drank before driving over. She was curious to find out what Lin Mei would make of all this. Rochelle knew Lin Mei had a pretty open mind on the topic of Voodoo, and on religious practice in general, but reincarnated zombies? It was so far-fetched, like something straight out of a campy B movie. Surely there was a more simple explanation, and she was hoping that as a psychologist, Lin Mei could conjure one.

"What's a gris-gris?" asked Lin Mei, as Titi exited Abeni's room and joined them in the observation room.

"Historically they've come in many forms," said Titi. "Based on what Kemi is describing, I surmise it refers to a small cloth pouch which can be enchanted for harm or protection. Most likely they'll need to obtain a piece of Jandro's hair or clothing, or blood, along with other ingredients, to enclose inside the pouch, after inscribing a spell inside the fabric and performing a ritual to enchant it. They intend to use it to trap Bram in human form."

"Interesting. So let me try to get this straight. This Bram demon is Christian? I didn't know demons could do that, choose a religion. I guess I never really thought about it." She took another sip of her coffee.

"The bokor called him a petro lwa," said Titi. "A highly aggressive, warring spirit. He doesn't practice a religion. He merely has a history of preying upon the repressed sexuality of the Puritans in order to indulge his fleshly desires."

"And now he's possessing Jandro?" said Lin Mei. "But... pimps aren't exactly Puritanical? Am I missing something?"

"No," said Titi, "but as Kemi pointed out, through Jandro, he has access to all the sex he wants."

"Oh, I see. Of course, that makes sense. Sorry, I must have missed that part. Haven't had enough coffee today. And what about our four vics?" said Lin Mei. "You said they're not demons, right?"

"Their possessing spirits are not demons—yet," said Titi, "although if they stay on this malevolent course, they may certainly become demons in time. Right now, they're only displaced human souls. Normally, when a soul dies, it returns to the spirit realm. This bokor, Nimbeau, is very powerful. Before they could die, he not only turned them into zonbis, he sent them into the *future* in pursuit of Bram. I've never seen anything like this. It may be Kemi speaks the truth, when she says that I'm in over my head. It's possible the solution is beyond my reach."

Rochelle was somehow relieved to hear this. "So it sounds like your work here is done," she said quickly. "Let Dr. Varma and the medical staff take it from here."

"I know we don't often agree," said Titi quietly. "But this time... I feel very fearful. I almost want to walk away from this. There's very dark magic at work here."

"Almost?" said Lin Mei. "What's stopping you?"

"It's Abeni," said Titi. "She's calling to me for help. I feel her. I know my cousin here is not a believer, so let's just call it a gut feeling. I think I can get through to her." Titi cleared her throat and paused. "Yes," she said, after a moment of further contemplation. "I think it's worth trying. Bram himself cannot be reformed, but once he's no longer possessing Jandro's body, it's possible that Jandro may have a chance at redemption. We must try to liberate their spirits from the human bodies, and send them back to the spirit realm. It won't be easy. Asking them to let go of a physical body will feel like death to them. But if we don't, these women will be dangerous if they're released from custody. If we make no attempt to save their souls, they will seek either to kill or more likely torture Jandro."

"They can't get to him," said Rochelle, shaking her head. "And anyway, he'll get his fair share of punishment in prison. God knows he deserves it."

"Malice is not necessary to restore justice," admonished

Titi. "And whether or not they succeed in punishing Bram, it's unlikely they'll want to surrender control back to the women whose bodies they stole. As I said, it's like a death sentence for them. But regardless of what happens to Bram or Jandro, these women deserve a chance to heal. If there's any chance we can give them that, we must try."

"They seem so calm," said Lin Mei. "Abeni—I mean Kemi?—is cooperating with your questioning. It's hard to imagine them doing harm to anyone."

"Try telling that to the nurses who had to restrain them last night," said Rochelle.

"They can be calm when they want to," said Titi. "If you anger them, you can expect them to respond with a temper, like small children."

"Did you say you can do a spell to force them out of the bodies?" asked Lin Mei. "I realize they don't want to die again, but they're supposed to be dead anyway, right? They say they were hanged in 1692, right? So technically you're not really killing them by taking their physical bodies away. The hanging is what killed them, and that's not our fault."

"When you say they're *supposed* to be dead, it's problematic," said Titi. "Because they *didn't* die, technically. They found a way to displace their souls, and it's not for us to say what was *supposed* to happen. They have bodies, and they feel alive, and they won't want to let go of that. But what I do know is that the bodies don't belong to them, and we need to return those bodies to the women they belong to."

"What are you proposing we do?" asked Rochelle, half curious, half not wanting to know.

"I would like to perform some daily healing rituals on the victims, and monitor them to assess their progress. If they're receptive, we can arrange baths for them using a special treatment of oils and herbs which I will prepare," said Titi. "This is to ready them for the exorcism. For that, we can request the assistance of Angelique. Our cousin Angie is a Haitian Vodou priestess operating a temple in Charleston," she added for Lin Mei. "She can provide the altar and sacrificial animal."

"Wait, what?" said Rochelle incredulously. "An *animal sacrifice*? Oh no. No. Do you actually think the U.S. government would be interested in sanctioning something like that? This is too crazy. I can't anymore with this."

"Is there some reason you can't perform the exorcism here in New York?" said Lin Mei.

"We need a temple, and the communal strength of a Voodoo congregation," said Titi. "Angie can help us with those things, and she and I have an established synergy. Seeking out an *ounfo*—a Voodoo temple—among strangers will prolong the process."

"Chelle," said Lin Mei. "We can get someone to pull the court records from 1692. There's an archive of everyone who was executed. If the names of these four women are on record, it would go a long way toward verifying if Abeni or her alter ego Kemi is telling the truth."

"Fine," said Rochelle. "If it will put an end to this ridiculous theory once and for all, I'll have my assistant get on it. But Titi, your work here is done. You asked to have your one conversation, and you got it. So it's time for you to go home now. Dr. Varma is perfectly capable of supervising their care without your assistance."

"Oh no. Don't even think about asking me to leave now," said Titi, her face growing hot in anger. "Shut me out and you'll regret it."

"Is that a threat?" said Rochelle, straightening her back. "What are you going to do about it?"

"It's what your karma is going to do about it that you need to be worried about."

"Whoa, come on, Chelle, let's take a step back, okay?" said Lin Mei, putting her hand on Rochelle's back in a gesture of support.

"I'm not the one who needs to step back," said Rochelle, pursing her lips.

"Okay," said Lin Mei, looking at Rochelle and then at Titi, searching her mind for a way to smooth things out. "Titi, for now let's just get you back to your hotel, okay? Give us some time to research the victim's claims. If what you're saying is true, it should all check out. Can you just bear with us a little bit longer?"

| Chapter Twenty-Three |

FLASHBACK : June 12, 1692
Salem Village, Massachusetts Bay

Charity Thorpe sat quietly in a finely carved banister-back chair, contentedly mending her children's clothes as she watched seven-year-old Temperance learn how to make a corn husk doll from her sixteen-year-old adopted daughter, Elizabeth. "And now for the belt," said Elizabeth, holding the corn husk doll in place while Temperance tied with her tiny fingers a long string around the waist to secure the skirt. "And there thou hast it! Well done, Temperance! What wilt thou name her?"

Temperance gazed thoughtfully at the doll. "Echo," she said, through her missing two front teeth. She walked over to Constance, the Yoruba woman who worked for the Thorpes as a housekeeper and nanny, and showed her the doll.

"Very pretty, baby," said Constance, smiling broadly at her sweetness. "It reminds me of a doll I had as a child. Hast thou rendered thanks to Miss Elizabeth for showing thee how to make it?"

Charity's other born daughter Abitha, age eleven, looked

up from her Bible reading and interjected. "Dost thou not mean to ask if she thanked Talisa's Indian family for teaching her how to make it?"

"Abitha!" said Charity sharply. "Why dost thou insist on calling Elizabeth by her birth name instead of her Christian name?"

"Her parents chose that name for a reason, so that is what we should call her," shrugged Abitha. "As Constance is also truly Kemi."

"Respect thy mother," said her father, Rufus, as he stood up from the sermon he had been preparing at his writing desk.

"Who told thee that, Abitha?" said Charity, shooting Kemi a disapproving look. "Was it thee, Constance?"

"Just because thou giveth them a Christian name, it doth not make them a better person," insisted Abitha, not allowing Kemi to answer. Kemi looked at Charity, shaking her head to reassure her.

"Thou art courting a world of trouble, young lady." said Rufus, opening the cellar door. "Shall I fetch the whip?"

"Thou mayest fetch the rye bread whilst thou art in the cellar, if thou pleaseth, my lord," said Charity, interrupting his scolding. "Goody Maypool hath fallen ill again, and I've prepared an onion sallet to bring to her. Elizabeth will join me, and Constance will give the girls a bath while we're away. We shall return in plenty of time to prepare supper."

"Very well," said her husband, giving Abitha a final reprimanding look before taking his hat and cape. "I shall join for supper on my return from aiding Sam Shore in the repair of his roof. Good day, then. Behave thyself, Abitha. Mind thy mother."

The property of their neighbor, Samuel Shore, was situated near the outer border of Salem Village, on the road to Andover, almost four miles from the Thorpe's two-story wood frame farmhouse. It took Rufus little over an hour to arrive there riding with his horse and cart, and he gave thought to his upcoming sermon as the summer afternoon sun kept him company on the journey.

As he made his way past Wilkins Pond, he began to feel an odd discomfort in his chest, and a burning pain in his throat. He pressed his hand to his chest, aiming to relieve some of the discomfort, which he took to be heartburn, just as an intense dizzy spell washed over him. He parked the cart and horse at the side of the road to try to quiet the powerful wave of sickness that had suddenly come upon him. While trying to get his bearings, he was jolted by the sudden awareness of an old woman standing next to the cart. Her body was draped with a large black cloak, and a hood hung forward, masking her face. The sight of her alarmed him.

"Thou hast been a very naughty boy, Rufus," said the woman, with a wicked cackle he immediately recognized as belonging to his deceased mother, Deliverance Thorpe. "Now thou must be punished!"

He screamed in terror. *Lucifer is playing tricks on me,* he feared, shutting his eyes tightly and hoping she would disappear by the time he opened them. But when he opened them, he was no longer parked on the side of the road, with Wilkins Pond in view, but rather back at home, sitting on his bed in his upstairs bedroom, alone. He looked down and realized his clothing had changed as well. Now he was wearing his pajamas, as if he were about to go to bed, only it was apparent through the window that there was still bright daylight outside. "What the Devil is happening here!" he shouted. Then he was alarmed once again to see the hooded figure of his mother sitting next to him on the bed. She reached up and pulled the hood back from her face, revealing not his mother, but a bizarre replica of himself, except younger, and more physically fit.

"Dost thou know who I am?" said the specter.

"Of course I do," he said defensively. "How it's possible,

I could not guess, but any simpleton can see that thou art but a younger version of myself."

"But I am not a younger version of thee, my good man," he replied, removing the rest of his cloak and revealing a finely tailored expensive suit. "I am thee who is yet to come. Thee who hast been elected governor of Massachusetts Bay."

Rufus laughed. "Now I know for certain that Lucifer is playing tricks on me, for I am far too humble a man for such a position."

"So thy nagging ninny of a wife would have thou believe."

"No," said Rufus, distraught by the unexpected criticism of Charity. "If ever there was a woman deserving of her name, it is most certainly my loving wife. It was her idea, after all, to lawfully emancipate our housekeeper Constance, to free her from slavery and offer her a proper salary for her services. And it was her kindness which convinced me that it was right to accept the squaw sachem's request that we adopt Elizabeth, instead of forcing her to resettle with the others, so she could learn to read English, have access to education and medicine, and receive military protections as a Protestant. No, sir, thou art plainly mistaken. Charity inspires everyone in the parish of Salem Village with her fine example."

"Ah yes. She can be quite persuasive in the name of the Lord."

"Well, yes, I suppose thou couldst say so."

"She would make a better reverend than thee, I'm afraid."

"I'm afraid so as well."

"Everyone in town whispers behind thy back that she makes all the decisions for thee, for thou art a coward."

"Oh no, thou hast gone too far. No, I don't think so," said Rufus, trying to find the truth in his own words. "I don't... think I am. Her benevolent actions are enchanted with good intention, and I saw no reason to oppose her."

"Thou wanted to stay in Salem Towne. Thou had every luxury there. Thou had no reason to move to the village. Look at how thou livest now. Not much better than a farmhand."

"I happen to agree with Charity that a humble and modest life of cultivating farmland will be more beneficial for the children's integrity. City life would breed idle conceit. The ground is more fertile here, and so are the hearts of the parishioners."

"Is that what thou truly believeth? Or is that what thy overbearing wife tells thee to think?"

"No, thou hast it all wrong. I'm a very lucky man. It's by the grace of God that a man like myself won acceptance from such as her... a God-fearing woman, hardworking and prudent in matters of law and finance. Thou knowest, of course, that her grandfather Milton hath great wealth, is well-known and well-respected. He brought his family to New England on the Mayflower, and with her lineage she could have chosen any suitor far more handsome than I, and far more wealthy without a doubt."

"Yes, I know. So thou likest to tell everyone."

"But she cares not for the material wealth which is her heritage. She chose me, because she cares more for her spiritual integrity."

"She chose thee because she likes to have a whipping boy around to make her feel important. Art not thou tired of being a whipping boy, Rufus?"

Rufus' face grew red with anger. "I won't stand for this."

"Indeed, thou shalt not," said his doppelganger, as he produced a large knife from thin air and plunged it into Rufus' gut. "For the time hath arrived for a real man to begin charting the course of thy life."

Rufus stared down at the wound in horror as blood began to soak his clothing. Dizzy as he fell backwards onto the bed, he closed his eyes as a wave of nausea passed over him.

When he opened his eyes, he was lying in a patch of tall grass next to Wilkins Pond. The knife wound was gone. The sun was shining brightly overhead, and as he shifted himself upright, his horse neighed loudly and stomped his feet in agitation, ears flicking wildly back and forth.

| Chapter Twenty-Four |

"Elizabeth," said Charity, looking out across a grassy knoll and squinting in the afternoon sun as the sound of hooves hitting the dirt punctuated their conversation and the warm smell of summer, of horses' sweat and dung, of floral scents wafting on the breeze, filled their nostrils and lungs. She paused a moment to weigh the gravity and propriety of the topic on which she wished to inquire.

Elizabeth smiled warmly in anticipation of her query.

"Hast thou been happy living with us, since thou hast left thy tribe?"

"Of course, Mother!" said Elizabeth, her eyes widening at the thought that Charity could think otherwise.

"It must have been so difficult to part from thy true mother as such a young girl. She was a brave woman to let thee go."

"Must we speak of her now?" said Elizabeth sadly, pushing away the grief to reassure Charity kindly, "Thou art my mother now, my one and only."

"It warms my heart to hear thou say that, Elizabeth. I wasn't sure... after Reverend Thorpe... disciplined thee not long ago."

"It was only the one time," said Elizabeth dismissively, even though the fiery sting of his whip was freshly vivid in her memory. "I know he only does so because he loves me. He said so. He wants to refine my conscience to know right from wrong."

"I'm glad to hear thou feeleth that way, Elizabeth." Charity was silent for a moment as she wondered if Rufus could ever whip his own flesh and blood with such fury. She shuddered with the realization that she wasn't sure of the answer. It was not uncommon for a man in their village to whip a child for discipline, but there seemed something hateful and monstrous about him in that moment. "Thou mustn't think ill of Reverend Thorpe, or of thy mother, for that matter," Charity continued at last, pulling herself away from her dark rumination. "Someday thou shalt have children of thy own, and thou shalt understand how hard it is to see one's child leave thee. She only wanted what was best for thee, and was brave enough to let thee have it."

"It's not a thing I can allow myself to contemplate, honestly," said Elizabeth meekly. "Except when Abitha insists on calling me Talisa. I'm very sorry, Mother. I've asked her not to, time and again. She also calls Constance by her birth name when thou and Reverend Thorpe are not around."

"Oh, Abitha!" said Charity, exasperated. "How that child is intent on vexing me! I'm grateful for thy forthrightness, Elizabeth. It's good of thee to set a fine example for the girls, as the Lord intends."

"But am I truly good?" questioned Elizabeth. "I'm embarrassed to say I don't believe I fully know yet what it means to be good in a Christian sense. Am I good enough? Will I be good enough? I try so very hard."

"But of course thou art, my angel," said Charity, squeezing Elizabeth's hand sympathetically. "To be good means to follow God's guidance, as best we can, for having been born into sin. But good enough, thou sayeth? What ever dost thou mean? Good enough for what?"

"Good enough for Jeremy Burroughs to want to marry me?"

Charity was speechless for a moment. She had no idea that Elizabeth fancied the young man. "Oh, my dear sweet girl," said Charity. "Thou wilt make a fine wife for any young man who is lucky enough to see thou for the treasure that thou art."

"I had a terrible dream last night, Mother. I was wearing a white dress, and was bound at the hands and feet in white cotton gauze. My head and face were also covered in gauze, but I could see faintly through the cloth that I was standing on the roof of a tall building, perhaps some sort of balcony. I heard them calling out 'witch' as some men threw me off of the roof, and I plunged a great distance into a nearby lake, where I drowned. I was so frightened at this that I was in tears when I awoke. What could possibly be the meaning of this?"

Charity warmly put her arm around Elizabeth and kissed her head. "It was only a bad dream, my dear child." But the heavy shadow of fear was already casting a cold wind across her heart, and her eyebrows tensed unconsciously. She sought comfort, as she often did, in the singing of a hymn from the 18th Psalm of David. Elizabeth quickly recognized the lyric, and joined her in singing:

Floods of ill men affrighted me,
death's pangs about me went;
Hell's sorrows me environed;
death's snares did me prevent.
In my distress I called on God,
cry to my God did I—

Elizabeth abruptly stopped singing as she caught sight of something moving outside of the horse-drawn cart. She sharply turned her head to see the tall grass bending in a strange manner, as though a large animal was moving through it, except it didn't move like an animal with legs, more like a slithering snake. Suddenly the horse lurched to a standstill, snorting.

"What is it, Charger?" said Charity, snapping at the reins. "Giddy up!"

Charger's ears stood erect and his eyes darted in fright at the movement in the grass around him. Suddenly, he reared up, squealing in terror before falling to the ground, paralyzed. Charity and Elizabeth were thrown from the cart into the nearby grass.

"There's something crawling on him!" cried Elizabeth, looking over at Charger as she helped Charity to her feet.

"What is it?" said Charity, turning to look, her heart thumping hard like a drum. "I don't see anything!"

"It's some kind of slithering white snake!" said Elizabeth. "It's killing him!"

Charity searched the brush for a weapon, seized an oak branch from the ground, and hurried over to Charger, pulling up her skirt to keep from tripping over it. "I don't see it! Where is it? Good Lord, please help us!" She stared in horror as Charger's breathing became more and more labored, but still no assailant was visible. "It's witchery," she whispered, falling back.

"It's coiled around Charger's neck!" said Elizabeth, tears escaping her eyes. "Come back Mother, lest it attack thee next!"

"What good is a stick when faced with a demon?" said Charity, tossing the branch away. She rushed over to Elizabeth and linked arms with her for support. "We must get back home by foot, and pray to the Lord for our protection. Come now, quickly!"

| Chapter Twenty-Five |

At the age of eleven, Abitha Thorpe was a contemplative girl, but when the rare occasion did come along that she had something to say, she spoke with fierce conviction, and her words often revealed a deeply perceptive nature.

It was almost time for supper, and Abitha called Kemi in to help her get dressed after her bath. It was true that Abitha preferred to call Kemi by her birth name whenever her parents were not around. She knew they would certainly not approve, but as far as she was concerned it was an inconsequential infraction, and only one of a multitude of ways that Abitha exercised a mostly invisible rebellion against the religious tradition practiced by the Salem Village community that surrounded her.

"Kemi," she started softly as Kemi brushed out Abitha's long, straight blonde hair and fastened it under a white linen coif. Abitha paused at length, thinking of how best to phrase her question.

"Yes, child?" said Kemi, picking up the white apron and helping Abitha to pull it over her arms.

"Which God dost thou suppose is the real one?"

"How dost thou mean?"

"Talisa told me that Mother Earth is the god of the Indians. But Mother and Father believe that the God of the Bible is the only true god. And He is male. So which god is real?"

"If thou asketh me, all who are believed and worshipped are real," said Kemi, taking a seat in the wooden chair next to the bathtub. She had grown accustomed to Abitha's philosophical questions, and enjoyed the way they inspired her to give her answers careful thought. She knew that the Thorpes would not approve of this conversation, but she trusted that the girl was discreet enough to not cause serious problems for her. Abitha climbed up onto Kemi's lap and rested her head onto Kemi's chest, something she would never do in the presence of her parents or townspeople.

"How can they all be real?" she asked thoughtfully, picking up Kemi's hand and pressing her palm into Kemi's palm, in a curious, playful way. "If they were, perhaps Mother Earth and the Christian God could get married."

"Perhaps each one becomes real once thou knowest them."

"Maybe none of them are real," said Abitha. "Maybe they're imagined."

"Oh my, what a notion. Thou wouldst be wise to keep thoughts like that to thyself. But if thou asketh me, I believe that imagining something is close to the same as it being real."

"But surely it's not the same. Temperance imagines a good many strange things," said Abitha, sliding off of Kemi's lap and standing up to straighten her skirt. "Certainly thou doth not suppose those things are real?"

"They are real to her," said Kemi. "And they are probably real in other ways too, ways thou mayest not understand."

"I wonder if she might be bewitched," said Abitha thoughtfully. "If she is, the townspeople might hang her."

"Oh no, thou shouldst not say such things. They wouldn't hang a child."

144

"Exodus 22:18," cited Abitha. "Thou shalt not suffer a witch to live."

"Your sister is not a witch, child. Thy mother is taking her to the apothecary tomorrow," answered Kemi, standing up to begin preparing supper. "But even though she says many strange things, I don't believe she is ill. She only hath a special way of seeing the world. She is like our village oracle back in Oyo. The oracle sees many things that are beyond common understanding."

"Why doth Temperance speak out in church, during the sermon? Why doth she not behave herself? And why doth she not get punished as harshly as I do?"

"Because thou knoweth better than she does," said Kemi gently. "What does it harm thee to just let her be? Those are enough questions for today. It's time to prepare supper before thy mother returns home."

"I don't feel well," said Abitha, holding the back of her hand to her mouth to stifle some gas that had come up from her stomach. "My belly aches."

"Go lie down," instructed Kemi. "Dinner didn't agree with me either. I'll brew some tea for the both of us."

Reverend Thorpe was in a terrible state when he arrived home. He seemed to be angry about something and ordered Kemi to keep Charity and the children from interrupting him while he worked in his study, slamming the door shut to make his point clear. He didn't even notice that it was after sundown when Charity and Elizabeth finally made it back to the house. As per his instruction, Kemi quietly alerted Charity that the reverend was of a foul temper, and while Charity would normally be inclined to try to cheer him, and tended to be successful in such endeavors, she was overwhelmed with her own thoughts of the day's events and decided to postpone recounting the terrifying incident to him in that very moment. She sent Elizabeth to bed and retired early herself, hoping to speak with Rufus after his work in the study was settled. Sleep didn't come readily, but with her prayers it did finally fall upon her, before Rufus joined her in bed sometime after midnight.

| Chapter Twenty-Six |

At 3 a.m., all was dark in the house, except for the gray, dusty panels of moonlight slipping in through the bedroom and kitchen windows. Everyone in Salem Village was asleep except for the Thorpe household. It was the third night in a row that little Temperance had awakened everyone with her screams.

On the first night it happened, Charity had leaped from her bed and run into the children's bedroom in frantic alarm, thinking a wild animal had somehow gotten into the house and was attacking the children. Instead, she discovered that Temperance had been having frightening dreams, and was afraid to go back to sleep. Kemi had come upstairs from the kitchen, and sat with Charity as she tried to comfort Temperance.

On the second night, Kemi offered to stay up with the fitful child, so that Charity could return to bed.

On the third night, Charity didn't bother to get up at the now-familiar sound of screaming. She remained in bed, listening to Kemi in the next room trying to calm the child with soft, soothing words. Next to Charity, Rufus was also awake, with his fingers pressed to his temples as he tried to shut out the aftermath of his daughter's repeated outbursts.

"Perhaps the medicine is doing her more harm than good?" said Charity to Rufus in the morning at breakfast. She put her palm to Temperance's forehead. "She's not running a fever. How feeleth thou, dear?"

"Bound and gagged, pierced with a thousand knives," said Temperance absent-mindedly into the space in front of her. "The ghosts of Bram's violence pouring from my mouth like vomit."

"That's enough," snapped Rufus sharply.

"They number in the thousands," continued Temperance. "Bram is swimming in their blood."

"Enough blasphemy!" said Rufus, slamming his palm onto the table. "Thou wilt learn discipline!" He stood up, walked over to her and took a forceful grip of her arm, pulling her away from the table as she shrieked in pain. "Go read aloud from thy Bible," he said sternly. "Don't make me take the switch to thy back side." Temperance wiped tears from her reddened face and quickly ran off.

As the morning sun was rising in the sky, Rufus left the house to run errands and Kemi took the girls out to work in the garden so Charity could lie down to recover from a migraine. "I heard thee say the name of Bram," said Kemi to Temperance, outside in the garden. "Is it someone thou knoweth?"

"Bram is the name of the demon," said Temperance, pulling an onion out of the ground and placing it in the wheelbarrow. "Bram Sylvrvysc. He lives with us now. He promised Father to make him governor if he allowed him to use Father's body for his own purposes."

"What purposes dost thou mean, child?" Kemi kneeled next to Temperance with grave concern.

"She means incest," interrupted Abitha, trying to be helpful.

"Hath thy father committed incest with thee, Abitha?"

"Yes, with me, and with Temperance too. But it wasn't

Father. He would never do such a thing. It was Bram."

"Bram hath lain with Elizabeth, too," said Temperance.

"When?" said Kemi. "Is that what she told thee?"

"No," said Temperance. "I saw it happen in my dream. He told her that if she tells anyone, he will cut her throat and blame her kin. He will do it again today when he goes to bring her back from the Churchill farmhouse."

"We must tell thy mother," said Kemi, picking up the wheelbarrow full of vegetables. "She will know the right thing to do. Let us wait until this afternoon, after Reverend Thorpe leaves for Sam Shore's house."

Once back inside, Kemi put a kettle on the fire to brew some chamomile tea for Charity, hoping it would help to calm her nerves. While Abitha brought the vegetables to the cellar, Temperance ran over to Charity, who was seated at the table, reading from her Bible. "Mother," she said, taking Charity's hand. "There's someone at the front door, seeking thee."

Charity looked over at the door. "I heard no one knocking," she said, feeling somewhat rattled at the turn of events over the last week.

"They're knocking with their *eyes*," said Temperance.

Charity sighed deeply, never knowing what to make of her youngest child's nonsensical utterings.

"Come now, Mother," urged Temperance. "Thou must come now."

Charity finally conceded and arose from the table. She walked over to the front door and opened it, letting out a sudden gasp as she clasped her hands in front of her mouth in horror. In front of the door, there were four wooden sticks spiked into the ground, each with the severed head of a crow impaled at its top.

"Is this someone's idea of a cruel prank?" said Charity gravely, but her eyes frantically searching the trees outside the house belied her calm tone. She turned to Temperance and shook her, tears beginning to escape her eyes. "Who did this?

Was it thee? Dost thou mean to frighten me? Because I am truly frightened at this."

"It wasn't me," said the girl defensively. "It was Bram."

Charity was certain that Temperance had gone mad from the medicine given to her by the apothecary. "These herbs have worsened thy illness. We must discontinue them immediately—"

"Mistress Charity," Kemi ventured carefully. "Temperance and Abitha have something important to tell thee. Go ahead, children."

The girls timidly recounted what they had revealed to their nanny earlier. "Impossible," said Charity, her heart racing with fear that her children had been practicing witchcraft. And yet, she stopped for a moment to ponder the renewed vigor and frequency that had marked conjugal intercourse with her husband of late. "I'll speak with thy father directly when he returns home from the Churchills'."

She was inclined to dismiss all of it as outright fabrication, and not only expected Rufus to deny it, but also intended to take his word for it, even though some part of her did recognize truth in the accusations—part of her that didn't want to be conscious of it. At the surface of her awareness, she was simply being led quietly, helplessly into darkness, like a lamb to the slaughter. Her words and actions no longer felt her own; she was only a puppet now at the mercy of a strange dream, one from which there was no escape.

Her thoughts turned next to the memory of the peculiar, menacing look on Rufus' face, days ago, as she had tried to explain that a wild animal had attacked and killed their horse on the road, while omitting the part that the assailant was somehow invisible to her. Rufus had seemed strangely titillated by the story, more so than upset by it. It seemed unlikely now that he would admit to anything untoward, and as such, what good could come of confronting him? Yet, she could sense no other path forward.

"Hast thou all gone mad?" said Rufus, when he came home that evening and heard the allegations. He looked into the fearful eyes of each of the girls in the room as if he had nothing to hide. "Incest? Rape? Adultery? Unclean acts with a savage? And worst of all, witchcraft? Thou all want to see me hanged, is that it?"

"Lord, I beg thy forgiveness for how grave the accusations are, but what would compel them to accuse thee so?" pleaded Charity.

"The explanation is simple," said Rufus. "Constance here is practicing witchcraft herself, and means to cover the transgression by accusing me."

"No," said Kemi, "It's not true, Mistress Charity, I would never."

"Rufus, I realize thou hast no real affection in thy heart for either Constance or Elizabeth," said Charity. "Thou never hast. But what reason could Abitha and Temperance, our own flesh and blood, possibly have for accusing thee of such things?"

"What reason indeed," said Rufus, "unless they too are practicing witchcraft! Three of them have confessed to intercourse with a demon, and the fourth bears witness. I will contact the magistrate at once and have them all jailed."

"Please, Rufus, they are only children," begged Charity.

"It's not him," said Abitha quietly. "He knoweth not what he does."

"They're better off dead now, anyway," said Rufus coldly. "How could any of them be sought for as a wife after what they've done?"

"Thou must forgive him, Mother," said Temperance, taking Charity's hand. "Thou must forgive us all."

"That sounds like a confession," said Rufus, wagging his finger toward Temperance. She only stared at him quietly in response, with a blank expression that Rufus found disquieting.

Charity was no longer listening. Her mind was elsewhere,

clinging to the memory of a time at dinner, weeks ago, when the six of them had shared a moment in laughter together. Frivolity of any kind was generally discouraged, but she remembered how it felt so freeing to just let go, and feel happy for a change. Maybe now she was being punished for that moment, somehow.

| Chapter Twenty-Seven |

Charity wept like never before, clutching helplessly at her apron, so much so that Elizabeth felt more sorry for her than for herself. Rufus stood stoically at her side as the sheriff and his men took their daughters to jail. The Salem jailhouse was full, so they were to be taken to a toolshed provided by a neighboring farmer which had been converted into a private jailhouse. Even though Constance and Elizabeth were not born to her, Charity felt as a mother to both of them, and was just as distraught over the thought of losing them as she was over losing Abitha and Temperance. At the trial she had no tears left, and only stared numbly into space as the magistrate announced the verdict. Four more witches to be hanged on Gallows Hill. She arrived home without a word to Rufus, and crawled into her daughters' bed, where she slept all night.

The moon was high in the sky, and the air in the toolshed-turned-jailhouse bore an unearthly chill. Abitha tensely dug herself into the straw-covered floor and huddled close to her jailmates for warmth, wondering if the chill was coming from the air outside, or from the knot in her stomach and the horrible memory of her parents' petrified faces as they silently watched the magistrate announce a hanging conviction.

Her mind wandered to morbidly wondering what it would be like to be hanged. She imagined that the pain would be over quickly, not like the pain of remembering her father heaving on top of her, with his terrifying distorted face and the blood red eyes of Bram glowing in place of his familiar features. She couldn't imagine that the God of the Bible would send her to Hell for a crime she didn't commit, nor for the trivial subversive acts that she committed in secret, such as running through the cornfield, screaming and laughing and dancing like a lunatic while everyone else was away at the meeting house for the Sunday sermon thinking she was ill in bed.

Whenever she prayed, she always asked God for His forgiveness for what seemed in her mind like such unimportant matters, but she knew they were important to her parents. Half the time, she wondered if He was even there, listening. Sometimes she believed that He was, but her ambivalence in that belief came and went like the wind.

Abitha often thought that her younger sister Temperance had a madness about her, and clearly she was not alone in that perception, but then of course she knew that she had her own madness too. Temperance's madness was different from her own though, she thought, more innocent perhaps. Abitha kept her own special madness a secret from almost everyone. Only Kemi was allowed to see it, and even Kemi was not privy to her every rebellion. Perhaps she and her sister were truly not meant for this world.

Meanwhile, Elizabeth seemed to suffer from all of the guilt and remorse that Abitha lacked. Kemi tried to assure her that it was no one's fault that Bram had chosen their family to prey upon, that Reverend and Goody Thorpe were truly good people, like many of the others in the congregation who had also been similarly cursed. "Thou art a good person, too," Kemi told Elizabeth, squeezing her hand tight. "We are all good people. We don't deserve to die."

As if in response to her words, a warm breeze entered the shed at that very moment, as if a fire was being kindled right there in front of them. Abitha noticed it first, and began to sit up straight, and lean toward the source.

"What is it?" said Elizabeth, protectively gripping her arms around Temperance.

"It's a bokor," said Temperance, not looking, and not moving either, but only blinking softly from the warm air.

"Thou art right, it is!" said Kemi, astonished. Her eyes widened in amazement as the shadowy figure began to materialize in front of them. The other girls still did not seem to be able to see anything; they squinted at the darkness while feeling their muscles relax from the warmth.

"Thou art good and wise, Kemi," said the bokor once his materialization was complete. The other girls gasped in surprise, as they still could not see him but only heard his voice.

"Why can we not see thee?" asked a curious and fearless Abitha.

"I don't want thee to be frightened by my appearance," said the sorcerer. His speech was friendly and warm, like the breeze that accompanied him. "My name is Nimbeau, and I have come here to help thee. Thy friend here, Constance, known to her people as Kemi, hath seen a bokor before, and will not be frightened by the sight of me."

"I will not be frightened by the sight of thee, either," said Abitha with confidence. "Show thyself."

"A brave girl thou art!" said Nimbeau. "And what of you others? Are you as brave as Abitha?"

"Yes," said Temperance, nodding her head.

"And thou, Miss Elizabeth?"

"Yes," said Elizabeth. "Show thyself."

"Talisa is braver than she looks," said Abitha.

"Abitha! That's not a very nice thing to say," Kemi said,

rebuking her. "Elizabeth is neither foolhardy nor impetuous, and thou ought to consider her fine example."

"I'm not saying it to be mean," insisted Abitha.

"I'm glad to see how brave all of you are," said Nimbeau, his appearance materializing for everyone present. By his features, they guessed that he was Black, but it was impossible to see his skin color, because he was painted with a pitch black paint over all of his skin, except for a white skull that was painted on his face, and white bones that were painted on his limbs. He wore an ornate necklace made of small bird skulls, feathers, and bones. His chest was otherwise bare, and his feet were bare too. On his head rested a large animal skull with long horns, adorned in the back with a plume of black and purple feathers. The tool shed was shrouded with the dark of night, yet there seemed to be a warm glow of light emanating from his skin.

"How dost thou know our names?" said Abitha.

"I have divined this knowledge through means that thou wouldst not understand," said Nimbeau kindly. "What is important to know is that I mean you all no harm. I want to help you, and to protect you and all future victims from the evils of this demon, Bram. He hath pursued this destructive path for centuries, and the blood of a multitude of women rests upon his wicked soul. I want to stop him, and I need your help to do so. Will you help me?"

"What dost thou want us to do?" asked Abitha.

"We must trap him in human form," said Nimbeau. "Every time his host body dies, he manages to escape through passage to a spirit realm—what we may call another dimension. This passage is a corridor that leads into another world. I need thy help to obtain a lock of hair, or a drop of blood, from the body he inhabits, in order to perform the ritual that will trap him in human form. I will send the four of you into the future as zonbis. It is there we will put a spell on him, a *gris-gris*, to force him to become mortal."

"Thou wanteth us to commit *murder*?" gasped Elizabeth.

156

Nimbeau thought carefully on how to respond. Bram had already eluded Nimbeau on six previous occasions, and each time it was because Nimbeau had failed to convince Bram's victims to carry out his plan. He kept being misguided by a certainty that vengeance should be a strong enough motive.

"He need not die by our hands," said Kemi, squeezing Elizabeth's hand in reassurance. "He will easily bring death on himself by his actions. We need only prevent him from escaping."

"That's right," said Nimbeau. "I sense the anger in thy voice, Kemi. Thou hast been conditioned for many years to silence thy voice. But the time to show thine anger is now. These children whom thou loveth dearly will die, and so wilt thou, and so will the daughters of hundreds more if thou doth nothing. I am the only one with the power to stop him, and I cannot do it alone."

"Why not?" inquisited Abitha.

"Because my presence is what we call astral, and my physical body is elsewhere. I am also limited by my ethics. The difference between me and Bram is that he will gladly force any woman to do his bidding, but I am asking you, my Queens, to help me of your own free will. And if you refuse, I shall be saddened by your deaths, and for this missed opportunity, and hope to have better luck the next time."

"Thou sayeth that Bram's host body will die," said Abitha. "But Bram hath taken possession of our father, and we don't want him to die. Isn't there another way?"

"I'm sorry, young Abitha," said Nimbeau sympathetically. "One way or another, thy father will die at Bram's hands. Once he taketh possession of someone's body, the only way for his spirit to be sufficiently compelled to escape back into the astral corridor is for the host body to die. I assure thee, there is no other way. We can make sure that Bram will die with him, but there is no way to save thy father now. Thy father may already be dead of a suicide by his own hand."

| Chapter Twenty-Eight |

Charity was awakened by the touch of a cold hand to her shoulder. She sat up slowly, as if in a trance, and found that she was still lying in the children's bedroom, alone. The night was still dark, with a sliver of moonlight coming through the window, and the house felt isolated and quiet, like the inside of a coffin. She arose from the bed and realized in a daze that she was still wearing the same clothes she had worn to the courthouse the day before. Walking over to the window to gaze out, she found herself unsurprised to see the reflection of Rufus standing behind her. She turned slowly to look at him, only to find there was no one there. She looked back at the window and the reflection was gone.

A thump downstairs caught up to her attention, and she called out to Rufus, but he didn't answer. Oddly, she felt no fear. The sound of Temperance's laughing echoed eerily through the house, and Charity reckoned with a strange bemusement that she herself was bewitched. A second thump obliged her to feel her way through the dark into the hallway, fingers dragging along the wall for guidance, heart beating in a quiet rhythm as she descended the stairs, plunging each foot into darkness and feeling her way for the next step.

At the foot of the stairs, she stopped and allowed her eyes to adjust to the dim moonlight coming through the kitchen window. The gray, shadowy figure of a man lying on the floor next to the fireplace seizing with some kind of fit materialized into view, and the confirmation that it was Rufus brought a small lump into her throat. His limbs were flinging about, occasionally kicking the kitchen table and causing it to thump against the hardwood floor. For a moment Charity stood by, quiet and calm in the knowledge that she was ever helpless to change the course of events.

"Auck!" he said, his voice throttled by the pool of saliva and bile gurgling forth from his stomach. At the sound of his voice, Charity walked over to kneel at his side.

She took his hand into hers and squeezed it tightly, smiling an odd incomprehensible smile and praying for God to save his soul. He writhed on the wood floor, gagging and gasping for air, until finally the last breath expired from his lungs. Partly cloaked in darkness, his face contorted into frightening, unrecognizable countenances, until at last, the glowing image of a distorted creature, naked and gnarled, with the head of a dead fish and inhumanly long limbs, which bent backward away from its body like those of an insect, came crawling out of him as though it were discarding a molted skin. It turned and hissed at her before leaping away, passing effortlessly through the wall and out of view.

She reached forward and touched the lifeless face of her husband with her fingertips, and brushed his hair away from his face. In the twelve years they had been married, she had not touched his hair once, although the desire to do so was ever present. It was simply far too sensual an act for her to deem it permissible. As a social woman with an inexplicable aversion to the restless malaise of solitude, she now felt more completely alone than ever before, and yet somehow, the melancholy of it was no longer insufferable.

As the sun rose, she saddled Meadow, their remaining horse, and delivered to the sheriff a death wish wrapped in a lie. The note contained her handwritten confession which said that she, too, had practiced witchcraft along with her daughters, and that now Rufus was dead by her hand. She asked that her last request be granted, that she should be hanged with her daughters. The magistrate arranged an immediate trial to entertain her plea, which was granted as an act of mercy.

| Chapter Twenty-Nine |

There were sirens blaring on the next block, and a couple of tourists talking and laughing loudly for a long time outside her hotel window on their way back to their room after a few drinks down the street, but it was the knocking at her door that woke Titi—she had grown accustomed to tuning out the night chatter and traffic noise that came with living above a nightclub in a tourist-heavy part of New Orleans.

Maybe they've got the wrong room, she thought, digging her face into her pillow, but the knocking persisted. Finally, she got up and put on the plush courtesy bathrobe. Her long, straight hair, which during the day she wore tucked under a headwrap, was now pulled back into a ponytail. She looked through the peephole and saw two police officers—a young Latina and an older Asian male—their vehicle parked out front with its lights flashing.

"Are you Titi Beaumond?" asked the woman officer, after Titi reluctantly opened the door. Once Titi confirmed her identity, the woman took hold of Titi's arms and cuffed them behind her back. "You're under arrest. You have the right to remain silent. Anything you say may be used against you in a court of law."

"Wait a minute! You must be mistaken," said Titi, her eyebrows knit tightly together, heart hammering her chest and eyes squinting from the brightness of the lights, half-awake thinking that there must be another Titi Beaumond in the city. "Are you sure you have the right person?"

"You have the right to an attorney," continued the woman. "If you can't afford an attorney, one will be provided."

"Did you hear what I said?" said Titi. "You have the wrong person! Do you have an arrest warrant?"

"Yes, we do, ma'am," said the male officer.

"Well? May I see it? Shouldn't you be showing me that to begin with?"

The two officers exchanged glances with each other and after a moment of deliberation, the male officer showed her a piece of paper, holding it up for her to read. "We're not required by law to show you the warrant, ma'am."

"Not required by law? Do you need a law to tell you how to use common sense? Apparently you do." She didn't have her reading glasses, so she squinted and leaned back from the paper to read aloud what it said.

"Affiant states that at 4:38 a.m. on September 4, 2016, a fire of undetermined origin occurred at the Glen Haven Psychiatric Hospital annex known as Ophelia's Wing. Surveillance video identifies suspect as having placed an unknown object against the side of the building near the southwest corner of Bethune and Greenwich Streets and engaging in suspicious activities at the fire's point of origin at 3:07 a.m. the same morning. Such evidence constitutes probable cause to believe that the accused did knowingly and intentionally commit the crime of arson in the second degree, in violation of New York State Criminal Code, Article 150.15, a class B felony constituting the destruction of property and the endangerment of all individuals present in the building at the time the fire occurred... *What? Arson?*" Titi paused for a moment, aghast. "Suspect presents symptoms consistent with paranoid schizophrenia, with history of attempted suicide. Affiant recommends 72-hour hold at a secure psychiatric facility pending immediate psychiatric evaluation." Titi frowned and shook her head. *What the hell is happening here?* she thought, her mind racing.

"Watch your head getting into the car, ma'am," said the woman.

"Wait," stalled Titi, pausing halfway into the car. "I have a psychiatrist, can I take a moment to call him?"

"You'll get your one phone call at the station. Right now we need you to come with us, or you can add resisting arrest to your charges."

"Wait a minute! If arson happened at this address," she said, pulling away from the officer's grip. "Wait, damn it! If there was a fire, it wasn't me! I was there assisting with a federal investigation. You can contact my cousin, Special Agent Rochelle Roy about that, she is fully aware of it and can clear it up for you. She works for the FBI."

"Save it for the judge, ma'am."

At the station, Titi was processed and put into an empty holding cell where she waited to make her one phone call. Carlos was the first person she had thought to call, but only because he was the best person she could think of to advocate for her mental health. He was white, he was male, he was a doctor, and his mother was an attorney. If anyone she knew had privilege, it was him. But Adrian was also an attorney, and she picked at her cuticles while contemplating whether to use her one call on Adrian instead of Carlos. They had been playing phone tag since she arrived in New York, and kept missing each other. She decided it was too embarrassing to involve him in this situation, especially after his complaining about his crazy ex-wife. *He said he had enough crazy in his life.* She took a deep breath, and dialed Carlos' cell phone number.

"I don't know what the hell is going on, Carlos. Could Rochelle seriously be behind all this? I don't know why, but she clearly seems to want to punish me for my beliefs."

"I understand why you think that, but I don't think so, T. I know you and Ro have always had tension between you, but I've also been living with her for the last year and I think I know her pretty well by now. They had to have pretty substantial evidence against you in order to issue an arrest warrant, you understand that?"

"Do you think I did it?"

"Did you?"

"Of course not! Maybe you think you know her, but you obviously still don't know me."

"I believe you, T. I still have to ask. I don't know all the details of what happened between you and her. Obviously, someone did do it, and might be trying to frame you. Are you okay with me asking my mother for legal advice?"

"Do you have to?"

"No, of course I don't have to. But if you want the best legal advice you can possibly get, then I'm sorry, but she's the one you want to ask. Her firm specializes in mental health advocacy. I doubt you'll find a more competent attorney in this field. How would you feel about her representing you at your hearing?"

"Oh, hell no. You're going to ask a racist to defend me? Are you out of your mind? What the hell are you thinking?"

"I'm concerned you might be stuck in a psychiatric facility for a long time if you don't get the right representation. I know my mother's not your favorite person, but she happens to be very good at what she does."

"I don't know, Carlos. I just don't know. I can't think right now. I know I can't afford a good lawyer. Do you honestly think she can get me out of here?"

"I know she can, without a doubt. The question is how

willing you are to put up with her stupid remarks."

"What kind of question is that? I don't like it, but I'm desperate. This case that Rochelle brought me in on is bigger than any of us, Carlos. I *need* to get out of here immediately, and continue my spells to help the victims. I can't risk the possibility of being trapped here. I'll do whatever it takes. If you know for damn sure that Veronica can get me out of here, then I'll suffer through her ridiculous microaggressions, not for my own sake, but for the sake of these four young women."

"Okay, I'm sorry, I wouldn't have even suggested it except that I might be able to persuade her to do me a personal favor and take the case pro bono, in exchange for my help with another matter. It will also help to guarantee that you'll get the best advocacy out of her. Let me talk to her, and we'll get the ball rolling on the formalities. Tell them you want to see your attorney *before* they perform any DNA testing, okay? Are you doing alright? Not suicidal?"

"I'm okay, Carlos. The only thing I want right now is to help these victims. That requires staying alive."

"I'm asking because I need to know for your hearing. I don't even know if my mother is available or willing to help out. She's dealing with some health issues. I don't want to get into details."

"Under any other circumstances, I would try to find another way, Carlos. They're going to transfer me to secure custody at Glen Haven. God only knows how long I'll be stuck there. I'm... also dating an attorney right now, but I think it's too much to ask of him to help me with this, this early in the relationship. If you think of any other possible solution, will you please let me know?"

"Of course. I'll do whatever I can to help."

"Thank you. I love you, Carlos."

"I love you too, T." He hung up the phone with a sigh. *Rochelle is not going to like this.*

| Act Two |

In obstinate cases, the student is taught to use the Imagination freely, until he is able to make a mental image or picture of the sub-conscious mind doing what is required of it. This process clears away a mental path for the feet of the sub-conscious mind, which it will choose thereafter, as it prefers to follow the line of least resistance.

Of course much depends upon practice—practice makes perfect, you know, in everything else, and sub-consciousing is no exception to the rule.

—Selected from *A Series of Lessons in Raja Yoga*
by Yogi Ramacharaka (1906)

| Chapter Thirty |

Dosed up and drowsy on haloperidol, Titi slept on and off, her dreams plagued with visits from Bram. Now he was attacking Rochelle instead of Adrian. "Keys in the car and no one around," said Bram. "Let's take this ride for a spin." Then Rochelle stabbed herself in the left eye with a letter opener. Titi woke in a lurch, only to find herself still confined to a secure psychiatric containment room at Glen Haven. She fell back asleep and then dreamed that Bram was taking Lin Mei "for a spin." He compelled Lin Mei to wade through a pool of liquid nitrogen until she shattered like glass into a thousand pieces.

A knock came at the door, waking her again, then the deadbolt turned and a security guard ushered in a young, slender woman in a white coat who introduced herself as Dr. Anjali Varma.

"How are you feeling today, Ms. Beaumond?" said Dr. Varma, taking a seat in the chair next to the bed.

Titi tried to open her eyes wider to look at her, but her eyelids felt weighted down. "What are you medicating me with? I feel like crap."

"We've given you an antipsychotic to help you with your

hallucinations."

"I didn't ask you to help me with my 'hallucinations.'"

"I'm sorry, but the state has mandated involuntary medication for your protection."

"How do you figure it's for my protection? I can't think like this. I can't meditate like this. You've taken away my access to psychic insight. I feel dead inside."

"Please, bear with us while we try to determine the best medication for you. It may take a little trial and error, but you'll be kept safe in the process."

"Safe from what? I need to be kept safe from you! I've already been through 'trial and error,' fifteen years ago. You can name any psych med you want, I've taken it. Talk to my psychiatrist about it. His name is Dr. Carlos Beaumond."

"Is he the one who prescribed you cannabis?"

"Yes, he is."

"He's your husband?"

"My *ex*-husband."

"Are you aware that cannabis has been found to increase risk of psychosis in users who are already predisposed?"

"No, I haven't heard of that. And I'm not psychotic, but you're assuming that I am, and treating me like I am. Whatever happened to innocent until proven guilty?"

"Ms. Beaumond, the police officers who transferred you here from the station reported that you were having conversations with yourself in the car. Can you tell me who you were talking to?"

Titi shifted uncomfortably. "I was speaking with the lwa. They're Voodoo spirits, not that it's any of your business."

"I see. Can you tell me what they were saying?"

"Not something I feel like sharing."

"Please allow me to rephrase. Did they give you any specific instructions to harm yourself or anyone else?"

"No, they did not."

"Did they tell you to set fire to the Glen Haven annex?"

"I didn't set any damn fire."

"Okay. I can see that you're becoming agitated."

"Does it occur to you that wrongful arrest gives me a damn good reason to be agitated?"

"Let's leave you to rest for a bit, alright? If you feel calmer later, we can talk some more."

The security guard came in to ask Titi if she wanted to join other patients in the dining room for breakfast or have it brought in to her. She opted to join the others.

"What you in for?" asked an elderly Caucasian woman with long, tangled silver hair and a mole on her nose. She picked up a small nugget of scrambled eggs with her fingers and shoved it into her face with a wide toothless grin, chewing with her mouth open as she thought about her dog Toto whom she hadn't seen in thirty years.

"Something I didn't do," said Titi, pursing her lips.

"That how they do. Yes ma'am. That how they do. One they got you here, don't let you go. Never. Not ever," said the woman in a slow drawl, shaking her head. "Not till you dead, and sometime not even then."

Titi caught sight of an elderly white man shuffling toward them with a walker. Once he got close enough for Titi to see the dried blood surrounding the knife wound on his neck, she realized with ghastly horror that he was a ghost.

"Don't mind my husband Wyatt," said the woman. "He been dead a good while now. They think I killed him. You only one who seen him now since he dead. Only one, other'n me."

"Did you kill him?" asked Titi, surrendering to a macabre curiosity.

"Don't rightly know. I walk that long road what lead to the doll house. One way in, no way out. Sometime doll get lost, I showed them the way. Look in my eye, you seen the way?"

With curiosity, Titi indulged her and looked into her eyes,

169

seeing only darkness in the pupils within her pale blue irises. The woman slowly turned her head until the window in the far corner of the room reflected in the center of her eye, giving the appearance of a distant exit within it.

"What does that mean?" asked Titi. She decided a pipe packed with some dank weed would be great right about now to help her decipher this cryptic message, which did somehow seem to conceal something meaningful.

"It be the way to the dollhouse. You seen them dolls, ain't you?"

"Which dolls?"

"Them four queens. They was here, but they done been moved. They done keep them a secret."

"Wait a minute, have you seen them? Who told you this?"

"You tell them goody-two-shoes Shelley sent you!" the woman said with a cackle, ignoring the question. "But shh. They won't believe you. None ever do."

| Chapter Thirty-One |

Meanwhile, Rochelle was at home, clutching a bottle of vodka on the couch. Although she had no idea who Titi might have told at this point, she was desperate to escape the pervasive feeling that haunted her adult life: that no one in her family ever seemed capable of understanding her decisions, decisions which made perfect sense to her, especially when, in her mind, she had been left without recourse. Having Titi arrested was an example of one such decision. Why couldn't someone just be on her side for once? She kept imagining her mother's voice saying, "You knew she wasn't going to get a fair trial." Her cell phone rang and she looked at the caller ID. It was Carlos.

"Hey babe."

"Hey."

"Is everything going alright?"

"No, it's not. When does your flight come in?"

"I'm... not flying back today after all." He wished to God that he was.

"What? Why not? What happened? I really need you right now, Carlos. Titi's been arrested."

"Yeah, I'm sorry... I heard."

Rochelle was struck in the chest by a combination of shame and indignation. "Who told you?"

He braced for impact. "Titi called me."

"Of course. I should have known." She sat silently struggling with how to feel about that. When he offered nothing to break the silence, she changed the subject. "So what's going on? Why aren't you coming back today?"

"I got a call this morning from Dr. Varma, the attending psychiatrist who's supervising Titi's custody at Glen Haven. The call started with her asking basic questions about her psych history. It ended with her notifying me that she'll be filing a complaint against me tomorrow morning with the New York State Office of Professional Medical Conduct. They'll launch an investigation to determine if I've been guilty of misconduct. I could potentially lose my license."

"For what?"

"For prescribing Titi marijuana when she has a history of psychosis."

"Oh." Rochelle face palmed herself. *It just keeps getting better and better.*

"Yeah. Just what I need right now."

"I take it this is the reason you haven't called me until now?"

"I'm just under a lot of stress, Ro. You haven't called me either, alright? I went to talk to my mom about the situation yesterday, to ask for her help. I've asked her to represent me during my misconduct investigation, and also act as Titi's criminal defense attorney."

"Oh, my God." She sat up straight and glared at the phone. "Carlos! Are you serious? Why would Titi even agree to that? Why would you... ? Surely there's another way?"

"My mother's just been diagnosed with stage four lung cancer; I only found out yesterday. I was going to talk to you about it in person, but because of this new development with Titi,

I need to tell you now. I promised my mother that I would take a sabbatical and spend some time with her here in San Francisco, helping her out at the firm while she's undergoing chemo. To repay the favor for representing me and Titi."

"Wow. I don't know what to say."

"I don't either. I have to go now. I'm on my way to my mother's house to discuss the details of the case. She'll be accompanying me back to New York next week for Titi's hearing."

"She's not welcome in my apartment, Carlos."

"She'll be staying at a hotel. And so will I." He left out the part about sharing a hotel room with his mother at her insistence. She needed him present to comfort her, she said. He also omitted that she would be paying his hotel and travel expenses, although he could afford to pay for a separate room and would have preferred to do so. He knew Rochelle would be quick to remind him that the "favor" would come with strings attached, but refusing his mother's financial aid in situations where she felt the need to assert complete control was never a simple matter. She would be offended by his refusal, accuse him of a lack of gratitude, say that he must not really love her, and he would never hear the end of it. He didn't challenge her anymore when she wanted to pay for something on his behalf. In this case, he expected his refusal would also jeopardize Titi's defense.

"Wait, so what are you saying? Are you breaking up with me? You know what, never mind. Fine. I guess I'll just talk to you later."

"I'm not trying to break up with you. This situation is just a lot for me to deal with, okay? Not thrilled about signing up to be a punching bag as my mother's dying wish."

"And that's somehow my fault?"

Carlos sighed. "It's not anyone's fault. It's not about fault. I'm not trying to punish you. It's not about you. I just don't know how to deal with this. I need time to sort things out."

She heard him saying the words but it still felt like punishment. "I need you right now. I'm falling apart over here. I don't know how else to put it, how to communicate to you how bad it is for me right now."

"I'm sorry. I believe you. My mom needs me, too. We can talk about it more when I get back, okay? I have to go now."

After getting off the phone, Rochelle walked to the corner liquor store and bought another six bottles of vodka.

"Having a party?" asked the cashier, hoping she might invite him.

"Something like that," said Rochelle as she grabbed the two bags and left.

| Chapter Thirty-Two |

Midori walked into the kitchen of the condo she was sharing with Lin Mei in Soho and found that Lin Mei was sitting at the dining table, pulling seeds out of strawberries using tweezers.

"Lin Mei," said Midori, her face contorted in horror. "What the fuck are you doing?"

"I'm taking the seeds out of my strawberries. Is that okay with you?"

"With *tweezers*? Seriously?"

Lin Mei stared at her, perplexed. "I don't like having seeds in my fruit."

"Please stop. Oh my God. Please just stop."

"Why?"

"I don't know, it's just freaking me out, okay! Seriously! Just stop it!"

Lin Mei stared at the strawberry and put the tweezers down as she struggled to maintain her composure. *Why not just go do it in the other room? Do you have to be so petty?* she asked herself, as if trying to resolve a dispute between two children. *You think I'm being petty? She's the one being petty.* "Midori,

I'm sorry it upsets you, but this is like a meditation for me. I've been looking forward to doing this all day. It helps calm my nerves."

"It's just freaking me out! You might as well be peeling the skin off a baby!"

With a sudden fury, Lin Mei picked up the plate of seeded strawberries and violently flung it across the room. A couple of crushed strawberries left a red smear on the wall before falling to the carpet. "Fucking everything has to be about you, doesn't it!" she shouted angrily as her face turned as red as the stained wall. "The *one* thing I have that helps me has to fucking freak you out! Of course it does! One thing! ONE! I'm fucking sick of it! I can't take this anymore! You're killing me here! Is that what you want? FUCK!"

Midori put the back of her hand to her mouth to stifle a response as tears welled up in her eyes. She tore out of the kitchen and ran into the bedroom, pulling her raincoat out of the closet and slipping her boots on.

"Wait, please!" said Lin Mei, running after her, trying to put her arms around her. "I'm sorry! Please! Don't go!"

Midori angrily twisted away from her. "I *told* you to leave me there in Tokyo! Why can't you just let me die! This is not what you want! Just admit it!"

"Yes it is! It's just not easy, okay? I'm doing the best I can. *Please* don't run off and do meth. What will it take for you to see how much I'm bending over backwards to help you?"

"I never asked you to do that!"

"Please, Midori," said Lin Mei, softening her tone. "I'm sorry. I can't imagine how empty my life would be without you in it. Please stick it out with me. There's a way through to the other side of this. Things can get better."

"I don't know, Lin Mei. There's something wrong with me. I just feel so bored without the meth, I can't stand it."

"It's not boredom. It's your mind trying to escape the

pain. It's that little girl inside of you that your dad used to beat up, trying to make a man out of you. He tried to convince her not to exist. But she's not a little girl anymore. She's a grown woman, and she needs so very much for you to be her hero right now."

Midori brushed a tear away from her eye. "My dad used to say, 'A real man stays at the top of the food chain.'"

"Yeah, well we have a name for that in psychology. Social dominance orientation. Fancy way of saying inferiority complex. In other words, someone who needs to prove that they're better than you to save themselves from feeling like a total failure in life."

"I can't take it when you yell at me," said Midori, changing the subject.

"I'm sorry. Let's get counseling together, okay?"

"And I can't take it when you give me the silent treatment."

I can't take it when you put your shoes on the couch. Lin Mei sighed. "It's not meant to be the silent treatment, Midori. I just have so many things weighing on me right now, I need time to process everything—" She was interrupted by her cell phone ringing. It was Reid, her boss. "I'm sorry, I have to take this. Please don't leave."

"I haven't been able to get a hold of Roy," said Reid. "Do you have any idea where she is?"

"I haven't heard from her since her cousin was arrested."

"Well, there's something mighty strange happening down at Ophelia's Wing," he said, his childhood Southern accent peeking out from behind years of New York conditioning. Lin Mei knew this meant he was excited but working to maintain his composure. "We've got four special agents in there—expert forensic nurses—assigned to security. I think you probably know Rahim, Lluc, and Trieu. Not sure if you've met Diego since he transferred in from the Hostage Rescue Unit. I call them my four kings. They're reporting some pretty unusual events. I need you and Roy to get down there and check it out."

"I assume she's at home," said Lin Mei, exasperated at the thought of having to leave Midori in a distraught state. "I can swing by her place and see if she's there."

"Don't bother. I'll send Jefferson over there to do that. I need you to get on down to Ophelia's."

"What kind of unusual events are they reporting?"

"They say they've been experiencing some... what they called, 'reality distortion and altered states of consciousness.' They're not sure if these are actual paranormal events, or hallucinations. But if it's truly delusional, they've all four got the same delusion."

"Just like the vics."

Midori leaned back against the wall and stared impatiently at the ceiling.

Lin Mei took hold of Midori's hand. "Please don't go," she mouthed to Midori.

"A paranormal explanation seems highly unlikely," said Reid, "but we need to cover all of our bases. Do you share Roy's opinion that her cousin is mentally ill?"

"Honestly, sir, it's hard to know what to make of it," said Lin Mei. "The persistence of her hallucinations clearly meets the diagnostic criteria for schizophrenia. I don't believe she started that fire, though. It also seems unlikely to be a coincidence. It's possible that schizophrenic individuals are acutely sensitive to things which may actually prove someday to be real. We just don't have the tools to detect them yet."

"So you're thinking something paranormal, then?"

"Maybe something that isn't truly paranormal, only beyond our current scientific understanding. I mean, once upon a time, it was considered witchcraft to practice herbal medicine. Much of the technology we have now would seem like magic to our ancestors. So maybe it's not paranormal at all, just another stage in human evolution. Maybe schizophrenic individuals are genuinely sensitive to phenomena existing on other planes, in other dimensions. Things the rest of us can't sense, but it doesn't mean they're not real."

"This might surprise you, Chen, but I'm open to that possibility."

"With all due respect, sir, if we're going to leave that possibility on the table, I urge you to consider Titi's recommendation of an exorcism. Really, if the vics consent to it, what does it hurt to try?"

"I'll think about it. Meanwhile, give me a status report once you get down there. Try to get a sense of what we're dealing with here."

| Chapter Thirty-Three |

Elizabeth Thorpe could feel the trickling return of sensation to her limbs as the sedative began to wear off, and as she opened her heavy eyes, she found that her arms were bound at the wrists, and her legs at the ankles, with leather straps attached to a hospital bed. *This is not my body,* she began to remember, staring oddly at her unfamiliar arms. *Why do I hurt all over?*

Wrestling with the straps and realizing that she was trapped, she looked around at the room to get a sense of where she was. There was a brushed steel toilet in the corner of the room, and a nearby drain in the center of the floor. No other furniture, except the bed.

She stared at the door, hoping that at any moment, someone would walk through it and release her, or at the very least explain the situation. A dream came to mind that she had told Charity about, the one in which she was bound at the hands and feet and thrown into a lake. *Perhaps I've fallen through the lake into another world.*

The memory of talking to Charity helped to remind her of where she came from, and she began to slowly remember who she was, and the events leading up to her hanging. This was definitely a new world. Something strange was happening, something unnatural and unholy. Why would they bind her hands and feet like this? *They must surely have mistaken me for a witch again.*

The body she was inhabiting at the moment was craving crack. There was a dull ache in her stomach, partly from hunger, partly from this body having repeatedly sustained physical violence over a number of years. The physical distress amplified a pervasive sense of anger and irritability, emotions that Elizabeth was accustomed to repressing, but which overwhelmed her now.

"Is anyone there?" she said, her voice hoarse and the words coming out in a whisper. She cleared her throat and spoke again, feeling the muscles in her chest labor with the exertion. "Is anyone there?" A couple of tears spilled out of her eyes.

Beep. Beep. Beep. *Where is that bizarre sound coming from?* She twisted her head as far back as she could manage, noticing over her right shoulder a box with numbers, strange symbols and blinking lights on it. *What is this place?* At last, she fell back against her pillow, exhausted, and tried to rest.

Within the hour, the undercover agent orderlies assigned by Reid entered the room to check on her, striking fear in her as she realized she was tied down and at their mercy. "Good evening, Quila," said the first one, Special Agent Rahim Aslam, a friendly, dark-skinned young man with Afrocentric features. Like his three counterparts, his face was clean-shaven, hair trimmed short, and his slender, muscular body was adorned in green scrubs.

"Who is Quila?" asked Elizabeth weakly.

"You are," said Special Agent Diego Miguel García Martínez. Diego was taller than the others and thin like a rail, his deeply perceptive brown eyes gazing at Elizabeth through silver wire-framed glasses, framed by thick eyebrows, dark brown skin and thick black hair. "Do you understand why we have these straps on your hands and feet, Miss González?"

Elizabeth shook her head no. "My name… isn't Quila. It's… Virgina." She didn't quite feel like Elizabeth anymore, and she didn't really know Quila very well either. It somehow made sense to her to have a new name, although she couldn't begin to guess how she had conjured the word.

"Vagina?" said Diego, puzzled. Something about this young woman was stirring him on the inside like a tornado, and he took a breath to keep his cool. He could see how fractured she was on the surface, and still, somehow, so rock solid, underneath so many layers of trauma. He wanted to know her. He couldn't resist a smile.

"*Vir*gina."

"Is that what you want us to call you?"

"Yes."

The third man, Special Agent Lluc Vives-Mares, regarded her quietly with hazel eyes surrounded by a light olive complexion, with a soft layer of wavy brown hair growing out atop a recent buzz cut. "You were in pretty bad shape a couple of nights ago, Miss," he said. "Do you remember that?"

Virgina shook her head again.

"You look much better today," said the fourth nurse, Special Agent Trieu Nguyen. His high cheekbones and long, pointed nose flanked by broad nostrils reminded Virgina of Elizabeth's eldest brother Maska, who was sixteen years old when she last saw him, the day she left the Massachusett tribe.

"May I use the toilet?" she asked cautiously, hoping they would leave the room.

"You're wearing a catheter, Quila—I mean, Virgina. So you can just go any time."

She didn't understand what he was saying, but the feeling of pressure from her bladder had seemed to subside, and she didn't question it.

"Talisa, can you hear me?" a female voice echoed in her head.

Virgina raised her head and looked around. "Yes, I hear you!" she said aloud. "Where are you?"

Rahim walked over and shined a pen light in her eyes. "She's responding to a hallucination."

"It's me, Abitha," said the voice. "Are you here somewhere? Can you hear me?"

"Yes, I hear you!" said Virgina again aloud, realizing that wherever she was, Abitha could not hear her voice.

"¿Con quién habla?" said Diego, asking her in Spanish who she was talking to.

"*Con mi hermana*," Virgina reflexively answered in kind, wondering what language she was speaking as she answered that she was talking to her sister.

"Is she a ghost?" asked Lluc.

"I don't know," said Virgina, staring at him blankly. "I think so."

"We'd like to remove the straps to see if you feel up to walking around," said Trieu. "Will that be alright with you, Quila? You don't want to hurt us, do you?"

"My name is Virgina. And no, I would never hurt anyone."

"Good. We're glad to hear that. We're going to remove the straps now, alright?"

More tears spilled out of Virgina's eyes as Rahim and Trieu walked over and unbuckled the straps. Rahim reached his arm forward for her to grab onto so he could help her stand up. Her body felt stiff and weak as she struggled to raise her arm in order to hook her fingers onto his bicep. Trieu put his hand on her back to give her some support.

"You're going to be okay," Diego said kindly in Spanish. "We're doing everything we can to help you."

Trieu reached down and pulled a small stepping stool out from under the bed. "Here, use this to step down."

Who is this Quila González? she wondered. *I wonder*

what she thinks about me using her body.

"Let's just take it slowly," said Trieu. "One foot at a time. Slowly. That's it, now the other one."

The muscles in her legs gave out and she wobbled, falling back onto the bed.

"Why does it hurt so much?" she asked, her voice cracking.

"Your body is beginning to feel pain for the first time in God-knows-how-long," said Diego. "You've been off the crack cocaine for a week now. It takes time for your body to adjust. You're doing good, though. We'll get you some more baclofen to help with the withdrawal symptoms. Let's just take things as slowly as possible. We're not going to let anything bad happen to you."

Crack O'Kane? thought Virgina, perplexed by the oddity of the situation. *Back low fin? What language is this?* "I don't want to be here," she said aloud, pushing herself up and sliding her bare feet toward the floor. Her eyes were fixated on the door to the room, and an intense sensation of desire to be on the other side of that door welled up in her chest and shot down through her spine, through her torso, and down her legs, like a flash of lightning. As soon as both feet touched the ground, she vanished into thin air.

A moment later, she found herself standing out in the hallway, facing the door to the room she had just come from. Rahim and Diego burst out of the room, slamming the door open. Astonished to find her standing there on the other side of the door, they quickly grabbed her and pulled her back into the room.

"Wait, no!" she pleaded. "Don't tie me down again, please! Please!" She screeched and twisted her body violently, resisting their efforts. "I'm not going to hurt anyone, I promise!"

"It happened when her feet touched the ground," said Diego, taking care not to injure her as she struggled to keep her feet in contact with the floor. "Lluc, grab her legs and swing them up here. I think if we keep her feet off the ground, she'll be okay."

Trieu stepped out of the room for a moment to retrieve a roll of gauze from the supply closet.

"What are you doing?" asked Lluc.

"I'm going to wrap some gauze around her ankles to help cushion them. They're chafing from the straps."

At the sight of the gauze, Virgina began screaming at the top of her lungs and kicking her legs violently.

"Getting a sedative," said Diego, exiting the room and returning with a syringe. As the needle pricked her arm and delivered the drug, her arms and legs went limp.

| Chapter Thirty-Four |

"Rahim, look," said Lluc, pointing down the hallway at Eka's room.

"What the hell?" said Rahim. An ethereal, glowing white light was emanating through the small window on the door to her room.

"Is Reid sending someone down here to check this out?" said Trieu.

"Dr. Chen is on her way," said Lluc.

"Getting another sedative," said Diego.

The four men gathered outside of Eka's room, trying to get a glimpse of what was happening through the thick glass, which was frosted for privacy, before entering the room.

"Are we ready?" said Rahim. "I'm opening the door."

From the hallway they could see Eka sitting upright in her bed, her arms and legs bound with leather straps, same as Quila's had been. Some kind of glowing white slime was oozing out of her mouth, and she kept coughing and vomiting up more and more of it as she stared blankly into the space in front of her. A cold wind was whirling around in the room, but the agents couldn't tell where it was coming from.

"Eka!" said Lluc from the doorway. "Are you okay? Talk to us! What's happening here?"

"Don't call me Eka," she said, wiping the luminous drool from her chin with the back of her hand. "I'm Mercurial." At this, she began heaving again, and with a gurgling "auck," a large white cloud of misty smoke billowed out of her mouth and began to form humanoid shapes in the room.

"What the hell are they?" said Diego, staring in astonishment at the figures as they morphed and grew before their eyes amidst the dancing swirling mist.

"I think they're ghosts," said Lluc, recalling a childhood memory of the first time he had seen a ghost, at the age of eight. The ghost, a Madrilenian great-uncle and former television actor who went by the stage name of Javier Domingo, gave warning through mime and gestures that his beloved niece Ivet, Lluc's mother, was in danger of drowning from swimming drunk on gin and tonics with oxycodone. Lluc raced downstairs to the swimming pool of his uncle's villa in Barcelona in time to save her life. "Look, they're taking the shape of women," said Lluc to his colleagues. "Deformed women."

One of the figures appeared to be missing part of her left arm, amputated at the elbow. Another was missing part of her right leg, amputated at the thigh. Another of them appeared to have a broken neck. Another had deep empty cavities where her eyes should have been, as if they had been gouged out. All of them had in common that their mouths were sealed shut, down-turned into frowns.

"Look at Eka's face," said Trieu. "Pardon, I mean Mercurial. They seem to be using her body as a portal into our world. It's causing her pain. Look at her face." Mercurial's face appeared to be screaming, but no sound was coming out.

"Get some gauze," said Diego. "Let's see if we can close up the portal by binding her mouth shut."

As the four men entered the room, the ghostly figures

shrieked and howled, twisting and grabbing at them in vain as they walked through. Trieu approached and pushed Mercurial's chin up to close her mouth, and then loosely wound a strand of gauze around her head, covering her lips. He then secured her mouth shut with several pieces of medical tape crossing over the top of the gauze. Within a minute, the ghostly figures disappeared from the room.

Without needing to look at her face, Lluc was sensing her pain on a vibrational level. He reached forward to rest the palm of his hand on her blanketed shin to help set her fears at ease. For a moment, she feared that it was a gesture of sexual aggression, but she could see in his eyes that it wasn't. Her heart, icy and rigid moments before from the piercing pain which plagued her all over, softened as she looked into his eyes. His touch was not only melting her, but somehow flowing along with her on the same current.

"It worked," said Trieu. "I just hope the gauze is enough to keep them contained."

"We'd better check on the other two," said Rahim. "Bring the sedative and gauze."

| Chapter Thirty-Five |

"How did you know where the safe house was?" asked Veronica, adjusting the video camera to fit Titi's face into the frame.

"Rochelle told me the building was called Ophelia's Wing," said Titi, begrudging the interrogation. "I found the address online." The sound of Veronica's voice was grating on her but she pursed her lips and reminded herself that perhaps karma had brought her here to give Veronica the opportunity to redeem herself.

"What was your intention in going there?"

"I intended to chant a prayer for the four trafficking victims, in as close proximity as I could manage. So they could feel my energy."

"And why did you go in the middle of the night?"

"I didn't want anyone trying to stop me."

"Miss Jameson, the surveillance video shows you placing an object against the building. What was it?"

"It was a box of chocolate truffles. An offering for the Marassa."

"The Marassa? What's that?"

"They're Voodoo spirits—the holy trinity of Voodoo. They look like children, but they're the most ancient of the lwa. Twins, yet they number three. A paradox."

"Hm. How quaint. And how did you choose the location for the placement of the offering?"

"The Marassa appeared to me as I was getting out of my cab. Two visible nonbinary children wearing matching yellow dresses, and a third who could not be seen, only felt. They led me to the spot where they wanted the offering left."

"Well, Miss Jameson—" Veronica again smugly took the liberty of addressing Titi by her maiden name.

"It's Beaumond," Titi corrected her this time. "I think you know how it's spelled."

Veronica subtly rolled her eyes, and opened a folder containing a copy of the arrest warrant. "As you know, the warrant says that you left an object at the fire's point of origin. The police initially believed it to be some kind of incendiary device; at least, that was the conclusion drawn by your cousin. But the fire investigation report says the burn pattern clearly demonstrates the fire originated *inside* the building, and burned outward until it reached the offering you had left outside of the building. Any ideas how that could be possible?"

"I do have some ideas, yes. But you just see me as crazy, so what's the point in setting myself up for more of your shade. If I may ask, what exactly caught on fire inside the building?"

"The report says it was a power outlet in a room where one of the victims in the case your cousin is investigating was sleeping."

"Can you tell me which of the vics it was?"

"There was an African woman sleeping there."

Titi was surprised to hear this. "You must mean Abeni. It makes me wonder if she's ever given birth to twins," she said thoughtfully.

"How strange. Why would you wonder that?"

"She attracted the Divine Twins to her aid. The Marassa led me to her. It's possible that Abeni reached out to me using some type of kinesis."

"A colorful theory," said Veronica with an abrasive laugh. "What we know to be fact is that the fire could not have originated from outside the building. So getting the charges dropped should be a fairly straightforward matter. But let me be frank, if I may. If paranormal abilities were actually real, science would have proven it long before now. Research has been consistently inconclusive on that topic."

"Some forces are driven by faith." Titi knew that the odds of persuading Veronica to challenge her own convictions were paper thin. Veronica ruled her emotions with an iron fist, like Franco ruled the Spain of her childhood. Titi forced herself to be patient in responding, although she kept returning to the same question in her mind that usually plagued her conversations with Veronica: *why do I even bother?*

She often guessed that Carlos must be the reason, because this woman had given birth to him, and she felt grateful for that enough that her efforts to appeal to Veronica on a spiritual level vainly persisted. "Faith is not something you can use science to prove," she continued. "It doesn't operate by the same rules as your material logic. Scientific experiments would of course fail. If you need a scientific experiment to tell you if you have faith, then you obviously don't have it."

"So it sounds to me like what you're saying is that it's nothing more than a crapshoot," said Veronica, raising her eyebrows as she closed the folder and placed it back in her briefcase. "Completely random coincidences leading to confirmation bias."

"What I'm saying is that you're limiting yourself by viewing it through that lens. It's not a crapshoot, it takes learning how to see with your heart instead of your eyes, learning to *feel* your way. It means understanding there's more to the picture than logic can provide. It's something you *have* to feel to understand. But I can see you're not feeling it. So never mind. Let's just get on with it. When can I get out of here?" said Titi, changing the subject. "I have a lot of work to do."

"Well, we have the matter of Carlos' misconduct investigation to tackle next. It's intricately wound with your current crisis and the question of whether marijuana is the best therapeutic option for your mental health. From what I've seen, it's clearly not. I've asked my good friend, Dr. Shannon Thompson, to evaluate you. She lives here in Manhattan, and she's an expert in schizophrenia. She can see you as soon as Tuesday."

"Let me guess. She's white?"

"Well, yes, she is. What does that have to do with anything?"

"Of course she is. Do you even have friends of any other race?"

"What an absurd and impertinent question. You know, I'm trying to help you here, but you've been nothing but hostile and confrontational. I never have this problem with white clients."

Titi cringed and laughed, shaking her head. *It never ceases to amaze me the things she's capable of saying with a straight face,* she thought, knowing Veronica's ego would enjoy hearing that. "That says more about you than it does about me. I'm just reflecting back to you the hostile energy you've been putting out there. Not just today, but since the day we met."

"I haven't the faintest idea of what you're talking about. I've always been nothing but kind and gracious with you."

"I could give a half dozen examples from this conversation alone, but what's the point? You won't acknowledge it. It just drains my energy. I'm not even sure why you decided to 'stoop so low' as to help me. I know it wasn't out of the kindness of your heart."

"If you must know, the simple answer is that I need my son right now," said Veronica matter-of-factly. "My assistance on this matter will give him some much needed closure with you, and, well, let's be honest," she said with a patronizing smile. "I think he needs that. After all, why do you think he ran straight into the arms of the one person who he knew could drive you away? Did you ever think about that?"

Titi couldn't help but gasp at the audacity. A surge of anger swelled in her chest. "You're not right," was all she could say, shaking her head.

"After his misconduct hearing," continued Veronica, "he'll be coming back with me to the West Coast, and staying with me the next few months. This trifle of rescuing you from your little quagmire is a small price to pay to ensure his cooperation. Does that answer your question?"

What kind of relationship would you have with your son if you couldn't coerce it out of him, thought Titi, while maintaining eye contact with Veronica.

Veronica raised an eyebrow and looked away.

"I ask if she's white because her privilege puts barriers between me and her ability to empathize with my situation."

"So you'd rather see a Black psychiatrist? That sounds quite racist to me. I don't know if you're aware, Miss Jameson, but psychiatry is a *science* with observable guidelines and methodology. It doesn't matter that Dr. Thompson is white. Anyone can learn the rules and practice them."

"Is she at least a spiritualist?"

"I wouldn't have a clue."

"Not much of a good friend then, are you?"

"Do you want my help or not, Miss Jameson? Dr. Thompson is who I recommend. She was kind enough to accommodate you for an evaluation at 7 a.m. on Tuesday. Tomorrow's a holiday, her schedule is full, and she's squeezing you in. You're welcome. The sooner we get you on a more consensus-based trajectory, the sooner you can get out of here."

"Carlos can show her the record of all the psych meds I've tried and failed," said Titi bitterly. "Smoking weed was the only thing that helped my depression and chronic pain."

"That may be true," said Veronica. "But let me be frank with you again. It still doesn't mean it's the best option. Our first order of business is establishing your care under a psychiatrist other than Carlos, and Shannon is who's available. Take it or leave it."

| Chapter Thirty-Six |

Rochelle felt water in her shoes, and looked down. She was sitting in her living room, in a chair she had never seen before. It was an upright, wooden, banister-back chair, and it was facing the television. Glancing around, she realized that all of the navy blue carpet in the apartment was soaked in several inches of water. It was yet another bizarre development in a seemingly never ending paradigm shift, and she was getting tired of it, too tired of it to be alarmed.

The television powered on in front of her, apparently of its own accord. After about five seconds of incomprehensible blobs morphing in the static like Rorschach inkblots, the image of Jandro's face appeared on the screen. "It's good to see you again, Special Agent Roy," he said with an unnatural, gleaming smile, one which expressed a sadistic glee rather than actual happiness.

A trickle of water tickled her knee. The water level in the room had risen.

"Tide's coming in!" announced Jandro with a wide-eyed chuckle, as if he were a game show host announcing the next round of contestants, or perhaps as though he were announcing what she had won.

"I don't care anymore," said Rochelle, staring at the television from under an invisible but thick layer of depression. "Let it."

"But what about your daughter?" said Jandro, his creepy smile dissolving into a puzzled frown as he raised his right hand and pressed six fingers to the glass of the television screen. His fingertips were pulsating, glowing and growing, and opened up like giant pores to reveal something brownish-green and slimy inside. Thick white worms slithered out of the pores like eels and slid into the water, circling Rochelle before closing in and attaching themselves to her body.

"Leave my daughter out of this," said Rochelle, realizing at last through her lethargy that she was waist-deep into a nightmare. Jandro's mention of her daughter triggered anger in her, but her words somehow came out slower than pond water, and her arms and legs felt weighted down. The slimy things seemed to be feeding on her emotional response like leeches.

"Tsk, tsk. You can't keep her a secret forever."

"You'll never find her." By now the water in the room had risen to her chest, but her body felt so tired and heavy, she couldn't compel herself to rise from her chair. "You'll never find her," she said again, clenching her teeth.

"What if I already have?"

The ceiling and roof had disappeared now, revealing towering ocean waves looming up over the sides of the building, threatening to crash in and flood the room at any moment. "But you haven't," Rochelle said, closing her eyes and opening them again, hoping the scene would change. It didn't. "You're not real. This is only a dream."

"Life is but a dream, isn't that what they say?" said Jandro, his face distorting into Bram's demonic grin before disappearing from the television and reappearing behind her, wrapping the six fingers of his left hand around her neck. "You think I'm in your dream right now? It's the other way around. You're in *my* dream. That means *you'll* do what *I* want. You're nothing more than a receptacle to fill with my pain. The sooner you come to terms with that fact, the better off you'll be."

"You mean the better off *you'll* be. Your lack of compassion makes you a robot," said Rochelle, throwing her head back with great effort, and laughing, beside herself. "Robots are predictable. Easy to defeat."

"Compassion?" Bram's face morphed back into Jandro's puzzled guise as he leaned in front of her. "What's that? Haven't seen much of it in my life. But I think you've got it backwards, my little cactus blossom. It's the compassionate ones who are predictable. You can't stand to see someone hurt without trying to fix it." To make his point, he touched the corner of his eye with one bulbous finger and traced a line down the side of his face like the path of a tear. A teardrop of blood fell down his cheek, following the trail, and dripped into the water as his mouth turned down into an exaggerated frown. "Makes you easy to manipulate, easy to control. Just have to bring on a little pain. Or pretend to."

Rochelle closed her eyes to shut out the grotesque image. "People with strong boundaries know where to draw the line," she said with her eyes closed, like she was trying to speak through a migraine. She opened them and said, "They can give *you* lethal injection for all I care. It won't break my heart."

"Such a barbarian!" Jandro covered his mouth in mock surprise. "I can see you have so much in common with your good friend Lin Mei. The murderer."

She closed her eyes again, wishing the nightmare would end. When she opened them, her entire apartment was gone and her chair was bobbing in the middle of a deep, dark ocean with nothing but obscure liquid below. "She's not a murderer..." she said, her voice coming from inside her head. "It was self-defense."

"That's what you tell yourself, isn't it?" he said, his voice now also in her head, disembodied, distant, surreal. "But deep down you've always believed it didn't have to come to that."

"She was just a child. Her father would have killed her and her mother both." Her chair was still bobbing but seemed to be dipping lower and lower into the water, coming up to her chest at first and then, gradually it seemed, up to her neck.

"Mm hmm. What if we talk about your pathetic excuse for a boyfriend?" His voice seemed to be coming from nowhere and everywhere.

"Carlos is a good man. There's nothing you can say about him that will make me think less of him." The water was dark enough that she couldn't see her feet, only darker shadows passing below her in the water, large oblong shapes, maybe fish, maybe sharks. She tried not to think about them, but she was slowly losing her grip on managing the fear.

"He chooses his mother's feelings over yours, every time. Am I wrong? He's constantly asking you to make allowances for her. Does he ask the same of her for you, I wonder?"

By now, the water was up around Rochelle's ears, and she tipped her head back to keep her face from being submerged. Her body still cemented to the chair, her heartbeat began to accelerate and she tried to meditate on staying calm. *This is just a dream. This is just a dream. This is just a dream.*

At last the water rose inches above her face, and she could now see the image of Jandro's face glaring down at her from above, distorted by the ripples of the water. She held her breath for as long as she could, but it was less than a minute before her motor control gave out, and her nostrils sucked water into her lungs. Her body succumbed, twisting to violent spasms before slowing to a complete still, floating face down in the water. A curious, quizzical thought dangled in Rochelle's mind. *When you die in a dream, do you die in real life?*

The sound of knocking echoed through the water, and

she could hear the voice of her partner, Jason, calling through the door.

"Roy! Are you in there? It's me, Jefferson!"

"It's your lover boy," said Jandro with a sneer, now suddenly underwater beneath Rochelle. Bubbles of sound emerged from his mouth as he spoke. "He'll have to come back later. We're busy."

Rochelle shut her eyes tightly and then opened them. She was still floating face down in the water, but Jandro was no longer lying underneath her. She could now see clear sand below her through the water, and noticed the feet of a Black man standing a foot or two away in front of her, submerged up to his chest in the water, and realized that she could probably stand up. Tightening her stomach, she swung her feet forward until they touched the ground, and brought her head up out of the water, looking around, coughing water out of her lungs. They were far out from any shore, and there was a full moon above shining brightly on the man in front of her. His face was not one she recognized. His muscular arms and chest were bare, except for a pendant necklace that seemed to be carved out of black stone, with the image of an eye in the center of it.

"Who are you?" she asked curiously.

"I'm Nimbeau," he said, taking her by surprise as he reached forward and grabbed hold of the front of her collared shirt and pushed her backward down into the water until her head was below the surface. This time, she believed would drown. Her arms and legs thrashed helplessly in panic.

The landline telephone began to ring, and she sat up in a lurch to find herself dry and sitting on her living room couch. There was a sharp pain in her forehead, and her heart was clenched like a fist.

The answering machine picked up the call, and the outgoing message came on that she and Carlos had recorded together, each speaking their own name. "It's Rochelle—and

Carlos—leave a message!"

Her mother Tanée's voice came on after the beep, mid-chuckle. "You two kill me with that corny message," she said. "Anyway, baby, it's your momma calling. I've got some news for you. Your daddy just got out of prison. He got exonerated by DNA evidence. You know I've said it a million times, I always knew this day would come. Thirty-one years wrongfully imprisoned, can you believe that? So he has some restitution money coming. He wants to come up there to New York to see you. Give me a call baby. Love you."

Rochelle decided this latest development warranted another trip to the liquor store, but as soon as she felt sober enough to locate her keys and wallet, Jason came knocking at the door again.

Chapter Thirty-Seven

"What the hell are you doing, Roy?" he said, after she invited him in. "Pull yourself together!"

"What do you care? Oh, wait, I get it now. You want me, is that it? Yeah, that's it. You want me, don't you," she said, pulling aside the collar of her shirt flirtatiously to reveal more of her neck.

"What? No! Stop it. This isn't you. You're better than this."

"You know what, Special Agent Jefferson, I regret turning you down before. So here I am. Yours for the taking."

"You're talking about something that happened, what, nine years ago? You know you did the right thing turning me down. You were my superior officer, I was a trainee. It was unprofessional then, and it's still unprofessional now."

"Yeah, you're right. Unprofessional. That didn't stop me from getting with Efren, though, did it. Maybe he'd be alive now if it wasn't for me."

"*You* didn't kill him," said Jason. "The cartel did. Don't get it twisted."

"So this is just payback, then? I rejected you so you have

to reject me?"

"It's not payback, Roy. I have Natasha. You have Carlos. We both have a job to do. We don't have time for games. Some crazy shit is going down right now at the safe house. Reid wants us to get down there right away. Speaking of Carlos, where is he?"

"He dumped me," she said dejectedly, checking the empty bottles on the floor to see if they had anything left in them. "He doesn't want me anymore. Oh, hey, I need to get down to the store. It was nice chatting with you. Gotta go."

"You know very well how enabling works. Carlos isn't here to enable you, is that what you mean? And I'm not here to enable you either. Look at what you're doing. Your talent and potential are being wasted. Is Carlos supposed to be okay with that?"

"Stop trying to lay a guilt trip on me. And give me a break. He's not trying to help me get sober. He's just mad at me for ruining his career."

"And how exactly did you do that?"

"Having Titi arrested triggered a misconduct investigation. He could lose his license."

"That sounds like that's *his* karma to bear. If he's as good as you say, then they won't find him guilty."

"Oh, because justice is always just? My dad spent thirty-one years in prison for a crime he didn't commit. Where's the justice in that? I wish everyone would stop trying to sell me on this farce you call karma. Sometimes the bad guys win and sometimes good guys suffer, regardless of what they deserved."

"Your dad was abusive to you and Titi. Don't paint him like he was a saint."

"You don't need to remind me of that. Titi reminds me enough. And that doesn't mean he deserved *that*."

"Look, that's not for me to decide. It's between him and God. Anyway, Carlos is wealthy and white. Let him worry about

202

himself. He can afford a good attorney. Your father didn't have that luxury." He paused to reflect on karma and her disdain for the notion. "You could think of it like there are two forces at work on the world, one is karma and the other is luck. They're not mutually exclusive. Without luck, it's like we're trying to play a card game without shuffling the cards. We need that element of randomness, or else the game becomes too predictable. We would get bored and lose interest in living. Just because luck exists doesn't mean karma doesn't, just like shuffling the cards doesn't mean the game play doesn't have rules. It just means that sometimes some people are dealt better hands. Karma knows the difference between the cards you were dealt and how you played them. And karma isn't always about what we deserve. Sometimes it's just about spiritual lessons that came due for us to learn in this lifetime, not as punishment but as coming of age."

"Well, did you hear what I said? I need to get to the store, Jefferson. This is between me and God. So step aside."

"I'm not going to let you buy more alcohol, Roy."

"Try and stop me."

"Don't think I won't—"

Before he could finish the sentence, she had lurched toward the front door and he lurched with her to block her exit.

"Get out of my way," she said, whipping around to snap her knee forward and unfold her leg into a kick toward his head, which he deftly blocked with his forearm.

"We don't have time for this," he said, leaning back to dodge a punch thrown at his face before reaching to get a hold of her body. He was much taller than her, and solidly built, but he knew that she was usually much more agile than this. Knowing firsthand the lethal precision she was capable of in hand-to-hand combat, he could see how much the alcohol was slowing her down. The sadness of it struck him painfully in the chest, like a psychic hit from within. Beads of sweat took shape on the brow of his shaved head.

When he leaned in to try to wrestle her toward the couch, she charged into him with her shoulder, and despite her impaired state, shoved him away from the door. She pivoted back toward the exit, put her hand on the knob and threw the door open while swinging another kick toward Jason's groin as he lunged forward again. He blocked the kick with his knee, amazed that she was still taking shots at him.

This last move was sloppy enough that he could have successfully grabbed her kicking leg, or swept her standing leg, and taken her down. But he realized he didn't want to. The sadness of it hit him again with another psychic blow. *I need a different approach.* He stepped back and threw his palms up in the air. "Okay!" he said. "Okay. You win. Just stay for a minute and talk to me, please? Just asking you to give me a minute."

She kept her eyes sternly locked on him, vigilant for another aggressive move, as she cautiously closed the door. "Stand over there, away from the door, and then we can talk." She looked at her watch. "You got one minute."

| Chapter Thirty-Eight |

Flashback: February 26, 1993
Garden District, New Orleans, Louisiana

Samson Bishop lived with his daughter Rochelle and his wife Tanée in a modest, single-story, shotgun-style house in the Lower Garden District of New Orleans until 1985, when he was arrested and found guilty of raping and murdering a prostitute. With her job as an actuary, Tanée Bishop could afford to continue living in that house after Samson was convicted, and was still living there decades later, when he was eventually exonerated by DNA evidence.

Titi stopped by her aunt Tanée's house to pay her mother a surprise visit. At the age of seventeen, Titi had dropped out of high school and moved in with her twenty-three-year-old boyfriend, Billy Charlotte, who had worked as a longshoreman before he started cooking and dealing meth out of his trailer in the Seventh Ward District. Titi knew her mother would be there at her aunt Tanée's, because her aunt Yolande was visiting from Haiti with her husband Andre and their three children, and they were all staying at Tanée's house. She also knew her grandmother Ruth would be there, and wanted to take advantage of the opportunity to visit everyone while they were gathered in one location.

"There she is!" said Ruth, who at five feet tall was both energetic and regal at the same time, and at the age of fifty-four was still turning heads when she walked down the street. "Get over here Titi and give me some sugar."

Titi smiled broadly at the sight of her beloved grandmother and hugged her tightly, kissing her cheek. The savory smell of shrimp and sausage gumbo simmering on the stove nearby wafted over, mingled for a moment with the scent of her grandmother's perfume, and gave Titi another warm and welcome hug.

"Good to see you Titi," said Tanée, squeezing Titi around the shoulders before turning to address Titi's cousins. "Did y'all thank your Maw Maw Ruth for buying y'all a Sega Genesis?"

Titi's cousins Andre Jr. and Samuel, ten and twelve respectively, looked up from playing Mortal Kombat with her sixteen-year-old cousin Angie, and Angie's high school boyfriend whose name she couldn't remember. "Thank you Maw Maw!" they said together, showing a wide smile by way of appreciation.

Ruth laughed and gave a single clap of joy. "Y'all are welcome babies. Y'all are very welcome."

"Thank you, Mom," said Tanée, planting another kiss on Ruth's cheek as she walked by the dining table where Ruth was seated. "But you don't have to spoil them so much. And you really didn't need to buy Rochelle a new computer. Make them work for it!"

"Aw, let them have fun once in a while," said Ruth. "Shelley's so smart, you know she's gonna do us all proud. Look at her over there, typing away. What you typing over there, baby?"

Rochelle smiled bashfully. "It's the World Wide Web."

"The World Wide what?" said Ruth with a laugh.

Rochelle, twelve years old, pushed her glasses up on her nose. "World Wide Web. I'm talking to people through the computer." She thought about explaining to her grandmother how a modem works, but decided against it.

"Oh Lord. Such a nerd," said Titi, rolling her eyes and pulling a pitcher from the refrigerator to pour herself a glass of iced tea. Her mother Sheila looked Titi up and down and gave her a look that said that she did not like the way Titi was dressed and would rather she hadn't shown up wearing that scandalous ensemble when her grandmother happened to be visiting. At the time, Titi was too stoned to care about her mother's disapproval, and didn't think it looked all that scandalous, but on some level that would eventually take decades to break the surface of her awareness, felt the sting of it.

Like Tanée, Sheila was also raising a daughter as a single mother, following her husband Clark Jameson's death from prostate cancer in 1983, which was determined to have been caused by his exposure to Agent Orange while serving in the U.S. Army during the Vietnam War. "Titi Anne," said Sheila, "why don't you get that white boyfriend of yours to come spray the oak tree out front for buck moths?"

"Sure, Momma," said Titi, retrieving a cigarette from a pack of Camels in her purse. She knew better than to light one up in her aunt's house, but the sensation of holding the little bundle of anticipation was comforting to her.

"That boy don't like to come around us," said Tanée. "He don't mind having a Black girlfriend, but he don't like her Black family."

"He's very busy with work," explained Titi, smiling graciously. "I'm sure he would love to come help out as soon as he's free."

"Titi baby, come over here and sit by me," said Ruth, patting the chair beside her. Titi obliged, taking a seat next to her at the dining table.

"Your momma tells me you plan to marry this boy. Marriage is a sacred bond, honey, you understand that, right?"

"Yes, ma'am."

"Your Paw Paw Charles and I were married thirty years. And he was married to Mary, his first wife, for twenty-four years before that, faithful to her until the day she died. And we was faithful to each other, too, until the day he died, and I still been faithful ever since. Think about what kind of man earns loyalty like that. This ain't no small achievement. There's a reason he was one of the wealthiest men in New Orleans. But wealth don't mean a thing without integrity. So I want you to promise me that you'll honor them wedding vows, you hear? Do me and your Paw Paw proud."

"I promise, Maw Maw."

"I done had the same talk with Shelley and with Angie. Same as I had with your mommas when they was your age. You stay true to yourself, you stay true to your man, and you find yourself a good man who's gonna stay true to you too."

"I will, Maw Maw." Titi nodded and digested the advice for a moment before getting up to go smoke her cigarette. Rochelle stared wide-eyed at the television from her chair in front of the computer, contemplating the terrorist bombing of the World Trade Center being reported on the six o'clock news. "I'm going to be an FBI agent when I grow up," she announced to her cousins.

"Little Miss Goody Two Shoes!" Titi jeered, sticking her tongue out at Rochelle as she walked past. Rochelle crinkled her nose and stuck her tongue out back at her.

"Don't listen to her, baby," said Sheila to Rochelle as she got up to join Titi on the porch. "You go on and join the FBI if that's what you want to do."

"You really love this Charlotte boy, don't you," said Sheila, sitting down next to Titi. "He got that long blonde hair, big brown puppy dog eyes, the heart of a rebel."

"I'm sorry Momma, it's just hard for me to get away."

"He got a tight grip on you, honey. It ain't healthy."

"That's not what I mean. It's just hard to get away because I miss him so much when I do. He understands me like no one else does. And I understand him."

"Let me guess, he was abused too as a child? Yeah, you got the soul of a healer alright. But listen baby, you need to be careful when touching the wounds of the Devil," said Sheila, looking in Titi's eyes with grave concern. "Lucifer might call himself the light bringer, but all that glitters ain't gold. The Lord cast the Devil down from Heaven for a reason."

"Maybe the Lord sent the Devil to Earth so he could get healed," said Titi, taking a long drag from her cigarette and then lowering her arm to flick the ash from the end of it while exhaling into the damp Louisiana air. "Don't you worry about me, Momma. I'll be just fine."

But Sheila did worry, and with good reason. It wasn't long after that day that Titi and Billy eloped, and it would be another three years before she saw her daughter again, addicted to meth, recovering from a marriage plagued by domestic violence, and a divorce that almost killed her.

| Chapter Thirty-Nine |

"How are you feeling this evening, Olena?" said Dr. Varma, checking the heart and blood pressure monitor mounted behind the bed before turning to look at her patient.

On making eye contact, Dr. Varma was met with a malignant scowl. "What the fuck do you care?" her young convalescent grumbled in a Russian accent. "And my name isn't Olena. It's Orna Mental. You can call me Orna for short. And stop looking at me like that."

"Am I looking at you a certain way, Orna?" said Dr. Varma, with a puzzled expression. "I apologize. I certainly didn't mean to—"

"You don't see me as the beautiful woman that I am. You see me as a whore. And you look down on me because of it. You think you're better than me."

"I think you have the wrong—"

"Your man's the one who can't keep it in his pants. It's just more convenient to blame the other woman. You blame the other woman, but him, you forgive."

"Really, I don't think—"

"Ask your precious Philip what he was doing last night

while you were working the night shift. See if a room at the Hotel Piscean rings a bell. He picked up a street walker and she did things to him that you would never do. And you know what else? He can't stand how skinny and insecure you are, and obsessed with losing weight. He feels too sorry for you to break up with you."

Dr. Varma stared at Orna, speechless and horrified.

"Yeah, I know, the truth hurts. But guess what? I did you a favor by letting you know. You can thank me later. Feel free to cry if you want."

Dr. Varma was no stranger to unstable patients saying disturbing things to her, but the mention of her boyfriend by name, together with the attack on her person, had gotten under her skin. She wanted to ask Olena, or Orna, where she had heard such things, but didn't want to give them any more power than she had already unwillingly done, in spite of struggling to remain calm. The gravity of the accusation had thumped her in the chest, and drained her body of energy. Suddenly, something slimy slithered around her neck, and without making a sound that would betray any sense of alarm, she reached up to push it away, stepping backward as it fell away from her to the ground. Wiping her hands on her white coat did little to remove its sticky residue, and tears coming to her eyes, she abruptly turned and ran from the room, without even looking to see what it had been.

Moments later, the four undercover agents entered. Diego carried a syringe full of sedative, and Trieu a roll of gauze.

"I see you intend to rape me with that," said Orna.

"We're not going to rape anyone, Olena," said Trieu. "We're just trying to help you."

"I'm Orna. Orna Mental. You mean you're trying to help me shut up, so why don't you just be honest? But you don't want honesty. You won't speak it and you don't hear it."

"What truth do you think we don't want to hear, Orna?" said Lluc. "We have nothing against the truth."

"Your mother faked the condom breaking so she could use her pregnancy to manipulate your father. Your daddy didn't want you. He never wanted you. That's why he left you. You spend so much time trying to act important when inside you just feel abandoned and worthless."

Lluc inhaled deeply and exhaled slowly. Rahim, who knew Lluc well enough to know she had struck a nerve, reached over and squeezed Lluc's shoulder.

"Maybe you should stick to telling truths about yourself," said Diego.

"Maybe you should tell them about the coke you took home with you for personal use after forensics was done with it," she said, shrugging.

Diego looked at the ground, silent for a moment. His father, Special Agent Eduardo García Hernández, was an immigrant from Guadalajara, Mexico, who joined and later retired from the U.S. Marine Corps before joining the FBI, from whom he received the FBI Medal of Valor when he put his life on the line to protect three of his colleagues from gunfire. Diego cringed to imagine the disappointment on his father's face were he to learn of this incident. Then he looked back up at Orna and spoke with summoned strength and pained sincerity. "It was an impulsive mistake that I regret."

"But you still haven't returned it," said Orna with contempt.

"We all make mistakes," said Trieu, coming to Diego's defense, all the while hoping she wouldn't call attention to his own indiscretions concerning a polyamorous affair with two female informants. "Why don't you ask Diego about the time he got stabbed defending his sister when an intruder attacked her with a knife? This man is a hero."

"Oh, I see," she said, laughing derisively. "You think I'm being too hard on you?" She looked around at their earnest faces with a menacing scorn, then tensed her eyes in anger. "You don't know the meaning of hard."

"It's not a contest. We all have wounds here," said Rahim, with a fire in his eyes that spoke to Orna of his own history of intense and prolonged sufferings. He was a widow; his cherished wife Salma whom he lovingly nicknamed "Misirlou" was killed by a suicide bomber in Baghdad. Her ghost still haunted him. A former prisoner of war in Iraq, and a survivor of childhood physical abuse, he was also no stranger to complex PTSD. "It doesn't change the fact that we're trying to do the right thing here. We're trying to help you. Look at us. Listen to what we're saying. *We're trying to help you.*"

The cold wind encircling Orna's heart grew more fierce as the agents noticed that Orna's eyes began glowing a pale icy blue, and Trieu snapped into action, winding the gauze around Orna's head, blindfolding her and gently securing it with a tie in the back.

"You can't keep us in this prison forever," said Orna. "Truth wants out."

"You're here for your protection," said Rahim. "To reduce the risk of you hurting yourself and others."

"It's not meant to be a punishment," said Trieu. "We're just trying to figure out how to give you the right kind of space, to let the pain come to the surface so you can heal. We're not going to give up on you, Olena."

"It's Orna," she said with an aggrieved impatience.

"We're not going to give up on you, Orna," said Trieu.

"We're going to leave you now to get some rest," said Diego. "We're not the bad guys, okay?"

"You're extremely perceptive," added Lluc. "So you know we're trying to help you."

"I see your intention," said Orna. "But you're fools if you think you can help us. You're better off getting as far away from us as you can." Orna's voice deepened into an unearthly, reverberating rumble, like a thousand voices speaking in a low-pitched chorus, "WE. ARE. CURSED." Rahim and Diego exchanged concerned glances in reaction as her voice slowly returned to its previous, angry, bitter timbre. "You will only suffer for having known us. I can promise you that."

"We don't believe that," said Trieu. "Just hold on, okay? Give us a chance to try."

At that, Orna began to scream at the top of her lungs, a piercing, screeching wail like an otherworldly siren blasting through the walls. Diego quickly administered the sedative, and the four agents left the room feeling shaken. Finally, while sitting alone in her bed, with her hands and feet bound by straps, and her eyes bound with gauze, Orna stopped screaming.

| Chapter Forty |

When Rochelle opened her eyes and lifted her head from the table, she found she was alone in her apartment, having passed out in a kitchen chair. Five handles of Absolut vodka were lined up in front of her, standing at attention, like empty soldiers.

Was Jason here in my apartment earlier? Or was I dreaming it?

She picked up a mostly full bottle of Absolut off the floor and chugged it.

Fuck it. Who fucking cares. I'm wasting my energy on a losing battle. I'm done with that.

A pile of unopened mail was staring at her from the kitchen counter. At the top of the pile was a green envelope with no return address. She knew who it was from.

A little Black girl that she didn't recognize walked over to her and took her hand. The girl looked like she was maybe five or six years old, and her afro curls were pulled into two puffs on top of her head. "Don't you want to talk to me, Mommy?" asked the girl.

"Of course I want to, baby," said Rochelle, gently

touching the girl's face. "I've missed you so much."

The little girl threw her head back and began giggling uncontrollably, clapping her hands and stomping her dress shoes.

Rochelle stared at the girl with curiosity as she shifted into the demonic shape of Bram with his nasty-ass fish head before taking the form of Jandro. "Oh, it's you," Rochelle said, drowsily. "You were much cuter before." She chuckled. "You keep hanging around here. You must really like me."

Suddenly she heard a loud boom, as if a bomb had gone off in the sky above her. She looked up at the ceiling as a jagged crack began to stretch diagonally across it. Giant leeches poured into the room through the crack. It was the last thing she remembered before she passed out.

"Roy. Roy. Wake up." Jason was standing over her on the couch, jostling her shoulder.

"How long was I out?" she slurred, struggling to sit up.

"A few seconds," he said. "I'm calling 911. We need to get you to a hospital, Roy." He glanced at the empty soldiers. "Are you trying to kill yourself?"

"No," she said, sliding back down into the couch with a dejected sigh. "But I don't feel any need to live, either. Tell Reid he was wrong. The world doesn't need me. All I ever do is ruin everything."

"Here, drink some of this water. Listen to me. Listen to me! Are you listening? You haven't ruined anything. Listen! You haven't ruined anything. I can get an ambulance over here, or I can take you in my car. I don't know how fast an ambulance can get over here in this traffic. Taking my car is probably faster, but I'm parked two blocks away. Do you think you can walk?

"I don't want to go to the hospital. I want to stay here."

"Staying here is not an option. You need medical attention."

"You can't make me go."

"I will if I have to. But it would be better if you went

willingly. What if we—"

Rochelle interrupted him with the face of someone about to vomit. As her stomach clenched in anticipation, and her gag reflex began to trip, he quickly grabbed a small plastic trash can nearby, and passed it to her.

"Don't look," she said, spitting and then waving at him to turn his head. "Don't want you thinking I'm a lightweight."

"You… are too much right now," he said with a snort, shaking his head. "Let me ask you this. Do you *want* me to help you?"

She stared blankly into the distance without responding.

"Roy," he said, moving his head directly into her line of vision. "Do you want me to help you or not? Do you?"

She took a deep breath and exhaled in several, choppy bursts. "Yes."

"Okay then. Let's start by having you drink some more of this water."

"Don't tell me what to do."

"Let me ask you again. Do you want me to help you?"

"I said yes."

"Then trust me, and drink some of this water. You've puked out enough that maybe we can hold off on going to the hospital right this second. Let's just keep re-hydrating and see how it goes. Okay?"

"Okay."

"Where's Carlos?"

"He's at a hotel. He doesn't love me anymore."

"Somehow I doubt that's true."

"Then why are you the one who's here, and not him?"

"You'll have to ask him that. But I can tell you one thing for sure. It's hard to see you in this state, Roy. You're one of the strongest women I know. If it was Natasha doing what you're doing right now, I don't know if I could take it."

"Nobody asked you to be here."

"It wasn't a criticism. It's just hard to see you suffering so much. I'm here because I choose to be, because I see so much potential in you. It kills me to see it go to waste."

"Potential for what? Potential to be the biggest loser on the planet?"

"Potential to be a happy, joyful person."

"Bahaha," she said, laughing. "Doubt it."

"Believe it," he said.

She heaved another choppy sigh.

"I didn't know you had a daughter," he said, taking a seat in the armchair facing the couch. He felt his cell phone vibrate, and looked at the caller ID. It was Reid. He silenced the call.

"Who told you that?" she said, glancing over at the kitchen counter. "Were you reading my mail?"

"What? No, of course not. You were out of it, and talking about her to someone. It looked like you were having a hallucination."

"I got a letter today from my friends Tim and Sandra, who adopted her twelve years ago," she said with some effort. "She wants to meet me."

"Twelve years ago? You mean... while you were at FLETC?"

"I got pregnant right after I graduated. Efren was the father."

"Holy shit. I wasn't that far behind you in basic, I had no idea. Does Carlos know?"

"No. I haven't told anyone. Not Carlos, not my family, not anyone. Except you. By accident. Now, if you'll excuse me, I need to go use the bathroom, if that's alright with you."

"Of course, go ahead."

While she was in the bathroom, he called Reid. "It's not looking good. She needs to take immediate medical leave, sir."

"Put her on the phone, Jefferson. That's an order."

She's punishing herself. Talking to you is going to make

her feel guilty, and make it worse. "With all due respect sir, I can't do that right now. Let me help her sober up, and I'll have her call you as soon as I can. I've never disobeyed an order before, you know that. But the state she's in right now is extremely volatile. I'm asking you to please give her some time, sir—if you will. She's too valuable to our team to risk sabotaging her willingness to get help."

"Fine, I'll trust your judgment on this. Do what you need to do, Jefferson. Check back in with me when you have an update."

"Understood." Jason pocketed his phone and looked at his watch. "Hey, Roy?" he said, walking over to the bathroom and knocking on the door. "You been in there a while, is everything okay?"

When she didn't answer, he tried the knob, finding it unlocked. "Roy?" he said, opening the door a crack and catching sight of her sitting on the floor with her back against the wall, fingers wrapped around a bottle of vodka. "What the hell! You had vodka stashed in the *bathroom*?" He pulled it out of her hand and poured it down the sink.

"Wait," she said half-heartedly, remaining planted on the floor. "I wasn't done with that."

He went back into the kitchen and came back with another glass of water, sitting down on the floor next to her. "Have some of this instead. It's going to be a long night."

| Chapter Forty-One |

"Abitha, do you hear me?" A deep male voice echoed in the darkness of Abitha's mind.

Abitha turned her head to locate the source of the sound, but all she could see was darkness through the blindfold, and the sound seemed to be coming from everywhere at once. "Yes, I hear you. Is it you, Nimbeau?"

"Yes, clever girl, it is I. What is your physical location, my Queen?"

"I'm not certain, but I believe they have us jailed at some kind of almshouse. Are you not able to project yourself here?"

"For some reason, I cannot. There's an electromagnetic pyramid surrounding the entire building, which prevents me from being able to get any closer to you. I'm now communicating with you telepathically, using a frequency that they must not have anticipated, or else I presume they would have taken measures to shield you from that as well."

"Who do you mean by 'they'?"

"Your jailers. I have to assume it is not by accident that they have you contained inside such a shield. They are more advanced in astral manipulation than I anticipated, although their efforts are still somewhat rudimentary. I see that they've also managed to bind Bram to his current body to prevent him from killing himself, which may work to our advantage. It would be best, nevertheless, to proceed with our gris-gris plan and not leave his fate in the hands of amateurs."

"What if leaving this telepathic frequency open was not an oversight? What if they've allowed it in order to eavesdrop?"

"A sensible theory. That would certainly be sly, but theoretically, I should be able to sense the presence of eavesdroppers. Nevertheless, since it's the only means we have to communicate at this point, it's a risk we have to take. As your abilities evolve, this form of communication will gradually become unnecessary."

"Nimbeau, am I a witch?"

"Yes you are, as are your three sisters, as are the women whose bodies you're occupying. Not for having been raped by a demon, but by virtue of your lineage. You descend from the children of Nephilim."

"How could we descend from the children of Nephilim if they were all destroyed in the Great Flood?" asked Abitha.

"That's a story for another day. Just know that the children of Noah fear your power, and they will attack you the only way they know how: through your physical mortality. They have no idea how much karmic power they've given away to you, cloaked within every mindless assault. They are the serpent and you are the bird. Your wings are your ability to influence events with the magic of your intention. You have the potential for so much more though, Abitha. You've all been kept in cages. I'll be able to show you and your three sisters whole new worlds once this matter of Bram is resolved."

"Like what?"

"There's not much time to explain. I have no choice but to leave you to discover and explore on your own. I will monitor your progress from afar. Your ability to communicate telepathically is already rapidly developing. You will discover other abilities in time. The important thing is to get to Bram as quickly as possible, initiate the gris-gris, and stop him before he does any more damage. Focus on that intention, and do not allow yourselves distractions."

"How are we to get to Bram? We're bound at the hands and feet, and that's not the least of our problems."

"Your mind has been conditioned to limit itself to the physical realm. Learn to quiet your mind. Listen to your body. Let yourself feel *good*. I know you've been discouraged from feeling good by Puritanical conditioning. They knew that feeling good would activate abilities in you that they wouldn't be able to control—powers of manifestation. Let go of what you think you know. Let yourself open naturally to new possibilities. You'll soon be able to navigate the astral realm, just as I'm doing right now. You can start by taking a look around. What do you see?"

"They have me blindfolded. I can't see anything."

"Even better. You've been gifted with freedom from the distraction of your physical vision. When you begin to see things with your astral vision, pay attention. Be aware of the vibrations in your body, and let them guide you. Remember, feelings, not words."

"My body is hurting all over. It's hard to concentrate on anything else. I don't know how to feel good like this."

"Get inside your magic, Abitha. I know you don't fully understand yet what that means, but it's all I can tell you for now. You'll find your way into it."

"Is there time for one more question?"

"Yes, what is it?"

"Are you sure the host body is okay with what we're doing? Her name is Olena. I can feel her. It's like she's sleeping inside of me, but I've been reliving her memories. I sound like her when I speak. It feels so strange. I'm not myself. Her pain is wrapped around me like a cloak. It's suffocating. It doesn't feel right."

"Do not be alarmed, Queen Abitha. She abandoned her body long ago. Had she not, we could not have borrowed it as we did. You must remind yourself that we're not borrowing it in order to bring her harm. We're borrowing it in order to bring her justice. He who strangled the life from her body is he who did the same to you. You're feeling her call to action. Let her pain keep your righteous anger alive. Do you think you can do that, Abitha?"

"I think so."

"Very good. I must take my leave now. I will contact you again in approximately twelve hours of Earth time. While the rest of the world goes to sleep, you and your sisters will be awakening. Thank you for your assistance, Abitha. I will speak with you again soon."

Abitha could sense Nimbeau's gradual disappearance like a dissipating mist. Once again, it was dark and quiet inside her head, inside her blindfold, inside her darkened room. And yet, the noise of her physical pain enveloped her with a deafening volume. She noticed a quiet trembling vibration in her chest, and focused her attention on it to help keep her centered amidst the flood of sensations.

A small blob of whitish blue light appeared in the center of her vision, and shifted, growing slowly larger until she felt she was swimming in it. It was casting a dim light into the room around her, and even though her eyes were still closed and the blindfold still in place, she could see in her mind's eye that the room she was in was now lit up with a pale blue-gray light.

She sat up and raised her right arm to take a closer look at her hand. The "skin" of her astral body seemed to be a transparent, swirling rainbow, like the surface of a soap bubble. The arm of her physical body had remained where it was, lying at her side with the leather strap buckled around it. *I'm coming out of my body,* she thought. On realizing that she could possibly walk freely around the room using her astral body, she had the desire to lift herself out of bed, but was suddenly unable to. Her mind was a flood of thoughts. *How was I able to lift my astral arm just now? How do I un-tether the rest of me? What am I saying? I've truly gone mad. Am I only a figment of Olena's dream? Abitha is dead. Abitha is dead. Abitha is dead.*

Olena's physical body began screaming again, and Abitha couldn't stop it. Her fingers dug into the sheets at her sides, every muscle in her body tensed, desperate for the suffering to end. Alarmed and terrified that something had gone terribly wrong, Abitha tried changing the course of her thoughts. *No! I'm not dead. I'm not dead. I'm not dead. We're not dead. We still have a chance. I'm going to help you, Olena.*

The screaming stopped.

My mind needs to stop talking and just listen. Stop that talking. Stop it! Be quiet. Be quiet!

After a few minutes of lying still, she was struck by how impossible it was to achieve silence by continually ordering herself to stop talking. *Do what Nimbeau said and listen to your breathing.*

The constant chatter of her thoughts slowly came to a standstill as she shifted her attention to the sound of her breathing. Tears began to fall silently out of her eyes as she listened intently to the shifting rhythm of her chest and diaphragm rising and falling as her muscles steadily inflated and deflated her lungs.

Staring up through her blindfolded eyelids at the astral ceiling above, she became aware that she was floating upwards, and slowly panned her head toward her left shoulder to see Olena's body lying in the bed below her. *I did it!* she thought, as her astral body snapped back into her physical body as if to say that no, she hadn't. *Okay, don't get discouraged,* she reassured herself. *I'm on the right track. I need to keep trying.*

After what felt like hours of silently listening to the sound of her breathing (but was actually only a minute or two), she felt herself floating upward again. Her astral body was similar to her physical human form, but radiating a pale white-blue light. Up and up she floated, until she passed through the ceiling and looked down like a giant eye on the room she had come from. There was a bright blue, glowing, astral pyramid housing her room, with Olena's body lying in bed in the center of it.

In the distance, she could see a translucent golden pyramid, and in the center of that pyramid was another woman lying in bed. *"It's Kemi!"* she realized. *"Kemi, it's me, Abitha! Can you hear me?"*

Kemi responded telepathically. *"Abitha! Are you alright? Where are you?"*

"I'm learning astral projection. I'm floating in the air above you. I'll come into your room where you are. Do you see me? I don't know how to explain it. But Nimbeau said there would be abilities awakening in us and the others as well."

"I can't see you, but I know that he speaks the truth. Last night, I was paying close attention to some type of fixture on the wall—I could sense the electricity pulsing through it. It was calling me. I raised my hands up and sparks came out of the palms of my hands like lightning. It connected to the wall fixture and it burst into flames."

"Oh, I know what that is! It's..." She paused as the word came to her. *"Electrokinesis."*

"I've never heard of that. How do you know this?"

"I don't know. I just know things somehow. It's as if I'm walking along a road and picking up words along the way, as they float by. Does it make sense to you, Kemi? I don't know how else to describe it. But what you have is the gift of electrokinesis. Maybe pyrokinesis too. I have the gift of astral vision. I'm not sure what else. It's like opening gifts at Christmas. You don't know what you're going to get!"

"Don't worry Abitha, it doesn't have to make sense. Just breathe and trust it. We need to figure out a way to get out of

here. Can you locate Talisa and Temperance?"

"I see a red pyramid in the distance. Temperance is trapped inside. Talisa's in an emerald green one. I'll travel to their rooms and speak with them. Kemi, the source of your power is literally in your hands. Whatever you do, don't let them bind your hands. Somehow that white gauze is limiting our powers."

"I won't. I believe I could create another fire, but we have to be careful. We were lucky the first time. They blamed the fire on the priestess and arrested her. If I repeat the act a second time, they may soon suspect that I was the source."

Abitha floated upward through the roof and took a broad look at the architecture of the building, and then returned to Kemi inside of her gold pyramid. "I see that you're in a room with a window," said Abitha. "At the foot of the building, beneath your window there is a gray box which supplies power to the entire building. If you can manage to send a power surge into the box, you could disable all of the electricity in the building, so no one will be able to get in or out. Now that the outside entrance has been sealed off due to the fire, the only way into the building is through an underground transit system which passes through an abandoned tunnel. All the windows and doors to the building are barred from the outside. Having the electricity disabled will buy us some time."

"Very well. I will practice developing my... electrokinesis. You go talk to Talisa and Temperance and find out what gifts they've opened."

| Chapter Forty-Two |

"Boss, we've got three of them bound in gauze," said Rahim, on the phone with Reid. "We're getting ready to go in to assess and bind Abeni, or however she's self-identifying now. Not sure if it's a good idea to remove the restraints, though, after everything that's happened with the other three."

"Restraint protocol calls for its use when harm to self or others is imminent," said Reid. "Have any of them tried to physically harm any of you, or themselves?"

"Physically? No, not really. Just manifesting some unpredictable, supernatural behaviors."

"Their restraint orders have expired. Varma's the one with the authority to renew them, but even if she does, you can't keep Abeni in restraints based solely on the behaviors of the other three. Let her get out of bed, get up and around. Stay vigilant. Keep that gauze at hand."

"Understood, sir," said Rahim.

"Good work, Kings," said Reid. "Chen should be arriving any time now to help get a read on the situation."

"I'll check back in with you after we finish assessing Abeni." Rahim hung up the phone, as Diego loaded up another syringe with a sedative.

"I'm a little on edge after Orna," said Lluc. "She wields words like swords."

"You okay?" asked Trieu.

"I'm okay," said Lluc. "Just caught me off guard. I'll live. Let's just get it done."

"Gauze?" said Diego.

Rahim held up a fresh roll. "Check," he said.

Diego reached over and unlocked the door to Abeni's room.

"Good evening," said Rahim.

Kemi stared with concern at the sight of four men entering the room.

"What do you want from us?" she asked.

"We're here to help you, Abeni," said Trieu. "Or, how would you prefer that we address you?"

"You can call me Sin Chronic."

"Nice to meet you, Sin Chronic," said Trieu, who caught himself staring for a moment. She reminded him of his best friend, Xuân, who was killed in a landslide in Long An, Vietnam, when she and Trieu were teenagers. "We're going to remove the leather straps. You don't want to hurt us, do you?" His voice was so gentle and earthy that for a moment, the blazing strength of her anger, fueled by the searing pain of inflammation all over her body, was slowed to a molten lava.

"No. You're not the ones I want to hurt. I *will* hurt you, though, if you try to stop me from getting to Bram."

"We mean you no harm," said Lluc. "Please trust us."

Sin Chronic drew a deep breath and exhaled as Trieu and Lluc approached to unbuckle her arms and legs. Gently, they pulled the straps away from her limbs and helped her sit up.

"I'm feeling so much pain," said Sin Chronic. "I need my crack pipe." Not having any idea what a crack pipe was, Sin Chronic wondered why those words had come out of her mouth.

"We can get you some more medication to help with the withdrawals," said Trieu. "They'll pass over time. We're just here to keep you safe while you ride them out. We want to help you recover your health."

"May I take a look out the window?" she said. "It's been so long since I've seen the outside world."

"Of course," said Trieu. "Here, use this stool to step down."

Holding onto the arms of Trieu and Lluc as they escorted her to the window, Sin Chronic wobbled the few steps. It was a clear night, and the city of Manhattan was teeming with lights. In the distance, she could see the top of the Empire State Building towering over its neighbors. She had never seen anything like it. Tears began to fall from her eyes as she tried to process the physical abuse she had experienced since she had taken over Abeni's body.

"Some day you'll look back on all of this like it was a bad dream," said Trieu gently. "I know it's hard right now, but I promise it will get better. Just breathe and hold on."

Sin Chronic's eyes followed the windowsill down the wall to the edge of the gray breaker box that she could dimly see below. "Yes," said Sin Chronic slowly. "I do believe that things will get better in time."

With a controlled burst of electricity, she sent a lightning shockwave from her palms through the biceps of Lluc and Trieu. They were thrown back against the wall and knocked unconscious, as a jolt of exhilaration surged through her. Her eyes widened as she stopped for a moment and inhaled deeply, speechless and awestruck by her own power.

"Quick!" said Diego, raising the syringe. "It's her hands!"

Sin Chronic whipped around to face them as Rahim and Diego each reached forward to take hold of her arms, but she swiftly dispatched both of them with an outward flick of her wrists, knocking them to the floor unconscious with bursts of electricity shooting from her palms.

After walking over to remove the keys from Trieu's belt, she looked out the window and focused her attention on the gray box at the foot of the wall. *I'm not trying to start a fire,* she guided herself. *Just enough to disable power to the building.*

She relaxed her mind and visualized an eruption of gold light, which filled her head and chest and then trickled into her arms. A warm, tickling sensation came over her hands and a bolt of gold lightning leaped from her palms, shattering the window glass, as she maneuvered it into the breaker box below. The fluorescent light fixture above her flickered for a moment and then went dark, like a candle being blown out. Leaving the four kings lying on the floor, she stepped out into the hallway and locked the door.

| Chapter Forty-Three |

Lin Mei's phone rang. It was Reid. "What's your status, Chen?"

"I'm here at Glen Haven. The power's gone down at Ophelia's Wing. We can't call the shuttle or communicate with anyone inside. Backup generators aren't working either, for some reason. All the windows and doors are barred from the outside. With all due respect, sir, why did we not move the vics to another safe house after the fire?"

"There's special telecommunications technology only in use at that location. I can't get into a lot of detail right now, Chen, it's classified. There are two secret fire exits not visible from the outside. The kings know how to access them, and so do the clinical staff. But moving the vics is not an option. How's it looking at Glen Haven?"

"We're on a separate power grid, sir. Power is still intact over here. Any luck getting a hold of Rochelle?"

Reid sighed. "Roy... is in the middle of a meltdown. Jefferson's over there holding space for her. Any luck finding a Voodoo consultant?"

I'm in the middle of a meltdown myself. "No, not at this

time of night. No one's answering phones. What's our next step?"

"We need to get a hold of Roy's cousin. She's in secure confinement, right there at Glen Haven. Find her, ask her what she needs, and get it for her."

"Understood. I'm on it." Lin Mei hung up the phone and tried to call Midori. It went straight to voicemail. Lin Mei heaved a heavy sigh. She was sitting inside a consultation room which was soundproofed for privacy, and staring blankly at the wall in front of her. If only she could just take a nap. It was excruciating to feel so tired. She rested her head against the wall and quickly fell asleep.

She had a nightmare that aliens were using a radio signal to take control of her body. In the dream, she was still sitting there in the same room at Glen Haven, and her surroundings looked so real that she could almost believe she was still awake. The sound of a radio frequency was squealing in the back of her head, mixed with the sound of static, like they were tuning the dial on an old analog radio, searching for the right frequency. Once they found it, they used her hands to pick up and unlock her phone and began looking at her email through her eyes, trying to read the phrase "Ophelia's Wing" out loud from a message she had received earlier that day, sounding out each syllable and repeatedly mispronouncing it. "Up... hill... I... as... why. Up hell... I as wing." The sensation of some other being manipulating her mouth to speak in her own voice—words that looked like English but sounded foreign—was so disturbing that she woke in a lurch.

She stared around the room, not sure at first if she was still dreaming, then noticed a ceiling vent blowing cool air into the room, creating white noise. With her scientist mind, she decided that her subconscious must have been incorporating that sound into her dream, and was trying to calm herself with that idea, when several pale, swamp-green, eel-shaped wraiths appeared in a flash, slithering on the walls, and then vanished from sight, as if a projector had turned them on and off.

This time she knew she wasn't dreaming, and her pulse accelerated. Before she could process their significance, a woman materialized on the other side of the room who seemed to be a clone of Lin Mei, wearing the same hairstyle and clothing, sitting across from her in another chair. "Dr. Chen," said the woman. "Aren't you the one with the gay husband?"

"No," said Lin Mei, tilting her head, perplexed at the question, not thinking too hard about her answer. "*I'm* the gay husband."

The skin of the woman's face began to distort and stretch and change into the form of her father as she remembered him during her childhood. Just the momentary glimpse of her father's tortured face brought a flood of emotions cascading over her, triggering the memory of his death when she was ten years old living in Taiwan.

Her father had never talked to Lin Mei about his post-traumatic stress from World War II; she only knew of it due to vague allusions her mother had shared with her years after his death. On the fateful day of his death, the details of which fleetingly overwhelmed her senses, Lin Mei had come home from school to find her father suffering, as he frequently did, from a bout of alcohol psychosis. Physical abuse toward Lin Mei and her mother was not unusual during one of his episodes, but on this occasion, he had her mother tied to a chair in the kitchen. Her face was bleeding. He was crying. He told Lin Mei he had been waiting for her to come home from school so they could all be purified by fire together. The room smelled of gasoline, and it didn't take Lin Mei long to assess the situation. She knew if he caught hold of her, she would soon be tied up as well; she quickly slipped out of reach and ran into her parents' bedroom, digging out his revolver from what he thought was a secret hiding place. She shot him between the eyes with it.

Her father's tormented visage disappeared as quickly as it had appeared, as the face of Bram and the shape of his fish head began to emerge instead atop the woman's body, which still otherwise looked like Lin Mei. It was as if the alter ego were a projection manifesting from within Lin Mei's subconscious, and Bram's face seemed to be struggling to take possession of it. But the form of the woman's head kept snapping back to that of mirroring Lin Mei, as if Bram was having trouble establishing a foothold. Lin Mei stared at the apparition dumbfounded, like a deer in headlights.

Still invisible, one of the wraiths began to slither across her shoulders. Shaken out of her stupor, she shrieked and quickly pushed it to the floor, lurching toward the door in a panic to exit the room.

Halfway down the hallway, she stopped to catch her breath, wondering if they would pursue. They didn't.

What the hell was that about? Christ. Should I tell Reid about this? He's seriously going to think I've lost my mind. Maybe I have lost my mind. But what about all this other paranormal activity? Everyone's going crazy at the same time? That's not it. I've got to pull myself together, get a hold of Titi and see if she has any idea what's going on.

| Chapter Forty-Four |

Lin Mei cautiously returned to the hospital lounge where some burnt coffee was still left in the carafe. Her hands shaking as she filled a paper cup and chugged it, she struggled to calm herself. The caffeine acted quickly in accelerating her pulse, but she still felt as exhausted as ever.

After several phone calls to find out exactly where Titi was being held, and several phone calls more to get the clearance to speak with her, Lin Mei at last arrived at Titi's secure containment room. She knocked on the door and a male orderly let her in. "Hi Titi. Rough night, huh? I'm sorry about what happened between you and Rochelle."

"It wasn't your fault."

"I sympathize. I don't know if it helps, but Rochelle honestly believed she was doing the right thing. She wasn't trying to hurt you."

"You came here to tell me that?"

"I came to ask for your help. The power is down at Ophelia's Wing. We don't have the first clue what's going on. Reid, my boss, said to find you, ask you what you need, and get it for you."

"What I need first of all is to get off these antipsychotics. They're interfering with my psychic and clairvoyant abilities. I feel dead inside. I don't know how anyone thinks they're helping me by giving me these drugs."

"I'm sorry they don't have a good regimen figured out for you," said Lin Mei. "For some people, hallucinations can be extremely cruel."

"I take issue with your calling them hallucinations, but let's just say they are. What's so damn wrong with having hallucinations if I'm not committing any harmful behaviors?"

"There's nothing wrong with it. You can't help what you see, I understand that. Reid understands. We also can't help that we just don't see the same things that you do. I'm here now to ask you to share your insights with us. We understand that we need you. Will you help us?"

"What will it take to get me out of here and get me off of these meds? I don't want to jeopardize Carlos' misconduct investigation. But I need to get out of here."

"I know of a great psychiatrist who might be able to help you. Her name is Dr. Sophia Pomme-Verte. She's African American—she immigrated to the U.S. from Cameroon as a child. She's also a spiritualist, like you. I'll see if she's available to meet with you tonight, or tomorrow morning."

"See if you can talk to Veronica about it and cancel my appointment with that other doctor she wanted me to see."

"Oh. Do I really need to speak with Veronica?"

"I don't blame you for not wanting to," Titi said with a tired laugh. "But she told me that she needs to get me established under the care of another psychiatrist who's not Carlos for the sake of the misconduct investigation. So please, I urge you, see if you can get this Dr. Pomme-Verte on the phone. I don't think I need to tell you, time is of the essence. We need to get through to these vics before they get through to Jandro."

"If they do get to Jandro before we get to them, and carry

out whatever it is they plan on doing, isn't it fair to say his karma brought it on himself?"

"If that's how it plays out, sure. But I'll be honest, Jandro is not my focus right now. The four queens and the displaced spirits piloting their bodies are walking a thin line. Their hearts haven't succumbed yet to pure evil. I can see in their eyes a speck of hope. If they indulge themselves in vengeful cruelty, a demonic euphoria will sink into their flesh like a vampire and consume their souls. We *must* stop that from happening, if we can. If we allow ourselves the sadistic pleasure of torturing Jandro for his sins, then the evil begins to take hold in us too."

"Let me make some more phone calls. I'll come back as soon as I can." She started towards the door, but then stopped and turned back to Titi. "Something really strange just happened to me downstairs. I was in the soundproof consultation room, and had a weird vision... eel-like creatures were crawling around on the walls. They disappeared from view, but then one of them slithered across my chest. It was still invisible but I could feel it. I pushed it off me and ran out of the room. It seriously freaked me out."

Titi frowned in concern. "I've seen them before, in a dream. They're connected to Bram somehow... like they're his minions. Or they could even be like a form of appendage that detaches from his body."

"They were circling the room, and didn't come near me until I started to panic."

"What caused the panic?"

Lin Mei was too ashamed to share the post-traumatic memory of her father. "I saw a vision of myself, like an alter ego, but I don't know if that's what caused the panic. It was the sight of those things crawling around on the walls that triggered something visceral in me."

"Hm. It's almost as if they revealed themselves in order to incite a fearful reaction."

"What would be the point of that?"

"I don't know. Maybe they're attracted to and feed on fear."

"Great. Do you think we can get rid of them by getting rid of Bram?"

"I have no idea. I'm a spiritualist, not a demonologist. But I hope so. Yet another reason we need to make preparations for Jandro to be exorcised along with these four. With the right ingredients of effort, hope, faith, belief and luck, we might succeed in banishing the demon back to the abyss from which it came."

"You think we have all that?"

"Those are the ingredients we need. It's not optional."

"What about this power outage at Ophelia's Wing? Any ideas?"

"I suspect the vics are working some type of psychokinesis. But I don't know how good any advice I give is going to be while I'm on these psych meds. My intuition is impaired."

"Okay. Let me step outside, get some fresh air and go make some phone calls. I'll be back when I have some news for you. We've got the four kings over there helping us, too."

"The who?"

"My boss calls them the four kings, I don't know why. They're special agents who have training as forensic nurses. They were assigned to work security at Ophelia's Wing. It's interesting that you call the vics the four queens."

"Four kings and four queens... just like the Tarot. Can I ask one more favor of you? Can I borrow your cell phone to check my voicemail? I'm just wondering if I've heard from Adrian. Someone I've recently started dating, back in New Orleans."

"Of course," said Lin Mei, passing her cell phone to Titi. Titi anxiously dialed her voicemail service and discovered she did have one new voice message, and it was from Adrian.

"Hey beautiful," he said. "Sorry I missed you again. I was tied up on a call with a client and couldn't get away. Something in the sound of your voice from your last message tells me you're tied up with something important too, so I'll just share this quote with you and catch up with you later. It's from a first-century Syrian poet named Al-Buhturi. He wrote, 'Is not the example of God's prophet, Joseph, a sufficient consolation for him who, like thee, is imprisoned on an unjust and false accusation? He long remained in bondage with patient resignation, and patient resignation made him master of an empire.'"

After a moment of silence, Adrian then hung up, or else the call dropped, without any closing remarks. Titi stared wide-eyed at the phone.

"What is it?" asked Lin Mei, concerned.

"Uh, it was Adrian."

"Do you want to call him back?"

"I… uh. I don't think so. Not right now. Do you know if Rochelle told anyone where I am?"

"She felt so terrible about the whole thing, I honestly don't think it's the kind of thing she would go blabbing to anyone who wasn't already privy to the information."

Was it a psychic insight? Or random synchronicity? If he really did somehow know the details of her situation, she felt more shame in it than consolation, and quickly brought her attention back to the urgency of the moment. "Listen, Lin Mei. Please, go make your calls. Thank you and Reid for helping me. I see how tired you are right now. Seeing an alter ego sounds like the beginnings of dissociation. You've been taking care of everyone except yourself—believe me, I know what that's like. Be kind to yourself," she said, taking Lin Mei's hand and squeezing it tightly. "I pray this nightmare will end soon, for all of us. *Ashè*."

| Chapter Forty-Five |

"Do you remember what it was that inspired you to become a special agent?" asked Jason, still sitting on the bathroom carpet next to Rochelle.

"Yeah," she said, beginning to sober up enough to answer his questions. "It was visiting my dad in prison at the age of seventeen. I was so angry with him. That was when I decided to legally change my last name to my mother's maiden name."

"So your pop's getting out of prison now, huh?"

"Yeah. Thirty-one years for a crime he didn't commit. Can you believe it?"

"God works in mysterious ways."

"Sure. Next you're going to tell me everything happens for a reason."

"I don't know if I would put it that way. What if I just tell you that silver linings can usually be found where you look for them?"

"Sometimes no reason will ever be good enough."

"Silver linings are not about justification. They're about finding something to live for, paving the way to move forward. When you get to the point where you find yourself looking for silver linings, that's how you know you're healing."

Rochelle felt inclined to change the subject. "What about you? What inspired you to become a special agent?"

"It started when I interrupted a rape at the age of eleven."

"Wow. I never knew that. That's rough."

"Yeah, it was," he said, stroking his chin as a way of mitigating his vulnerability. "It was behind the apartment building where we lived back in Chicago. At least I stopped it by shouting for help, but the guy got away. I wasn't happy about that."

"It's not your fault. You were just a kid. What you did was brave. Don't be so hard on yourself."

"It's not that I think it's my fault. It just awakened something in me. Something like a sense of responsibility."

"How can you feel responsible for something if it wasn't your fault?"

"I think of responsibility as ability to respond. Response-*ability*. An inner calling to be part of the solution, even if I didn't cause the problem. The idea of punishing who's at fault is problematic for karma and other reasons. Justice needs to be about restoration, not retribution. It needs to be about the healing, not inflicting more pain. And blame rarely falls on just one person. We can look at parenting and societal shortcomings, ignorance, illness, cycles of abuse, and all kinds of other contributing factors, but I think responsibility can be more than simple than that. Blame can take us in never ending circles. I mean, don't get me wrong, holding someone accountable for harmful behaviors means measures should be taken to protect public safety while we sort out how to heal the wound. All I'm saying is leave out the hate, and the vengeful, sadistic intention to punish. Our focus needs to be on setting the right boundaries for everyone to heal."

"Hm." Her attention was clearly elsewhere.

He smiled. "Maybe now is not the right time to talk

about this."

She leaned forward and attempted to stand up. "I think I need to go for a walk. You're welcome to hang out here if you want. I just need some fresh air."

"Some fresh air on the way to the liquor store?" he said suspiciously, remaining seated.

"You don't need to treat me like I'm a two-year-old, alright?"

"You said you'd accept my help, Roy. Do you still want me to help you?"

"Yes."

"Okay, then let's hang out here for a while, is that alright?"

"Does Natasha know you're here?"

"Yes, she does."

"I mean, what are you *really* doing here, Jefferson? What do you want from me? What do you expect to get out of this?"

"I'm holding space for you, Roy. Because I can, and because I want to. And because you need that right now."

"Holding space."

"Yeah."

"For how long?"

"However long it takes for you to consider getting some professional counseling and maybe checking into an outpatient rehab."

"You'll be waiting a while then."

"If that's what it takes."

"I got a letter from Sandra today. Where is it?"

"I wouldn't know. Where did you see it last?"

"I guess it was in the kitchen. It was in a green envelope. Her letters come in green envelopes. She's my daughter's adoptive mother."

"Let's go get it, and have a seat on the couch. You should try to drink more of this water."

"I need to go for a walk."

"Stick it out with me here, Roy. Please? We can get through this. Things can get better. Just give it a chance."

Feeling too tired to argue anymore, Rochelle pulled herself to her feet, retrieved the green envelope from the kitchen counter and moved to the living room couch.

"The envelope is still sealed?" said Jason. "I thought you said you read it already?"

"I did?"

"Yeah, you said that your daughter wanted to meet you."

"I must have been dreaming."

"Are you going to open it?"

"Yeah. Just give me a minute. I think I'm too sober for reading this right now."

"How about if you just try to get some rest. The letter can wait."

"It's okay, I want to read it now. But do you mind if I fix myself some coffee?"

"Go ahead."

She dragged herself back to the kitchen and pulled a mug out of the cabinet. Peeking around the corner to see if Jason was watching, she pulled another bottle of vodka out of the cabinet and poured it into her coffee mug.

"Hey! Whoa! This is what you call coffee?" said Jefferson, catching sight of her and running into the kitchen. He pulled the bottle out of her hand and poured it down the sink.

"You're no fun," she sulked.

"Don't you get it, Roy? We *need* you. Whoever it was that made you feel worthless, they were *wrong*. You hear me? They were wrong. You don't need them to tell you what you're worth. You just need to look in the mirror and see it for yourself. Don't you know how much of a rare jewel you are? To me, to everyone on our team. You've got this gold crown on your head and you don't even know. We've always been blinded by your light. Everyone loves you. What will it take for you to love yourself?"

"I don't know," she said, her voice trembling as tears came to her eyes. "I wish I could care, but I just don't anymore."

"You're depressed. You can get on an antidepressant. You can get therapy. Trust me, help from a capable therapist can make a world of difference. It's nothing to be ashamed of."

"I don't want any medications."

"What do you think alcohol is? You're self-medicating with alcohol. It's making your depression worse, not better. There are other paths you can take."

"There's nothing I can do to help anything. It's like you've said before. It's a never ending cycle. We arrest one crime boss, another pops up. I'm tired of fighting this fight. It doesn't matter to me anymore. The world can go on without me. It doesn't make any difference."

"It matters to the victims you've freed from slavery. Every single one of them has the opportunity to turn their lives around, thanks to you. It matters. You matter."

"I wish I could believe that. But I feel too ashamed of what I've done. I can't forgive myself."

"Forgive yourself for what?"

"For giving my daughter up for adoption. She must think I'm the worst mother on the planet. I know I do."

"There are far worse things a mother could do. Give her a chance to understand."

"She won't forgive me. She'll never forgive me."

"Something tells me it's not your daughter you're talking about that won't forgive you."

"I need to go for a walk, Jason."

"Okay, fine. I'll come with you, okay? Let me just take a piss before we go."

When he came out of the bathroom, she was gone.

| Chapter Forty-Six |

Lin Mei stepped out of the revolving glass doors that connected the Glen Haven welcome lobby to the outside world, and took a deep breath of the balmy autumn air.

There was a tall, slender Black woman wearing a colorful headwrap and small round glasses, standing a close distance away on the sidewalk, facing the entrance and gazing intently at Lin Mei, who gave her a cursory glance before looking awkwardly down at her phone to make a call.

A melodic ringtone began to ring, and the mysterious woman raised her cell phone to her ear to answer it. "I've been expecting your call," she said, as Lin Mei suddenly realized that the woman's voice was the same as the one coming from the speaker of her phone.

"Are you... Dr. Sophia Pomme-Verte?" said Lin Mei, half speaking into her phone before fully registering that the person at the other end of the line really was standing right in front of her. She hung up the phone and walked over to the woman.

"Please, call me Sophie," she said, gracefully pocketing her phone and offering her hand.

"I'm Dr. Lin Mei Chen," said Lin Mei, shaking her hand, then adding with a quizzical smile, "or... did you know that already?"

"I don't know who you are, or in what way I'm to help you. But I've known for quite some time that I should meet you here in this exact place, at this exact hour. To do what is yet to be revealed."

"Well, we definitely need your help. I'm a forensic psychologist at the FBI Human Trafficking Unit. We've been working a tough case that appears to have some kind of... supernatural element. If you could please follow me inside, there's someone I would like for you to meet. I'll explain on the way."

From the moment Sophie entered the room, a sense of calm washed over Titi.

"Ms. Titi Beaumond?" said Sophie, reaching her hand out for a handshake. "Dr. Hagia Sophia Pomme-Verte. But please, call me Sophie."

Titi stood up and straightened out the hospital pajamas she was wearing before reaching forward to shake Sophie's hand. "Thank you for seeing me on such short notice."

"The honor is mine," said Sophie. "And now, Dr. Chen, I encourage you to go home and get some rest. Someone you love is there, waiting for you."

Even though she was worried about seeming unprofessional, Lin Mei couldn't help stepping forward and offering Sophie a hug, which Sophie warmly accepted. "Thank you," said Lin Mei, feeling hopeful. "I'll keep you both in my prayers, and the four queens too."

"We're going to begin by chanting some Vedic mantras," said Sophie after Lin Mei left. She reached into her bag and pulled out a fountain pen and a small notebook. "I've instructed the hospitalist to discontinue your antipsychotic medications that were scheduled for 8 p.m.—I'm glad that we were able to begin your chanting therapy before that happened. I'm going to phonetically write some Sanskrit words for you to chant with me. As you may already know, chanting, like singing, will stimulate your vagus nerve, and help to alleviate symptoms of depression or anxiety that you may currently be suffering. The difference between this and singing is that you'll be chanting a mantra which has the focused intention to liberate you from malevolent influence. We'll begin chanting in five-minute increments and gradually work our way up to longer stretches, until you're able to comfortably chant for an hour."

"Why do we have to start in such small increments? Let's just do an hour."

"It's not as easy as it sounds," said Sophie. "It's going to release some emotional tension at first; you may feel the need to meditate or grieve afterward to process it. We'll monitor your reaction to it and set the pace by how strongly it's impacting you."

Titi nodded, her eyes open wide at the prospect of getting off of the antipsychotics. "Are you... Buddhist?" she asked as Sophie jotted the mantra to paper.

"In Cameroon, I was raised in the Baha'i Faith," said Sophie, looking up at Titi with smiling eyes. "The Baha'i Faith is syncretic, in many ways, like Voodoo. But nowadays, I call myself a non-denominational spiritualist. A pantheist, if you like."

"Not that I mind at all," said Titi, "I'm loving it, to be honest—but isn't it a bit unusual for a psychiatrist to rely on faith-based treatments in place of pharmaceuticals?"

"I have nothing against pharmaceuticals, and am happy to prescribe them when they're needed. That includes cannabis, MDMA, and psychedelic medicine, to name a few. Pharmaceuticals are useful tools when applied properly. But unless we as prescribers work in harmony with the spiritual worldview of the patient, then these tools aren't as effective.

Obviously, beliefs can vary greatly based on spiritual and religious orientation. Dr. Chen tells me you're a Vodouisant, and I can see that you're no stranger to the practice of healing. So it helps for me to understand your paradigms, as best I can, to help fortify your sense of faith, because faith in what the future holds is essential to anyone's recovery. I would not hesitate to recommend antipsychotic medications in the appropriate contexts."

"What about cannabis? It's been the only thing that's really helped me with my PTSD and depression."

"I don't doubt it. But I suspect that you've been using far more than the optimal therapeutic amount. As a result, your ability to stay grounded in your body can sometimes become impaired, which in mild cases, can manifest as paranoia, and in extreme cases, may appear as psychosis, even though inwardly it may be a meaningful experience. As the Haldol begins to wear off, we'll have you begin a micro-dosing regimen of orally ingested cannabinoids to help mitigate the effects of the withdrawal. In other words, you'll take edibles, instead of smoking it, as this form allows us to closely monitor the dosing and adjust up or down as needed."

"Do you think this plan will help Carlos with his misconduct investigation?"

"If it can be shown that cannabis does help you, and is necessary for your recovery, I do believe it will help exculpate him. But ultimately, our goal is for you not to need the cannabis anymore. If, in the future, you wish to experience it as a recreational form of exploration, you must keep mindful of the fact that it is also, at the same time, numbing you. As with any pain reliever, it masks your body's ability to perceive the subtle sensations which guide your intuition and psychic awareness. Some pain-relieving drugs may create the experience of enhancing awareness, but in reality, as with any numbing agent, they're actually fading out other areas of perception to strengthen your ability to focus on certain details. A magnifying glass can be a useful tool, but you wouldn't want to drive a car that has the distortion of a magnifying glass as its windows. You may *feel* good, but escape from pain is not the ultimate goal. Both feeling good and feeling pain are important steps in refining your ability to navigate by intuition. Ideally, you want to get to a place where you don't need to self-medicate. As awareness of your pain slowly returns to you, you'll begin to re-experience the grief you've repressed. Get ready to do a lot of crying, as the need arises."

"I don't have a problem with that. I cry all the time."

"That's good, because your tears will take you to where you need to go. Let them lead the way. Those painful sensations which you once felt the need to mask will catalyze magic that you can harness. That's where you want to be, seated in the driver's seat, rooted in your magic, not distanced from it. Unfortunately, trauma sometimes forces distancing between consciousness and the body; then medication perpetuates that distance. Sometimes it can't be helped—the wound is so intense that medication is necessary. But when self-medicating, you run the risk of becoming complacent with the wound, and never healing from it. By distancing your consciousness from your body, you're also making yourself a magnet for malevolent spirits who would love to make use of your magic while you're not paying attention."

Titi nodded in agreement. "As a Vodouisant, I'm no stranger to magic and the need for spiritual protection."

"It's to your advantage. Your self-healing journey would be prolonged if you didn't know how to use magic to protect yourself. Once you heal your wounds and wean yourself from the need to self-medicate, not only will your fear of pain greatly diminish, because by learning not to tune it out, you'll gain confidence in pain's value and your ability to manage it, but your magic will also become even more powerful, and you'll be better able to defend yourself and those you love from malicious spirit attack. Demon possession is a pretty extreme and rare example. Thankfully, most people will never know the battle that comes of having a demon invade their lives. And yet, as I'm sure you know, there are many other types of parasitic spirit creatures less powerful than demons which will readily take advantage of a body in want of a lucid driver, and work your magic to their own benefit without you even being aware of it."

"Respectfully though, I know how to ground, and meditate. I've been doing it for years, even while using cannabis. So what's going to be different?"

"You've been grounding only to a limited degree. You've still kept some distance between yourself and your emotional wounds. As the cannabis gradually leaves your body, you'll have to work, and I mean *work*, to keep increasing your body awareness, decompartmentalizing, feeling your pain, slowly learning how to co-exist with your emotions, swimming in them rather than drowning in them, until you heal to the point where you don't feel the need to self-medicate anymore. It's not going to be a simple thing that happens overnight. It's like going to the gym, only you'll be lifting emotional weight instead of physical weight. You have to start small, work your way up, exercise a lot of discipline and perseverance before you'll even *begin* seeing results. But the psychic muscles you're going to develop through this awareness of subtlety of sensation will begin manifesting your desires beyond your wildest dreams."

"I don't know, Sophie. What you're saying resonates, but I can tell you that I've had some really bad times when I was unmedicated. I joined a convent when I was twenty-five, hoping to fortify my faith and find some structure. I fell in love with a priest there, his name was Father Matthew. A sweet and loving man who was more compassionate than anyone I had ever known. He told me that he loved me, but that honoring his vow of celibacy was important to him, and that he was going to ask to be transferred to another diocese in order to protect himself from temptation. That's when I tried to kill myself. I stabbed myself in my barren womb, and laid down on the floor of the sanctuary to bleed out before the altar of Christ." Titi stared sadly at the ground for a moment, remembering. She looked back at Sophie. "I don't want to go back to that place."

"That sounds like a very painful experience," said Sophie gently. "And it sounds like a lot of other painful experiences came before that one. Feeling nervous is understandable. It might help to keep in mind that you've gained some distance from those wounds—fifteen years, right? And you've found some validation through your work as a healer, which means you've developed some healing skills that you can apply to yourself. You've been exercising empathy for others your whole life. The time has come now to work some more on your *self-*compassion. It won't be the same this time around. And you'll be under my psychiatric care and supervision. With the right support and guidance, and taking gradual steps in the right direction, you can get to the other side of your grief."

Titi took a deep breath and nodded. "What do these words mean that we're chanting?"

"This is known as the Rahu Shanti mantra. The legend behind this chant tells of a powerful and malevolent demigod by the name of Rahu who was devouring Surya, the sun deity, and Chandra, the moon deity, causing them to eclipse. They prayed to Buddha to come rescue them. Buddha heard their prayers and compelled Rahu to release them. Ever since, Buddhist monks have used the mantra as a prayer for protection. It's also known as a prayer of unveiling."

Titi sighed again as her body welcomed the idea. "I need all the protection I can get right now."

"I'll do all that I can to help you, Titi. Let us begin."

| Chapter Forty-Seven |

"*Orna. Where are you? Can you hear me?*" Sin Chronic leaned back against the wall in the darkened hallway, pressing her palms to the wall at her sides, and listened for the sound of Orna's voice in her head, but there was no response, and she began to wonder if she had imagined it before. Abruptly, her thoughts were interrupted as she found herself in a wolf's body, running through a night forest surrounded by snow, sucking cold air into her lungs, heat peeling away from her body in ripples from the wind, the skin of her feet pounding the ground as she pursued the scent of her prey with a singular objective, leaping through the air as her teeth met their mark, vicious in tearing open the pelt of an elk whose antlers spanned the length of a hospital bed, ravenous in feeding on its flesh together with the other wolves in her pack whose eyes also blazed a fiery red. Seized by the brutality of her hunger and the taste of blood in her mouth, her pulse was racing and all thoughts of her humanity vanished.

"*Sin Chronic. I hear you. I see the four kings in your room. Are they dead?*"

The sound of Orna's voice jolted Sin Chronic out of her

reverie and back to Ophelia's Wing, where she found herself crouched on the floor like a sprinter on the starting blocks. Bewildered, she pulled herself upright and struggled to remember what had happened to the four kings. Had she killed them? *"I... I don't think so. I shocked them unconscious, but they were still breathing. Help me find my way out of here, Orna. I'm having violent thoughts. I don't want to run into any security guards."*

"I am too. I was an eagle and attacked a bear. My wings were enormous! I crushed its skull and ripped its head right off with my claws. It was breathtaking! It was glorious! I wonder if I can do it again? Dr. Varma and the nurse Maisie have left our floor, taking the stairs to go find help. They're moving very slowly because of how dark it is. They'd better not come near us. When you come out of your room, follow the hallway to the left, and take the first doorway on the left. Virgina is in that room. After you release her from her restraints, come get me. I'm in the room directly across the hall. From there, I'll show you where Mercurial's room is. She's down the hall and around the corner."

Heart trembling, Sin Chronic cautiously felt along the wall to find the door to Virgina's room, and fumbled with Trieu's keys to find the one that would open the door.

"Virgina," she called in a low voice as she entered the room. "It's me, Sin Chronic. Are you alright?"

"I'm having scary visions," said Virgina with tears coming to her eyes as she struggled to shake the memory of taking the shape and fury of a green python forged of rock solid muscle as it wrenched the life out of a lion, blood spurting and bones snapping one by one. "I'm so relieved to see you. Orna told me you were coming. Help me remove the restraints and gauze, so my feet can touch the ground. Somehow my gift needs my feet touching the ground in order to work."

Sin Chronic promptly unbuckled the leather straps, and pulled the stool out from underneath the bed to help Virgina step down. She reached her hand out to help her up, and as soon as

Virgina's foot touched the ground, Sin Chronic felt a rush of energy come up through Virgina's hand and into her own body.

"What was that?" said Sin Chronic, her eyes wide with euphoria. "What just happened?"

"I don't know. It's like my feet are taking in power from the ground."

"I felt the energy rush into me, through touching you. Something miraculous is happening." Sin Chronic raised her hand in front of her face and stared at her fingertips as a bluish gold light began to form just above the tips of each finger. She looked back at Virgina and intuitively reached over to touch her arm. A surge of electricity passed into Virgina's arm and energized her entire body.

"That was a million times better than smoking crack!" said Virgina, her pupils dilated and heart racing.

"What's happening to us?" said Sin Chronic, feeling a wave of panic pass through her, then taking a deep breath to let it leave her body without holding onto it.

"We're leaving our cocoons and becoming butterflies," said Virgina, her voice and spirit suddenly light with joy. Her feet left the floor as her entire body began to float in the air, inches above the ground.

"You're flying! How did you do it?"

"By feeling happy, I guess! Yay!" Virgina tested her theory with another joyful laugh and felt herself rise again, closer to the ceiling.

Sin Chronic frowned. "I don't seem to have that gift."

"I wasn't able to do it before. It was when you touched my arm and sent a surge of electricity into my body... something changed inside of me."

"It's my gift... electrokinesis."

"I wonder what mine is called!"

"It's called flying!" They both laughed, before clutching at their sides. Cramping pains all over their bodies suddenly demanded their attention, dampening their elation with a cruel reminder of their wounds.

"*Sin Chronic! It's me, Orna! Are you coming to get me or not?*"

"*Sorry baby! We've been distracted! Coming right now!*"

"Wait! Where is her room?" asked Virgina, taking Sin Chronic's hand.

"It's directly across the hallway. Why do you ask?"

"Because," she said, and before she could give a reason, the two of them had teleported together into Orna's room.

"What do you call that gift!?" said Sin Chronic, catching her breath.

"That's teleportation," said Orna, still blindfolded. Sin Chronic and Virgina rushed over to her and quickly removed the gauze from her eyes and the straps from her arms and legs. "And Virgina, what you were doing before is called levitation."

"Eavesdropping were you!" chided Sin Chronic, relieved and cheered to be reunited with her adopted sisters. "Naughty girl!"

"I had to see what was taking you so long!" said Orna, rubbing her chafed wrists with a weak smile and stepping down from her bed. "Let's go get Mercurial. She's not doing well, she needs our help. Her gift is hydrokinesis. We need to put all of our gifts together if we're going to stop Bram."

They found Mercurial trapped in a nightmarish trance, convulsing in seizures with the sensation of eviscerating a blue whale—one that was singing, no less, a song the sentiment of which resonated deeply in Mercurial's soul, a haunting melody that said without words, "I exist, but not for long; I leave you with my song." Ripping into its flesh with her orca teeth together with a pack of other killer whales, blood spilling into the water and whipping into a froth at the ocean's surface, saddened and terrorized her so much that her mind was a whirlpool of other images—Eka's memories of autumn, visiting the sulphur baths in Old Town Tbilisi, Temperance's recollections of the harvest festival in Salem, floating paper boats on Wilkins pond, all mixed together with the ferocious hunger of the killer whales and agonizing empathy for the whale—working frantically to help her compartmentalize as water began seeping from the walls and pooling on the floor around them. After releasing her from her restraints, her sisters put their hands on her back to help her stabilize and sat with her as she fell into uncontrollable sobs.

Once her crying subsided, the walls stopped crying too. She knitted her eyebrows in anger, and said with a deep voice rumbling in her gut the words "Mori Erit," rolling the R's in a way she never had before, emphasizing each syllable like no truer words were ever spoken, not knowing what the words meant and not caring either. For all she knew it was the language of witches, and whatever it meant was truth, and all she could feel while saying it was the intense desire to sink her fingernails into Bram's chest and rip out his beating heart. Orna recognized it as Latin, although how she knew that, or that it meant "He will die," she could not begin to guess. Her sisters neither felt the need for translation nor contemplation, and by instinct only echoed the sentiment, repeating in agreement, "Mori Erit." Joining hands, they then joined energies to launch themselves into the astral realm.

| Chapter Forty-Eight |

Meanwhile, Rochelle was sitting on the pavement behind a dumpster, and it was starting to get cold. She didn't want to go back to her apartment, even though she wasn't sure whether Jason would actually be waiting there for her or if his entire visit was just a false memory. She didn't feel like finding out. The hard, cold sidewalk felt no different from the world as she knew it, and she no longer felt the compulsion to seek anything else.

The ghost of a dead girl—Abitha—eleven years old when she died, her blackened eyes sinking back into her skull, cruel rope burns carved into her neck, long blonde hair caked with dirt—approached slowly and stood beside her.

Rochelle leaned her head back against the concrete wall of the building housing the liquor store next to her apartment, resting the heel of a just-purchased bottle of Patrón, already half-empty, on its edge on the pavement. Another ghost child approached—Temperance—age seven, with long muddied red hair, her neck bent slightly to one side. The ghost of Temperance took her place at Abitha's side and reached forward to take her hand. A few feet behind her, the ghost of a sixteen-year-old girl born with the name of Talisa stood quietly staring through dead eyes. To her right, the ghost of 26-year-old Kemi stood casting a dispassionate stare. Without words, they pleaded with Rochelle to save them. The physical pain they felt in their current host bodies was far worse than anything they had ever felt in Salem. They didn't want magic, or vengeance, or war. They only wanted sleep.

Whatever part of her wanted to feel guilty about them was helping to fuel her desire to drink. "I can't help you," she said, taking another shot of tequila to commiserate. "This one's for you."

"That's it?" said the specter of Jandro, materializing in front of her, ignoring the ghosts and kneeling to peer closely at Rochelle's face. "You're giving up? Just like that? What if I tell you that I need you, Special Agent Roy?"

"You mean you need someone new to victimize?"

He shook his head. "You've got the wrong idea. That's Bram. That's not me. I mean sure, Bram could find someone new to torment easily enough. Your dad's been drinking a lot since he got out of prison. Got all that restitution money and plenty of time on his hands, spending a lot of time home alone now with your dear, sweet mother. It would be a shame if something happened to them."

Rochelle's face contorted in helpless anger and disgust. "Don't act like I have any control over your sick mind games. Like I'm buying that 'Bram' decided to step out for a second so you and I could have this little heart-to-heart. You're gonna do whatever you're gonna do."

"Bram can't be everywhere at once. He's busy with something right now. So I'm asking you nicely and sincerely, Special Agent Roy. Please don't let them kill me for what Bram did."

Rochelle laughed. "Let who kill you? Your victims? The state of New York?"

"Whoever."

"Why should I care if they do or don't?"

"Because I was coerced into committing violent acts against my will. Before Bram, it was the cartel. It was kill or be killed; it's not what I wanted. My first kill brought me to tears, can you believe that? You think it makes me less of a man?"

Rochelle looked intently in his eyes, suspicious of an emotional booby trap. "It takes strength to cry. More strength than a lot of people have."

"I was so ashamed. For killing, for crying, for what Quila might think of me. So my cousin Danny got me high on coke, said it would pick me up, boost my confidence. That's when Bram showed up. Special Agent Roy, I love Quila more than anything. I want her to be safe, and happy."

"You could have found a way out."

"Sure. Easy for you to say. When you've got a demon inside you, come tell me again how simple it is. I'm just thankful he never killed her. There were so many others he killed. Or mutilated. Not sure which is worse."

"I've heard enough," said Rochelle, taking another swallow of tequila. "He never killed her because he's you. *You* chose to spare her life. Anyway, demon or no demon, you're asking me for more than I have to give. There's nothing I can do to help someone who can't or won't help themselves. Energy vampire waste of time bullshit."

"Right. This is why women shouldn't be in law enforcement," he said, looking around with a shrug, as if addressing an imaginary audience. "They just don't have the balls for it."

"You don't know shit about having balls," she snapped. "You torture women because you're too much of a fucking coward to feel your own pain. So get the fuck out of my face."

"That's the spirit!" he said with a wicked laugh, his body growing in size and towering over her as his human head morphed into that of a dead fish. "There's some fight left in you!"

He raised the six bulbous fingertips of his right hand and closed his eyes as the slithering wraiths oozed out of them, sliding along her legs and pushing their fangs into her flesh to feed. She leaned her head back against the wall, in part too weary and inebriated to work up the effort to fight back, and in part fighting back with a show of indifference.

At that moment, the sound of a woman's voice singing came vibrating through the air, halting the movement of the creepy crawlers. Bram shrieked in horror and covered his ears until finally he scampered away on all four limbs, taking his minions with him.

It was a sad and beautiful angelic voice, and the melody spoke to Rochelle of loneliness and coming of age. The otherworldly lyrics of the song were in a language she couldn't understand, and she imagined they were of a language beyond human, the language of angels and gods. A bright light began to materialize in front of her, and from inside the light, the shape of a woman's body began to materialize and grow until Rochelle finally began to make out her features.

"*Titi?*" said Rochelle, pulling herself into a more upright position. "Is it you? Is this real? Or am I just imagining this?"

"Yes," said Titi, her smiling face glowing with a golden light. "All of the above. I'm here by virtue of astral projection. I need your help, Chelle. We all need your help."

"What's astral projection?"

"It's a way of traveling through other planes of existence that share the same Earthly space with us."

"I'm not thinking straight right now, Titi. I don't think I can be much help."

"Yes, you can. You throw that tequila in the trash and go back to your apartment. Jason is there waiting for you to come back. We need to move quickly. The four queens have freed themselves from their restraints and will soon be on their way to the federal prison to confront Jandro. We may be able to stop them if we can make an appeal to their host bodies. We have to give them something real, something worth living for, something worth fighting their way back for. For Abeni, it's her son. Quila and Olena each have a younger sister whom they love dearly. Eka loves to sing. I think we can connect to her through singing, as I did with you just now."

"How are we supposed to find Abeni's son? We don't even know her last name."

"You've got to find it in you to believe me when I say it's possible. Without faith, all hope is lost. Go on now and get yourself sober. The answers will come to you. If you trust them, they will."

"But you hurt me."

"I did what?"

"You hurt me, Titi."

"How on Earth did I hurt you? Did I ever steal your husband?" With these words, the glowing light around Titi's face began to dim, and her appearance began to fade.

"You called me a Goody Two Shoes. You blamed me for my dad abusing you. He abused me too, in case you forgot."

"Your father left me unable to bear children. And here you are, perfectly capable of having children, and you go and give yours up for adoption. I'm not going to lie. It's a cruel irony. A slap in the face."

"That's why I never told you. Because I knew you would blame me. I knew you would never forgive me."

"You didn't need to tell me. I could sense it."

"If you could sense it, then you know why I did it. And if you know so much, then what do you need me for?"

"I don't know everything, Rochelle. All I know is that we both have been carrying around resentment and never having the conversations we needed to have."

"It's not my fault."

"I don't know whose fault it is. Either way, I'm sorry. Do

you hear me? I'm sorry."

Tears came slowly rolling out of Rochelle's eyes.

"I mean it, Rochelle. I'm sorry."

Rochelle heaved a deep sigh. "I'm sorry too."

"Sorry for what?"

Rochelle brushed the tears away from her eyes and sniffled and laughed. "Sorry for stealing your husband."

Titi heaved a sigh too, as the light around her face continued to flicker. "You didn't steal anything that didn't want to be stolen," she said sadly, as the glow began to return. "That's the part that hurts the most, and I know that's not your fault. So let's just be done with it. My heart is opening for someone else now." Titi stepped forward and wrapped her arms around Rochelle, blanketing her in a warm, comforting astral hug that revitalized Rochelle from the inside out. She set the bottle on the ground.

"I have a gift for you," said Titi, extending the palm of her left hand, in the center of which rested a Jerusalem cricket. "By way of gratitude for having me arrested, which led me to Sophie, my new mentor."

Rochelle extended her own palm to receive it as the ominous insect hopped into her hand. "You're giving me a potato bug?" said Rochelle, fighting an urge to laugh until the bug fixed the hypnotic gaze of its skull-shaped face upon her. As she moved in closer with an odd stare, it leaped forward and bit the left side of her neck with excruciating vice-like jaws, its abrasive legs scraping her skin before hopping away. She shrieked and shot Titi a dumbfounded look as she clutched at her neck in pain.

"To help you heal," said Titi. "May it lead you to silver linings."

Thanks, don't do me any favors, Rochelle wanted to say, but she was too floored by the insect bite to speak. She knitted her eyebrows tightly together, trying to process what was happening in her body, overcome by a strange trembling from deep within that she at first wanted to dismiss as the chill of the night air, but became alarmed as cube shapes swelled up and moved painfully under her skin like some kind of bizarre allergic reaction. Gradually, they began to subside. It was more than she could try to digest in this moment.

"I'm going to work on reviving the four kings," continued Titi. "I don't know where Reid found these guys. They've got good intuition, but aren't very skilled yet with their magic. They tried to perform binding spells on the four queens and were unsuccessful. Right now they're lying unconscious at Ophelia's Wing. I've got to find a way to revive them. We could use their assistance with performing the healing spells. It would really help if you could get to work on finding those lost family members." With those words, Titi vanished, and Rochelle was left alone, staring down at her unfinished bottle of tequila.

| Chapter Forty-Nine |

The doorbell rang, and a bewildered Adrian consulted the time and wondered who could be on his front porch at this hour. He put his reading glasses down on his mahogany desk where he was reviewing deposition transcripts for a case that was about to go to trial. On peering through the peephole of his front door, he was even more surprised to see his ex-wife, Candace in a body-conscious gold cocktail dress with a low neckline that showed off her fine jewelry.

"Candace!" he said, gesturing her in. "What are you doing here? I just gave you an alimony check last week. If you're here for Jericho, he's not here. He's spending the night at a friend's house."

"I'm not here to see Jericho, Adrian. I came here to see you. Is that alright?"

"Sure, of course. Come on in. Can I offer you a non-alcoholic beverage?" It was a strange relief to see her not angry.

"I'm okay, thank you. Listen, I just wanted to tell you I'm really proud of you for sticking with your sobriety for so long. I realized I was kind of hard on you the other night. I was in the neighborhood, so I wanted to stop by and apologize in person."

"You didn't have to do that, but I appreciate it. I know being with me wasn't easy. I should be the one to apologize."

"I don't know how to say this, but seeing you turning over a new leaf like this has got me feeling... I don't know. Some type of way. You look good, Adrian. You sound good, you... smell good. What do you think about dinner this Saturday? I could get our old table at Andaluz." She bit her lower lip in a playful, seductive way Adrian knew all too well.

Adrian looked at her as though she had just asked him if he had a spare penis laying around she could use as a toothbrush. "I don't understand... I thought you and Malcolm were really hitting it off?"

"I thought we were too, but it turned out he was hitting it with a side chick. I'm done with that. Now that I think about it, I think he was really just a rebound to help me get closure with you."

"Sorry to hear that, babe... I mean, Candace. He's a fool for not realizing what a good thing he had."

"I'm glad you feel that way," she said, stepping forward and sliding her hands up around his neck.

"Whoa, wait," he said, taking her hands and pulling them away from his face. "I told you, I'm seeing someone new now. I think it could be serious, I really don't think—"

"Ugh!" she said, that familiar indignant look coming back. "The one who's a fool here is me. I don't know what the hell I was thinking coming halfway across town to see you. I'm not a priority in your life. Never have been, never will be."

"That's not true, and that's not fair. You and Jericho were always my priority."

"That's a damn lie. Your only priority was your first love. Drinking."

"You were my first love, Candace. And I'm sober now, what do you want me to say?"

265

"I want you to say you'll give me another chance to know you, now that you're sober. You deprived me of that opportunity before. Don't you think you owe me that, after everything we've been through?"

"I'm happy to give you that chance, Candace, but it'll have to be through friendship."

"*Friendship?* What the hell do you know about friendship? Your idea of a friend is Pete Hill."

"I think you should probably go now."

"Oh, you think? You got that right. Good luck with Miss Might-Be-Serious. She has no idea what she's getting herself into. You know, I should invoice her for fifteen years of my emotional labor that went into making you her Mr. Right!"

"Is that right? And what part of me getting sober do I get to take credit for? What part of my struggle gets to be about me and the choices I made, choices that I had to fight for? You're the one who didn't want me! Someone else does, so now you suddenly want a second chance?"

She looked him in the eyes. "She can keep my sloppy seconds."

He shook his head and took a deep breath to stay calm. "Good night, Candace. That's all I'm going to say. Drive safely home."

"Ugh!" She stormed out and slammed the door behind her.

Adrian stared at the closed door in disbelief. *What does she want from me, another apology? How long is she going to keep being angry? How long do I need to keep apologizing?* Before he realized it, he had pulled his keys out of his suit jacket pocket and settled down into the driver's seat of his lunar blue Mercedes Benz convertible.

His phone rang and he looked at the caller ID. It was Jericho.

"Hey Dad. Is everything alright?"

"Yeah. Everything's good. Everything alright with you, son?"

"Sure, I guess so. I just had a feeling that I should call you."

"I just had a little disagreement with your mother, but it's done now."

"Okay, well don't take it personally, okay Dad?"

"Don't take what personally?"

"I mean, don't punish yourself, you know? It's not worth it."

"You know me too well, son. But I'm okay."

"You sure, Dad? How's Titi? Can't wait to meet her."

"I don't know, Jay. I haven't heard from her in a while."

The distant sadness in his father's voice deepened Jericho's concern. "I'm sure there's a good reason," he said gently.

"Have a good night, son." Adrian hung up the phone and started the car. Not thinking about where he was going, all he knew was that he wanted to clear his mind and get out of the house for a bit. Ten minutes later, he found himself parked in front of Dave's All Night Liquor store.

| Chapter Fifty |

Flashback: January 19, 2004
Douglass Mansion, Charleston, South Carolina

"Don't make a sound if you want to live," said a man's voice from behind Rochelle's right ear, as he pressed the cold barrel of a Glock against the skin of her face. "Get undressed."

Is this guy for real? she thought, distancing herself from an emotional reaction. *Could he have picked a worse target?* Little did he realize that the woman he had chosen to assault was not only well-trained in self-defense and armed, but was also in active radio communication with a special forces team operating out of a secure room downstairs in the same building, the historic Douglass Mansion where a federal diplomatic ceremony was taking place today. *I knew my first secret service detail would be memorable, but dude you're making it too easy.*

She sized up the assailant in her peripheral vision, glancing past the match-grade gun barrel against her face. No silencer meant he either had no intention of firing the weapon, or else he had a foolproof escape plan. Or maybe he was just a gambling man.

For someone whose life was being threatened at gunpoint, she appeared unconcerned, which may have been due to both her training and keen ability to read people. Frankly, there had been a few training scenarios at the academy which rattled her far worse than this. In this particular moment, her lack of fear surprised even herself.

"Special Agent Roy," came a voice from her left earpiece, fashioned to look like an ear-climber earring. "We've got infrared visual on your assailant. Are you in need of assistance? Signal with your left hand. One finger to acknowledge, two to request back up."

Rochelle closed her eyes and meditated. The assailant didn't have the subtext of any narcotics addict she had ever seen. His voice had a strong timbre to it, not the weak tremor of someone in ill health. *Hitman?* She imagined that any one of the dignitaries at the event could potentially be a target. But that wouldn't explain why this particular hitman would have the rape of an undercover agent on the itinerary. *Not very professional behavior for a gun-for-hire,* she thought, perplexed. She carefully extended one finger of her left hand.

With an unaffected sigh, she leaned forward to remove her shoes and pivoted her head in a subtle way to get a better view of him in her peripheral vision.

He jabbed her face with the gun and cautioned, "Don't even think about resisting."

His hands were covered with gloves; his upper body sported a fitted turtleneck. Enclosing his face was a plastic Halloween mask of a baby doll head, painted like white cracked porcelain, with small red circles for cheeks and black scowling eyes. His hair appeared to be pulled back into a ponytail, or maybe it was slicked down under the mask, but from where she was positioned, she couldn't see very well what color it was. Maybe black, or dark brown.

Even without being able to see his face, she guessed by

the way he held the gun and barked his orders that this wasn't his first rodeo. She estimated his age to be mid- to late twenties, from his slim build and the tonal quality of his voice. *But why here? Why now? There are armed agents everywhere...* Then it dawned on her. *He's getting off on the danger. Thrillseeker... adrenaline junkie.*

"Maybe you can't tell from the couture gown I'm wearing. Let me let you in on a little secret," she confided in a barely audible whisper. "I'm a federal law officer. In the line of duty, no less. So, let's not do something foolish, alright? I'm going to give you the benefit of the doubt here. I'm sure you didn't know any better. So I'll tell you. You're already committing a felony by using a weapon to threaten me. If you kill me, too? Life in prison."

"I don't care if you're fucking Gandhi. Get moving."

"Okay, fine," she said calmly, putting her finger on his pistol, and pushing it gently away from her face. "I'll do what you want, alright? You can't help yourself, I get it."

"Bitch, you don't know me, so stop trying to get in my head," he said, shoving the gun harder against her face, his voice betraying his anger. "You're just hiding how scared you are to try to mess with my head. I know how your kind are. Manipulators."

"Oh, my kind? I have a kind?"

"Yeah, your kind makes me sick. Apparently they'll let just anyone in here."

Rochelle wasn't sure if her kind referred to being Black or being female, but she seized the opportunity to try to get a rise out of him. She raised an eyebrow and glanced over at him. "Apparently."

Later, in retrospect, the assailant would berate himself for taking the bait. But unfortunately for him, something pathological was calling the shots. She was right that he couldn't help himself. "Don't get smart with me, bitch," he snapped. "I will not hesitate to—"

He was unable to finish the sentence. As he raised the pistol in anger to strike her with it, she deftly knocked it from his hand to the floor and took hold of his arm, flipped him onto the ground, and procured zip-cuffs from a secret thigh compartment under her gown. Moments later, two armed guards arrived to take the perpetrator into custody.

Returning downstairs to the ballroom, her silver gown barely rumpled, Rochelle was approached by a server holding a tray of bubbling flutes. "Champagne, Miss?" said the server.

"No, thank you," said Rochelle, catching sight of Reid Shelton. The director of the Federal Law Enforcement Training Center from which Rochelle had just graduated the month before was an unexpected guest for today's event. She wondered if he was working an undercover assignment as well. She remembered thinking when she met Reid her first year at the academy that he seemed like the kind of person she wouldn't mind working for—a sentimental man, encased in an old-school hard shell.

"Did you find the toilet?" he asked as she approached, posturing for the sake of her cover.

"Yes I did, thank you," she said, playing along, remarking to herself that these Secret Service assignments were certainly not dull.

"Good. Listen," he said, lowering his voice. "I'm not here for a social call. I'd like to speak with you privately, if you don't mind coming with me, this way, to a secure conference room."

Before taking hold of the conference room doorknob, Reid slid his palm over the fabric of his khaki pants to take the sweat off of it, same as he would do before shaking someone's hand.

The odor of burnt coffee wafted by Rochelle from an old drip machine sitting near the conference room door, triggering sudden intense nausea. She raised her hand to block her nostrils as her stomach turned.

"Have you toured the Douglass suite?" asked Reid, casually gesturing Rochelle to follow him into a hallway leading to a secure room. Some kids playing on the lawn outside the one-way window caught his eye for a moment as he closed the door behind her.

"Director Shelton," she said, taking advantage of the pause, as she drew in a deep breath and prayed for the nausea to pass. "What a surprise. To what do I owe this honor? Was there a problem with my transcripts?"

"Oh no, ma'am, nothing like that. My reason for this visit is two-fold. Let's start with the bad news, shall we? It has recently come to my attention that you were designated by Special Agent Efren Bautista as emergency contact and next of kin."

Rochelle held her breath as she maintained eye contact and held back a panic attack. After a long pause, she responded. "Yes, sir. It's true, Efren and I were in a relationship. Will there be disciplinary action?"

"Well, there might have been, if FLETC had learned of it sooner. Instructors dating their students aren't providing a constructive environment, you understand that, don't you Roy? But that's water under the bridge. I'm sure you already know that Special Agent Bautista was deployed to an undercover DEA assignment immediately after your graduation. I'm sorry to inform you that he was killed yesterday in the line of duty. I'm not able to provide any other details at this juncture. I'm sorry for your loss, Roy. Once his autopsy is complete, they'll fly him in from Juárez for the memorial service. My secretary will get in touch with you to give you the exact date and time."

Silence. Hand over her mouth to keep from screaming.

Reid cleared his throat. "There's another reason for my visit, Roy. You probably remember me attending your graduation? I certainly remember you. Honor graduate in the

272

top percentile of your class. 300 on Firearms. Sure, I've seen other students with a perfect Firearms score, although they're few and far between. But I've never seen another student with your general aptitude during my 25-year career. Your parents must be very proud."

"Thank you, sir. Yes, sir. My mother is very proud."

"Listen, Roy. The FBI has just tasked me to head up their new human trafficking division, and I want you to come work for me. I saw noted in your file that you've recently requested a transfer to the Office of Women's Violence? You're looking for a *desk job*? Did I read that right?" Reid shook his head. "It'd be a crying shame, and a real waste of your talent, Roy. I'm assembling a top-notch team, and it's clear to me that you belong on it. The world can benefit, not just from your talent and skill, but also from your perspective as an African-American woman. And this isn't coming out of some quotas initiative, alright? I'm not asking you to be the token Black woman. I want a superlative problem-solving team, Roy, not an echo chamber. That means men and women from diverse backgrounds, who have the aptitude for this kind of work. A diverse team means diverse perspectives, and diverse approaches to problem-solving. These are critical to our success and survival. I've got Dr. Lin Mei Chen on board as our forensic psychologist. Maybe you've heard of her—she's a prodigy, like you. And a few others; I'm waiting on confirmation. I know I've just given you a lot to process, but would you please give it some thought? It's a standing invitation. Take your time, think it over."

This time it was Rochelle who cleared her throat. "I'm sorry, Director, but you should know that I'm pregnant. With Efren's child. My due date is in August. I'm getting out of law enforcement so I can raise this baby. It's important to me, now more than ever. Please don't try to convince me to do otherwise, sir. I've already given it a lot of thought."

"Ah. That explains why Bautista listed you as primary

beneficiary before he left. Good man. And that's an admirable decision on your part, Roy, but I know you know there are plenty of special agents who have families to take care of. Balancing the time between work and family, as a single mother no less, is not an easy task, I'm aware of that. But let me be blunt here. The world needs you. Not just anyone can do what you can do. Do you truly understand the importance of that? Do the world a huge favor and give it some more thought. You want to make this world a safer place for your daughter, am I right?"

"What makes you think it's a girl?" said Rochelle, concerned that her voice betrayed her desire to be somewhere else. *Efren thought the baby was going to be a girl, too.* "It's still soon to tell."

"Eh, it's just a hunch," said Reid. "Hunches can be wrong, but they usually aren't. And if it is a girl, you got a name picked out?"

"If it's a girl, Shani. If it's a boy, Sean. After Efren's father. It was the name Efren wanted. I'll give him that, especially now that he doesn't get to have any more say in the matter."

"Alright then," said Reid. "That's enough small talk for me. Not exactly small talk, I know, but let me just take this excuse to skedaddle out of here and let you think things over. We need you Roy. The world needs you. Think hard about it. Get back to me when you have an answer that you feel certain about."

After Reid left the room, Rochelle sat motionless waiting for the wave of morning sickness to subside. For the sake of the baby, she resisted the urge to order a scotch from the bar. Her mind was a spinning tornado of thoughts, feelings and memories. Oddly, no tears came to surface, and Rochelle stopped to wonder what was wrong with her. Efren was the greatest love of her life. *What kind of person doesn't cry at a time like this?*

She believed Reid when he said the world needed her. He was the second person in her life to tell her that. The first was Efren. Efren didn't want her to take a desk job, either. He was angry about it; said it was a waste of her potential. They had had long talks about the pregnancy before he left for Mexico. She knew that her mother, and especially her grandmother Ruth, would find completely unacceptable the news of a pregnancy out of wedlock, and Rochelle had intended to keep the pregnancy a secret until she and Efren could hastily arrange a wedding. Her heart sank with the realization: *There won't be a wedding now.*

Needless to say, the pregnancy wasn't planned; the condom had broken. She fully wanted to be a mother, and had intended to become one later in her career. Just not now, not at 23. Not when her work could leave her child an orphan at any moment. But she wasn't just worried about her daughter losing a mother, and now her only parent. Rochelle worried about Shani becoming a target for the enemies that come with this line of work. Crime bosses looking to leverage power, vindictive parolees looking to punish those who put them away. She didn't want to expose her to that risk. She would raise her daughter herself. A desk job was the only acceptable solution.

But time has a funny way of challenging even the most hardened convictions.

| Chapter Fifty-One |

"If you feel comfortable taking my hands," said Sophie to Titi, kicking her shoes off and planting her feet flat on the floor, "I can help ground you. I see that you're struggling with disorientation from the psych meds. You're destabilizing."

Titi took hold of Sophie's hands and closed her eyes.

"Let's do some energy work to help clear your mind," said Sophie. "Your thoughts are racing all over the place, obscuring your vision. Are you feeling guilty about your cousin?"

Titi nodded, her eyes still closed. "I've been punishing her all this time for what her father did to me. It wasn't just the abuse. Our fathers came back from the Vietnam war, and mine died of cancer. But her father got to live. She's able to bear children, I'm not. It all seems so unfair. But it wasn't her fault, and I acted like it was. I didn't mean to, I just wasn't aware I was doing it. It was like an unconscious reflex coming out of my wound. I regret it. In a way, she and I remind me of Mambo Erzulie Freda and Mambo Erzulie Dantó. Do you know of them? They're lwa—Voodoo spirits—sisters who are often at odds with each other. Erzulie Freda is a goddess of love, extremely emotional. Erzulie Dantó is a maternal goddess—aggressive and a strict disciplinarian, but also a passionate protector of women and children. It's almost like our lives are a manifestation of their stories, their energies. Maybe by making peace with each other, we can help to bring peace to their conflict as well."

Sophie nodded thoughtfully. "As I'm sure you know, there were also parallels observed between the lwa and the Catholic saints. They were seen as corresponding manifestations of spirit which made syncretizing them possible," she said. "I mean, it makes sense. Spirits animate. Their energies are so powerful that it doesn't surprise me that we could also find parallels with them in our own lives." She paused for a moment, reading Titi's demeanor. "But I sense that you still feel unresolved about something. Is it Carlos?"

"No, it's Adrian." Titi paused with concern as the image of Adrian setting himself on fire flashed through her mind. "Something just happened to shake his sobriety. I can feel it. I'm not sure what it is."

"I'll step out into the waiting room, so you can spend some time alone to reconnect with him. It's possible that your astral visit with your cousin left him vulnerable to attack by Bram."

"I don't understand," said Titi, opening her eyes. "How could that be?"

"When you astral project, you distance your consciousness from your body. It may have temporarily weakened the psychic bond between you and Adrian. It's a risky maneuver when you have a vigilant demon ready to exploit the opportunity. Don't blame yourself, though. There was no way to know if or where he would strike, and we do also need your cousin's help in finding the family members of the four queens. She knows things that she doesn't know she knows. Plus, she has the resources to seek them and bring them here. Take a moment now to let Adrian feel your energy, to revitalize your connection. I would suggest that you share some psychic visualizations with him that will help lift his spirits, and yours as well."

"What kind of visualizations would you suggest?"

"Positive experiences that you've had together, optimistic visions for the future, whatever feels good to you."

"I can do that."

"I'll step out into the waiting room."

After Sophie left, Titi took a deep breath and called the image of Adrian into her memory. "Come to me," she said, projecting her feelings toward Adrian. "You are protected, and loved so very much. We're going to have an amazing time together when I get back." Then, words fell away as she conjured images in her mind of listening to his poetry, going to a Saints game with him, and meeting his son. She felt the firmness of his arms holding her, and the tenderness of his kisses, while calling to memory the smell of his cologne. She pictured slow-dancing together, laughing together, and growing old together. They were such beautiful imaginings that she couldn't help crying. Her tears escalated to sobs and then eventually slowed until at last she took a deep breath and knew that the danger had passed. Her mind and heart felt supremely lucid. It was at that moment that Sophie intuitively re-entered the room.

"Very good," said Sophie, seeing the change in Titi's manner. "Let's take a moment to think about the four queens. Do you know where they are? Can you sense them?"

Titi inhaled deeply and slowly exhaled. "Yes. I'm picking up on something, but it's faint."

"Take your time."

Titi again inhaled deeply and exhaled. And again. And again. "The police are trying to get into the access tunnel that leads to Ophelia's Wing, but it's flooded. It's Eka… she's flooded the tunnel using hydrokinesis. There's water leaking out onto the street from the side of the building where the fire happened. The hospital staff are trapped on the upper floors. They can't get to the emergency exits." Another deep breath. And another. And another. "Olena... is clairvoyant. She's used remote viewing to identify the location of the prison. Their abilities are rapidly evolving because of Abeni... her electrokinesis is giving them power and transforming them. Quila tried to teleport them there at first, but it didn't work. Now the four of them are holding hands and... flying astrally over the city, to the prison."

"What is the next step, Titi?"

| Chapter Fifty-Two |

No sooner had Sophie spoken these words, Titi found herself standing at the top of an enclosed, indoor emergency exit stairwell on the fourth floor of a building which she immediately recognized to be Ophelia's Wing, after having caught sensations of it during her previous visits to the location, and from the clairvoyant insights she had just experienced moments before. She would have recognized it by sight as well, except that it was very nearly pitch black inside, due to the power and emergency backup power being out. Words from a poem she had written weeks ago came to mind:

I know this place from my dreams
Where everything is what it seems.

The next step, Titi would have answered Sophie, was to revive the four kings, whom she knew to be rendered unconscious on the third floor. Somehow she had projected herself here using means she didn't quite yet understand. But why she had arrived on the fourth floor instead of the third, she did not know.

The steps descending in front of her in the darkness were

bringing on an unexpected panic. Still as stone, she stood at the top of the stairs, staring into the descending void, struggling to breathe, until a dimly glowing vision of a little Black girl she recognized to be her own ten-year-old self materialized in front of her. The girl was standing a few steps below the landing, and she looked up at Titi before turning to walk down the stairs.

Titi stepped hesitantly to follow the vision halfway down the stairs to the lower floor, but stopped when she heard a man's voice that she recognized as that of Rochelle's father. "Titi!" he bellowed gruffly. He was drunk.

Titi responded aloud as if in a trance. "Uncle Sam?" she said timidly, startling herself with the sound of her own voice. For a moment, she wondered if she would catch the little girl's attention again, but the girl had simply stopped, looking down the stairs.

"Get in here," said Samson. His voice seemed to come from beyond the door which led to the hallway into the third floor. The little girl obediently continued down the stairs and passed through the door out of sight, leaving Titi alone in darkness again.

Titi knew very well what moment was being reenacted in this apparition, which was confirmed shortly thereafter by the sounds of her ten-year-old self screaming from the other side of the door. Tears immediately welled up in her eyes, and she shook her head, struggling to summon the strength to move forward. *The four queens are depending on you.* The remaining steps fell ahead of her into darkness and she braced herself against the handrail to finish descending to the entrance to the third floor hallway.

Her hands trembled as she used both of them to take hold of the doorknob to open it. It was locked. To the right of the door perched a numeric keypad, but she couldn't begin to guess what the entry code could be. She turned her head to the right to think for a moment of what to do. *Do I need this code?* she wondered. *Am I physically here? Can't I simply pass through the door?* She placed her left hand against the surface of the door, but it felt solid.

Suddenly, she caught sight of a dimly lit image reflected in the darkened stairwell window to her right. She knitted her eyebrows together to focus her vision, as an apparition of Adrian became clear. He was holding up three Tarot cards, the three that had been drawn when she did a reading for him: Death, The Tower, The Devil. "Now is the time to be brave," whispered Adrian, fortifying her while at the same time sending a chill down her spine. Then he vanished.

She closed her eyes. *Be brave.* She took a deep breath and exhaled slowly. *Death is the 13th card of the major arcana,* she recalled, turning back to look at the keypad. *The Tower is 16. The Devil is 15. 13-16-15. Could that be it?* She typed the combination into the keypad, and the door unlocked.

On the other side of the door, there was no sign of her uncle Samson or her childhood self. The third floor hallway stretched out in front of her mostly into darkness. Unfamiliar sigils inscribed themselves in blood on the walls at each side, as if drawn by an invisible finger and dimly lit by a candle that was nowhere to be found. The sigils were whispering to Titi things she didn't know how to put into words, things ancient and beyond her understanding, things waking fear.

In the distance, a Black woman, seated at a vanity in the middle of the hallway, looked at the reflection of her face in the vanity mirror, a face which Titi could see from where she was standing, but not recognize. Titi took some steps forward to get closer to the woman, and saw that a little boy was standing at the woman's right side.

"Do you like my pink flowers, Adrian?" said the woman, turning her head so he could see she had placed in her afro two dainty pink rosebuds which matched her pink crepe ascot blouse she had purchased by mail order from Sears.

"Yes, Momma," he said.

"I want my hair to look pretty for the funeral. Does it look pretty?"

"Yes, Momma. But whose funeral is it? Huh, Momma?"

Titi's face contorted when his mother didn't respond. She knew whose funeral it was for. *His mother had just poisoned herself and was about to die in front of him,* she realized sadly. The scene faded into darkness as a metal sphere the size of a tennis ball came flying toward Titi, as if launched from somewhere behind the scene she had just witnessed. It was flying fast toward her, and she barely had time to think about dodging it when it thumped her hard in the chest.

She shrieked in pain and looked down, discovering that somehow, over the top of her pajama top and pastel green patient robe, she had come to be wearing a magnetic breastplate of armor, to which the metal ball had continued clinging in the place where it struck her. She tried to pull the ball away from the armor, but it was heavy, and the magnetism was too strong. Before she could think too much about what had just happened, another metal ball came flying toward her from the distance, and struck her again just inches to the left from where the first one had, remaining again in place.

She gasped, trying to catch her breath from having the wind knocked out of her. Intuitively, she quickly pulled her arms out of the breastplate and threw the armor onto the floor, just moments before another ball came whizzing toward her, and this time hit the breastplate as it lay on the ground, seemingly guided there by its magnetism.

Feeling shaken, but even more determined, her confidence boosted from having had the sense to remove the armor, she proceeded forward into the darkened hallway until at last she came to a door on the left that she sensed was the room she needed to enter. She felt water seeping into her treaded, non-slip hospital socks and the hems of her cornflower blue drawstring pajama pants, and looked down to see that a thin pool of water had traveled down the hallway toward her from the opposite direction. *The water is rising in here. I need to act quickly.*

She put her ear to the door to see if any movement was happening inside the room, and on doing so, she could hear a thumping sound which seized her heart with fear. *Someone is having a seizure.* The haunting memory flashed through her mind of her uncle Samson lying on the floor, convulsing from alcohol withdrawal, his foot unintentionally kicking the wall. An irrational thought occurred to her. *What if it's not Uncle Sam? What if it's Adrian?*

She tried to dismiss the fear, but it was strong. *What if it's Adrian?* Tears came to her eyes again, and she gave in for a moment to release them. Feeling more lucid after she had escaped the weight of her tears, she took a breath, sniffled for a moment, and brought herself back to her center. *I can't let fear do the driving.*

She tried the doorknob. It was locked. This time there was no keypad. The knob clearly needed a key to open it. She started to cry again. *Why is this so hard?* The water level had by now risen to her ankles. *I can't think. I'm running out of time.* Before she could contemplate why she was doing it, she guided herself to confront every painful memory she could think of, every single memory that she had spent her life running away from, one by one, so she could wash away the confusion with her tears and somehow arrive at the solution.

She braced her hand against the wall as traumatic memories erupted through her like thunder, detonating like landmines, rocking her soul. There were memories of physical pain, of being raped by her uncle, of Billy's fists against her face, and the knife slicing through her flesh when she wanted to die. There were memories of heartbreak, like the day she realized that Carlos was cheating on her, years before Rochelle ever came into the picture.

She recalled the news of death that struck twice when she was eight years old—first when her grandfather Papa Charles passed in the early fall that year, and then when her father died of cancer a couple of months later. Recalling the memory of his kind face and old soul those days he would come home from work and she would run to him with a leap into his arms—being carried with him into the house as he would greet her mother with a kiss—the grief overwhelmed her. "I miss you Daddy," she cried. Her tears fell and fell and fell like raindrops into the water at her feet, as the flood water level steadily rose.

At last, when her whole body ached and she felt she could bear no more, she heard the lock of the door unlatch. She took a deep breath to gather her strength, and opened the door, expecting to find someone on the other side of it who had unlocked it. She didn't see anyone but the four kings, lying unconscious on the floor, but sensed that her father and grandfather had paid her a visit, as had Adrian.

A surge of excited energy welled up inside of her. She now knew exactly what to do. She walked over to Rahim and took his right hand in hers. "Rahim, King of Fire. Awaken!" Slowly, Rahim opened his eyes and began to sit up as Titi quickly moved on to Diego. Placing her hands on his head, she called out to him, "Diego, King of Air. Awaken!" Next, she moved on to Lluc. Placing her hands on his chest, over his heart, she called, "Lluc, King of Water. Awaken!" And finally, placing her hands on Trieu's feet, she called, "Trieu, King of Earth. Awaken!" And awaken they did.

| Chapter Fifty-Three |

Feet on the ground is better, thought Virgina, looking down on Manhattan as they soared over the towering buildings toward Hell's Kitchen, and the federal prison to which Jandro had been remanded into custody awaiting trial. Contemplating the world through her astral vision triggered the memory of seventeen-year-old Jandro showing fifteen-year-old Quila what the world looked like through night-vision goggles. For the first time in more than a decade, she felt a moment of grief over the loss of her first love.

"If you ever truly loved Jandro," telegraphed Orna in response to Virgina's sorrow, *"you must help to free him from Bram's torment."*

Virgina wished there was another way, one that didn't require taking Jandro's life, but quietly opted not to verbalize this.

"There's no other way," responded Orna. *"What must be done must be done. You'll feel better after. We all will. It's for the best."* These words lifted their collective mood, keeping the four of them buoyant in the astral realm and preventing them from snapping back into their physical bodies with the weight

of grief.

Sin Chronic was the first to understand that the four queens had arrived at a place in their minds where they no longer needed words, and it felt antiquated to hear the occasional thoughts of her sisters projecting around her in the form of words. The only things salient to her right now were visceral things like the emotion of heat and desire, the burning fire of wanting things with passion and determination. Right now, the red-hot gleam of a single intention guided her, and that was to destroy Bram.

As soon as their bare feet touched the roof of the prison, a quaking energy rocketed out through Virgina's legs which sent waves of force into the concrete below them. The men in their cells cheered at the chaos as part of the roof caved in, knocking unconscious the two correctional officers who were patrolling the top floor where Jandro's cell was located.

Mercurial giggled at the sight of the prisoners through her astral vision, who seemed to her like baby goats jumping around in slow-motion, as if moving underwater, yet they were shrieking with delight, and butting their heads against the bars of their cages. Her perception was growing more and more fluid by the minute, and subtle ripples of air were passing over her skin like a thick, underwater current, or maybe the ripples were coming from under her skin, as now she could sense every pulse of blood flowing through her veins.

The baby goats reminded her for a moment of Temperance tending goats on her father's farm, then shifted into the shapes of otherworldly creatures for which she had no name—creatures with tentacles gripping the steel bars of their prison cells, sharp teeth that they knocked against the bars, blue-green bioluminescent rippling skin that flickered with excitement, and eyes that seemed blind with death—creatures such as one might find in the very deep sea—before shifting back into the shapes of men.

Jandro's cell stood alone at the far end of the room, like

the head of a dinner table, and his guests were the inhabitants of the rows of cells on either side. Once the roof had been torn open, the four queens dropped down through its cleft and gracefully landed like gymnasts on the ground facing Jandro from the opposite head, with the dinner guests now become captive audience.

Jandro's eyes glowed red and his body grew and shifted into the shape of Bram, as he took a deep, savoring breath. "I can smell your blood through those feeble pyramids warding your flesh. Come to Papa, infirm little souls," he said in his grating, unworldly voice, raising his left hand and releasing a barrage of leeches which slithered through the air toward the four queens. The penned spectators jumped up and down and shrieked with glee.

Trusting her instincts, Mercurial stepped behind Virgina and put her left hand on her back, as Virgina did the same to Sin Chronic, who did the same to Orna. Orna put her palms together and manifested a longsword which glowed with a gleaming, silver light. She raised the sword and pointed it at Bram. "Meet your death, demon," she snarled.

"Orna, no! Stop!" The sound of Diego's voice rang through the air as he began to materialize in front of them. "You mustn't kill him, unless you want his evil to become your own!"

"You think you can stop us?" hollered Sin Chronic. "You have no army!"

"He does," said Rahim, materializing to Diego's right and placing his left hand on Diego's shoulder. Trieu quickly appeared to his left, and Lluc surfaced beside him. Rahim cupped his hands together and thrust a heatwave toward the four queens, hoping to knock them off their feet as Lluc blew soundwaves to deflect Bram's leeches. With a lightning reflex, Sin Chronic shot her right hand up into the air, creating an enormous electromagnetic shield which she swung down in front of her sisters to absorb the impact of the heatwave and dissipate it.

"You protect *him* by attacking *us?*" shouted Sin Chronic. "Where's the justice in that!?"

"We're not trying to hurt you," said Rahim. "Only slow you down, so you can reconsider what you're doing."

"It's not right!" cried Virgina, her anger winning out over her grief. "He must be stopped!"

"Yes, he must be stopped," said Titi, materializing behind them. "But evil cannot be destroyed. You can only take a stand against it. To think otherwise is a trap. This wrath won't bring you peace, it will only bring your own anger back on yourselves for allowing yourself to do what you condemn him for. Hate seems like the easy way out, but you have to fight the evil within. It's the only way. The intoxication of vengeance is fleeting, it won't bring you strength. You could know magic of your own that's far more powerful than what this bokor has shown you."

"You know nothing!" said Sin Chronic, her hand still held aloft, as if to call a halt to the nonsense she was hearing. *"Ut sanguine suo solvat qui nobis inrogaverit!* Only his blood will settle this debt." She paused for a moment, seething in ire to the point of tears. "We have touched the teeth of the piranha. There's no coming back from that. How can you funnel violence into us and not have it ricochet? There's only one way to be rid of him, and that is to be rid of him." She fired a bolt of lightning in Titi's direction, and Titi was knocked to the ground, clutching her stomach in pain. The four kings rushed toward her, but Sin Chronic pushed them back with another wave of electromagnetic force.

"Orna," ordered Sin Chronic. "Kill that demon!"

Orna lowered the tip of the sword to the ground then swung it upward, guiding its trajectory with her eyes as it flew through the air toward Bram, whose appearance was flickering erratically between Jandro's physical self and Bram's monstrous spirit form.

With grounding energy flowing into them through Trieu,

the three other kings quickly placed their hands on Lluc's back as he blew another wall of soundwaves in the direction of the sword, changing its course enough to barely miss striking Jandro and hit the back wall of his cell. Bram cackled at the spectacle.

"Abeni, I know that you have a son," said Titi gently, summoning the strength to pull herself to her feet. Sin Chronic turned and looked at her, dumbfounded, the anger slowly draining from her face.

"His name is Abeo, am I right?" said Titi. "We can find him, and bring him to you. Olena, we can find your sister Maryska, too. And, Quila, your sister Vanessa. Do y'all remember them?" She looked at each of their saddened faces and knew the answer. "For you, Eka, I only have a song. Will you sing it with me? I think you know the words." Eka's eyes softened as Titi began to sing. "I've got the blues, I feel so lonely. I'd give the world, if I could only... make you understand. It surely would be grand. Baby, won't you please come home?"

| Chapter Fifty-Four |

"Miss Beaumond? Are you alright?"

Titi opened her eyes and was confronted by the concerned face of Dr. Varma. "Yes, I'm fine," said Titi. "Why do you ask?"

Dr. Varma smiled and searched for a diplomatic way to reply. "You were singing. Rather than answering my question."

"Where's Sophie?"

"Who is Sophie?" asked Dr. Varma.

"My psychiatrist. The one that Lin Mei had brought in to see me."

"Do you mean Dr. Chen?"

Titi was losing patience. "I mean the woman from Cameroon that Dr. Chen brought to see me."

"Let me take a look at the visitor log. I'll be back." Dr. Varma stepped out of the room, closing the door behind her.

Something's wrong, thought Titi, frowning as a wave of anxiety washed over her.

"The log doesn't show any record of visitors, either from Dr. Chen or anyone else," said Dr. Varma on re-entering the room.

"What about the power outage at Ophelia's Wing? The

tunnel getting flooded?"

"I didn't hear anything about Ophelia's Wing. It's been shut down for decades. The tunnel? What tunnel do you mean?"

"Never mind. What am I doing here?"

"You were brought in yesterday on a psychiatric hold after you were arrested for destruction of property."

"What destruction of property?"

"There was a fire in your hotel room."

"Wait—in my *hotel room*? Something is definitely wrong. I need to talk to my cousin Rochelle. Special Agent Roy. Please."

"Ms. Beaumond, I'm sorry this news is so hard to accept, but as I told you before, your cousin died earlier this evening of alcohol poisoning. She was found in an alley next to her apartment building. It's understandable to be in shock."

"No," whispered Titi, her eyes falling closed from the weight, tears falling out, face contorting in horror, as her breath erupted from her chest. Rochelle was just a little girl laughing not that long ago it seemed, laughing at Saturday morning cartoons, doing cartwheels in the front yard, running around listening to her CD walkman. *What happened to her?* She grew up. *Where is she?* She's gone. *How can she be gone?* She's not coming back. "No," said Titi again through her tears, mournful, indignant and adamant. "I don't accept that. That's not right. May I please speak with Dr. Chen?"

"It may be impossible to reach her at this hour," said Dr. Varma with a kind and reassuring voice. "And it appears your dosage of the antipsychotic medication is still too low. It takes time to build up in your system. I understand that it may not seem so to you, but we genuinely want to help you, Ms. Beaumond. Please be patient while we try to find the right regimen for you."

When Titi opened her eyes, Dr. Varma was gone. She caught sight of Bram standing in the corner of the room, staring down at her with his horrible dead fish head. The six fingers of

292

his right hand were spread out across his chest.

"Your loverboy Adrian is getting wasted out of his mind as we speak," he said, with a low-pitched rumble in his voice. "Tsk, tsk. If only you would have returned his calls. Now he's convinced you've simply moved on, and drank himself to oblivion to forget you. And guess who else left the keys in the car? Your beloved cousin. Guess she won't be any help to you now."

"No," said Titi, staring sadly at the floor in front of her, struggling to find an explanation. "You're playing tricks with my mind. None of this is real."

"Sure, you'd like to believe that, wouldn't you? It's a lot easier than admitting that you're just a psychotic, delusional, paranoid schizophrenic who's angry at the world, the same world that violated your trust, just like your uncle did, just like your mother did by not calling the police when he raped you, like Billy did when he beat you and beat you and beat you until you were almost dead, like Carlos did when he cheated on you, like your cousin did by giving away the baby you were meant to have. The list just goes on and on, doesn't it?"

"No." Titi couldn't help the tears. Her forehead tensed and eyes fell closed as she tilted and rocked herself forward and back to comfort herself, all the while losing the strength to keep going, ready to sleep and never wake up.

"Oh yes," said Bram with mock pity. "Poor, pathetic wretch, now you've got your hopes up over yet another man who'll tell you anything he thinks you want to hear, just to keep having you around to exploit and abuse. And all the while, God just stands by and does nothing but laugh at your suffering."

"No," said Titi again, opening her eyes, feeling a rise of indignation in her chest. "Don't you dare try to paint Adrian like yourself. And don't try to reduce God to your own hateful reflection, either. That's how I know you're lying. Get the fuck out of here. Get out. Get out!!" As her words crescendoed into a high-pitched shriek, the specter of Bram vanished through the window, like a wraith being sucked out by a vacuum cleaner.

"We're going to try adding some lithium to your regimen," said Dr. Varma, who was once again sitting in her chair in front of Titi, in the same location she had been previously, her eyes wide with concern.

Suddenly, Titi remembered the Vedic chant that Sophie had taught her, and began chanting it aloud.

"Interesting. The Rahu Shanti mantra? Where did you learn it?"

Titi stopped chanting for a moment to answer her question. "Sophie taught it to me last night."

"You must have been exposed to it at some point before, in order for you to recall it during a hallucination."

"It wasn't a damn hallucination."

"Okay, I'm sorry. I didn't mean to upset you. Do you want me to give you some space right now?"

"Do what you feel is right," said Titi, indifferent. "I'll be here, chanting."

Dr. Varma quietly exited the room as Titi continued intoning the mantra.

In the next moment, Titi felt herself being sucked out of the room as Bram had been, as if she were being pulled from one dimension into another.

She found herself in the center of a medical consulting room, and Lin Mei was sitting in a chair to her left. She looked around, and found that a clone of Lin Mei was sitting in another chair to her right. Neither of them seemed to be aware of Titi's presence. Titi recalled the incident that Lin Mei had shared with her of interacting with her alter ego, and wondered if she had traveled back in time.

The Lin Mei clone to her right began to shapeshift into the figure of Bram, and Titi reflexively raised the palm of her right hand to block Bram's ability to take control of Lin Mei's alter ego. Titi didn't understand what was happening or how she was doing it, but somehow she blocked him long enough for the real Lin Mei to escape the room.

Titi sensed that somehow she had also similarly protected Adrian from attack by Bram earlier when she felt something shake his sobriety, except with Adrian she didn't have any visual of what was happening, only a similar array of subtle psychic sensations in the back of her head that paralleled those she had just experienced with Lin Mei. An intricate tension, then a release when the danger had passed. She could almost draw a three-dimensional map of it.

Something was also feeling different about the physical sensations in her head. Her consciousness felt centered and locked in. It was like she had at last found her way back into the driver's seat of a vehicle she had only ever been a passenger in. After reflecting on it a moment, it occurred to her that the lightning bolt Abeni had struck her with had potentially catalyzed more karmic power in her.

Now with intention, she slowly closed her eyes and then opened them, finding herself now in a different hospital room, with five people sitting around her. One of them was Sophie, and the rest were the four kings.

"Sophie!" she said with relief. "I think I shifted into another reality."

"I know it's not easy," said Sophie gently. "But it's crucial for you to stay tapped into this timeline—a timeline with the most optimal outcome. You've been shifting in and out of corrupted timelines with less favorable outcomes. Keep visualizing positive results."

"It's hard not to be angry, I'm sorry."

"You don't have to be sorry. Being angry is a natural response, there's nothing wrong with that. It's vital to be aware of it, and acknowledge it. Your frustration is valid. The four queens have a good reason to be angry too. But acting on or even dwelling on vengeful or malicious impulses depletes your karmic power. The more you focus with discipline on your hopes rather than your fears, the better you'll be able to heal and protect yourself, and use your magic with intention to manifest your desires. Rochelle, Lin Mei and Jason will be arriving shortly. We'll be discussing the arrangement of the exorcism."

"The last thing I remember was traveling astrally with the four kings to go to the prison. I was singing a song to Eka."

"The song you sang, and the things you said to bring their bodies back to consciousness were effective," said Diego. "It caused the connection between the zombified spirits and their control of the trafficking victims to be destabilized. As a result, the astral plane experienced a powerful wave of distortion in that moment, and all of us were kicked back to our physical bodies."

"And Jandro?" said Titi. "Bram?"

"The four kings succeeded early on in binding Bram to prevent Jandro from killing himself without killing Bram along with him," said Sophie. "That will enable us to perform the exorcism without jeopardizing Jandro's life."

"Where did you four kings come from?" asked Titi. "Have you always practiced magic?"

"Reid chose us and trained us in magic," said Rahim. "Not enough to resolve the situation without the help of a clairvoyant such as yourself. Reid never had any formal training, so what we know is limited to what we've all read about and discovered doing research on our own. Our newest recruit, though, Special Agent Alo Archer, is the descendant of a *povosqa*, a Hopi shaman. He's been the hierophant on our team."

"Speaking of which," said Sophie, "I'm noticing that your abilities have developed in leaps and bounds since I last saw you, Titi. I have much to learn from you. In the meantime, the exorcisms must be our first priority. Even though Bram's spirit is bound to Jandro's body, his magic is still powerful enough to conduct telepathic thought manipulation on the unguarded.

Until he's exorcised, we must all take extra measures to protect ourselves. *Quod amor protegat*: that love may shield us."

| Chapter Fifty-Five |

"Carlos?" said Rochelle, struggling to open her eyes. Titi's astral presence had momentarily curbed Rochelle's desire to drink, but the compulsion returned after Titi left. She had finished her Patrón and for the moment, lacked the energy to go buy more.

There would come a day in the not too distant future when Rochelle would look back and feel unforgiving that she had allowed herself to spiral so far out of control, but for now she was completely unbothered to find herself still lying on the pavement behind the dumpster in the alley between her apartment building and the liquor store. Better than having Jason getting on her case all night long, she figured. Except for some liquor bottles and cigarette butts that had been left by a couple of high school students earlier that evening, and a flattened cardboard box formerly belonging to a homeless man named Regular Joe who had passed away the night before, the alley was empty. "Oh," she said, to no one in particular. "I thought you said something to me."

How did I get here?
You've been asleep.
He left me.
You didn't want to remember anymore.
She wins.
You've lost some feelings.
Whose voice is this?
Buried.
Fading.

Rochelle blinked, and for a moment found herself remembering the green envelope from Tim and Sandra, her daughter's adoptive parents, sitting on the kitchen counter. She was both hopeful at the thought that she could potentially reconnect with her daughter, and at the same time mortified to imagine that her daughter would be disappointed to learn of the unwell state she had been in for longer than she could remember. Her fear was bullying her hope, and fear was winning.

She struggled to open her eyes again and glanced around the darkened alley. Staring absently into the dark end of the alley, away from the street, she saw a faint, nebulous shadow shift and move in a peculiar, serpentine motion. At first, she thought it was a snake, maybe a cobra, but the more she stared at it, the more she thought it looked like the form of a disfigured man, laying on the ground, waving his hand at her. Was it a greeting? Or a call for help? Or the spirited beckoning of Death? As the shadow approached and took a more definitive shape, she realized it was nothing more than a small black kitten exploring the alleyway, foraging for food. The kitten climbed up into her lap and greeted her with a tiny "Mew!"

It licked its paw, then tilted its head and looked into her eyes. "You want to find Abeni's son," said the kitten telepathically with the voice of a little girl. "Listen carefully. You must go to the African country of Aanu which borders North East Nigeria.

The name of the country means Mercy. You must search there for a village called Idariji, but know that you will only succeed on this journey if you first forgive yourself. Seek out a woman who lives there by the name of Ẹtu Ìwo Ọkan. She is the Antelope with One Horn. Ask her for Agbaiye Omi Ọgbọn Inu. The orb of water knowledge will be needed to help you find him. Quila's sister, Vanessa Ladorada, the Golden Butterfly, will be easier to find. She's a well-known news broadcaster in Mexico City. Olena's sister is Maryska Kovcheh Danya, a schoolteacher in Kiev. She is the Ark, God's Gift of the Sea."

The words were coming through as jumbled up gibberish to Rochelle, but dreamlike images unfolded in her vision of an antelope with one horn, an orb of rippling water, a golden butterfly, and a shimmering ark atop a vast ocean.

An Isabella tiger moth alighted on the kitten's head and the kitten gently nudged the creature of fiery orange wings onto her paw and held it close to her ear—as if it were whispering something important to her—before it flew away. "Don't worry about trying to remember the names," the kitten continued. "Your mind is too far away for that. Your angels will remind you with riddles when the circumstances are more favorable. Just recognize them when you see them."

You're not real.
Banished.
A trap.
Anchor.
Treachery.
Veiled.
Illusion.
Muted.
I don't believe in fairy tales.

Rochelle's heartbeat and breathing were slowing down and her consciousness was fading in and out. "No," she said abruptly, startling herself and the kitten, who sprinted away into the darkness. "I don't want to die," she said, struggling to keep herself from slipping away. "Please, God, help me," she pleaded tearfully. "I don't want to die."

In the darkness to her left, somewhere off in the direction where the kitten had departed, she could hear the sound of a shovel hitting dirt. Looking over in that direction, she saw what appeared to be a Black man's head sitting on the ground, wearing a black top hat decorated with yellow, green and purple beads and feathers, the colors of Mardi Gras. His face was painted with a white skull, but by the shape of his features it wasn't Nimbeau. He lifted the shovel and rested it over his right shoulder, and she then realized that his head was not sitting on the ground, but rather he was standing inside a deep hole that he had been digging.

"*Now* you fucking tell me!" he ranted, following his exclamation with a hearty laugh. With his left hand, he raised a fat cigar to his mouth, and toked on it as Rochelle regarded him curiously.

"Oh yes, I know you, doll, but you don't know me. They call me Baron Samedi. And I'm almost done digging your grave, sugar lips. Want to try it on for size?" He snapped his fingers and she found herself lying in an open coffin at the bottom of a hole in the Earth, six feet deep.

Her arms slowly lifted of their own accord and crossed over her chest to indicate that the time had come now for her mortal repose, and a gradual vanishing began taking hold of her body, inch by inch, beginning with her toes and winding its way upward around her, an invisible slow-motion tornado swallowing her whole, a burial shroud dressing her in oblivion.

Dreams of simple things like wanting to someday learn to play the piano, and the hope of seeing her daughter smile ever again grew more and more distant. The sadness of this at last flung open the gates of her grief, and wave after wave after wave of tears passed through her like a tsunami, and the delirium slowly drifted away, and a dull, aching pain seeped in from the cold concrete beneath her. Baron Samedi had made his departure and taken the coffin with him. Her body felt too heavy to leave the ground.

"Help," she said, quietly at first, clearing her throat as her muscles shuddered from the chilling night air. "Somebody help me, please?" she said, with more volume. "Somebody help me."

"Roy!" shouted Jason as he walked past and caught the sound of her voice. Had her plea for help happened a moment earlier, he wouldn't have heard it, on account of his cell phone catching his attention. It was his girlfriend Natasha, and he had silenced the call. Had her plea happened a moment later, he also wouldn't have heard it, on account of a bus passing by. As it happened, he walked by at exactly the right moment, and heard her calling from behind the dumpster. He stopped dead in his tracks and peered into the darkness of the alley. "Oh my God, Roy," he said, catching sight of her and rushing over to kneel beside her. "What happened to you? Why did you leave like that? Are you alright? Did someone assault you?"

She shook her head no as she continued to cry, and he sat down on the pavement and put his arm around her and gave her a hug. "Okay. That's okay. You're okay. It's going to be okay. Let's get you to the hospital, alright? Are you able to walk?"

The next thing she knew, she was being admitted to Glen Haven's substance abuse rehab center, and wheeled into a room on a gurney where she was transferred to a hospital bed. She had a vague awareness of a nurse inserting a needle into her forearm to start her on an intravenous drip of vitamins and nutrients to re-hydrate her, and to administer a sedative to help discourage the urge to drink. Sleep came quickly, and for Jason too as he sat with her through the night. He was still asleep in the chair next to her bed when she woke up around 2:45am.

Sitting atop a pile of her neatly folded clothes on the wheeled table next to her bed was her cell phone, and she reached over to pick it up, careful not to wake Jason with her movements. Low battery. Her voice mailbox was full. Six messages from Carlos, two from Lin Mei, two from her mother, one from Reid, and one from Sandra, her daughter's adoptive mother. *Oh no,* she thought, immediately regretting having looked at her phone, and tossing it back on the pile of clothes. *I can't. The world will have to wait.*

| Chapter Fifty-Six |

FLASHBACK : July 3, 2015
Kenner, Louisiana

What was he going for with this decor? Carlos mused as he looked around the rustic space his colleague Dr. Tom Slepen had thoughtfully dubbed "The Listening Room." There was a soft, embroidered pillow thing sitting on the couch that looked obviously homemade—*quaint,* thought Carlos. It had a house with a door, two windows, and a chimney adorning it in red thread. *'Mom and apple pie' motif, I guess. Does this usually make people feel safe? Certainly not the kind of thing my mother would ever make.*

"What brings you to see me, Carlos?" asked Tom, entering the room and taking a seat. "It's been a while. How have you been?"

"Not great, I guess," said Carlos, chuckling while not finding any humor in it. "Obviously I wouldn't be here, if things were hunky dory."

"Of course, so let's talk about that. You said on your phone message that you're currently going through a divorce?

I'm sorry to hear that."

"Yeah, it's been… complicated. I was having an affair with Cassandra, one of my colleagues at the hospital. Something about her brought out the worst in me."

"Could you say more about that?"

Carlos shifted uncomfortably and cleared his throat. "It's hard for me to talk about. Let's just say I was exhibiting some abusive tendencies toward Cassandra that I thought I had overcome after kicking my cocaine habit."

"Physical abuse?"

"No, it was psychological, never physical. I was constantly psychoanalyzing her without her invitation. Backhanded compliments, undermining her self-esteem, things like that."

"Could you give an example?"

Carlos stared at the floor, rubbing the back of his head. "What comes to mind off the top of my head is the last fight we had before we broke up. I was treating her like she was an imbecile for calling me out on some legit grievance—my usual. My standard defense was to accuse her of misunderstanding things I had said when I knew very well their meanings were clear. 'Do you even understand English?' I said. 'Supposedly you're so smart.' Calling her dumb was the worst. She looked at me like I had punched her in the gut. She walked out the door and never spoke to me again."

"Sounds like some gaslighting was going on too?"

"I don't know, Tom. Maybe? To me it was more like pathological lying."

"Where do you suppose this anger came from? Were you angry at your ex-wife?"

"God, no. I could never imagine being angry at Titi. She's the sweetest person you could ever meet. I'm angry at myself for disappointing her. But mostly I was angry with my mother. I still am. Cassandra was just a convenient outlet. And she's white, and a closet racist. She reminds me a lot of my mother, come to think of it, except my mother is openly racist. It was different when we first met. We had a whirlwind affair at first. She was so amazing, full of energy, exciting. She didn't seem saddled with all this emotional baggage, and I feel bad for saying that—I mean it wasn't Titi's fault, all the terrible things that happened to her. I was just so desperate for something light and easy for a change. I showered Cassandra with attention, and gifts. I promised I would initiate divorce proceedings once Titi's mental health was more stable, but it just never seemed like the right time. And then I met Rochelle—Titi's cousin. She came down to New Orleans at Christmas, and it was actually the first time we had ever met, even though Titi and I had been married ten years. Rochelle was always just so busy with work, she missed a lot of family events, including our wedding. She and Titi weren't exactly close. But she and I hit it off immediately. I didn't have any qualms about filing for divorce after that. And I ended it with Cassandra too."

"As a psychiatrist, I'm sure you're familiar with the concept of grooming victims for abuse?"

"I'm familiar with it, but I hate to think of it that way. It's like asking me if I was gaslighting, it sounds so intentional and predatory. On a conscious level, it's not what was going on, although Silvia would probably say it was. Cassandra probably would, too. I wasn't like that with Titi, that I know of. I mean, you could ask her. I don't think I was."

"So what was going on at the conscious level?"

"With Silvia? Cocaine is what was going on. With Cassandra? It wasn't grooming. I just thought I was in love. Everything was always perfect and wonderful at the beginning, with all of them. I wanted to be their everything. But it never takes long for the wounds to take control. I was aware of becoming abusive with Cassandra, but I didn't know how to stop or walk away. She just made it so convenient. It's part of the reason I'm here. I want to break the cycle, especially now, going into this new relationship with Rochelle."

"I recall that you had met your ex-wife under somewhat controversial circumstances, am I remembering that right? Could you remind me of how you met?"

"I met her in a grocery store, in New Orleans. She was wearing a flattering tank top and buying avocados. She recognized me from the hospital, but I didn't know who she was, so she introduced herself. Stunningly beautiful."

"She was your patient?"

"Not technically. I was overseeing her care, but it was an intern who was treating her. I had never met her."

"An attempted suicide, is that right?"

Carlos cleared his throat. "That is correct, yes. But not the reason we met at the grocery store."

"But still, it's safe to say she saw you as being in a position of authority?"

"I suppose."

"She's Black?"

"Yes, but what does that have to do with anything?"

"And now you're dating her cousin? So your current girlfriend—Rochelle, is it?—is also Black? You have a thing for Black women?"

Where is he going with this? "I have a thing for intelligent women who challenge my assumptions. Titi just happens to be Black. And my girlfriend before her was also Black. It happens when you live in New Orleans; the odds of dating a Black woman are much higher there than in San Francisco. Anyway, why are you asking me this? I guess white men feel entitled to questions like this? It makes me feel like I'm not where I'm supposed to be."

"Are you suggesting that I'm a closet racist, too? Seems to me more like a convenient way to derail your therapy."

"Are you suggesting I'm suffering from some kind of

white savior complex? Not a bad theory, Tom, but there's too much context to prove that's not the case. Titi saved me in more ways than I could ever save her. But yes, racism is a good topic for us to discuss, because my mother is openly racist, and a psychiatrist. How can people of color go to her and trust her advice, knowing that she sees them as lesser human beings?"

"And if I were racist—and I don't think it's fair to suggest that I am, but let's just consider the possibility as a hypothetical—ultimately, as your psychiatrist, does it matter if I am, or am not a racist? Whatever is true or not true about *me* is separate from what ails *you*, don't you think? 'Narcissism and Stockholm Syndrome,' I believe were the words you used previously to describe your relationship with your mother. Don't you think I could help you with that, racist or not?"

"Ultimately, Tom, it matters. How can you ask me if it matters? Sure, maybe you could help me with it if I decided to overlook that my ex-wife or other partners wouldn't get the same quality of treatment from you. Hypotheticals and playing devil's advocate are just smoke and mirrors to obscure the need to take a stand against our national inferiority complex. Clinging to subversive narratives veiled as hypotheticals only serves to protect you from the vulnerability of endorsing a narrative you actually care about."

"What if subversive narratives are what I really care about?"

"Are they, though? I'm guessing not, if you're couching it with 'what if.' If you can't take a stand on it, then this is just another hypothetical, more playing devil's advocate, isn't it? It's a mind game, a foundation for a never ending debate which is not what I'm here for."

"What is it that you think I'm trying to subvert?"

"It's a subversion of empathy. A failure to acknowledge the inhumane impact of systemic racism."

"You're speaking of systemic racism against Black

people? I'll be honest, Carlos, I'm not sure that that kind of anti-Black racism still exists in this country at the systemic level. It did a long time ago, sure, but not anymore, not to the degree you seem to be suggesting. I mean, let's talk about how the history of anti-Semitism and anti-Irish sentiment broadly affected white populations in America at a systemic level. Not to mention the fact that people of color can be racist, too. What do you think about that?"

"Yes, any kind of prejudice fucking sucks, anyone can be racist, and anyone can be a victim of racism, but *systemic* racism in the United States clearly works in favor of keeping white people in power, and the statistical evidence of its widespread existence—in sentencing disparities, wage disparities, health care, home ownership, education, corporate power, political power—is all astronomically undeniable. The list just goes on and on. It doesn't take much to recognize the radical imbalance of power that's been in place a very long time. I think I'm wasting my time trying to convince anyone of a truth so self-evident."

"Does it occur to you that the statistical inequities you would probably use to prove this 'self-evident' truth might be explained by collective social inadequacies? That perhaps white people might simply be more success-driven than people of other races?"

"You actually think skin color has that effect on our biology?" Carlos shook his head in disbelief. "Part of me wants to get up and walk out of here right now, Tom. The other part of me wants to try to educate you, if that's even possible."

"Give me a chance. Educate me."

"Have you heard of résumé whitening?"

"No, I haven't."

"There's been a recent Harvard study which found that Black and Asian job seekers were more likely to get interviews just by whitewashing their résumés. In other words, by changing their names to sound more white, and by removing any references to their actual race, they actually had a better chance of getting a callback, not on the basis of their job qualifications, but because of how white their names sounded. Don't tell me this is about white people being more success-driven, Tom."

"Hm, well, I'd be curious to read the study and share my thoughts on it."

"Titi used to tell me that she wished I could spend just one day walking around being a Black man, just to see how vastly different the experience is in the way people treat me. I think you could benefit from having that experience too. And until that ever happens, I think I need to find myself a different therapist. If the empathy is only there for white people, the moral injury is just going to add up over time."

"Could it be said that you only have empathy for Black people?"

"I have empathy for people who have empathy, regardless of race. You can check out that Harvard study and tell me your thoughts on it in a social setting, on your own time, not on my dollar. Meanwhile, I'll be looking to align myself with a therapist who's a little more pro-diversity."

"I'm not a bad guy, Carlos."

"Everyone's capable of being a little ignorant," said Carlos. "God knows I've been guilty of that where systemic racism is concerned. Therapy is just not where I want to spend my time, and money, educating you. Take care, Tom."

| Chapter Fifty-Seven |

Her apartment seemed different when Rochelle got home. More quiet. Empty. She picked up her phone and opened her news app. A headline, which read "Wildlife rescue team releases one-horned antelope after rehabilitation," grabbed her attention, although she didn't know why. She also didn't know why she turned her head to look out the window in time to see a butterfly with gold wings flutter by, which struck her as something she had seen before, maybe in a dream, but she couldn't recall the context. Nonetheless, gears began shifting in the back of her head, just beyond her awareness.

Her cell phone rang and she looked at the caller ID. It was Reid. "Roy here," she said, taking the call.

"Hey, there she is," said Reid good-naturedly. "What's your status, Roy?"

"I'm okay," she said, wrestling with a tremor in her hands. "I just got home. They've got me on Librium to help me with the withdrawals. It's still pretty rough."

"You're alive and talking on the phone with me, Roy, so I'm just going to thank God for that."

"Thank you, sir. I'd like to request that we assemble

a team to investigate familial contacts on the four vics. Titi is going to do some healing work with them while they're in rehab to see if we can find out more details about their origins. I might have some leads myself. I also formally recommend arranging an exorcism as soon as possible, per Titi's advice. I know it's unconventional, and I'm not about to officially endorse any particular belief about the paranormal, but whatever rational explanation there may or may not be, for the sake of what they themselves believe, I feel convinced it's what will help them the most."

"Understood. I'll talk to the four kings about it and have them organize a team, post haste."

"I'm curious, sir, why do you call them the four kings?"

"They remind me of a story my mother used to tell me as a child. Remind me to share it with you someday. In the meantime, I want you to take it easy. That's an order."

"Sir, I think we need to have a talk about my early retirement. I can't keep going like I've been going. I've been trying so hard not to let you down. I'm so sorry. I really tried."

"Nonsense, Roy. You've exceeded my expectations in every way since the day I met you. I don't expect that to change any time soon."

"It's kind of you to say, sir, but I've let myself down. I don't know if I can forgive myself."

"Well, it's a damn shame if you don't, but that's between you and your therapist. Listen, I know you've got supernatural strength, and I'm being dead serious, but it doesn't mean you can't take time off now and then to take care of your health. It's a downright necessity. So you do that, and there will always be plenty of work here, if and when you decide to come back to it. Right now the priority needs to be getting back on your feet. For the time being, let it sink into that stubborn head of yours that you haven't let me down."

"I'll see what I can do, sir."

"One more thing. My gut's been telling me you weren't happy with how I responded to Chen giving your cousin the case file. You think I wouldn't have cut you the same slack?"

"I don't know, sir. Since you brought it up, I'll admit that sometimes I wonder."

"I haven't given her any leeway that I wouldn't have given you, or Jefferson, or anyone else on our team, given the extraordinary commitment to doing the right thing you've all consistently shown me all these years. I haven't lost any faith in you, Roy. That's a fact."

"Thank you, sir. I really appreciate that."

"Don't be a stranger, alright? By way of the sparrow, we shall be free."

"By way of the sparrow? What does that mean?"

"I don't rightly know, to be honest. Just another something my mother used to say to me as a child. I guess it's just a poetical way of saying to let go and trust the process."

"I like that, sir. By way of the sparrow, we shall be free."

"You take care, Roy."

"You too, sir."

After she hung up the phone, it rang again. "Hey Midori," she said, after glancing at the caller ID.

"Hey Rochelle. I was wondering if you could have a talk with Lin Mei? There's something wrong with her. She's been sitting on the couch in the same position ever since last night. She won't eat or sleep or anything. I can barely get her to talk. She's only said two words to me since she got home, and they didn't make any sense. I'm really worried."

"What were the two words?"

"Stop Theraazh."

"Stop the what?"

"Theraazh."

"I'm sorry, I don't understand what you're saying. Something that rhymes with garage?"

"Yeah, I was thinking it might be French, so I Googled it and found Geoffroy Thérage, the executioner who burned Joan of Arc at the stake. She was sentenced to death for cross-dressing. It's my best guess."

Rochelle jotted the words down on a piece of paper and realized, by the unintentional space she had left between the E and the R, that she had written down 'STOP THE RAGE.' It struck her as significant, but it was too much to process at the moment. "I don't mean this the wrong way, Midori, but what could I possibly do to help? She never listens to me anyway."

"What do you mean? You're the *only one* she ever listens to."

Rochelle stared silently at the empty wall in front of her, as the truth of Midori's words sank in. "I'm sorry, I'm just not in good shape right now. I want to help, but I just got out of the hospital myself. Jason is on his way here to pick me up to go see my cousin, who is also in the hospital. I honestly don't know if I can help Lin Mei. I'm afraid of making it worse. It sounds like she needs immediate medical attention."

"Should I call 911 then?"

"Can you call a cab? Can she walk?"

"I tried to get her up last night and bring her to the bedroom to lay down, and she started screaming at the top of her lungs, then cried for ten minutes, then went blank like she is now. She won't eat, she won't talk. I'm really scared right now."

"Ok, you'd better get an ambulance. They may need to medicate her. Put her on the phone, I'll talk to her. After we're done, you call 911, okay? Have them bring Lin Mei to Glen Haven and admit her."

"It's my fault, Rochelle. It's all my fault. She should have left me in Tokyo."

"It's not about fault, alright? We're all doing the best we can with some crazy circumstances. Just put her on the phone and get an ambulance over there when we're done."

"Here she is."

"Hey girl. It's me, Rochelle. You okay? Talk to me."

Lin Mei opened her mouth to speak but the sound came out in a cracked whisper. Tears began to roll out of her eyes. "Chelle, I... I... don't feel well. Something's wrong with me... I... can't move."

"Okay, don't panic, you're gonna be alright. Midori's going to call an ambulance. You just sit tight and hold on. Can you do that?"

"Yes," Lin Mei whispered, her voice cracking again. She cleared her throat and said it again. "Yes."

"You're extraordinarily strong, Lin Mei, you know that? You're one of the strongest women I know. To survive what you survived as a child... I don't know many who could do what you did. So you just hold on now. All you have to do right now is breathe, and hold on. You hear me? Love you."

"I love you too, Rochelle." Tears were streaming from her eyes. She sniffled. "I'm not strong like you."

"You don't need to be strong like me. You need to be strong like you. Now let me talk to Midori. You get yourselves down to Glen Haven and get some help, okay? I'm on my way there myself, so I'll meet you there."

"Goodbye."

"No, don't you go saying goodbye on me. See you later. Right? I'll see you later."

Midori got back on the phone. "It looks like she's done talking now," she said, biting her lip anxiously.

"Call 911. I'll meet you down at Glen Haven later. Text me her room number. Stay strong, Midori. Keep the faith. You've got this."

After she hung up with Midori, she heard the key turn in the front door, and Carlos walked in to find her sitting at the kitchen table with the envelope from Sandra open in front of her. He came over and gave her a hug, but she didn't feel like hugging him back.

"Jason called and told me what happened," he said. "You're okay now? You're going to do outpatient rehab?"

"Where were you? You abandoned me when I needed you most."

"Now you're sounding like my mother."

"Thanks. What happened to your hand?"

"Um, dog bite."

Rochelle sensed that he was lying and glared at him.

"Let's not fight, okay?" he said, the bags under his eyes becoming more noticeable. "I've been staying with my mother at the hotel. You know how demanding she is. I'm sorry, it was impossible to get away. And in case you forgot, she's going to be dead soon, and you won't have to deal with this anymore."

"I didn't forget. Thanks for the reminder."

"Thanks for the sarcasm."

"I think it's best if we spend some time apart."

"You won't get any argument from me there, since I'm going to be staying with my mother a while on the West Coast."

"Fine."

He breathed a heavy sigh and settled down into the chair across the table from her, staring off into the kitchen behind her.

"There's something I need to tell you, Carlos. I have a daughter."

"What? When? Where is she? Who's the father?"

"Efren was the father. I gave her up for adoption right after I graduated from FLETC."

His eyebrows furrowed together as he tried to process the information. "How come you never told me?"

"I was... ashamed for giving her up for adoption. I never told anyone, not even my mother. Don't worry, I'm not asking you to take care of her."

"I didn't think you were, for Christ's sake. Look, sorry. It's been a stressful night, alright?"

"You think you're the only one who ever suffers?"

"No, I don't. But it doesn't change the fact that it's been a stressful night." He stood up and pulled a box of cigarettes from his pocket, then dug out a lighter. On any other occasion, Rochelle would have been upset at the thought that he was smoking again. Right now, she didn't care.

"I got a letter from her adoptive mother. She said Shani's a child prodigy. Twelve years old and gifted in astrophysics and engineering. She's about to become the youngest person to pursue a bachelor's degree at MIT. She wants to become an astronaut."

"I can't say that surprises me, considering she has her mother's genes."

She scoffed. "I don't know if that's a blessing or a curse."

"Give me a break. It's a blessing, Rochelle."

"I miss you, Carlos."

"I miss you too. This thing with my mother… is more than I can handle right now. I'm sorry. I need to distance myself or else I'm going to end up taking out my frustration on you, and I don't want that."

"Okay. I get it. I need some space too."

At that moment, Rochelle got a text message from Jason that he was waiting in his car out front to take her to Glen Haven.

"I gotta go. Will you be here when I get back?"

"I can't. My mother's waiting for me. We're heading back to San Francisco for her surgery."

"Of course. I guess I'll see you when I see you. Take care, Carlos." At that, she picked up her keys and her phone and walked out.

| Chapter Fifty-Eight |

"Thank you again for inviting me to come stay at your place," said Titi, setting her suitcase down in Rochelle's spare bedroom. "I feel honored, truly. It's beautiful here. What an amazing view."

"I'm sorry I didn't invite you sooner," said Rochelle, turning on the lamp in the room to show Titi where the switch was. "It's been kind of tense between me and Carlos lately. I didn't want to make things any more awkward for you than they already were."

Titi took her coat off and hung it in the closet. "I appreciate that," she said with a reassuring smile, "but you don't owe me any apology. I did some reckoning with myself while I was in the hospital. I think it's safe to say things will be different now, moving forward."

Rochelle looked down with a half-smile. "Yeah," she said, looking back up at Titi. "Things feel different for me, too. Are you hungry? Want to get some take-out? There's a great noodle house around the corner."

"Do they do ramen? I could go for some ramen."

"Um, I think so. Yeah, I'm pretty sure they do. If they

don't, we'll go find some."

"Nah, don't worry about it. I'll try whatever you're having. I'd rather get to bed early tonight and not do a lot of walking around."

"We're getting old, Titi."

"What you mean, getting old?" said Titi, laughing. "We're just getting started. We're just getting out of the hospital, that's what you mean. A little rest won't kill either of us. By the way, have you heard any news from Carlos about Veronica?"

"Last I heard, she was recovering from surgery. I didn't ask too many questions. It's been a really touchy subject."

"I hope she comes to realize that death isn't the only way to find some peace."

"You're more kind than I am about it," Rochelle said as she looked down again with a half-smile. "I guess that's between her and God."

Titi knitted her eyebrows together in sympathy. "How are Lin Mei and Midori doing?"

"Midori checked into a 90-day rehab that Lin Mei found for her, one that will respect that she's transitioning. I think seeing Lin Mei in such a fragile state really catalyzed her into wanting to turn things around. Lin Mei's doing okay, she's still at Glen Haven. Her neuropsych testing isn't complete yet, but it's sounding like complex PTSD which developed into bipolar disorder. She wanted me to tell you they're expecting to discharge her tomorrow morning. She was hoping to see you before you head back to New Orleans."

Titi nodded again. They both stood quietly for a moment, feeling the weight of a lifetime of things unsaid.

"Well, hey," said Rochelle at last. "Let me grab a quick shower before we go eat, if you don't mind. Or are you really hungry? We could go now. Unless you want to get a shower in too before we go?"

"I'm fine," said Titi, smiling again by way of reassurance.

"Go take your shower. It'll give me a chance to get unpacked, so I can just relax when we get back."

"Feel free to make yourself at home. And hey. I'm glad you're here, Titi."

"Thank you, Chelle." Titi leaned forward and gave her a warm hug. "I am too."

Rochelle smiled and turned to leave the room, and Titi walked over to the guest bed and sat down on it. It was so comfortable that sitting down quickly turned into lying down, and feeling genuinely relaxed for the first time in a really long time. Her cell phone rang, and she retrieved it from her purse, another smile dawning across her face as she saw Adrian's name on the caller ID.

"Hi Adrian," she said, her heart aflutter.

"Hey beautiful. God, it's so good to hear your voice. How are things going in New York?"

"Better now. It's a long story. And it's really good to hear your voice too, you have no idea. I'm sorry I've been out of touch, there's been a lot going on. This case we've been working on has been out of this world. My cousin and I are getting ready to go out to eat right now, but I'll be back in New Orleans soon. I'll tell you all about it when I get back? Just to give you some incentive to take me out on a third date."

He could hear the flirtatious smile in her voice, and couldn't help smiling himself in response. "I know something profound was happening. Can't wait to hear all about it. Before you go, I just want to tell you: Thank you. You've helped me more than you know."

"I can say the same of you," said Titi, gushing. "Thank you, Adrian. These last few days have been a real awakening."

"For me as well," he said, with a quiet sense of reverence. "Have a safe flight, angel. I'll talk to you soon."

| Epilogue |

Special arrangements were made for Jandro's exorcism to take place in a secure space at the federal detention center, after which the remaining four exorcisms were conducted by Titi and Angie at the Voodoo temple in Charleston. All five were successful in liberating the host bodies from the possessing spirits, who were sent back to where they originated, although a long and difficult road toward healing now lay ahead for all of them. Some residual magic abilities remained in the four queens, who used them—as did Titi and the four kings—to forge protection for themselves and their loved ones against paranormal attack, but as of this writing, nothing yet as powerful as what they had experienced while hosting the possessing spirits.

Abeni reunited with her son, a former child soldier, and Quila and Olena with their sisters, although as one might have expected, these were bittersweet reunions. The four kings immediately resumed their work on Reid's covert paranormal investigations team. Lin Mei followed Rochelle's lead and retired from her work at the agency in order to focus on recovering her health. A few weeks later, Jason was promoted into Reid's role as director of the Human Trafficking Division so Reid could focus his efforts on leading and developing his Federal Investigations Committee for Unexplained Phenomena.

Lluc and Eka remained close friends, sometime later began dating, and are still together. Eventually, Eka became a popular recording artist and released her debut album entitled, "Progeny of Witches: Daughters of Nephilim." Rahim was the guitarist on the album. She hired Trieu, a culinary expert in his free time, as private chef for their long recording sessions, and Lluc sang backup harmonies on some of her songs.

Abeni embarked on a career in electrical engineering, while Olena found her calling as a civil rights attorney. Quila, who dated Diego for about a year, went on to medical school to study Indigenous health, and eventually returned to Glen Haven to work there professionally, all the while keeping in close contact with Jandro, frequently visiting him in prison. She told the others that she remembered the Jandro from before Bram came along, and was devoted to helping him remember him too.

With Olena's help, Quila also formed a New York-based non-profit organization for the protection of Indigenous land and cultures. She had come to realize that the narrative Talisa had been fed as a child regarding the relationship between the colonists and the Indigenous tribes was biased in favor of the colonists and left out many details, which inspired Quila to do her part to help restore power to Indigenous people in Talisa's honor.

Titi returned to New Orleans to continue her work as a Voodoo consultant, and a few years later, she and Adrian were married. Lin Mei and Midori continue to be married to this day. Rochelle and Carlos continue to be estranged. With Bram no longer a menace in their lives, Bokor Nimbeau never came calling again, although his impact on their lives would continue unfolding in ways that were yet to be revealed.

The weeks following the exorcism were a time of quiet respite for Rochelle. She went to New Orleans for a while to reconnect with family, and stayed with Titi while she was there. Adrian invited her and Titi to come with him to an AA meeting so they could see what it was about. It inspired her to continue attending meetings on her return to New York.

The four queens had gifted Rochelle a planter box full of yellow chrysanthemums which now decorate the view from her living room window, through which she could hear children playing in the alley below as a warm breeze carrying the earthy sweet scent of the mum blossoms wandered in. Hopeful, as she once again picked up that fateful green envelope, the one which contained her first letter from her daughter Shani, she took a deep breath before opening the paper sleeve to reveal its contents one more time.

Shani talked about how she had graduated from high school at the age of eleven, and how her adoptive parents had begun to share with her more details about her biological mother, because they felt so inadequate and humbled by the magnitude of her intellectual development. It was awful, she said, to know that they felt that way, but she confessed that it was fascinating to learn that both of her parents were special agents of the FBI who had made dear sacrifices in taking a stand against evil. This is what Sandra told her on the day she gave Shani a letter which Rochelle had written to her daughter twelve years before, when she gave her up for adoption.

In the letter, Rochelle talked about how the Rhodes had been trying to conceive for such a long time, and how they were discouraged by their inability to afford adoption fees through the agency. In learning their plight, she came to feel that God had brought her into their lives for a reason. She was grateful that Shani could be raised in a stable home with two warm and loving parents. If or when the time came that Shani felt she wanted to meet Rochelle and get to know her better, she said, she welcomed the opportunity, and said that Tim and Sandra would have special instructions for getting in touch with her so she could make all the necessary arrangements without jeopardizing Shani's safety. She begged Shani's forgiveness for having abandoned her.

The day Shani Rhodes met her biological mother was sparkly, Shani said, like a fairy tale. She had worn her favorite dress for the occasion, a cap-sleeved tea dress in pale brown satin, which she had paired with a pair of burgundy high-top sneakers. Her dark brown curly hair was braided in rows which culminated in a loose ponytail fastened with a caramel-colored bow.

Sandra's charcoal Honda Civic pulled up to the restaurant where Rochelle and Shani would have lunch, and on seeing Rochelle wave from outside, Sandra gave Shani a long, tight hug and dropped her off at the corner. A wide smile revealing a mouth full of braces lit across Shani's face when she saw Rochelle, because she was so beautiful, even more beautiful than she had imagined. Also amazing to Shani was the fact that Rochelle had unwittingly chosen a tawny brown and burgundy floral print blouse to wear which matched Shani's ensemble, a coincidence which delighted Shani to no end. Somehow the food at her favorite restaurant even tasted better, no doubt owing to her unbounded anticipation.

Even though she maintained near perfect composure the whole time, Rochelle periodically dabbed the tears in her eyes with her folded napkin, as they talked about how Shani's freshman year was going at MIT, and how Shani wanted to be an astronaut. Rochelle told her she was proud of her. Now that she had retired from her work as a special agent, she wanted to get to know Shani better, if she was open to that. Shani smiled and said she would like that.

END OF BOOK ONE

Acknowledgements

Excerpts from "The Thunder: Perfect Mind" poem, translated by George W. MacRae, republished with permission of Brill publishing company, from *The Coptic Gnostic Library: A Complete Edition of the Nag Hammadi Codices*, edited by James Robinson, 5-volume set, bilingual edition, published March 8, 2002; permission conveyed through Copyright Clearance Center, Inc.

Excerpts from "Baby, Won't You Please Come Home," jazz/blues song performed in 1923 by Bessie Smith/Clarence Williams, written/published in 1919 by Charles Warfield/ Clarence Williams, republished without copyright restriction (public domain).

Excerpt of hymn from the 18th Psalm of David, republished without copyright restriction (public domain) from *Psalms of David in Metre*, published by Mathew Carey and Joseph Charless by authority of the General Assembly of the Church of Scotland, Philadelphia, 1805.

Excerpts from "The 10th Lesson: Sub-consciousing" by author Yogi Ramacharaka, republished without copyright restriction (public domain) from *A Series of Lessons in Raja*

Yoga, published by The Yogi Publication Society, Chicago, 1906. Excerpt from poem 86 by first-century Syrian poet Al-Walīd ibn Ubaidillah Al-Buḥturī, republished without copyright restriction (public domain) from "Ibn Khallikan's Biographical Dictionary, Volume 1," writing completed in the year 1274 C.E., translated and republished by William MacGuckin of Ireland (also known as Baron de Slane) in 1867.

Gratitude

Special thank you to Stephanie for blessing this work with your editing talent and for being the amazing, loving, supportive sis that you are. Thank you Mom and Dad for bringing me into the world and blessing me with your love, strength and wisdom. Thank you Sean for your faith, love and support. To Sean, Chris, Whitney and Luis: thank you for encouraging me to write.

Thank you to Mary, Roman, Michelle, Sabine, Charlie, Pennie, May, Kaye, Brad, Karen, and the numerous other practitioners who have participated in healing me throughout my life.

To the cast and crew of the Land of the Haunted Dolls short film, who helped to breathe life into these characters so dear to me, and whose faith in this endeavor helped to inspire me on many days when the horizon seemed bleak: thank you. To the festivals who selected the short film, helping to spread love and hope amidst a devastating pandemic: thank you.

Thank you Carmen, Michelle, Hazel, Roberto, Dave, Anne Marie, and other friends and family for your support through the short film's and novel's creative process. To Sean, Anne Marie, Vanessa, Jason, Luis, Merrillynn, Clarissa, Dane,

Bob, and others who shared constructive feedback on respective chapters and sections: much appreciated.

Most of all to our glorious Creator the greatest storyteller of all time, to my subconscious and my Higher Self, to the guardian angels and other divine intercessors, and to my supportive ancestors, thank you for your blessings and guidance. To those loving and those beloved, for all your gifts immaterial.

Much love and gratitude to you all.

Appendix A: Additional Recommended Reading

"Explaining AP Style on Black and White" by Associated Press :
http://landofthehaunteddolls.com/reading/apstyle.html

"The Opposite of Addiction Is Connection" by Robert Weiss, PhD, MSW :
http://landofthehaunteddolls.com/reading/connection.html

"Why We Feel Shame and How to Conquer It" by Margaret Paul, PhD :
http://www.landofthehaunteddolls.com/reading/shame.html

"11 Things That Will Help You Hold Space for Someone" by Reaca Pearl, MA, LPC :
http://landofthehaunteddolls.com/reading/holdspace.html

"How to Have Boundaries with Someone Who Doesn't Respect Your Boundaries" by Juliette Virzi : http://landofthehaunteddolls.com/reading/boundaries.html

"Meet the Real Narcissists (They're Not What You Think)" by Rebecca Webber : http://landofthehaunteddolls.com/reading/narcissists.html

"Why Stockholm Syndrome Happens and How to Help" by Sharie Stynes, PsyD : http://landofthehaunteddolls.com/reading/stockholmsyndrome.html

"In Accusing All Creeps of Gaslighting, We Dishonour the Real Victims" by Barbara Ellen : http://landofthehaunteddolls.com/reading/gaslighting.html

"Nobody Is Beyond Redemption" by Deena Guzder : http://www.landofthehaunteddolls.com/reading/nobodyisbeyondredemption.html

"Can Weed Make Meditating Easier? Experts Weigh In" by Melissa Pandika : http://www.landofthehaunteddolls.com/reading/cannabis.html

Links to Statistics on Systemic Racism and Other Additional Links : http://www.landofthehaunteddolls.com/reading

Appendix B:
List of Dual Roles

Characters who are intended by author to be played by the same actor or actress in a television series or feature film based on the novel:

- Mambo Erzulie Freda / Titi
- Mambo Erzulie Dantó / Rochelle
- LaSirenn / Angelique
- Papa Legba / Adrian
- The Marassa / Kemi
- Baron Samedi / Jason

The pages that follow have been intentionally left blank